IN THE LAST DAYS

IN THE LAST DAYS

RONALD SAVAGE JR.

I want to thank God for giving me the talents and resources to write both this book and this series. I want to thank my family and friends for their continued support. I want to thank those who have given me my own life experiences – good and bad – to help me write the life experiences of others. I want to thank the readers for taking the time to engage with this story.

Harrison Genealogy

This is the genealogy of the Harrisons, the founding family of Creeke.

Abraham Creeke, founder of Creeke and its church, took for a wife a woman by the name of Angelica; and begat a son, Nathaniel, and a daughter, Laverne. Nathaniel died at the age of sixteen. Laverne married Franklin Harrison, who had no prior familial roots in Creeke. Thus, the line of Creeke became the line of Harrison through Laverne's marriage to Franklin.

Franklin begat a son, Lionel. And Lionel took for a wife, Judith Morris. Lionel begat Derrick Jermaine Harrison. And Derrick took for a wife, Kiana Danette Barnett, whose father was Barry Barnett, whose father was Bartholomew Barnett, who took Ana for a wife.

Barry begat three daughters - Kiana, Paulette Jean, and Nancy Mae – with his wife, Kimberly. Nancy married Joseph Keaton. Joseph begat a son, Joe Keaton. And Joe begat two sons – James Edmond Keaton and Jordan Elias Keaton – with his wife, Helen. Thus, the line of Barnett became the line of Keaton through Nancy's marriage and became the line of Harrison through Kiana's marriage to Derrick.

Derrick begat two sons, Marlin Trevor Harrison and Malcolm Drew Harrison. Malcolm begat a son, Derek Drumaine Harrison.

Marlin took for a wife Soleya Naima Perry, whose father was Bernard Perry. Bernard begat two daughters – Soriah Noelle Perry and Soleya – with his wife Sophia Estelle Tolbert, whose mother was Estelle Tolbert, whose father was Deacon Tolbert. Soriah was married to Quincy Marcellus Campbell. And Quincy begat a son, Marcellus Bernard Campbell. Thus, the line of Perry became the line of Campbell through Soriah's marriage and the line of Harrison through Soleya's marriage to Marlin.

Marlin begat three sons, Matthias Jamal Harrison, Deidrick Aaron Harrison, Derik Tremaine Harrison, and one daughter, Allison Queen Harrison. This is the genealogy of the Harrison family, the founding family of Creeke.

Green Genealogy

This is the genealogy of the Green family of Creeke.

Alan Green took for a wife, Laurie. And Alan begat two sons, Arnold Green and Alfred Green.

Arnold married Ruth-Anne Grace Parker, whose parents were Damian Lee Parker and Marianne Solomon Jones. And Arnold begat one daughter, Naomi Leigh Green.

Alfred married Athena Warren. And Alfred begat four daughters, Cynthia Pearl Green, Gloria Diamond Green, Diana Rubylynn Green, and Althea Esmeralda Green.

Dow Genealogy

This is the genealogy of the Dow family of Creeke.

Lawrence Dow took for a wife, Eula. And Lawrence begat one son, Samuel John Dow.

And Samuel took for a wife, Christine Robinson, whose parents were Henry and Elaine Robinson. And Samuel begat one daughter, Kameryn Elaine Dow, and adopted one son, Samiel John Dow Jr., and one daughter, Latasia Laminah Williams.

And Samiel's biological father was Kasey Ferguson.

And Latasia's biological parents were Antonio and Brittany Williams.

Townsend Genealogy

This is the genealogy of the Townsend family of Creeke.

Raymond Townsend took for a wife, Patricia. And Raymond begat one son, Benjamin Raymond Townsend, and one daughter, Charmaine An'genelle Townsend.

PART 1:

IN THE LAST DAYS OF HIGH SCHOOL

Samiel Dow Jr.

Samiel Dow Jr. was eighteen and about to graduate high school in a few weeks. His adult life would start after he walked across that stage.

But Samiel did not know what he wanted to do with his life at all. His life had always been going to school and obeying his parents. And that was exactly what they hoped his next step would be.

His parents wanted him to go to college. They wanted him to get the full four-year experience at a nice university. But they both wanted it for different reasons.

Mrs. Christine Dow had gone to college. She always loved sharing about her glory days on campus and how exciting it had all been. And she wanted Samiel and his sisters – Latasia and Kameryn – to have that same experience.

Mr. Samuel Dow Sr. had never gone to college. Instead, he had gone straight into the workforce. He wanted different and better for his kids, so he pushed them all towards college.

Samiel did not know what he wanted. He had been an average student. And some colleges had already accepted him.

But he also had a good reason for wanting to stay home too.

Samiel was leading a song at church on the first Sunday in May. As he sang, he looked out at the congregation. His eyes fell on his reason for wanting to stay home.

Sitting behind his fifty-year-old adoptive father was Samiel's forty-four-year-old birth father. Kasey Ferguson. Samiel had only known him for about a month.

Samiel first learned about Kasey two weeks before his eighteenth birthday. Up till then, Kasey had never even existed to him.

But Kasey knew all about him. And he had not been what Samiel expected.

Samiel had expected someone like an unprepared young parent who had since gotten his life together. But the man who showed up was Kasey. A single, homeless, unemployed, former drug addict.

Despite being rougher than expected, Samiel loved Kasey and was grateful to meet him. And he was grateful for the family he had grown up with. Samiel's biggest wish was to one day have his whole family together.

But he could not do that if he was not around.

"Praise The Lord," said Pastor Forrest Hall when the choir had finished. "Give it up for the choir y'all. Weren't they phenomenal today?"

Everyone clapped.

Church carried on as usual. There were announcements, tithes and offerings, and lots of prayer. Then, Pastor Hall took his text.

Pastor Hall preached a sermon on First Corinthians Chapter ten, verses twenty-three and twenty-four. It was to encourage the graduating seniors to consider every choice they made going into their adult lives. However, Pastor Hall also applied the text to the older adults, encouraging them to also examine their life choices. He made it clear that until their lives ended, there were always areas in life to deal with, no matter the age.

"We're going to go ahead and release the Townsend family early so they can begin preparing for the lunch rush that's sure to be coming their way," said Pastor Hall as he neared the end of his sermon. "And if y'all could just set Pastor his usual plate to the side, that would be greatly appreciated."

The congregation laughed. Samiel waved to his best friend, eighteen-year-old Benjamin Townsend, as he passed by him. After service, Kasey offered to treat Samiel to lunch at Patty's.

"You did so good today," said Mr. Dow.

"Thanks Dad," said Samiel, feeling his cheeks grow hot. He had once believed his dad was embarrassed of him and his singing. Since then, Mr. Dow had made it clear how much he truly loved Samiel *and* his singing. "Can I go with Kasey? He wants to take me to lunch."

"Okay," said Mrs. Dow.

"But not too long," added Mr. Dow. "Your grandparents are coming to visit later and–!"

"I'll be back by then," interjected Samiel, running off to catch up with Kasey. His dad tended to 'circle the airport and never land the plane' as Youth Pastor Derrick Harrison put it. Samiel did not want to risk missing lunch with Kasey because of it.

Kasey's car was old. So old that it had crank windows and a radio that only played the local stations, CDs, or cassette tapes.

Kasey typically liked listening to the hip-hop station. Occasionally, he would flip to the old school station. But during that drive, they listened to the hip-hop station.

At least they did until a song about drugs began playing.

"Nope," said Kasey, turning down the radio. "Hand me something to play."

"CD or tape?" asked Samiel.

"Doesn't matter," answered Kasey. "I'm not listening to that."

Kasey was sensitive about anything drug-related because of his past drug addiction. He was eight years drug-free and hated anything that encouraged drug use.

They arrived at Patty's and got settled in. Samiel ordered a more modest meal in Kasey's budget compared to his usual Sami Special. Although Kasey worked at his best friend – Mr. Marlin Harrison's – barbershop, he did not get paid much.

"How's your job search going?" asked Samiel.

"Eh," grumbled Kasey. "I knew it was going to be rough."

"Well, don't give up," said Samiel. "Remember, the goal is to not be sweeping Mr. Marlin's floors for the rest of your life."

"I know," said Kasey. "Marlin's a good guy and he's looked out for me. But there's only so much he can do for me, and I don't want to rely on him forever. I want to get on my own two feet at some point."

"You'll get there," said Samiel. "You know, I still can't believe he knew about me this whole time. Now it makes sense why he always looked at me strangely. He could've at least said something."

"Don't blame him," said Kasey. "He was just following the agreement me and your parents made."

"He still could've helped a brother out by saying something. Even just a small hint instead of looking at me all weird."

"He helped you by getting the Dows to adopt you. If it weren't for him, we might not have ever had the chance to meet."

Samiel had to agree. Mr. Marlin had told the Dows, a couple struggling with infertility, about Samiel's upcoming birth. That led to them adopting him.

And it was Mr. Marlin who was currently letting Kasey use his barbershop as a temporary home. Kasey slept on the couch in Mr. Marlin's office. Since Mr. Marlin also managed Creeke's recreation center, he let Kasey in before hours to use the showers in private.

"Well, I'm glad you're here now," said Samiel.

"Me too," said Kasey. "It's strange how much I wanted to get away from here when I was younger, only to get older, come back, and now never want to leave again."

"Has Creeke changed much since you were younger?"

"A little but not too much. Most of me wanting to leave was really just me wanting to get away from my parents."

"Do you ever think about your parents?"

"About as much as they think about me," snorted Kasey. "And knowing them, that's a big, fat 'never'."

"So, you never think about them?" questioned Samiel. "You're not even curious about what might've happened to them?"

"Does it look like they cared about what happened to me?" said Kasey bitterly. "They're the ones who disappeared on me. But I don't care. As far as I'm concerned, all the family I need is sitting right here with me."

"Well, look at you!" gushed First Lady Leilana Hall as she approached the table. "Out here having some family bonding time, I see."

"Hey Lana," said Kasey. "Nice hat."

"Thanks," said First Lady Hall, adjusting the yellow church hat on her head. "Forrest bought it for me. It goes well with my dress."

"Mhmm. What you doing here?"

"Having some family bonding time too," chuckled First Lady Hall. "You know this is the town hotspot after church."

"I can see that."

"Sami, you did so good up there today!" congratulated First Lady Hall. "It makes me so happy to see that you've gotten pass your stage fright!"

"Thank you, ma'am," said Samiel, blushing.

"You know, I was a little surprised when I came back to town and they told me you were the First Lady of the church," teased Kasey. "I was like 'Nah, not Lana! Not the party girl that only went to church on Christmas, Easter, and Mother's Day!'"

"What can I say?" said First Lady Hall with a shrug. "Life is full of surprises."

"Ain't that the truth," agreed Kasey. "But you're pretty good at this First Lady thing."

"Thanks Kasey," said First Lady Hall. "That really means a lot. Well, I won't take up too much time. I just wanted to say hi."

"Hi," said Kasey.

"You're so goofy," snorted First Lady Hall. "Oh! By the way, I heard they're building a new factory just down the road and they're looking for workers. You might want to look there since I heard you were looking for work."

"Thanks," said Kasey. "I'll check it out."

First Lady Hall walked away to find a table for her family. Minutes later, Pastor Hall passed by with his daughter, Layla, stopping for a bit to talk to Kasey and also congratulate Samiel. After them came Adrianna and Antoine Brown, who glared at Samiel as they passed without bothering to speak.

The final member of the Brown family to pass by the table was Andre Brown, who was wiping his damp hands on his pants.

"Hey Dre!" said Mr. Kasey. "I haven't seen you in a hot minute! How's it going?"

"I'm good," said Andre. "If you'll excuse me..."

"Well dang," said Mr. Kasey as he watched Andre walk away. "I guess Brown still doesn't want him talking to me."

"Don't worry about him," griped Samiel.

"Why'd you say it like that?"

"No reason."

Samiel's friendship with the Brown siblings had soured. Losing Andre, Adrianna, and Antoine as friends had been more annoying than sad. And he had barely talked to their older sisters – Karla and Mary – to begin with. But losing their oldest brother Drake as a friend had crushed him.

Drake Brown had been like the cool older brother Samiel had never had. They had related on so many things and Drake had always been someone Samiel could go to. But all that ended around the time Kasey came to town.

Samiel knew it was because he had made it clear to Andre that he did not want to share Kasey with him. Andre had accepted it, cooperated, and not made any fuss about it.

But all of Andre's siblings, especially Adrianna, had treated Samiel like he was some devil for doing that.

Samiel did not understand why they were so bothered by it. Kasey was *his* father who was there to get to know *him*. He should not have to share *his* father with anyone else, especially not with someone who was not his son.

"Listen," said Kasey.

"What's up?" asked Samiel.

"You know it really means a lot for me to be here with you, right?"

"Yeah."

"But if I can't get a good job to support myself staying here, I'll have to go where I can."

"Meaning what?"

"Meaning I'd have to leave town."

"But First Lady Hall just told you about the factory!"

"That won't be ready for a while. And even then, there's no guarantee I'll get hired there once it's done. I need something now."

Samiel silently exhaled his annoyance. He knew Kasey was working hard to find a good job that would allow them to stay together in Creeke. But Kasey's old prison record was making things hard for him.

"What'd you even get locked up for anyways?" questioned Samiel.

"Nah, I'm not telling you that," said Kasey.

"Why not?"

"I want to leave that in the past where it belongs."

"Doesn't look like it's staying in the past to me," said Samiel. "And you do know I can always go look it up right? I'd just rather hear it from you."

"Well, if you must know so badly," said Kasey. "The first time I got locked up was right before you were born. I was around twenty-six and got busted with drugs on me."

"And you didn't know about me, right?"

"Nope. I didn't find out about you until after you were born. And by that point, I was locked up and you were already adopted."

"What happened the other two times?"

"Second time was also for drugs around twenty-eight. Marlin shoved me in rehab after that, but I ended up relapsing. He tried again, I relapsed again. Third time was the charm. Then I got put in jail for a really bad fight at thirty-six."

"A really bad fight?"

"Yeah. Listen, don't be out here fighting over girls, alright?"

"You were fighting over a girl?"

"Not just any girl."

"Who was she?"

"Your mother Sammie."

"Her name is Sammie?"

"Samantha," said Kasey. "Samantha Wallace. I call her Sammie though."

"Huh," said Samiel. "When's the last time you talk to her?"

"This morning. I've been telling her all about you. She's glad you're doing well and ended up with a good family. She also thinks it's ironic that your name is also Sami."

"So, you talk to her all the time then?"

"Yeah."

"And you told her you were coming here to meet me?"

"Yeah."

"Why didn't she come too then?"

"She's not ready yet," said Kasey. He handed Samiel his phone, which showed a recent picture of Kasey and Samantha together on the screen. Samiel could see that he favored Samantha more than Kasey.

"What's she like?"

"Sammie is...," began Kasey. "For starters, her life is a lot more together than mine is. She's a teacher, and she lives in this nice condo. Got a nice ride too. Nothing like that hoopty I got out there."

"How'd you two end up together?"

"We met at a party at her college," explained Kasey with a chuckle. "She was a junior. I was just there, high out of my mind and looking for a good time. We got drunk and I woke up next to her in her dorm. We dated for a bit. Then I got locked up. I didn't want her seeing me like that, so we talked through Marlin, and that's how I learned she was pregnant. After I got clean, we reconnected. It's been on and off ever since."

"Are you two broken up right now?"

"Kind of," said Kasey. "It's complicated."

"And you were fighting over her?"

"Yeah. Like I said, it was really bad."

"What happened?"

"Some dude was being disrespectful and tried to get tough with her, so I had to get tough with him."

"When was this?"

"Right after we reconnected."

"And now you can't get a job because of it."

"Yeah," said Kasey glumly.

"I can help you look for a job," offered Samiel.

"No, that's alright," said Kasey. "I'd rather you'd focus on finishing school."

"It's the end of the school year though," said Samiel. "At this point, we're not doing anything besides waiting for school to end."

"Well, then that's what you need to be doing," said Kasey. He gave Samiel a reassuring smile and said, "It'll be alright. I'll figure something out in no time."

That evening, Samiel sat with his family in the living room. They had just finished eating dinner and were trading stories and life updates. His grandparents – Papa Lawrence and Grandma Eula Dow – had just finished tag-teaming on a story about the "good ol' days".

"How are things down at the department, Sam?" asked Papa Dow. Papa Dow had been a police officer like his son and had almost become chief. But when Mayor Perry arrogantly let the town choose the next chief, they chose the much younger Mr. Terrence Parker instead. After that disappointment, Papa Dow retired from the force.

"Things are...," began Mr. Dow, seeming to contemplate his words.

"Sam?" questioned Mrs. Dow when her husband's hesitation lasted longer than she liked.

"Honestly, things aren't good at all," answered Mr. Dow.

"What do you mean 'things aren't good'?" asked Grandma Dow.

"I wasn't going to say anything yet, but it's probably going to come out soon anyways," sighed Mr. Dow. "Mayor Perry is gutting the department."

There was a silence as the words sunk in.

"Gutting the department?" repeated Mrs. Dow. "As in replacing you and Terrence?"

"As in completely shutting it down for good," said Mr. Dow. "He claims it's too expensive to maintain a police department with only two officers in it. He plans to turn over the policing of Creeke to the county."

"Can't say I blame him," said Papa Dow. "I read in the news that departments in both big cities and small towns are struggling to keep officers. And Bernard has never been a dummy when it came to money, so I'm not surprised he's made this decision."

"But think of how this will affect the community," said Mrs. Dow. "Everyone knows and trusts Terrence and Sam because they grew up here and live here. They're part of this community and care about it. Bringing in outsiders who don't care about Creeke beyond a paycheck could backfire."

"Well Chrissy, there's nothing we can do about it," said Mr. Dow. "Mayor Perry has already started the process."

"Terrence isn't going to fight it?" asked Papa Dow.

"I don't think so," replied Mr. Dow. "He's tired of fighting with Perry."

"He can't just give up!" cried Mrs. Dow. "Especially not to someone like Bernard Perry!"

"Like I said, he's tired," said Mr. Dow. "We've been in this thing together twenty-eight years and he's been fighting that man since the day we started."

"Maybe it's for the best then," said Papa Dow. "If Terrence is at his wits end, it's only a matter of time until he loses it. He is Gabriel Ray Jones' grandson after all."

"Whew Lord," said Grandma Dow. "That's the last thing this town needs. Gabriel would've just beat the brakes off of Bernard and been done with it."

"Mhmm," agreed Papa Dow. "Would've put that man in the ground and gladly went to jail with a smile on his face."

"Can we not be so gruesome in front of my kids?" said Mrs. Dow quietly.

"Sorry darling," said Papa Dow. "But you remember how Gabriel was. And that was after he got saved. I remember how he was before he got saved. Heck I still remember the day he shot that hole in the church stop sign as a *warning shot* to Calvin Brown. That Gabriel had a quick temper and his daughter and all his grandkids and all *their* kids are the same way. That's why I'm so surprised Terrence made it this long without snapping."

"All I know is, I've got to figure out my next step fast because Mayor Perry is wasting no time with this," said Mr. Dow.

After dinner, Samiel and Kameryn ended up in Latasia's room. Normally, she would have a fit about them being in her "space". But after what they had learned that night, she just let it be.

His sisters' reactions to their father's news were as opposite as could be. Latasia was calm, while Kameryn was panicky. Samiel was somewhere in the middle, but he had to remain calm. He was the oldest and the man, after all.

"What's going to happen to us?" questioned Kameryn.

"What do you mean?" asked Latasia.

"Dad is losing his job," explained Kameryn. "We can't live off just what Mom makes."

"Dad's going to find another job."

"But how long is that going to take? And what if it doesn't pay as much? What if we lose our house? What if you guys get taken away?"

"First of all, I'm eighteen," said Samiel. "I can't get taken away. Second of all, you're overreacting. We are not going to lose the house and we're not going to get split up."

"I am not overreacting!" cried Kameryn. "I don't know if you've noticed Samiel but it's very hard to get a job right now!"

"Well, Dad's been working for a long time. I'm sure he'll get something with all his experience."

"Not if they say he's overqualified!"

"Why do you know so much about the job market?" questioned Latasia. "You're not even old enough to work yet!"

"I will be next year when I turn sixteen!" countered Kameryn. "I need to know what I'm getting myself into!"

"Well, right now you're fifteen and you need to relax."

"I can't relax! This is terrible!"

Samiel could not deal with Kameryn. Especially because she was saying what everyone was thinking, and he could not let his sisters see him getting all worked up. So, he went to see his father, hoping he had a plan.

He found his father pacing in the living room. That was a good sign. Mr. Dow and Kameryn both paced when they were thinking.

"Man, oh man, your mama is heated with me," said Mr. Dow when he saw Samiel. "I think I might be sleeping on the couch tonight."

"Why?" asked Samiel.

"She said I shouldn't have waited this long to tell her about losing my job. But she doesn't understand that I just found out myself. And I can't just come home and say I lost my job with no game plan in place for what to do next. I guess I need to start pounding the pavement for a new job or else we'll all be out on the street."

"Pounding the pavement?" repeated Samiel.

"Yeah," said Mr. Dow. "You know, get out there and start looking for a new job. Turning in applications, shaking hands. That type of thing."

"Why would you do that?"

"Because that's how you get a job?"

"No, it's not."

"Yes, it is. That's how I've gotten all my jobs."

"When's... the last time you applied for a job...?"

"Shoot when I was what, twenty-one?"

"Dad, that was almost thirty years ago."

"And?"

"Job hunting doesn't work like that no more."

"How would you know?" snorted Mr. Dow. "You've never had a job before."

"And you haven't applied for one in a long," said Samiel, deciding not to point out it was his dad who told him not to worry about a job and focus on school. Samiel had applied for some jobs out of curiosity when he turned sixteen. He never heard back from any of them. So, he gave up and did what his dad said. "Now you just go online and apply. And they tell you not to call or email either."

"That's ridiculous," scoffed Mr. Dow. "How are you supposed to show them you're interested if you can't get in contact with them?"

"You just got to hope they like your application enough to contact you," said Samiel.

"Uhn uhn," disagreed Mr. Dow. "I'm going to go pound the pavement like I've been doing. It's worked before, so it'll work again."

"Okay...," said Samiel. "And while you're doing that, I could get a job to help out around here."

"No sir," said Mr. Dow quickly. "You need to focus on finishing school and getting ready for college. And if you do get a job, then you're putting that money toward your own college education."

"I don't mind helping out, Dad."

"Well, I do. This is for me to deal with, not you. Understand?"

"Yes sir."

Samiel decided not to fight with his father. But he also knew he could not just sit by and watch his family struggle.

Monday morning, Samiel walked the halls of Creeke High School on his way to his first class. He reminisced on his time there as he walked. In a few weeks, he would be forever done with high school.

Samiel felt excited about life after high school. But he was also nervous because he had no idea what to expect.

Part of him was also scared that he would end up in the same position as his fathers. His dad had been a policeman for thirty years, while Kasey had drifted wherever life took him. Yet, they both ended up in the same spot: unemployed and unsure of what was next.

Samiel was in the same boat, and he hoped that twenty years later he would not still be there.

"Beep beep," said a voice from behind Samiel. He turned around to see his eighteen-year-old best friend, Derek Harrison, wheeling himself up the hallway in his wheelchair. His same-aged cousin, Allison Harrison, walked beside him carrying a stack of posters.

"What are those?" asked Samiel.

"Our prom posters," said Allison. "You know we're running for king and queen."

"And here I was considering running for prom king myself," joked Samiel. "Now I really stand no chance with my boy running here."

"My chances are a little shaky too," said Derek. "I'm running against Justin."

"And I'm running against Stacy and Mariana," added Allison. "I'm not too worried about Mariana, but Stacy is another story."

"I honestly don't care if I win," said Derek. "I'm just running because Queenie thought it'd be cool if both of us won."

"Well, it would!" said Allison. "When has a pair of cousins ever won prom king and queen at the same time?"

"Andre and Mariana could also easily do it."

"Oh please. Those two would never make it through a campaign together. Andre always says stuff without thinking while Mariana just doesn't care what she says, and they always talk crazy to each other. And it's crazy because Mr. Brown and Mrs. Garza are like this."

Allison crossed her fingers to show what she meant.

"Like I don't think I've ever seen them argue," continued Allison. "But their kids argue all the time."

"Well, that's just how the Browns are," said Derek. "They'll throw down with anybody including each other. But let anyone else come at one of them and you'll have the whole family trying to get at you."

"Mhmm," agreed Allison. "But I just thought it'd be cool if we won. Besides my parents won prom king and queen together and I want to carry on the tradition."

"You know this won't matter once we graduate, right?" said Derek.

"We haven't graduated yet, so it matters," said Allison. "Let me enjoy the last few weeks of high school that we have left. Because once it's over, it's over."

"I can't wait," said Derek. "Because the faster we get out of here, the faster I'll get back to using my leg again."

"You shouldn't be in such a rush," said Allison. "You should enjoy the moment while it lasts."

"Let's see you get your leg broken and not be in such a rush to use it again."

"Oh my gosh!" huffed Allison. "Do I have the wrong Derek with me? Are you really Dee-Three pretending to be D-Money?"

Derek stared annoyedly at Allison, who returned the same look. Samiel glanced at them both and started laughing.

"What's funny?" asked both Harrisons.

"You two!" laughed Samiel even harder. "You guys are funny!"

The Harrisons rolled their eyes at Samiel and the three continued toward the spot designated for prom posters. When they arrived, they found Allison's best friend, Stacy Gilbert, hanging hers.

"Alright Stacy!" cheered Allison. "That looks good!"

"Thanks girl!" said Stacy.

"You took this at that expensive photo studio in the city?"

"Yes ma'am. This cost me three-hundred dollars."

"Oh Lord," groaned Derek as he pretended to faint.

"That three-hundred dollars was worth it," Allison said. "This looks like a movie poster. I don't even want to hang ours now after seeing this."

"It can't be that bad."

"Compared to yours, ours looks like an arts-and-craft project."

"Let's see it."

Allison showed Stacy one of their posters. It was a colored poster board decorated with stickers and colorful stenciled lettering. At the center was a printed selfie of the Harrison cousins.

"It's cute," said Stacy.

"Mhmm," muttered Allison unconvinced. "Prissy helped me make them."

"Okay Prissy," complimented Stacy. "Here, let me help you hang them."

Samiel watched as the girls hung the poster. Mariana Garza also came with her best friend, Jada Graham-Hernandez, to hang her poster.

"Oh, that's cute!" gushed Stacy when she saw Mariana's poster. "Okay Mariana, I see you!"

"Thank you...," said Mariana, blushing.

"Are we the only ones who didn't go to the photo studio?" joked Allison.

"Looks like it," said Derek.

"Need some help?" asked Samiel to Mariana.

"Not from you," spat Mariana.

"Mariana," chided Jada.

"No!" snapped Mariana. "I don't need his help since he thinks my family is so stupid!"

Samiel annoyedly pushed air through his nose. He could not believe the entire Brown family was *that* upset with him. Especially because Andre had yet to say anything to him.

"Dang," said Derek once Mariana and Jada left. "Those Browns are on your head."

"I'm not worried about them," said Samiel. "Can I come hang at your place this Saturday?"

"You know you don't have to ask," said Derek. "What's going on?"

"It's Lala's turn to host LSS."

"Oh. Yeah, you can come over."

"Thanks."

Later that day, Samiel got called to the guidance counselor's office. The high school guidance counselor was Ms. Greta Nelson. She had been the counselor since Samiel's sophomore year.

Samiel learned from his mother that Ms. Nelson had started her career as a kindergarten teacher. Then she taught middle school for a bit. Eventually, she went back to school to become a guidance counselor.

Samiel liked Ms. Nelson as a counselor. She was a great listener and always gave good advice. And she was a lot more open with the students than her twin sister, Coach Gretchen Nelson-Brown.

"Hello Sami," said Ms. Nelson.

"Hi Ms. Nelson," answered Samiel.

"I'm meeting with all the seniors to discuss your plans after graduation," explained Ms. Nelson. "Do you already have an idea of what you want to do?"

"I'm not really sure yet," said Samiel.

"Okay. That's not unusual. I know plenty of people who didn't figure out what they wanted to do until they were *well* into their adult lives. Are you thinking about college?"

"Yeah," said Samiel glumly. "But I didn't receive any scholarships or anything."

"That's okay," said Ms. Nelson. "There are other options for paying for college. The one most people automatically go to is student loans. And since you specifically aren't sure what you want to do yet, you could also consider community college."

"Community college?"

"Yeah. It's cheaper and you could complete most of your general classes while figuring out your next step. And if you don't mind commuting, you could stay home. There's also the option of going to trade school and learning a trade. There's plenty of options out here for you to choose from."

"Did you know what you wanted to do when you were my age?"

"For the most part, yeah."

"And you ended up doing it?"

"Some of it."

"What about the part you didn't do? Do you ever wish you had done it?"

"I used to. But I've learned that had things gone the way I wanted them to, I probably would've been miserable."

The meeting with Ms. Nelson left Samiel with a lot to think about. His parents had always pushed going to a big university as his next step after high school. He had never even considered another possibility.

What stuck with him most was what Ms. Nelson said about community college. It would be a great middle ground between what he wanted and what his parents wanted.

He started researching when he got home. And he found that community college was significantly cheaper than university. It was something for him to seriously consider if he wanted to save his family some money.

Samiel researched until his father got home.

"Hey Dad," said Samiel. "How'd pounding the pavement go?"

"It went well," said Mr. Dow.

"So, you were able to get something?" asked Samiel hopefully.

"Not exactly," said Mr. Dow, scratching the back of his neck. "But I was able to talk to some people."

"And they said they'd hire you? Interview you at least?"

"That *could* happen," said Mr. Dow with a hypothetical tone. He scratched the back of his neck again and asked, "How was your day?"

"My day was fine," said Samiel dismissively. "I want to know how your job hunt went. Who'd you talk to?"

"That's not important," laughed Mr. Dow nervously. "Just know I'm on my way to landing something."

Mr. Dow's vagueness confirmed to Samiel that he had been right. But it was not a sweet victory for him. He had been hoping his father would be successful.

"Dad, have you ever learned a trade?" asked Samiel.

"A trade?" repeated Mr. Dow. "No, not officially. Why do you ask?"

"Ms. Nelson was telling me about other options I had besides going to college."

"Hm," said Mr. Dow with a slight nod. Samiel knew that was his father's way of showing disapproval. "Learning a trade could help but I still say it's best you go to college."

"I know," said Samiel. "That's why she also told me about community college. She said that was cheaper and I could use the time to figure out what I wanted to do. And I could stay close to home."

"Community college *is* cheaper," said Mr. Dow with another slight nod. "But don't you want the full college experience? Getting to live on campus and make friends and memories?"

"Not if it'll bankrupt our family."

"Nothing's going to bankrupt our family," said Mr. Dow sharply. "Now Samiel, as a young man you are free to choose what you want to do. But I don't want you limiting yourself all because you're worried about money. You figure out what you want to do and let me and your mother handle the money. Understand?"

"Yes sir."

Samiel knew his father meant well. But Samiel believed he had a responsibility to his family.

He did not want to do something that would hurt them financially. Plus, going to community college would allow him to stay home near Kasey. It gave him everything he wanted and was something to seriously consider.

That Saturday, Samiel went to Derik's house. It was Latasia's turn to host the Little Sister Society club meeting. And it was understood that all men leave the house whenever the girls met.

Samiel caught Derek's father, Mr. Malcolm Harrison, on his way out the door. He was dressed nicely. And he smelled nice too.

"Hey Mr. Malcolm," said Samiel.

"Hey Sami," said Mr. Malcolm. "Derek's in his room. DEREK!"

"YEAH?"

"SAMI'S HERE! I'M OUT!"

"ALRIGHT!"

"Alright," said Mr. Malcolm. "Bye Sami. Keep my door locked. And make sure my house was the same way it was when I left."

"Yes sir," said Samiel as Mr. Malcolm left. He went to Derek's room and said, "Hey. Where's your dad going?"

"Date," answered Derek.

"With who?"

"Ms. Nita. He met her on a dating app last summer. She's like fifteen years older than him and has no kids."

"Your dad sure has a thing for older women," chuckled Samiel.

"Yeah," laughed Derek. "You think we'll still be like that at thirty-three?"

"Thirty-three is such a long time a way," laughed Samiel. "I don't even know what I'll be like next week. Have you met his older woman?"

"Not yet. But the way he talks about her, she seems alright."

"Cool," said Samiel. "Listen, I need your advice on something."

"What's up?" asked Derek.

"My dad is losing his job," confided Samiel. "And Kasey might have to leave if he can't find a better job."

"Why is your dad losing his job?" asked Derek.

"Mayor Perry says the department is too expensive," griped Samiel. "And Kasey's having trouble finding work because of his record."

"Well, that sucks."

"Yeah," sighed Samiel. "I want to do something to help them, but they both just told me to focus on finishing school."

"Then maybe that's what you should do."

"Dude, these are my dads we're talking about here. I can't just sit by and do nothing. Especially not after all my dad's done for me. And if Kasey leaves then how will we get to spend time with each other?"

"Well, what are you trying to do?"

"I don't know. I'm kind of considering getting a job and going to community college. That way my parents will be happy, and I can still be around to help out."

"Yeah, but how does that help Mr. Kasey?"

"I don't know," groaned Samiel. He ran his hands down his face and said, "This wasn't supposed to happen."

"Yeah, I know how you feel," sighed Derek.

There was a knock at the front door.

"Can you get that?" requested Derek. "It's Benji with my food."

"Your food?" questioned Samiel. "Since when does Patty's do delivery?"

"Since one of their loyal customers had his leg broken by an evil jerk."

Samiel let Benjamin in. Whatever Derek had ordered smelled good.

"Hey," said Benjamin when he saw Derek. "Here's your food."

"Thanks," said Derek. "You're such a good friend."

"I can't stay long," said Benjamin. "I'm going prom shopping later."

"You got a date?" questioned Samiel.

"I'm going alone," answered Benjamin.

"Me too," said Samiel. "What about you, Derek?

"If it weren't for the fact that I was running for king I probably wouldn't go at all," said Derek.

"Why not?" asked Samiel.

"Because what am I going to do all night on a broken leg?"

"You've only got two more months to go till it's all healed up."

"Prom is in two weeks and graduation is the week after that," said Derek. He exhaled frustratedly and said, "I wasn't supposed to spend my senior year with a broken leg. I was supposed to be having fun! And now I ain't even got no one to go with anymore. So, what's the point?"

"So, you and Adrianna are *done* done?" asked Benjamin. "Or are you guys just on a break?"

"It's complicated," answered Derek. "I still like her. But the time isn't right."

"What if she moves on?"

"She won't."

"How do you know?"

"I just do."

"I don't know," said Benjamin. "Why don't you try dating other people?"

"I don't want to," said Derek. "Honestly, we'd still be together now if it weren't for that shoe-throwing daddy of hers. He's the reason we're in this mess!"

"I believe it," agreed Samiel. "The Browns are honestly nothing but drama."

"Mmhmm," uttered Benjamin, unconvinced.

"You don't agree with me?" questioned Samiel.

"I don't know," answered Benjamin. "I just remember things differently, I guess."

"Are you talking about what happened between him and Andre?" asked Derek. "Because I thought everyone was over that. Andre seems like he's moved on to me."

"His whole family still doesn't like me and always gives me dirty looks," stated Samiel.

"Well, that's your fault," said Benjamin.

"Whose side are you on?" remarked Samiel.

"No one's," said Benjamin. "But what you did was messed up."

"Well, how come he's not still mad at me too then?" asked Derek.

"You apologized," said Benjamin.

"You see how petty it is?" asked Samiel. "If he has such an issue, why doesn't he just be a man and come talk to me about it?"

"The same way you did?" asked Benjamin.

"Yes! I went to him and told him what was up!"

"After you tried to clown him in front of everyone at my video shoot."

"And made me look stupid in the process," added Derek.

"So what?" griped Samiel. "Why can't he just get over it like everyone else?"

"All I'm saying is, the Browns don't just have drama out of nowhere," said Benjamin.

"Whatever Benji," scoffed Samiel. "Don't you have shopping to go do?"

"Don't get mad at me just because you know I'm right," said Benjamin before leaving.

"Am I wrong?" asked Samiel. "Like is it so wrong for me to not want to share *my* father?"

"I don't think you're wrong about how you feel," said Derek. "But you could've handled it better."

"How would you have handled it?"

"A fight to the death."

"Haha," said Samiel sarcastically. "But really, how would you have handled it?"

"I would've just talked to Andre straight up," said Derek. "I honestly don't know why you didn't just do that to begin with. I'm sure he would've understood if you had just talked to him from jump."

Samiel did not do that because there should not have been a need for a talk in the first place. He felt like it should have been understood by everyone that Kasey was there for him and him only.

But Samiel also could not help but wonder how things would have gone if he had handled them differently.

When he got home, he found his sisters watching television in the living room.

"Hey," said Samiel. "How'd the meeting go?"

"Annoying," said Latasia.

"What happened?"

"It was just annoying," said Latasia.

"And it's none of your business anyways," added Kameryn.

"Rude!" said Samiel, starting for his room. He said over his shoulder, "Nobody was worried about y'all little meeting anyways!"

He ducked fast enough to avoid a pillow tossed at his head.

"You missed!" teased Samiel.

"Whatever Sami," said Latasia. "We're not in the mood."

Samiel went to his room. He was not sure what was wrong with his sisters. But whatever it was, they did not have to take it out on him.

Sunday service started interestingly. During praise and worship, Mr. Terrence became very emotional.

For the first time, his singing did not sound bored and uninspired. There was passion in his voice and in his piano playing. Tears rolled down his face as he sang.

The whole service ended up becoming a worship service. People cried, prayed, and comforted each other. Samiel took the time to think more about his situation with Andre.

It had been on his mind since his conversation with his boys. He wondered more and more if he should have approached things differently.

Samiel decided to seek another perspective. He needed to talk to someone from Andre's side of things. So, he approached Antoine after the service ended.

"Hey," said Samiel.

"What do you want?" remarked Antoine.

"Dang," chuckled Samiel. "I guess all preacher's kids *are* mean."

"Why are you over here bothering me?" snapped Antoine.

"I wanted to talk."

"Talk about what? I ain't cool with you."

"That's why I wanted to talk," said Samiel. "Why are you guys still holding on to something that happened months ago? Especially when Andre's been moved on."

"Well, I ain't Andre," said Antoine, crossing his arms. They were developing muscle from all his time in the gym. "You came at my brother for no reason and ain't apologized or nothing. You think I'm going to be cool with you after that?"

"But he doesn't care though."

"How do you know? You haven't talked to him."

"Well, he hasn't talked to me about it either."

"Maybe because you hurt his feelings," said Antoine sarcastically. "Would you want to be friends with someone who hurt your feelings and then acted like nothing happened? And we still don't even know what your problem was in the first place for you to do all that!"

"I told him what was up."

"Well, he didn't tell us," said Antoine. "All I know is, until you apologize to him, we're not cool. And that goes for *all* of us because we all feel the same way."

The conversation left Samiel feeling annoyed. It would be one thing for him to apologize if he had hurt Andre's feelings like Antoine said. But Andre himself seemed like he had moved on, which is why Samiel felt like what he did was not a big deal.

However, what stuck out to him in the conversation was how Antoine said none of the Browns were cool with him. He knew they stuck together when they needed to. Just like his own family stuck together when they needed to.

He wondered if his situation with Andre had anything to do with his sisters' bad attitudes the day before. Adrianna was the president of The Little Sister Society. They could have gotten into it over him.

"Lala," said Samiel when they got home from church. "Are you and Adrianna still cool?"

"Yeah, but we're not as close as we were before," sighed Latasia.

"Why?" asked Samiel. "Is it because of what happened between me and Andre?"

"I wish," snorted Latasia, rolling her eyes. "At least then the mess would make sense."

Samiel quietly exhaled relief. Whatever happened between them was not his fault. But then he wondered what had happened between them.

Whatever it was he would not get it from his sister. Latasia would not say anymore after that.

That Monday, Samiel went with Kasey to the library. Kasey liked the library. He said it was the only place he had never been thrown out of when he was struggling.

While there, they ran into Andre who was waiting around for Mary to get off work. He was looking at the science books. When Kasey saw him, he approached him with Samiel close behind.

"Dre!" greeted Kasey. "How you doing?"

"I'm doing fine," said Andre. "If you'll excuse me..."

"Come on Dre," whined Kasey. "You can't stop to talk for at least a few minutes?"

Andre exhaled strongly through his nose and glanced at Samiel. It struck Samiel how much Andre resembled his father, Mr. Torrance Brown, then. The furrowed eyebrows, the pursed lips, the annoyed eyes.

"No, I can't."

Andre's harshness shocked Samiel. He had never known Andre to be so harsh with anyone. By the time he recovered, Andre was gone.

"Alright," said Kasey, shoving his fists in his pockets. "I think it's safe to say me and him aren't on speaking terms anymore."

"He didn't have to talk to you like that!" snapped Samiel.

"It's okay," sighed Kasey. "He's already told me a few times not to talk to him anymore. I guess I'm just hardheaded and that's what I get for it."

"No, that's not right!" argued Samiel. "I ought to give him a piece of my mind!"

"What for?" asked Kasey. "He didn't do anything wrong. Brown told him not to talk to me and he's just trying to follow his dad's rules.

He probably told him all the terrible things I did to him when we were younger to prove his point.”

Samiel felt annoyed that Andre had acted like that toward Kasey. But he also knew it was not right to let someone else take the blame for what he had caused.

“That’s not why he won’t talk to you,” grumbled Samiel.

“It’s got to be,” said Kasey. “I don’t know what else it could be.”

“*I* told him not to talk to you anymore,” said Samiel guiltily.

“What? You did?”

“It was back when you first came back. You were spending a lot of time with him and not me, so I asked him to back off a little. I guess he didn’t like the way I said it, so he just completely backed off.”

“I don’t remember spending that much time with Dre,” said Kasey confusedly. “In fact, I’m pretty sure we only talked a handful of times before he completely went cold on me.”

“It seemed like a lot more times than that to me. It felt like you were here for him more than me. So, I told him to stop spending so much time with you.”

“That’s messed up,” said Kasey. “Sami, regardless of how much time I may seem to spend with someone else, you’re who I’m here for. You’re my son, not Dre.”

“Well, it’s too late to do anything about it now,” said Samiel. “Now, he doesn’t like me.”

“Did you try apologizing to him yet?”

Samiel did not answer. He just looked at the ground.

“Take it from me, Sami,” said Kasey. “The longer you let this go on, the less likely he’ll be willing to hear you out. I think you should try making things right.”

That evening, Mr. Dow invited Mr. Terrence over for dinner. His wife was away on business and his kids were out and about.

Mrs. Dow had taken Latasia and Kameryn to visit her mother, Granny Elaine Robinson. Granny Elaine used to live in Creeke with her husband until he died. Their yard had a big tree that Samiel and his sisters would take turns climbing.

Then her dementia started setting in. Mrs. Dow made the hard decision of putting her in a nursing home. She only did so because she was not able to care for her mother the way she needed to be.

Since then, Mrs. Dow regularly visited her mother. Normally, Samiel would also go, but that time he chose not to. So, Mr. Dow declared it a "guys' night in".

"Man, I ain't never heard you sing like the way you did yesterday," said Mr. Dow. "They ain't going to be able to say you're the sibling who can't sing anymore after that. No sir, not anymore."

"By 'they', you mean 'you'?" said Mr. Terrence.

"N-now wait a minute!" said Mr. Dow, flustered. "I-I never said you couldn't sing! I said you sounded weird when you sang! Those are two different things!"

"Sure Sam. Okay."

"It's true! Half the time you be up there singing like you don't want to be up there! But this Sunday you were on fire! Why can't you sing like that every Sunday?"

"I wasn't trying to do anything special," explained Mr. Terrence. "I honestly was just having a moment with The Lord."

"Well, you need to have a moment with The Lord every Sunday from now on."

Mr. Terrence smiled and shook his head.

"Yes sir," continued Mr. Dow. "That really touched me."

"I'm glad it touched you, Sam."

"Yes sir, it did," said Mr. Dow, eyeing Mr. Terrence knowingly. "But it probably touched me so much because I know what caused it."

Mr. Terrence dropped his smile.

"Everything's going to be alright," said Mr. Dow. "We'll get through this together."

"I know," said Mr. Terrence. "But I just don't like stuff like this. That jerk sprung that news on us and got us scrambling for our next moves, while he's chilling in his mansion."

"Like I said, everything will be alright," reassured Mr. Dow. "God's making a way for us as we speak."

"I don't understand how you're so calm about this."

"Because I know God's going to take care of us," laughed Mr. Dow. "He's not going to leave us out here stranded like this. Especially since He answered my prayer to have mouths to feed in the first place, you know what I'm saying?"

Mr. Terrence chuckled.

"But believe me when I say I know how you feel," continued Mr. Dow. "I'm old, only got a high school diploma, and the only big job I've ever had was that one. I can't join the force in the city, because they want young guys like Junior. So, I ain't got no choice but to believe God will make a miracle happen because it's going to take a miracle to get something with those stats."

"Tch," sounded Mr. Terrence, sucking his teeth. "I didn't think Junior would last in the academy because of how goofy he is. But he's hanging in there and determined to make it through."

"Ain't you happy about that?"

"Yeah. I'm proud of my boy. But sometimes I wonder if he realizes just how stressful this job really is. That's the only bright side of losing it: losing all the stress that comes with it."

"Ain't that the truth," agreed Mr. Dow. "That's why I'm glad all my kids are going to college. They'll have way more options than we had."

"Don't assume you know what your kids will do," warned Mr. Terrence. "I thought all my kids would go to college too but the only one that went was Angie. Junior's following in my footsteps and I don't know what MikeMike's doing. He's talking about becoming a truck driver!"

"What's wrong with that?"

"The farthest Michael has been outside of Creeke is the city. That boy ain't ready to be no truck driver!"

"Well, what do you want him to do?"

"I don't know."

"Hey, maybe he can hook you up with a job at his job," suggested Mr. Dow.

"As a delivery driver?" questioned Mr. Terrence.

"It's better than nothing."

"If that's the best you've got, we're in serious trouble."

"I've been out here pounding the pavement. Something will come. We just have to keep pushing."

Listening to his dad's optimism made Samiel sad. His dad did not deserve to be in this type of position after working so hard to help others.

Samiel decided to take matters into his own hands and do his own pavement pounding. He looked in the newspaper's classifieds sections and saw that Mr. Jacob Payne was hiring. The Brewers and the Townsends were also hiring.

Working for the Brewers or the Townsends would be a more positive experience. But Mr. Payne paid the most.

So, Samiel decided to pay Mr. Payne a visit the next day after school.

"Hello Mr. Payne," said Samiel.

"Samiel," said Mr. Payne, smiling in a disarming way that made him seem innocent. But Samiel knew better. Everyone in Creeke knew better. He could practically see the devil horns and pitchfork as Mr. Payne asked, "What brings you to my office today?"

"I saw you were hiring," said Samiel, handing the newspaper to Mr. Payne. "I know a few people who need work."

"Well, you came to the right place," said Mr. Payne. "I'm always willing to help my fellow man... for the right price, of course."

"Yes sir."

"So, these people who need work. Do they know you're here on their behalf?"

"Not exactly. I wanted to find out more information before I told them about it."

"Well unfortunately, I can't help you then. I don't like middlemen. I'm sure you understand."

"What if I was looking for work?"

"Then we'd have something to talk about," said Mr. Payne. He motioned for Samiel to sit, adding, "But only if you're truly interested. I don't like my time being wasted."

"What do you have available?" asked Samiel, sitting down.

"I have some things to offer," said Mr. Payne with feigned innocence. He smirked and eyed Samiel coyly. "But what I need most right now is an assistant."

Samiel could not wait to tell Kasey his news. He had found a way to keep Kasey in Creeke that also paid well. All Samiel had to do left was help out his dad.

Samiel decided to treat Kasey to dinner at Patty's. He did his best to contain himself while he waited for the right moment to tell Kasey.

"I've got some good news and some not so good news," said Kasey.

"I've got some good news too," said Samiel. "But you can go first. Just tell me all of it at once."

"You sure?"

"Yeah."

"Okay...," said Kasey hesitantly. "I found some work for the summer and–!"

"Really?!" gasped Samiel. He felt disappointed that his efforts had been for nothing but was still happy for Kasey. "That's great!"

"But it's not here."

"Not here?" repeated Samiel. "You mean like it's in the city?"

"No. I mean it's not in this area at all."

It took Samiel a minute to process what Kasey had said. Once he did, he felt all his excitement leave him.

"So...," said Samiel. "You're leaving?"

"Only for the summer," said Kasey. "I'll be back before you start college."

"But I thought you were here to stay."

"I was. And I still am. But I've got to take this if I want to get on my own two feet."

"You couldn't find *anything* around here?"

"You know I would've if I could've."

"Well, where's it at then?"

"It's in Atlanta where Sammie is... She's the one who got me he job..."

"Oh," said Samiel. "Are you two getting back together?"

"No," said Kasey. "But she did offer to let me stay in her guest room."

"Oh," repeated Samiel.

"Like I said, it's only for the summer. I'll be back before you know it."

Samiel nodded. He did not know how to feel. Part of him was glad Kasey had finally landed something.

But another part of him was mad that Kasey had to leave to do it. He wanted Kasey to stay.

"Would you consider working for Mr. Payne if it meant you could stay here?" asked Samiel hopefully.

"*Mr. Payne?!*" cried Kasey, scrunching his face. "As in *Jacob Payne?!*"

Samiel's hopes died. Even Kasey was aware of Mr. Payne's terrible reputation.

"It was just a suggestion," said Samiel. "I saw he was hiring in the paper."

"Well, I ain't interested, that's for sure," said Kasey disgustedly. "Ain't enough money in the world to convince me to work for him."

"Okay," sighed Samiel. "When are you leaving?"

"The day after your graduation."

"That's so close!"

"I know. Everything's just happened so fast."

"Well, this is just great!" scoffed Samiel.

"Sami, don't be like that," said Kasey. "I'm not going to be gone forever."

"You might as well be," muttered Samiel. "You just got here and you're already leaving."

Kasey did not say anything after that. The rest of the dinner was quiet and awkward. Samiel returned home in a sour mood.

"What's wrong?" asked Mrs. Dow when she saw him. "Did something happen with Kasey at dinner?"

"He's leaving," said Samiel sulkily. "That's what happened."

"Where's he going?"

"Atlanta," said Samiel, unable to resist showing his annoyance when he did. "He couldn't find work here so he's going where he could."

"Oh. For how long?"

"He said it's only for the summer. But who knows if it'll stay like that?"

"It'll stay like that," reassured Mrs. Dow.

"How do you know?"

"Because I know how hard Kasey's worked to be in your life," said Mrs. Dow. "When we first adopted you, Kasey was in jail and still battling with his drug addiction. Because of the terms of the adoption, he couldn't have contact with you until you were eighteen. We told him we wouldn't keep you from him when the time came, but if he wanted to be in your life, he had to beat his addiction. He did that and he's worked too hard to be in your life just to leave only after a few months. So, if he says he'll only be gone for the summer, then he'll only be gone for the summer."

Samiel felt a little better after the talk. But he was still a little sad and annoyed.

And then there was Mr. Payne. Mr. Payne had given Samiel the information expecting to hire someone. But Kasey was leaving, and his dad certainly would not work under Mr. Payne.

That left him.

Samiel wanted a job to help his family. And Mr. Payne paid well.

But Mr. Payne was also not trustworthy. Samiel did not want to work for someone like him.

But Samiel also felt obligated to produce someone to hire. And the job *did* pay well.

It was something for Samiel to seriously consider.

Prom was that Friday.

Samiel had decided on a dark green fitted suit with khaki loafers. His dad made jokes about how the suit looked on him.

"Back in my day, pant legs went past our ankles," joked Mr. Dow. "We wouldn't be caught dead in high-waters like you young boys today."

"Dad, I saw your prom photos," said Samiel. "We wouldn't be caught dead in that highlighter suit you wore either."

"Hey!" cried Mr. Dow. "I looked fly in my suit!"

"And I look fly in my suit too."

"Shoot, you better," said Mr. Dow. "You know how much that suit cost?"

"How much?"

"Enough that if you didn't look good in it, you weren't getting it."

Samiel snorted. But he also wondered if the suit had cost a lot of money. He did not want to be spending the family's money on unnecessary things.

That was why he had decided to take the job as Mr. Payne's assistant. By making his own money, his family could put the money they would have spent on him to better use.

Prom was being held in Creeke High School's gym. The theme was "Keep It Regal".

The gym was decorated with red and gold colors meant to look like a royal ballroom. Samiel thought it looked nice.

Benjamin was dressed in a classic black suit. He had his dreadlocks styled in two braids that went down the back of his head.

Derek seemed to be dressed in a gray plaid suit. But once he made it past check-in, he removed his suit jacket to reveal his actual prom outfit.

He wore a red floral-patterned satin suit vest with gray plaid pants. On his head was a gray wide-brimmed fedora, and on his feet were red spiked velvet loafers. For accessories, he had on a simple golden chain to match his golden grill.

Allison matched him by wearing an off-shoulder velvet red dress. It flared out below her knees into a feather-lined train.

"Well, if there's one thing we can always count on, it's for you to be the most uniquely dressed," said Benjamin to Derek.

"This ain't even want I wanted to wear," griped Derek. "All because of this stupid leg! And Nanna had to undo and re-sew my pant leg onto me just so I could get into them!"

"You still look good," reassured Samiel.

"That's what I've been telling him," said Allison. "You know full well if you looked a mess I'd tell you."

"Yeah whatever," grumbled Derek. "I'm only here to see if we won."

"We better," said Allison. "I look too good to lose."

"I look too good to lose too," said Stacy, approaching them. She was wore a sequined pink dress that went well with her pixie cut.

"Right?" said Allison. "You are *wearing* that pink."

"And you are *wearing* that red."

The next people to enter prom were Andre, Mariana, and Jada. Andre wore a plain black suit while Jada wore a black dress with silver straps.

But all eyes were on Mariana. She wore a sequined dark blue gown, and her hair was styled in a braided updo on her head.

"And she is *wearing* that blue," said Stacy. "And I mean *wearing* it."

"She does look good," said Benjamin. Samiel thought he saw Benjamin lick his lips when he said it but he was not sure.

"She's always been pretty," said Allison. "If she wasn't so slick at the mouth, she'd be alright."

The three of them walked up to the group.

"Hey hey!" greeted Jada. "Everyone looks good tonight!"

"So do you!" said Stacy. "And you too Mariana!"

"Thanks," said Mariana.

"Hey, what about me?" joked Andre.

"You look like a boy," teased Stacy. "Doesn't he, Allison?"

"Mhmm!" laughed Allison. "But a nice-looking boy."

"Yeah, a nice-looking one," said Stacy.

Everyone made small talk and danced. Despite his earlier disappointment, Derek seemed to also have a good time in his wheelchair.

But Samiel had something on his mind throughout the night. He snuck glances at Andre, thinking about how things had gone between them.

Finally, Samiel decided to address the issue once and for all.

"Hey Andre," said Samiel, when everyone else was on the dance floor.

"Hello," said Andre.

"Can we talk?"

"What about?"

"Us?"

"Us?" repeated Andre.

"Come with me to the bathroom."

Samiel led Andre to the restroom, where they would hear each other better.

"What about 'us' is there to talk about?" asked Andre.

"You haven't talked to me since March."

"And?"

"So, you're just going to hold a grudge forever?"

"I'm not holding a grudge," said Andre, glaring at Samiel. "You wanted me to stay out of your way and out of Mr. Kasey's way and I'm doing that."

"Well, I was wrong," admitted Samiel. "But you were wrong too. You shouldn't have spoke to him like that at the library."

"Spoke to him like what?"

"Like he was getting on your nerves just for wanting to talk to you!"

"Is this what you brought me in here for?" griped Andre. "To argue?"

"No, I brought you in here to talk this out so we could get back to being friends."

"Friends?!" cried Andre.

"Yes, friends."

"Was I your friend when you treated me like that for no reason?"

"Dude, he's *my* father," said Samiel. "How are you mad that I wanted you to spend less time with my father so I could actually spend some time with him?"

"That's where you're wrong," said Andre. "I had three conversations with him, and they were all about how I was doing in school. If that's all it takes to come between you and him, then that's sad. And if you were a real friend, you would've just straight up told me it was bothering you instead of trying to embarrass me in front of everyone. Real friends don't do that."

"Andre," said Samiel with a laugh.

"Talking about some they just giving out diplomas," ranted Andre. "I worked hard for my grades! You know how much stress I've been under just trying to keep them up, let alone being salutatorian? That's the real reason Mr. Kasey kept talking to me! He was worried I was going to end up drugged out on the street somewhere like him!"

"I didn't know that," said Samiel.

"Of course not because you were too busy thinking somebody was trying to steal him from you!" snapped Andre. "For your information, I've already got a dad and a stepdad, so I don't need yours! Now if you'll excuse me, I'm going back to enjoy my prom!"

"Hey wait!"

"What?!"

"I'm sorry," said Samiel. "I was wrong."

"Okay."

"Friends?"

Andre glared at Samiel for what seemed like forever.

"I'll think about it," said Andre before leaving.

Samiel had no choice but to accept that. He had let his jealousy cause him to mistreat his friend.

When he returned to the gym, they were preparing to announce the king and queen.

"And your prom king and queen are..."

Samiel looked around at all the candidates.

Allison and Derek looked relaxed like it did not matter to them if they won or not. Stacy was smiling nervously. Justin looked like he did not want to win at all, while Mariana looked like she desperately wanted to win.

"Derek and Allison Harrison!"

The room filled with cheers. Samiel and Benjamin patted Derek on the back excitedly while all the girls huddled around Allison gleefully.

When the Harrisons went to be crowned, Samiel noticed Mariana off to the side with a sad smile. Then came time for the king and queen to have their dance.

Derek and Allison returned to the table.

"Congratulations," said Mariana, shocking Samiel. He was sure she would have been the most bitter about losing.

"Thank you," said Allison. "Do you mind if I steal your date for my dance?"

"Me?" asked Andre.

"Yes you," said Allison.

"Take him," said Mariana.

Allison led Andre to the dance floor where he danced with Allison in Derek's place.

"Everyone's right," chuckled Derek. "They would be cute together."

"Don't let her hear you say that," cackled Stacy. "She'll have a fit."

After the dance finished, everyone else joined them on the floor to slow dance too.

"I think I'm going to ask Mariana to dance," said Benjamin.

"Why?!" cried Samiel.

"Man, look at her," said Benjamin. "She looks too good to just be standing on the side watching all night."

"Hey, go for it," said Derek. "You only get one prom."

"Thanks man," said Benjamin.

"Ain't this something?" snorted Samiel. "That boy's never looked her way and now she shows up here with her hair and makeup done and now he wants to be all up under her."

"Don't be a hater, Sami," chuckled Derek. "Let the mean boy have his dance with the mean girl. You only get one prom."

Samiel decided Derek was right. So, he made the most of the rest of prom. And it was one of the most fun nights he ever had.

The next day, Samiel decided to tell his parents about his plans after high school. He sat them down in the living room and got straight to it.

"I decided to get a job," said Samiel.

"Sami, that's wonderful!" cried Mrs. Dow. "Where?"

"Mr. Payne hired me as his assistant."

"Mr. Payne's assistant," said Mrs. Dow, less enthusiastically. "Don't you think that's a little much for a summer job before you go to university?"

"That's the thing," said Samiel. "I'm not going to university yet."

Both his parents' eyes grew wide. Before they could react, Samiel finished his explanation.

"I've decided to go to community college first and then transfer to university. It's a cheaper option than going straight to university. And I can be close to home for when Kasey comes back.

His parents did not say anything. Mr. Dow got up and left the room.

"I don't know what to say," said Mrs. Dow. "Are you sure about this, son?"

"Yes," said Samiel. "I've made up my mind."

"Well, alright," said Mrs. Dow. "If this is what you want to do then I guess there's nothing left to say. I'm just proud that you've made such a responsible decision."

"Thanks Mom," said Samiel, feeling a little better. He hoped his dad would feel the same way.

Mr. Dow had retreated to his bedroom. Samiel tried to avoid going into his parents' bedroom out of respect, but he needed to talk to his dad.

"Dad, I'm sorry," said Samiel. "I know this isn't what you wanted me to do."

"You're right, it isn't," agreed Mr. Dow. "Especially not working for no Jacob Payne. That's the type of job you take when you got no other options. And you *had* options."

"I know."

"But even still, I'm not mad about it," continued Mr. Dow. "I was just a little surprised that's all. Shoot, I'd rather you have a job than to be laying around doing nothing, or out running the streets doing God knows what."

"Is that what this is about?" asked Samiel. "You were afraid I'd turn out like Kasey?"

"What?" cried Mr. Dow. "No. This has nothing to do with him. If anything, I don't want you turning out like me."

"What's so bad about being like you?"

"Well," said Mr. Dow. "When I was your age, your grandfather told me the same thing I told you. He wanted me to go to college and get a degree and a good job. But I didn't want to do that because I was sick of school and had always wanted to be an officer like him. So, I worked a small job until I was old enough to join the force. And although I don't regret joining the force, I do regret not listening to my father about getting a degree. Because now I'm out here looking for work and without that degree, I'm limited on where I can go. And I don't want that for you. And I also know the longer you wait to go back to school, the less you'll want to do it. I am proud of you Sami, I really am. But I just don't want to see you end up where I am. Especially not from dealing with a crook like Jacob Payne. That man only cares about himself and his money and he wouldn't hesitate to screw you over in a heartbeat. And if he screws you over then I'm knocking a few screws loose in his head and we'll all be in trouble. But at least with a degree you could bounce back, you know what I'm saying?"

"Yeah, I know what you're saying," said Samiel.

"I wish you had chosen a different job," said Mr. Dow. "And I wish you would get that full college experience. But if this is what you want to do, all I can do is respect it. Because there's worse things you could've chosen to do."

Mr. Dow hugged Samiel. Although he knew it was not what they were hoping for, Samiel was glad his parents supported his decision anyway.

The final week of school was a blur. Before Samiel knew it, he was graduating.

He sat in his seat, eagerly waiting for the ceremony to start. Then it began.

Ms. Nelson was the emcee, and there were several speeches to sit through by the administrators. Then came time for Andre's speech.

"Yellow everyone," said Andre. "I am Andre Brown, this year's class salutatorian, and I won't lie: I didn't think I'd be up here giving this speech. These past four years have probably been some of the most challenging and chaotic of my life. And I'm sure my fellow graduates would say the same. Honestly, this won't be a long speech because most of you who know me, know I get distracted and can get off topic quite easily.

Everyone laughed.

"There is one thing I want to say though to my classmates. We're getting ready to enter a new chapter in our lives. In these past four years, we've gone through a lot of growth and changes. We've lost old friends and made new ones. We're beginning to need our parents less and less, and learning to make our own decisions... unless you have a dad like mine. Love you Dad..."

Everyone laughed again because they knew what Andre said was true.

"But most importantly, were getting ready to be adults. Thankfully I have three older siblings and a lot of older cousins who have no problem telling me how hard adulthood really is. So, I can tell you with full confidence, that adulthood is going to be really hard according to them. But I want to tell all of us that even though it looks hard, we have no choice but to be adults. Because we can't go back to being kids anymore. So, I say to all of us, congratulations on making it this far. Let's rock out and get ready for what's next."

After Andre's speech came Allison's valedictorian speech.

"Good evening," said Allison. When no one answered, Allison held a hand to her ear and repeated, "Good evening."

"Good evening," answered the crowd.

"Thank you," said Allison. "I regret to inform you that my speech won't be nearly as exciting as Andre's but I do believe it will be just as inspiring. You see, I don't believe it to be a coincidence that a preacher's stepson and a preacher's granddaughter were the top students of our class. Some may say it was due to our hard work, my granddad would say it was also because God preordained it. And I don't take it lightly that I represent the best of what our great town has to offer of my generation. I am a descendent of the founder of our town, I am a preacher's granddaughter, I am the only daughter of my parents, and I am the top student of this class. It would seem I am preordained by God for greatness, and I believe it to be so. But of all those things that make up my identity, what I am most proud of about myself is that I am not above anyone else in this room. I have never acted like I was better than my classmates, and I am proud to call many of them my friends. And that's what I want us all to remember for the rest of our lives. None of us are better than the other. We are all equal and we are a community. I hope that as we continue on in life, we'll always be able to lean on each other and help each other out as we've done these past twelve years in school. And as we get ready to start our journey beyond high school, I hope we'll always be able to look back at these years with fondness and remember all the good times we had in and out of the halls of Creeke High. With that being said, my fellow graduates, I love you, I cherish you, and I can't wait to see what we go on to do. Now let's graduate!"

Everyone cheered as the graduates lined up to receive their diplomas. The crowd was asked to hold their applause until the end, but Samiel knew no one would listen to that.

"This year's graduating class would like to present this special honorary diploma to the family of Simon Peter Stone," said Ms. Nelson, holding up a diploma. "He is dearly missed by those who loved him."

After that, the diploma portion began. Samiel watched proudly as his friends received their diplomas.

"Andre Joel Brown."

Andre walked across the stage and waved to his family. Samiel hoped that Andre would consider giving their friendship another chance.

After the Cs and some of the Ds, it was Samiel's turn.

"Samiel John Dow Jr."

Samiel heard his family cheering loudly for him. He could not believe he was finally in this moment. When he spotted his family, he waved to them as he crossed the stage.

After receiving his diploma, he turned his tassel, took his photo holding his diploma, and returned to his seat.

It was over. He had finally graduated high school. Samiel was officially an adult.

More people crossed the stage routinely until something interesting happened in the 'G's'. Mariana and Jada stood beside each other in line with Stacy behind them.

Samiel thought it was odd because Stacy's last name came before Jada's.

"Mariana Isabela Garza."

"WOOOOOOOOOOOOOOOO!" screamed Jada.

"Aww, I did the same thing for my sister at our graduation," laughed Ms. Nelson. She looked at Mariana and said, "You realize you have to do that for her now, right?"

Mariana laughed and nodded.

"Jada Maria-Chanel Graham-Hernandez."

"WOOOOOOOOOOOOOOOO!" screamed Mariana.

"Stacy Lanae Gilbert."

"WOOOOOOOOOOOOOOOOOOOOOOOOOOOOOO!" screamed Allison.

"Now isn't this something?" joked Ms. Nelson. "How'd all the best friends end up next to each other?"

The girls all laughed.

"Allison Queen Harrison."

"WOOOOOOOOOOOOOOOOOOOOOO!" screamed Stacy and Derek.

"Derek Drumaine Harrison."

"WOOOOOOOOOOOOOOOOOOOOOOOOO!" screamed Allison.

"AYYYYYYYYYYE, THAT'S MY BOY!" hollered Samiel as Derek hopped across the stage on his crutches. Derek flexed his bicep and flashed a big grin at everyone as he accepted his diploma.

"Justin Holmes."

Justin tried to rush quickly across the stage. However, he could not get through the handshakes fast enough to avoid being the center of attention.

Samiel tuned out as he waited for everyone else to graduate. He only tuned back in for one last name.

"Benjamin Raymond Townsend."

"AYYYYYYYYYYE, THAT'S MY BOY TOO!" hollered Samiel.

After everyone had received their diplomas, they were asked to stand.

"This concludes this year's graduation," said Ms. Nelson. "Congratulations to this year's graduating class from Creeke High School."

Everyone tossed their caps in the air. After graduation, Samiel searched for his family outside. Many of his classmates were hugging, congratulating, and crying with each other.

Jada's Aunt Hannah, Uncle Riley III, and some of her friends from her old high school had come to watch her graduate. Some people who he had never seen before were congratulating Stacy. They seemed kind of nerdy to Samiel.

And there was an interesting scene with Mariana. She and her father's family from New York were going back and forth in a mixture of English and Spanish. From what Samiel could gather from the English portions, they were making fun of each other's shoes and outfits.

Then they all laughed. Samiel understood then why she was always so blunt.

His family was waiting for him by the car. They congratulated him and gave him gifts. Then it was time to party.

Samiel had a great time at his party. Many people visited the house with well-wishes. But in the back of his mind, all he could think about was how Kasey was leaving the next day.

And the next day came. Kasey stopped by the house to say goodbye. Samiel hugged him for as long as possible, not wanting to let go.

But eventually, he had to. He followed Kasey to his car. Before Kasey pulled off, he rolled down his window.

"I'll be back before you can even miss me," said Kasey, flashing a big smile.

But Samiel knew that was not true. Because as he watched Kasey drive away, he realized he missed him already.

Latasia Williams

Seventeen-year-old Latasia Williams inhaled deeply as she waited for her interview. It was the first week of summer. But Latasia had one last thing to do at school before she could start her break.

She did not understand why she was so nervous. Especially because she was going out again for a position she currently held.

She was captain of Creeke High School's varsity cheerleading team. Going into her senior year, she wanted to remain captain. The only other person who stood a chance of snatching the spot from her was her best friend, Nicole Brewer.

Nicole had already said she did not want the position. But that did not make Latasia the automatic winner. Especially because Coach Gretchen Nelson-Brown had surprised everyone by choosing Latasia for captain the previous year.

"Lala?" called Coach Nelson-Brown. "You ready?"

"Yes ma'am," answered Latasia as she followed Coach Nelson-Brown into her office.

Latasia liked Coach Nelson-Brown. Coach Nelson-Brown had taken over the cheerleading program Latasia's freshman year. Before that, community volunteers had run the program.

What Latasia liked most about Coach Nelson-Brown was her professionalism. She was fair to everyone and looked out for all her girls.

The only thing about Coach Nelson-Brown was that she approached students differently than her sister. Ms. Nelson was more easy-going and understanding with students. It was the adults she was less patient with.

Coach Nelson-Brown was the opposite. She held high expectations for the students and held them responsible for their actions. It was the adults she tended to be more understanding with.

But Latasia did not mind. She felt like she had grown into a better person under Coach Nelson-Brown's leadership.

"How are you doing today?" asked Coach Nelson-Brown.

"I'm doing good," answered Latasia.

"Good. You excited about your senior year?"

"Yes."

"That's good. Are you already thinking about after high school?"

"Yes. I'm already looking at some colleges to apply to."

"That's good. How about we get started with this interview?"

"Okay."

"So, you already know the preliminary questions. The first is why do you want to be on the team?"

"I want to be on this team because I've been a part of it since my freshman year and I want to finish out my high school experience how I started it. Since being on this team I've gotten to see how the team has grown, and I've also gotten to experience the difference we make in the community."

"Okay. What is one quality a good cheerleader should possess?"

"A good cheerleader should be smart. We should be able to use our brains for more than just memorizing our cheers and routines."

"What do you believe is something you can improve on during your time on the team?"

"I believe I can improve on...," began Latasia. She always hated this question because she never knew what to say. Her focus was always on just doing a good job. "...continuing to learn and grow as a person..."

"What are three things you can bring to this team?"

"I can bring to this organization a positive attitude, work ethic, and the ability to be a team player."

"What are you doing outside of this organization to help your community?"

"I'm a founding member of The Little Sister Society which is an organization me and some of the other girls in town have put together to help our community. Some of the things we do include helping clean houses and community areas, we deliver groceries, we help out with watching and mentoring little kids, we raise money for different things in the community."

"Alright, now we get into the good part."

"Okay."

"So, I want to talk about how your leadership of the team went this past year and what your plans are if you're selected again to lead this upcoming year."

Latasia's ears perked up at the word 'if'. As far as she knew, she was the only person up for the captain position.

"So last year, I'd say you did a pretty good job as captain," continued Coach Nelson-Brown. "Your teammates respond well to you, you apply every critique I give you, and overall, your impact on the team has been positive. The only thing I'd say you need to work on is your risk taking. You tend to play it safe and avoid trying new things. This year, if you're selected again as captain, I would like to see you take more creative risks and bring more of your uniqueness to the team."

Latasia nodded her understanding.

"Other than that, I have nothing else to say. I think you did a great job last year, and if you're selected this year, I believe you'll continue to do a great job. If there's nothing else, that concludes our interview."

"Thank you for your time," said Latasia.

She left the interview feeling more unsure than she had when she went in. Nicole was waiting for her in the gym with the other girls who had completed their interviews.

"Did you apply to be captain?" asked Latasia.

"No," answered Nicole confusedly. "Why?"

"Because Coach kept saying 'if' I'm selected again, and I can't think of anyone else I'd be up against."

"Well...," said Nicole.

"What?" questioned Latasia.

"You might just want to see for yourself," said Nicole, gesturing toward the gym doors leading to the restrooms. Latasia watched as Priscella Payne walked through them.

"What's she doing here?" asked Latasia.

"I guess she's trying out again," said Nicole. "She might've applied too."

"There's no way she'd be a better captain than me," remarked Latasia. "One of the newbies be done asked her a question and all she'd do is tilt her head and say 'huh'?"

"Oh my gosh," snorted Nicole. "Why'd you sound just like her?"

"You know it's true," chuckled Latasia.

"Mhmm," agreed Nicole. She glanced at the gym doors again and gasped out, "Oh my gosh!"

"What?" asked Latasia, turning to see what had her attention. Upon seeing who it was, Latasia exclaimed, "Oh, I know you lying!"

Entering the gym was Danielle Lee.

Latasia could not believe her eyes. Danielle had caused so much drama and talked so badly about Coach Nelson-Brown after being cut at the last tryouts. And yet, she was back.

"What is *she* doing here?" questioned Nicole.

"I don't know," answered Latasia. "Ain't no way she's trying out again."

Latasia did not know how to feel. Seeing two of her former best friends brought up many memories of how the four of them used to always be together.

She remembered when they were little girls, holding hands everywhere they went. They had seen it in a movie and thought it looked cool. And they had always walked in the same order: Nicole, Latasia, Danielle, Priscella. Someone once joked they had organized themselves from darkest to lightest.

It all stopped in middle school. Danielle had claimed it was weird and for little kids. Instead, she started walking a little faster to always appear in front of them. The unmistakable leader of their group.

That's how things were up until the split. Latasia always feeling like she was fighting to keep up with Danielle. It was not until sophomore year that Latasia started finding her own path.

She had grown tired of things always having to be Danielle's way. Especially since Danielle felt untouchable because her dad was the principal. So, when Coach Nelson-Brown warned Latasia and Nicole about being mindful of who they called a friend, it was not hard for Latasia to distance herself.

"Listen up!" called Coach Nelson-Brown, getting everyone's attention. "These are the people who've been selected to move on to try-outs."

As Latasia half-listened for her name, she glanced at Danielle and Priscella. They sat as far apart from each other as possible. The previous year all four of them had sat together.

It amazed her how much could change in one year.

And it was all because Danielle failed her interview. She claimed she had been unfairly cut and wanted the girls to quit in protest to try and get her back on the team.

Latasia had just been named the captain of the team. There was no way she was giving that up.

The only person to side with Danielle was Priscella. That led to their friend group breaking in half.

A year later, Latasia and Nicole were still close. Priscella and Danielle had fallen out. Danielle ended up replacing them all with the Garza sisters and Jada. She fell out with all those girls too. Her only friend left was her boyfriend, Derik Harrison.

Priscella ended up becoming good friends with Allison and Jada. And she seemed to be gaining more friends as time went on.

"Nicole Brewer."

"Yes," cheered Nicole quietly, pumping her fist.

When they reached the Ls, Latasia listened for that dreadful three-lettered last name.

"Danielle Lee."

A small smirk appeared on Danielle's face.

"Priscella Payne."

Latasia pursed her lips. The thought of having to potentially deal with those two for a whole year annoyed her.

"And finally, Latasia Williams," said Coach Nelson-Brown, finishing her list. "If you were called, please go to the locker room and change. If you were not called, thank you for coming. At this time, you may leave."

"This is *interesting*," whispered Nicole.

"Mmhmm," agreed Latasia.

The next three days were grueling. But that did not stop Latasia from giving her best.

She executed the tryout dance, jumps, and cheers effortlessly. Her time in the one-mile run was the fastest. And she encouraged her teammates.

By the end of the week, Latasia felt like she had more than earned her spot on the team. But her aim was much higher than just getting a spot.

That Friday, she would finally find out if she had reached her goal of getting captain again.

"I want to thank you all for working hard this week," said Coach Nelson-Brown. "I will now announce those who have been selected to be on this year's teams."

The junior varsity announcements came and went. Varsity co-captain was another senior Latasia got along well with. She inhaled nervously, waiting for the announcement of the varsity captain position.

"This year's varsity captain...," began Coach Nelson-Brown. After what seemed like a long dramatic pause, she continued, saying, "will once again be Latasia Williams."

The room erupted in cheers as everyone congratulated Latasia.

Coach Nelson-Brown announced the rest of the team. Nicole made it again. But so did Priscella and Danielle.

"Girl, she had me scared for a second," laughed Nicole as they walked out to the parking lot.

"Had *you* scared?" cried Latasia. "Girl, you should've felt how fast my heart was beating! I just knew she wasn't going to call my name! But the real question is, how did they make it?"

Latasia and Nicole watched as Priscella drove away, while Danielle hopped into the passenger seat of her boyfriend's car.

"Technically, Prissy made it last year, so I'm not shocked she did again this year," said Nicole. "But Dani..."

"I'm surprised she even showed up after all that smack she talked last year," remarked Latasia.

"I know!" agreed Nicole. "I'm even more surprised she got passed interview. Her attitude is worse than it was last year! I wonder how she managed to pull that off."

"That's what I'd like to know," said Latasia. After thinking about it, she added, "What if Principal Lee pulled some strings to get her on the team?"

"No way," said Nicole. "If he didn't do it last year, why would he this year?"

"He probably got tired of hearing about it."

"Well, I know one thing. She better keep it cute this year. She's not going to ruin my senior year with her mess."

"Mine either," said Latasia. "You ready for our meeting tomorrow?"

"After all them jumps and flips I just did this week?" cried Nicole. "Girl, I need a rest!"

"How about this," said Latasia. "After the meeting tomorrow, we go celebrate."

"Ooooh!" squealed Nicole. "Me, Miki, and Ralphie were planning to go hang out at the creek tomorrow."

"Perfect," said Latasia. "There's always something happening down there. Let's get this summer started!"

Latasia entered her house and found her whole family waiting for her at the door.

"How'd it go?" asked Mrs. Dow.

"I'm captain again," announced Latasia.

"Oh!" squealed Mrs. Dow, hugging Latasia. "I knew my baby could do it!"

"That's my girl!" cheered Mr. Dow, adding himself to the hug.

"Congratulations Lala!" said Kameryn and Samiel, adding themselves to the hug.

Latasia relished the embrace of her family. Especially because they were the only family she had really ever known.

She had little memory of her birth parents, Antonio and Brittany Williams. All she knew about them was that they were a young married couple in their twenties.

They had died when she was four, and she had been their only child. After their deaths, Latasia was placed in foster care. The Dows were her first, and only, family.

What was supposed to be temporary ended up becoming permanent. They had always wanted a son and a daughter, which they had with Samiel and their miracle baby Kameryn. But the Dows had fallen so in love with Latasia that they decided to keep her too.

They had chosen not to change her last name out of respect for her birth parents. It made Latasia sad when she was younger, not having the same last name as her siblings. But being older, she was glad to have that small piece of her birth family with her.

However, that's where her connection to the Williams family ended. Unlike Samiel, she did not have a burning desire to find more of her birth family. Her family was right there in Creeke, and she could not imagine her life without them.

"Oh, this just makes me so happy," said Mrs. Dow after everyone had settled down. "And I have even bigger news."

"What?" said Latasia.

"The registration for Miss Teen Creeke has been extended an extra week," said Mrs. Dow gleefully. "So, if you and your sister want to do it, there's still time to get you in."

"Mom," sighed Latasia. "We already told you we didn't want to do it."

"I know," said Mrs. Dow. "But I was just hoping you'd both... change your minds."

Latasia tried her best not to look annoyed. The Miss Teen Creeke pageant was important to her mother. Especially because Mrs. Dow had won Miss Teen Creeke when she was eighteen.

That was thirty-one years ago. The last Miss Teen Creeke pageant had been twenty-five years ago when Mrs. Soleya Harrison had won.

Back then, she was sixteen-year-old Miss Soleya Perry. But her win had caused such a scandal that the pageant had been retired indefinitely.

The town mothers fondly remembered competing and wanted to bring the pageant back for their daughters. And every girl between the ages of thirteen and eighteen wanted in, including Latasia and Kameryn.

But they were both skipping it.

The cost concerned them. Mr. Dow was still looking for a new job, and the girls did not want to waste money on a pageant.

"Mom, I just don't think this is a good time to do the pageant," said Latasia. "I really just want to focus on getting ready for senior year."

"Okay," said Mrs. Dow disappointedly. "But if you change your mind..."

"Maybe next year."

"Okay," said Mrs. Dow.

She walked away sulkily making Latasia feel a little sad. But Latasia knew she and her sister were making the right decision for their family.

Saturday afternoon, Latasia and Kameryn went to Nicole's house. They were meeting for their monthly Little Sister Society meeting.

The Little Sister Society was an idea that Adrianna and Tamara came up with. That was why Adrianna was the leader of it.

They recruited Latasia, Althea, Nicole, and Charmaine to become members. Latasia recruited her sister to become a member too. Allison and Jada joined the club much later.

"I cannot believe you made me late," griped Latasia as they waited on the porch to be let in.

"I had to do my hair," argued Kameryn.

"All you had to do was put a hat on like I did!"

"Whatever Lala. It's not my fault I care about my appearance, and you don't."

"Girl!"

Nicole opened the door with a frown.

"Hey," said Latasia, giving Kameryn a 'you-better-be-glad-we're-in-front-of-company' look. "Sorry we're late. Someone just *had* to do her hair."

"You're not the only ones that's late," muttered Nicole.

"What you mean?"

"See for yourself."

Latasia greeted Mrs. Brewer and followed Nicole to her room. The only person in there was Althea Green.

"Where is everyone?" asked Latasia.

"I don't where they are, but I know where they aren't," said Nicole annoyedly. "I only know where Adrianna is because she had dance practice with Miki at the church for Founder's Day. But if I'd known everyone else was going to skip, I'd have slept in!"

"I'm sure there's a good explanation for everyone's absences," said Althea.

"Em is probably at home with her mom," said Latasia. "Do Allison and Charmaine work today?"

"Maybe," said Nicole. She huffed out, "But they still could've said something."

"All that leaves is Jada," questioned Latasia.

"She couldn't make it," said Althea. "She's busy."

"Mmhmm," uttered Latasia, glancing at Nicole to see if she was just as unconvinced.

"That's what she said when she called me," said Althea. "And if she had something come up, then that's her business."

"This is ridiculous," declared Latasia. "We were supposed to talk about what we were going to do for our bake sale at Founder's Day next week."

"It's okay," reassured Althea. "We'll just reschedule."

"The bake sale is literally next Saturday," said Latasia.

"Everything will be okay," said Althea. "I'll set up a meeting for next Friday. It'll be at your house since it's Kameryn's turn to host."

"Great," said Kameryn sarcastically.

"Don't worry," said Althea. "Everything will be fine."

After Althea left, Latasia looked at Nicole knowingly. She had a hard time buying Jada's excuse for not being at the meeting.

When Jada first moved to town, she became fast friends with Danielle and the Garza sisters. Her friendship with Danielle did not last long, but she was still close with the Garzas.

Latasia did not like any of those girls. And Jada so easily befriending them made her questionable to Latasia.

"Jada could've at least come up with a better excuse than 'she's busy'," snorted Latasia.

"Right?" agreed Nicole. "And then Thea talking about some whatever she got going on is her business. Like no, she's supposed to be here."

"Right? But you know how Thea is. She just got to be Miss Friend Of The World to everybody."

"Mmhmm. Just like how she was spending a lot of her time with Dani last month?"

"Girl don't even get me started on that. I'm convinced she was only hanging out with that girl because she felt sorry for her because she ain't got no more friends."

"Well, that's Dani's fault. She's the one chased everybody away."

"And she'll probably end up chasing Derik away too. I don't even know what he saw in her in the first place to even want to date her."

"You know how boys are," snorted Nicole, rolling her eyes. She flipped her hair and added, "They just pick whatever."

"Well, since ain't nobody here, you want to go eat?" asked Latasia.

"Might as well," said Nicole.

Latasia, Nicole, and Kameryn went to Patty's. Charmaine stood at the cash register taking orders.

"Charmaine An'genelle Townsend," chastised Latasia. "Why didn't you tell us you were working today?"

"Because I just found out today, Latasia Laminah Williams," said Charmaine. "It was supposed to be Benjamin's day to work but he had something to do so I had to cover his shift."

"Oh girl, I know how that feels," sighed Nicole.

"I'm sure you do Nicole Jameisha Brewer," said Charmaine.

"Okay, you didn't have to throw my full government out there," said Nicole. "I'm not the one came in here fussing at you."

"Girl, you and Lala do everything together," chuckled Charmaine. "Whatever she does, you're right behind her."

"Right beside me," corrected Latasia. She did not like the idea of having followers. It reminded her too much of how people saw her when she was with Danielle.

"Either way, y'all are always together," said Charmaine. "She's Latasia Laminah and you're Nicole Jameisha, since I'm Charmaine An'genelle."

"I wish I'd gotten a cute middle name like An'genelle," complained Kameryn. "Instead, I got an old lady middle name. Elaine. What girl around our age do you know named Elaine?"

"Elaine is our grandma's name," said Latasia sternly.

"My point exactly!" cried Kameryn. "I'm named after an old lady!"

"My grandma is the one who named me Charmaine," said Charmaine. "My father wanted to name me Angel and my mother wanted to name me Janelle. An'genelle was the compromise, and my grandma didn't like that, so she just randomly picked Charmaine, and everyone just gave up and called it a day."

"Now, why would she do that?" laughed Latasia.

"I don't know," answered Charmaine. "Are y'all getting y'all's usuals?"

"Yeah," said Nicole.

"Alrighty," said Charmaine. "It'll be out in a few."

"How do you just remember what everyone gets?" wondered Latasia.

"It's a lot easier than you think," snorted Nicole.

"It sure is," agreed Charmaine. "After you see the same person a few times, you start to remember what they always get."

"And if they're a difficult customer?" said Nicole. "Oh, you'll remember everything about them. What they got, what they wore, what they said, how much your feet was hurting!"

"Oh my goodness," cried Charmaine. "If you don't remember nothing else, you'll remember how much your feet and back hurt from standing all day!"

"And how much your mouth hurts from doing all that smiling."

"Mmmhmm!"

Someone entered the restaurant causing the bell above the door to ring. The girls moved aside so the customer could get to the counter. It was Priscella.

"Hey Prissy," greeted Charmaine. "What can I get you?"

"I think I'm going to get some wings," said Priscella.

"Okay. I'll have them out for you in a bit."

"Okay, thank you."

Priscella glanced at the girls before looking around unsurely.

"Prissy!" called a voice. Latasia looked to see that Mariella Garza was waving Priscella down. "We're over here!"

Priscella went to join the Garza sisters.

"When did they become friends again?" asked Latasia.

"Girl, who knows?" scoffed Nicole. "Do you know the Garzas came to the store the other day apologizing for trying to steal all those months ago?"

"Really?" said Latasia. "I guess even a broken clock is right twice a day."

"Right?" said Nicole. "I appreciate that they tried to make things right, but I still don't like them. They can all have each other for all I care."

"Y'all could've at least said hi to her," said Charmaine.

"For what?" asked Nicole. "I ain't got nothing to say to her."

"Me neither," added Latasia.

"Me either," added Kameryn.

"There's nothing wrong with being nice," said Charmaine.

"Easy for you to say, you like everybody," said Latasia.

"Not everybody," said Charmaine. "But I can still at least be cordial."

"Well, it's just certain people I can't be cordial with," said Nicole. Latasia nodded in agreement.

The girls went to find a place to sit. As they waited for their food, they started discussing their summer plans.

"Are you guys entering the Miss Teen Creeke pageant?" asked Nicole.

"No," answered Latasia.

"Why not?"

Latasia just shrugged and shook her head.

"Well, I'm doing it," said Nicole.

"Then I'm going to root for you to win," laughed Latasia. "Hey, if I applied for a job at your store, would your parents hire me?"

"Yes," said Nicole. "We need more workers."

"I think I'll apply then."

"You should."

"Last one hired is the first one fired," said Kameryn. "Just remember that."

"Well, that's not going to happen at our store," said Nicole. "My parents love you guys and wouldn't do that. Not like *her* parents."

Nicole eyed Priscella to emphasize who she was talking about.

"You know Sami took a job with her dad as his assistant?" said Latasia.

"Why?" cried Nicole. "He could've worked here at Patty's or the store with us!"

"I don't know why he did it. But I know Mr. Payne better not pull no funny mess. I don't play about my brother."

"Me either," said Kameryn.

"What are you doing this summer, Kami?" asked Nicole with amusement.

"Chilling," answered Kameryn. "I wanted to do take this art class for teens at an art school in the city, but I can't."

"Why not?"

"It costs too much," muttered Kameryn.

"Dang," said Nicole.

Latasia frowned. Their dad losing his job had changed all their summer plans. With her and Samiel getting jobs they could at least be pay for some of their expenses.

But Kameryn would not be sixteen for another year. And there was no telling how long it would take Mr. Dow to find another job. It made Latasia sad for her sister.

That evening, Latasia went with the Brewers to the creek.

The creek was Creeke's main hangout spot. During the summers, people played music, barbecued, and had a good time.

"Alright you guys," said Ralph, lugging a small cooler in his hands. "Remember to meet back here at nine. Don't do anything illegal, don't lose your phones, and don't accept drinks from strangers. Especially you two, Nicki and Lala"

"Whatever Dad," snorted Mikayla teasingly. "We're not little kids, you know."

"No, but you're twenty-one," said Ralph. "And they're seventeen. Both the perfect ages for making terrible decisions."

"First of all, you're only one year older than me," said Mikayla. "You're not going to ruin my night being a buzzkill. I'm going to meet up with Bri and Jonny. I'll be back by nine, so don't worry."

Ralph shook his head as Mikayla walked away.

"We'll be careful, Ralphie," said Nicole.

"Keep your cell phone *on*!"

"I *will*!"

Latasia followed Nicole away from Ralph.

"Gosh, he can be so annoying sometimes!" griped Nicole. "He acts like we're five-year-olds that always need to be watched!"

The girls walked over to the area where the picnic tables were. Latasia could smell something barbecuing as they got nearer.

Someone was blasting music through their car speakers. A small crowd of people were dancing and taking pictures.

Meet me on the dance floor

Meet me on the dance floor
Meet me on the dance floor
Meet me on the dance floor

"Ooooh this is my song!" cried Latasia. She started bouncing around and rapping the lyrics to DJ Mousie's EDM-inspired dance track, 'Meet Me On The Dance Floor'.

The song transitioned into another one and the girls looked for an empty picnic table. While searching, Latasia noticed another group of girls.

Priscella and the Garza sisters were dancing to the music. But her focus went to Jada, who was standing to the side filming and hyping them up.

"Oh wow," snorted Latasia. "Look who's here."

"Who?" asked Nicole. When she looked where Latasia was pointing, she said, "Oh, so she can come party, but she couldn't be bothered to show up to the meeting?"

"I'm saying."

Latasia briefly locked eyes with Priscella. Priscella flipped her hair, turning away to continue partying with her friends.

"Oop!" chuckled Nicole. "Did you see that?"

"Mmhmm," said Latasia. "She's feeling herself now that she done got some friends and made it back on the team."

"Right?" laughed Nicole. "You know what? We ain't even worried about them."

There were no picnic tables available. So, the girls decided to go walk down by the creek. They came across Derik and Danielle standing by the water, kissing.

"Ugh!" gagged Nicole, pretending to vomit. "Some people have no shame."

"Says the girl who kissed him in front of a room full of people," teased Latasia.

"That was different!" cried Nicole, blushing hard. "That was just a little birthday kiss! This is nasty!"

"Sure Nicki," chuckled Latasia. "Alright."

Nicole stomped away in the opposite direction. Latasia followed after her, chuckling.

"Nicki, it was just a joke," said Latasia.

"I don't care," said Nicole. "I should be able to walk around in public without having to be forced to see those two sucking each other's faces!"

Latasia eyed Nicole suspiciously. It seemed like every time Derik and Danielle got brought up, Nicole became moody.

The girls ended up back at the picnic tables. One had become available, so they took it. They played card games and danced to the music. Latasia looked around at all the young adults who were also having a good time.

"I can't wait to be grown," said Latasia. "It must be so cool to be in your twenties like your brother and sister."

"'Ralphie' and 'cool' don't ever belong in the same sentence," snorted Nicole. "He is such a dork. And Miki is annoying so she's not very 'cool' either."

"Okay, but they're your brother and sister, so of course you think they're annoying," said Latasia. "I was just saying it must be cool to be grown. You get to do whatever you want, you can move out on your own, you can make your own money, and nobody can tell you what to do."

"True," said Nicole. "Ralphie and Miki can just leave whenever they want and stay out as long as they want. But I've got to give a full presentation on where I want to go and have to be back by curfew. And I can't work as long as they can so they're paychecks are always bigger than mine."

"See? And then doesn't Miki only have classes three times a week in college? Versus us who have to go to school all day for five days a week?"

"Yeah."

"And I bet they don't have to deal with the same issues we do. They're so mature."

"I wouldn't say all that now... Those two are far from mature."

"Okay but there's other people in their twenties around here who are mature."

"True. I guess I see what you mean."

Latasia and Nicole went back to the car when it was time to go. Mikayla was already there, waiting for them.

"Have a good time?" asked Mikayla.

"Yeah," said Nicole. "You?"

"Yeah."

"Miki, what's it like to be in your twenties?" asked Nicole.

"Why do you want to know? You'll find out soon enough."

"We were talking about it," said Latasia.

"Whew girl," said Mikayla. "Look, just enjoy being seventeen, alright? And make all your mistakes now. Because once you get grown things are going to be way different and people won't be as nice when you make mistakes."

Ralph walked up to them, lugging the cooler.

"You're late," said Mikayla. "You said be here at nine. It's nine o'two."

"First of all, I'm grown," said Ralph, putting the cooler in the trunk of the car. "And I've got the keys. The meetup time was for y'all."

"Ooh Ooooooh," uttered Mikayla. "You get on my nerves!"

"You get on my nerves too," said Ralph.

Mikayla shoved Ralph, who lightly shoved her back. Before Latasia knew it, the siblings had each other in headlocks.

"See?" said Nicole. "I told you they weren't mature at all."

The next day, Latasia went to visit her friend, Tamara Kane. Tamara and her sister, Tamela, were taking care of their sick mother.

Latasia knocked on the door and smiled when Tamara answered.

"Hey," said Latasia. Holding up the food container in her hand, she said, "I've got food."

"What is it?" asked Tamara.

"Salad."

"Oh, she'll love that," said Tamara sarcastically.

"She better because my dad worked hard on this salad," laughed Latasia. She was glad to see Tamara acting like her old self. "How is your mom?"

"She's in one of her better moods today," explained Tamara. "You want to see her?"

"Sure," said Latasia.

Tamara went into her mother's room. Seconds later, she motioned for Latasia to come in.

Mrs. Frances Kane was sitting up in bed, watching soap operas. Blankets smothered her body while a headscarf covered her head.

"Latasia," said Mrs. Frances. "It's so good to see you."

"Hi, Mrs. Reesy," said Latasia, giving her a hug. "How are you?"

"I've seen better days," said Mrs. Frances. She smiled and said, "I heard you're the cheer captain again."

"Yes ma'am."

"Congratulations. If only I could get these daughters of mine to go out and do stuff more often too."

Tamara did not say anything. Instead, she gave a small smile.

"I was just telling Emmy the other day that she should be enjoying her summer with the rest of you. Not cooped up in this house with me all the time. You should take her out with you some time Latasia."

"Sure, if she'd like," said Latasia, knowing Tamara would never agree to it.

"I'm holding you to it," said Mrs. Frances with a smile. "So, what'd your parents send you over here with?"

"Salad."

"Okay," said Mrs. Frances, a slight sigh in her voice. "Tell them thank you. Between your family, the Greens, The Browns, The Harrisons, and The Townsends, y'all been keeping me and my girls fed and taken care of."

"Of course," said Latasia. "We want you to get better."

"That's so sweet," said Mrs. Frances, in the same tone one used with an imaginative child. Tamara teared up and left the room, and Mrs. Frances shook her head. "Those two aren't taking it well at all. Emmy's a little better at hiding it than Tammy is, but I've been trying to be more careful with what I say around them."

Latasia nodded her head with understanding.

"I can be honest with you Latasia because you've been through some things already," said Mrs. Frances. "My time is almost up. I've accepted it. But I just want to make sure my girls are good before I go."

"You can't give up Mrs. Reesy."

"I ain't giving up," said Mrs. Frances. "I'm just trying to get to where The Good Lord got the good wigs at. Because these ones down here ain't cutting it."

A chuckle escaped Latasia's mouth. Mrs. Frances reminded her a lot of her Granny Elaine.

Granny Elaine used to always make funny jokes during serious moments. Sometimes she still did. But most times she was quiet and in her own little world.

And Granny Elaine was close to her end just like Mrs. Frances. It made Latasia sad to see such great women have such sad ends to their lives.

"Go ahead and laugh," laughed Mrs. Frances. "I know I'm bald. This ain't my first rodeo with this. But if you really want to make me happy, take Emmy with you to Founder's Day and make sure she has a good time. Tammy already talking about she ain't going and I'm not about to be ran ragged by both my girls fawning all over me."

"Yes ma'am. I'll take her with me."

"Good. I don't want her missing out on life on my account. Tammy either but you know that girl is stubborn as they come."

After a few more words, Latasia met Tamara in the kitchen.

"Sorry," said Tamara with a sniff. "I just had to step out for a second."

"It's alright," said Latasia. "Your mom wants me to take you to Founder's Day with me."

"I'm not going anywhere," said Tamara.

"Well, I already told her I'd take you so..."

"Dang it."

"Why don't you come to the meeting Friday? We're going over what we're doing for the bake sale."

"Friday? I thought it was last Saturday."

"We had to reschedule it," grumbled Latasia.

"Why?"

"Nobody showed up."

"Why not?"

"Everyone had reasons. Some better than others."

"Hmm...," uttered Tamara. "Will everyone be there this Friday?"

"They better be," said Latasia. "Founder's Day is Saturday, and we need to discuss how our bake sale will work."

"Alright then," said Tamara. "I'll be there."

That Friday, all the girls gathered at Latasia's house to discuss their plan for the bake sale.

Surprisingly, even Jada was there. Latasia had not seen Jada since the day at the creek. She wanted an explanation for why she was not at the last meeting.

They went over the tenets of the club. Each girl had to give one if they wanted to be a member. The tenets of being a Little Sister were being courageous, smart, gracious, helpful, honest, positive, respectful, authentic, and independent.

After that, they got to why they were there.

"Let's talk about the bake sale tomorrow," said Adrianna.

"Before we get started, I just want to know where everybody was at the last meeting," said Latasia.

"I was at dance practice," said Adrianna.

"Um, did y'all not visit me at work?" snorted Charmaine.

"I was at work too," said Allison. "I ended up having to go in earlier than I thought, and I didn't have a chance to say I couldn't make it."

"Jada?" demanded Latasia. "What about you?"

"I was busy," answered Jada.

"With something more important than being at the meeting?" questioned Nicole.

"Yes."

"Well, what was it?" asked Latasia.

"She doesn't have to answer to you," said Allison.

"I'm part of this group, and my time was wasted," said Latasia.

"Exactly," agreed Nicole.

"Mmhmm," added Kameryn.

"She's not the only one who didn't show up though," said Allison.

"But she's the only one without a good reason," countered Latasia.

"Why are y'all doing all of this?" complained Charmaine. "She said she was busy, leave it at that."

"Because she doesn't have a good reason," said Latasia.

"And who are you that she has to explain herself to you?!" cried Allison.

"Girls, wait!" called Althea. "I think we need to focus back on why we're here, which is the bake sale."

"No Althea," said Adrianna. "I want to know why it's such a big deal too."

"Because we just want to know what was so important that she couldn't show up," explained Nicole. "What's wrong with that?"

"Because it's none of y'all's business," argued Allison. "And then Lil' Bit over there throwing in her little two cents like she got something to say."

"First of all, don't talk about my sister like that," said Latasia.

"Girl, what I have to say about your sister is nothing compared to what I have to say to you and Nicki because I'm about sick of both of y'all," said Allison. "Y'all been coming at this girl all year for no reason and it's not right!"

"Well, what's up?" challenged Latasia. "What you got to say?"

"Wait, hold on," said Jada. "We're not supposed to be arguing each other. We're supposed to be discussing the bake sale."

"Oh, now you care about the bake sale?" snorted Latasia. "Did you care when you skipped the last meeting for no reason?"

Jada pursed her lips and exhaled frustratedly. Latasia watched as she exited the room.

"Y'all should be ashamed," said Allison, standing up to follow Jada. "That girl ain't did nothing to y'all for y'all to be this nasty towards her. I'm leaving."

"Me too," said Charmaine.

"Me three," said Adrianna.

The girls walked out. Althea gathered her stuff and shook her head at Latasia and Nicole before also leaving.

"Can you believe them?" said Latasia.

"No for real," said Nicole. "They act like we're supposed to be all buddy-buddy with her."

"I just want to know what Jada did to y'all to make y'all dislike her so much," said Tamara.

Latasia whipped her head around. She had not realized that Tamara was still there with them.

"Look," said Latasia. "All I'm saying is, any girl that can become friends with Dani, Prissy, and The Garza sisters is someone I'm not trying to be friends with."

"You two were friends with Dani for years," countered Tamara. "And after today, I can see why. You're both just like her."

"No were not!" argued Nicole.

"You are too!" snapped Tamara. "And I guarantee y'all if she came back tomorrow apologizing and begging to be friends again, y'all would be right back following behind her like nothing happened!"

"No we wouldn't!" declared Latasia. "I don't follow behind nobody! Especially not her!"

"Right?!" agreed Nicole.

"Listen, I'm not going back and forth with y'all," said Tamara, standing up. "I've got way more important things in my life to focus on. But you two need to get it together. Because for y'all to complain about how badly Dani treated y'all, y'all sure are treating Jada the same way and that's sad."

Tamara left.

"This is unbelievable," griped Latasia. "We still don't have a plan for the bake sale all because girls want to be up under Jada!"

"We'll figure something out," said Nicole.

"Yeah," said Kameryn. "We don't need them since they want to be fake and hang out with the enemy."

"At least someone has my back," said Latasia.

But deep down, Latasia felt off. The way Kameryn had said 'the enemy' did not sound right to her at all.

About half an hour later, Mrs. Dow called the girls to the living room. Jada was back with her mother, Mrs. Serafina Hernandez-Graham.

"What's going on?" asked Latasia.

"I want to know what happened over here today," demanded Mrs. Serafina. "My daughter left home in a good mood and came home in a bad mood and the only place she's been today is here."

"Mom, I told you–!" began Jada.

"Hush!" commanded Mrs. Serafina. "I don't care what you told me. I'm your mother, you think I can't tell when you're in a bad mood? I want to know why."

"And I do too," added Mrs. Dow, crossing her arms.

The mothers looked at the girls expectedly.

"Uh...," uttered Latasia, looking to Nicole for help. "We uh..."

"We just um...," said Nicole.

"They wanted to know where I was and I didn't want to tell them, so I left," said Jada.

Latasia's stomach dropped. She knew trouble was ahead for her and her friends.

"Then what's the attitude for?" asked Mrs. Serafina

"I'm just having a bad day," grumbled Jada.

"Well then, you better make it a good day and fast, young lady."

"Yes ma'am."

"Chrissy, I'm so sorry I came over here like this," apologized Mrs. Serafina. "But she was stomping around and slamming doors and she never does that."

"It's alright, Fina," said Mrs. Dow. "I completely understand. I'd be the same way."

"Okay. Are we still on for–!"

"Of course."

"Okay, I'll see you then."

"Yeah, I'll see you then. Tell Zack I said hi."

"I will. You tell Sam the same."

"I will. See you later."

"See you later."

Mrs. Dow smiled and waved from the door. After closing the door, she walked past the girls, maintaining that pageant-winning smile. But her eyes when she glanced at them sent a different message.

"Why do I feel like we just got in trouble?" whispered Nicole when they were alone.

"Child," answered Latasia, lowering her head as if her mother were still glaring at her.

For the rest of the day, all Latasia could think about was the way Jada had rescued her. And she also thought about how her mother looked at her. She had given her that 'this-your-last-chance-to-get-it-together-before-I-get-you-together' look.

Nicole spent the night. That way, they could both go to Founder's Day together to set up.

Around midnight, Latasia found that she had trouble falling asleep. She kept thinking about the way Kameryn had said 'the enemy'.

It was the same way Danielle treated everyone. "Us" versus "them". And the only way to be part of "us" was to follow behind her.

Going against her meant becoming part of "them".

"Nicki?" whispered Latasia. "You sleep?"

"No," answered Nicole.

"Do you think Em's right?"

"About us being like Dani?"

"Yeah."

"I hope not. I don't want to be nothing like her."

"Me neither."

"You know, Jada could've really got us in trouble," said Nicole.

"Yeah," agreed Latasia. "But she didn't. I wonder why?"

"Maybe we were wrong about her. Maybe she's not that bad after all."

"Yeah, maybe."

Latasia wondered when she had started treating people as "us" versus "them". And she wondered why she had allowed her sister to think it was okay.

"Us" versus "them" is why she had stopped being Danielle's friend. It had been the cause of all the drama between them.

Latasia could not stand the thought of being anything like Danielle Lee. So, she decided to do something Danielle would never do.

Founder's Day was being held at the recreation center. The main hub was in the gym. When she arrived, Latasia found all the girls had shown up for the bake sale. But none of them spoke to Latasia, Nicole, or Kameryn.

Latasia and Nicole went up to Jada. They had both agreed on what they would say and do. And they would mean it too.

"Jada?" said Latasia. "Can we talk to you?"

"Sure," said Jada. "What's up?"

"We wanted to say we're sorry," said Latasia. "We didn't give you a fair chance and that wasn't right."

"And we also wanted to thank you for not getting us in trouble yesterday," added Nicole. "Can you forgive us?"

"I don't know," said Jada. "The first apology you gave me turned out to be fake. Why should I believe this one is real?"

"Because we realize we've treated you really badly," said Nicole.

"We've been mean girls," admitted Latasia. "And we're really sorry."

"Okay," said Jada.

"That's it?" cried Latasia. "Just 'okay'?"

"Yeah," said Jada. "I'll forgive you. But actions speak louder than words, so we'll see eventually if you're sincere or not."

"I guess that's fair," muttered Latasia.

"Now if you want to start proving yourselves, I could use some help setting up this display table," said Jada. "Since we never actually discussed what we were going to do, we're all just winging it."

The girls got to work putting their bake sale together. Charmaine and Nicole were salesgirls due to their experience. Allison and Jada would direct people to the bake sale because of their personalities. Althea would keep track of their money. All the other girls would fill in as necessary.

"Sorry, I'm late," said Adrianna, running toward them with Mariana and Mariella. "Dad was being Dad. I can't stay long because I have to go get ready for our dance. But I brought extra help to cover for me. Hopefully a certain *someones* don't mind."

"They apologized," whispered Jada.

"For real?" gasped Adrianna. "Did they actually mean it this time?"

"Yes," said Latasia, rolling her eyes.

"Well, alright then."

"Here comes Prissy with more stuff for us," said Allison.

Priscella skipped up to the table and dropped a basket on it.

"I've got bakeries," sang Priscella.

"You've got what?" snorted Mariella.

"Bakeries," said Priscella. "Baked cookies."

Adrianna and the Garza sisters scrunched up their faces in confusion.

"Um Prissy," said Mariana. "What's the difference between a baked cookie and a cookie?"

"Well duh," said Priscella. "A baked cookie is a cookie you bake in the oven."

"But don't all cookies get baked in the oven?" questioned Mariella.

"No. There are some cookies you can make without baking them."

"Oh," said Mariana.

"Alright, I'll give it to her," said Adrianna, throwing her hands up. "She got us with that one."

"Here want to try one?" asked Priscella.

"Sure," said Mariana, accepting the cookie and breaking it into three pieces to share with her sister and cousin.

As Priscella waited for their response, she looked at Latasia and Nicole.

"Do you want to try one too?"

"Uh... sure," said Latasia.

Priscella fished a cookie from the basket for them to split.

"I want to give this to you guys as a peace offering," said Priscella.

"A peace offering?" repeated Latasia.

"Yes," said Priscella. "I don't want to fight anymore. We don't have to be friends, but we don't have to be enemies either. And since we'll all be together on the team again this year, I want us to all be able to work together."

Latasia stared surprised at Priscella. Priscella had changed so much since the previous summer. She had gone from being Danielle's dumb shadow to making peace offerings on her own.

"Do you accept?" asked Priscella.

"Okay," said Latasia. She split the cookie with Nicole and Kameryn.

"Oh!" cried Nicole, after tasting the cookie. "Wait a minute, I like this! Hold on!"

"Yeah, this is pretty good!" agreed Latasia.

"Thank you," said Priscella.

"Let me find out this is how you got the Garza sisters to be friends with you again," joked Latasia.

"Actually, Jada was the one who got us to be friends again," said Mariella. "She made us realize we didn't have a real issue with each other. It was Dani that was the issue."

Priscella decided to stay and help with the bake sale. Along with what the girls brought, Mr. Bud Vaughn also gave them some baked goods to sell. They had more than enough to sell to the community.

The bake sale would last until noon. That was when most of the girls would leave to start getting ready for the pageant.

They did really well with their sales. In the last remaining hour, Derik Harrison dropped by their table.

"Can I get two cookies and a chocolate swirl cake for my lady?" ordered Derik.

"Sure," said Allison. "You've got to try Prissy's cookies. She really threw down with these ones."

Derik ended up staying a few extra minutes to talk with his sister. Then Danielle came to the table.

"What is taking so long?" complained Danielle. "It doesn't take that long to get cookies and cake."

"I was talking to my sister."

"You literally live with her! You can talk to her any other time!"

"First of all, I can talk to whoever I want, whenever I want."

"Okay, but I'm over there waiting on my cake though. And you're sitting up here chitchatting with your sister!"

"So? If you wanted the cake so badly, why didn't you come get it yourself?"

"Because she probably ain't want to see us," snorted Nicole under her breath.

"Girl, ain't nobody worried about you," declared Danielle.

"I didn't say you were," said Nicole. "I said you didn't want to see us."

"Like I said, nobody is worried about you," said Danielle. "If anything, you probably don't want to see *me* standing up here next to *my* man because he chose *me* over *you*."

"Girl!" laughed Nicole.

"Why don't you take your cake and go away?" said Latasia, defending Nicole. "This is supposed to be a positive event. We don't need you over here spreading negativity."

"You're one to talk because you've been sitting up here talking about all these girls behind their backs but y'all supposed to be a sisterhood," argued Danielle.

"And what kind of sisterhood do you have?" argued Priscella. "We were all your friends, and you turned on all of us!"

"Because y'all are fake! All of you stabbed me in the back!"

"How did I stab you in the back?" questioned Priscella. "I had your back! But you kept calling me 'stupid' and 'dumb' like you were better than me or something!"

"Well sweetheart, when you ask stupid questions, what do you expect?"

"I expect you to act like a real friend like I was to you!" said Priscella. "But that's alright! Because I've got real friends now who don't treat me like I'm stupid and I don't need you!"

"Well, good for you," snorted Danielle, giving Priscella a mocking applause. "I don't need you either. I don't need any backstabbers on my team."

"Dani, you are the queen of backstabbing so what are you talking about?" countered Mariana.

"Don't even talk to me," said Danielle. "Because I let you and your sister be my friends because you were so desperate to be friends with me. And not only did you try to use me for my popularity, but you also stabbed me in the back by becoming friends with girls I'm not cool with!"

"We can be friends with who we want," said Mariella. "And we don't want to be friends with you. And for your information, you asked us to be your friends. We didn't come to you, you came to us!"

"See?" cried Danielle. "Y'all even talking like her now! But that's fine! I don't need any of you! I can be by myself!"

"Good!" screamed Priscella. "We don't need you either!"

Danielle and Priscella both stormed away from the table in opposite directions.

"Go after your girl," grumbled Allison.

"I'm not chasing behind her," remarked Derik. "She started this mess."

"*Go*," repeated Allison, handing him the cake he had ordered for Danielle. "*Now*."

Derik rolled his eyes and walked away.

"Y'all better than me," said Latasia. "Because if it was the other way around, she wouldn't be coming to check on us."

"Sure wouldn't," added Nicole.

"Well, sometimes you just have to be the bigger person," said Allison. "I'm going to go check on Prissy."

Allison walked away from the table. Things slowly got back to normal. Within the last few minutes of the bake sale, Mr. Jeremy-Micah Brown stopped by.

"Howdy, young ladies," said Mr. Jeremy-Micah Brown.

"Hello Uncle Mikey," said Mariella. "What can we get you?"

"I don't know, I just want something sweet," said Mr. Jeremy-Micah. "What should I get niecey?"

"If you want something sweet, then you should get some of Prissy's cookies," said Mariella. "They're really good."

"Eh, I don't know," said Mr. Jeremy-Micah, dramatically dragging out each syllable. "I don't think I want nothing that came out the Payne house."

"And what exactly is wrong with my house?"

Everyone looked up to see Mr. Jacob Payne standing right behind Mr. Jeremy-Micah.

"Well, for starters, it's your house," answered Mr. Jeremy-Micah. "For all I know, them cookies is poisoned."

"Do you really think I'd let my daughter sell poisoned cookies to the town?"

"Yeah, if it'd make you some money. Shoot, you probably poisoned your daughter first as a test run to make sure it worked."

"I ain't got time for this mess," said Mr. Payne, pushing past Mr. Jeremy-Micah. "Give me one of my daughter's cookies. And where is my daughter anyways?"

"First of all, I'm not done ordering yet," said Mr. Jeremy-Micah, grabbing Mr. Payne's arm to pull him behind him. "You need to wait your turn."

"Don't touch me!" snapped Mr. Payne, yanking his arm free from Mr. Jeremy-Micah's grasp. He pointed his finger in Mr. Jeremy-Micah's face and said, "I don't know who you're grabbing like that but it ain't me."

"Boy, calm down," snorted Mr. Jeremy-Micah. "We both know you ain't going to do nothing."

"Touch me again and see what happens."

"Oh really? Because we can do this if you want."

"Of course you want to fight, because the only thing you Browns know how to do is act stupid in public."

"Well, at least we ain't as crooked and backstabbing as you Paynes are!"

"Okaaaay!" said Mr. Lee, stepping in between the men. "What is happening over here?"

"What's happening is your boy is about to get beat up if he keeps talking to me crazy!" ranted Mr. Jeremy-Micah.

"Beat up?!" cried Mr. Payne. "Over a cookie?!"

"Quit talking to me!" argued Mr. Jeremy-Micah.

"Or what?"

"What you mean 'or what'?" questioned Mr. Torrance Brown as he approached the argument. "My brother said quit talking to him, so quit talking to him. What's there to be confused about?"

"Oh Lord, now here come the family chihuahua acting like he's going to do something," instigated Mr. Payne.

"Excuse me?!" cried Mr. Brown, snatching his glasses off.

"Boy, put your glasses back on!" taunted Mr. Payne. "You know you can't see without them!"

"Come over here and I'll show you just how well I can see without them!"

"Man, I ain't got time for you two," said Mr. Payne, picking up a cookie from the table. "You two are just a couple of clowns."

Mr. Payne walked away from the ranting Mr. Browns. A few of the other men came to calm them down and lead them away from the table.

"What just happened?" asked Latasia, as they began cleaning up.

"Girl, I don't know but I want every last detail," cackled Nicole. "That was juicy!"

"No, because this is crazy," said Latasia. "First Prissy, and now her dad. What they got going on?"

"Shoot, I want to know too."

After they finished cleaning up, Latasia walked with Nicole to the theatre space where the pageant would be held.

"Nicki," said Latasia. "You're my girl, right?"

"Of course!" said Nicole.

"So, we can tell each other anything, right?"

"Duh!"

"Alright. Do you like Derik?"

"What?!" cried Nicole in a high pitch.

"Do you like Derik?"

"Girl!" laughed Nicole, her voice still high. "You're funny! Let me go get ready for this pageant."

Nicole walked into the dressing room, still laughing. But Latasia found it hard to believe that the laugh was real.

The rest of Founder's Day was eventful. There was the praise dance, the Founder's Day play, and then a small speech given by Pastor Derrick.

The praise dance was beautiful. And even though the play was the same every year, Latasia still enjoyed it. Learning about the origins of the town she grew up in never failed to make her emotional.

But Pastor Derrick's speech was the true highlight. He talked about the founding of Creeke more in-depth and why it was important to maintain its legacy. And he talked about how Creeke changed throughout time, and how change was not always a bad thing. By the time he finished, Latasia was full of pride for her hometown and the people in it throughout history.

Then it was time for the pageant. Everyone gathered to see the first Miss Teen Creeke crowned in twenty-five years. "Good evening and welcome to the Miss Teen Creeke pageant," said Pastor Hall. "Before we start, I'd like to open with a word of prayer."

Pastor Hall gave his opening prayer. Then he introduced the emcee.

"Our emcee this evening will be Mrs. Athena Green. Mrs. Green is the wife of Alfred Green, and mother of four beautiful, smart baby girls: Cynthia, Gloria, Diana, and Althea. She is a previous Miss Teen

Creeke contestant, competing under her maiden name, Miss Athena Warren. She is happy to be the emcee for the continuation of this tradition. Everyone, Mrs. Athena Green."

Everyone applauded as Mrs. Green took the mic.

"Hello Creeke!" said Mrs. Green. "Are y'all ready for our first pageant in twenty-five years!"

Everyone cheered.

"Me too," said Mrs. Green. "But first, we've got some business to take care of."

Mrs. Athena read off the rules.

"Now, we will have our previous Miss Teen Creeke give her final walk," said Mrs. Green. "Please welcome, Mrs. Soleya Harrison."

Mrs. Harrison took to the stage.

"I am your reigning Miss Teen Creeke, Soleya Naima Harrison," said Mrs. Harrison. "When I was crowned, I was sixteen and my name was Miss Soleya Naima Perry. Some time has passed since I was crowned, but I am more than honored to be granted the opportunity to place the crown on the next Miss Teen Creeke tonight."

Mrs. Harrison gave her final walk. Latasia was in awe of her grace and elegance as she watched her.

"Hello, Mrs. Soleya," said Mrs. Green, when Mrs. Harrison joined her for her final interview. "It's been twenty-five years since you won this crown over me."

Everyone laughed.

"Okay, but seriously," said Mrs. Green. "Your daughter is competing tonight. How does it feel to know that the next queen coming after you could potentially be her? Are you hoping she wins?"

"If my daughter wins, I will be just as happy for her as I would be for any of the other young ladies who may win tonight," said Mrs. Harrison. "What's most important is that everyone has fun and gains confidence from this."

"She's still got it y'all!" laughed Mrs. Green. "That's exactly how she beat me twenty-five years ago. That's alright. We know you're rooting for your baby. Just like I would've been rooting for mine if she were up here."

Latasia chuckled as Althea's face reddened with embarrassment. Althea had also chosen not to compete because of her shyness.

"We'll now introduce our contestants," said Mrs. Green. "First up is contestant number one."

Nicole walked on stage and smiled.

"Hi," said Nicole. "I'm Nicole Jameisha Brewer, the youngest daughter of the Brewer family, and I'm very happy to be here as your contestant number one."

"Hola!" said Mariana. "Soy Mariana Isabela Garza, la hija mayor de Alejandro Garza y Marie Garza. I'm your contestant number two."

"Hola," said Mariella. "Soy Mariella Adelaida Garza, la hija menor de Alejandro Garza y Marie Garza. I'm your contestant number three!"

"Hello," said Adrianna. "I'm Adrianna Ernestine Brown, the youngest daughter of Mr. Torrance Brown and First Lady Leilana Hall. I am your contestant number four!"

"Hello," said Danielle. "I'm Danielle Amaya Lee and my parents are Arthur and Tasha Lee. I'm your contestant number five."

"Hi!" said Priscella. "I'm Priscella Leah Payne, daughter of Jacob and Rachel Payne. I'm your contestant number six!"

"Hello," said Charmaine. "I'm Charmaine An'genelle Townsend, the daughter of Mr. Raymond and Mrs. Patricia Townsend. I'm your contestant number seven."

"Howdy everybody!" said Allison. "I'm Allison Queen Harrison, the only daughter of Mr. Marlin Harrison and Mrs. Soleya Harrison. I'm your contestant number eight!"

"Hello," said Stacy. "I'm Stacy Lanae Gilbert. My dad is Stephen and my mom is Tracy, and when you put that together like they did, you get Stacy, your contestant number nine."

"What's up?" said Jada. "I'm Jada Maria-Chanel Graham-Hernandez, daughter of Mr. Zackariah Graham and Mrs. Serafina Hernandez-Graham, and I am your contestant number ten."

Latasia felt a little sad watching her friends compete. She wished she could have also been up there. So, she decided that next year, she would definitely be up there.

"Just a reminder that no one is allowed in the dressing rooms except the contestants and volunteers," said Mrs. Green. "If an emergency happens, a volunteer will come and notify the parents or guardians of the contestants. Restrooms are located in the hall. And now it's time to meet our judges who were anonymous to the contestants until earlier today when interviews were conducted."

Mrs. Green introduced the judges, and then the pageant started. There was casual wear, evening wear, a question, and then talent. As Latasia watched, it became obvious the frontrunners were Allison, Mariana, and Stacy.

Then, it was time for the awards. Allison won the People's Choice Award. The contestants voted for Jada to win Miss Congeniality.

Then came the time for the big awards.

"Now, it's time for second runner-up," said Mrs. Green. "You know I was a runner-up. It was last runner-up, but hey, I was in line for the crown.

The crowd roared with laughter.

"Second runner up for Miss Teen Creeke... is contestant number nine, Miss Stacy Gilbert!"

Everyone cheered as Stacy accepted her prize.

"Our last award of the night is Miss Teen Creeke," said Mrs. Green. "First, I will announce the two finalists for the crown. The finalists for Miss Teen Creeke are... Allison Harrison and Mariana Garza."

Allison and Mariana stepped forward.

"The next name I call will be Miss Teen Creeke, who will receive a crown, a sash, and a cash prize. The other young lady will be first runner up, and she will receive a medal and a cash prize."

Everyone waited for the announcement of the winner. After what seemed like ages, Mrs. Green opened the envelope and read the name.

"This year's Miss Teen Creeke is... *really* Miss Teen Creeke. Miss Allison Harrison!"

Allison's mouth hit the floor. Latasia cheered for her, happy she was the winner and not Mariana. Even though they had just squashed their issues, it would take some time for her gut reactions to adjust.

And that's what she felt with all the "mean girls" as Allison and Derek called them. It would take time for her to come around to being cool with Priscella, Mariana, Mariella, and Jada.

But there were two things she knew for certain. One was that she would never *ever* be cool with Danielle ever again. And the other was that she would work hard to never be like her either.

Althea Green

The Green family was a sports family. Every Green was somehow tied to a sport. Althea Green was no exception.

Her father, Mr. Alfred Green, was Creeke High School's head football coach. He had been a budding football star as a boy. But after an injury in college killed his career, he settled down with his wife and four daughters.

Althea's oldest sisters, Cynthia and Gloria, had also been athletes. Cynthia had played volleyball in high school like their mother, Athena. Gloria had done track and field.

Althea's third oldest sister, Diana, had not played any sports. But she loved watching them. She would be the loudest person in the stands on game days.

Althea herself had played basketball for a season when she was younger. But she knew she was no athlete, so she did not keep up with it.

Still, she knew most sports like the back of her hand. But football was the one she knew best. Football was the supreme sport in the Green household.

It was her sports knowledge that let her write more for Creeke's newspaper, The Creeke Courier. Her Uncle Arnold Green originally employed her to temporarily write the teen column. That was when Derik Harrison had been kidnapped and could not do it.

But Althea had liked writing for the paper. And when Derik came back, he was more than happy to let her have the teen column. So, her employment went from temporary to part-time.

Since then, Uncle Arnold had expanded the teen column into the youth section. Both Althea and Derik covered stories for it. But sometimes, they got to cover things outside of the youth section.

Althea liked it most when she got to cover sports stories. Usually, Uncle Arnold wrote the whole section himself.

But sometimes he would get in a jam and call Althea for help. Those were the times that excited her most.

Writing for the sports section allowed her to express all her interests. She got to write, read, research, and use her sports knowledge all in one place. It was perfect for her.

But it was mid-June. There were few sports-worthy stories taking place. So, Althea had to be content with the youth section.

"I was thinking of asking Mr. Arnold to let us write more for the paper," said Derik, stopping by her desk for their usual daily chat. It was the Monday after Founder's Day weekend. "He just wants to confine us to the youth section."

"Well, it makes sense," said Althea. "We can't work as long as Ralphie can, nor do we have the same level of experience as him."

"Yeah, but we're still able to do more than just the youth section," griped Derik, sucking his teeth. "Like I'm the editor-in-chief for the Creeke High Gazette, for crying out loud!"

"What do you want to write?"

"I want to write for the entertainment section. And I'm sure you'd want to write more in the sports section since you're way better at covering sports than Ralphie is."

Althea would never describe herself as a better writer than Ralph. But she did want to write more for the sports section.

"Uncle Arnie has way more experience than us," said Althea, choosing to be sensible. "If he wants us to only write for the youth section then we should follow his lead."

"Well, of course," said Derik. "But I don't think it'll hurt to ask."

"Thea!" called Uncle Arnold, walking over to her desk.

"Yes?" answered Althea.

"I've got an assignment that I'd like you to cover," said Uncle Arnold. "Justin Holmes is giving a football training camp for the young boys in the town. Get me that story and get me good pictures, you hear?"

"Yes sir," said Althea.

"And see if you can get me something about his college football plans too," added Uncle Arnold. "Derik, I want your article for the youth section on my desk before you leave."

"Yes sir," said Derik. When Uncle Arnold walked away, Derik quipped, "Now ain't that something? I'm over here wanting more to do, and it just falls in your lap."

All Althea could do was silently nod.

"I guess I better go get this done," grumbled Derik.

Justin Holmes was holding his football camp at Creeke Middle School. He was holding the day's final group huddle when Althea arrived. She collected interviews from parents and took pictures as she waited for him to finish.

Watching Justin in action always amazed Althea. His confidence was so strong on the field that no one would believe how incredibly shy he was off of it.

Althea wished she could be confident the way he was when she needed to. The only times it seemed to kick in for her was when she felt annoyed or needed to be polite. Or even sometimes both.

When Justin ended camp for the day, Althea approached him.

"Hi," said Justin with a smile.

"Hi," replied Althea, also smiling. "My uncle wanted me to cover your camp for the paper. Do you mind if I record our interview?"

"Go ahead," said Justin. "It's all on the record."

Althea giggled at Justin's journalism joke. Justin had been a part of the Creeke High Gazette all four years of high school. He wanted to be a sports broadcaster one day.

"Okay Justin," began Althea. "What made you want to hold this camp?"

"I just wanted to do something for the kids," answered Justin. "School's out and I wanted to give them something to keep them out of trouble, you know what I'm saying?"

"Yes," said Althea. "Why was it important that you hold this camp now?"

"Like I said, it's summer," said Justin. "It's not always a lot for kids to do around here, you know what I'm saying? And I just want to do my part to help our community and show the kids that they can do something positive with their time and energy instead of running around in the streets doing God knows what."

"What are you hoping the kids take away from this experience?"

"I hope the kids take away from this that they can do something productive with their time," said Justin. "They don't have to get wrapped up in crime and getting dirty money. There's ways to make clean money and live right."

"Yes," said Althea. "So, what are your plans after the camp?"

"Well, I've got a lot of training to do for this upcoming season in the fall," said Justin.

"I saw you committed to a school I've been looking at. How many offers did you have?"

"I had quite a few."

"What made you commit to this one?"

"It just felt like home. They recruited me and evaluated me for months and they liked what they saw. The coaching staff there just seemed invested in us as more than just players. Like they care about us as people and care about how we represent ourselves and show up for ourselves not only on the field but off the field too. And that's something that was important to me especially after playing for four years under your dad, you know what I'm saying? Not to mention they have a really good journalism program there. That's something that's also important to me once my sports career on the field is over, you know what I'm saying?"

"I do," agreed Althea. "What are your plans for future football camps here in Creeke?"

"I don't have anything set in stone right now," said Justin. "But I'd like to do more."

"That's all my questions," said Althea. "Now, all I need from you is a picture."

"Okay," said Justin.

Althea had to stand on her toes to get the picture because of how tall Justin was. The sun lit Justin's dark-brown skin richly. He pressed his full lips into a closed-mouth smile and did his best to focus his eyes on the camera.

"Thanks Justin," said Althea, after taking the photo.

"You're welcome," said Justin, returning to his normal, shy self. "I'll walk you to your car."

"Okay," said Althea.

"Um," uttered Justin when they reached the field entrance. Althea listened as he asked her whether she had read a particular book.

"I just finished it," answered Althea.

"Was it good?" questioned Justin. "I want to read it, but I haven't had time."

"It was great," said Althea.

"Now you're making me want to read it even more."

"Here's my car," said Althea. She extended her hand and said again, "Thanks Justin."

"You're welcome," said Justin, taking her hand.

Althea watched as their hands shook and then remembered what her father told her about giving eye contact during handshakes. She quickly raised her eyes to Justin's face and found him simultaneously doing the same.

They both smiled. Then Althea got in her car and left.

"Have fun on your little special assignment?" teased Derik when Althea returned to the office.

"Yes," answered Althea.

"Dani called while you were out. She wanted me to tell you thank you for helping her with her interview skills. It really paid off."

"It was no problem."

"That's not what I told her."

"What'd you tell her?"

"Well, if I said to you what I said to her, then I'd be called a cheater," said Derik with a smirk. "But I did tell her she was welcome on your behalf."

"Okay then...," said Althea.

"I also talked to Mr. Arnold about writing more for the entertainment section," said Derik proudly. "He said he'd give me a crack at it."

"That's wonderful," said Althea.

"I think you should ask him about writing for the sports section."

Althea nodded. Part of her wanted to ask. But another part of her feared her uncle would say no.

"I should get this article done," said Althea.

"Alright," said Derik. "I'm serious though. Ask him. The worst he can say is no."

Althea shook her head as he walked away. They had grown up together. So, she viewed him as a younger brother she always had to keep track of.

Much in the same way Cynthia viewed his older brother, Matthias. And Derik was becoming more like his older brothers every day.

It did not take long for Althea to write her article on Justin's camp. In fact, she found herself putting more effort into it than usual. She secretly hoped her uncle would read it and give her more opportunities without her having to ask.

"Here's my article Uncle Arnie," said Althea, placing the copy on his desk.

"Thanks baby girl," said Uncle Arnold. He removed his glasses and rubbed his eyes. "Tell your dad I'm not making it to dinner tonight. It's going to be another late night for me and Ralphie here."

"Yes sir," said Althea.

"Mimi should still be coming over though. Your Aunt Ruthie's working late at the hospital."

"Okay."

"You know Derik asked me about writing for the entertainment section?"

"He told me."

"I told him I'd give him a crack at it," said Uncle Arnold with a nod. "That boy has a lot of ambition, and he sure isn't shy about asking for what he wants. I like seeing that in a young person."

The conversation grew quiet. Uncle Arnold stared at Althea, causing her to look at the floor.

"Tell your dad I'll make dinner up to him," said Uncle Arnold with a small sigh.

"Yes sir. Have a good night."

"You too."

Althea could hear her sisters arguing from outside the house. Cynthia and Diana argued a lot ever since Cynthia chose to take a college semester off and stay home.

Diana had gotten used to being the oldest sister in the house. But with Cynthia back, Diana was back to being the middle sister. And she did not like it.

"Diana!" yelled Cynthia. "Didn't I tell you to take the trash out?!"

"First of all, you don't tell me to do a thing!" argued Diana. "I am grown, and you are not my mama!"

"Well, I hope you'll be ready to explain to your mama why you didn't take this trash out when she gets home!"

While her sisters argued, Althea took out the trash out. Outside she met Matthias Harrison coming up the driveway.

"Hey," said Matthias. "Let me get that for you."

"Thank you," said Althea, handing the trash bag to Matthias.

"Is Cynthia home?"

"Yes, she is," answered Althea, wondering if he could hear her sisters arguing.

"Okay," said Matthias. "I'll chill out for a bit then."

Althea and Matthias returned to the house. Diana and Cynthia had moved their argument to the living room.

"Don't get mad at me because you're lazy!" argued Cynthia.

"I am not!" hollered Diana. "If anyone's lazy it's you!"

"How am I lazy?! You're the one who didn't do your part!"

"I did do my part! It's not my job to take out the trash!"

"It doesn't matter who's job it is! If you see it needs to be done, you should do it!"

"Why didn't you do it then?!"

"Because I asked you to do it!"

"You don't tell me what to do!"

"First of all...!"

"I wonder how long it'll be before they notice we took it out for them," joked Matthias, causing Althea to quietly giggle.

"What is going on out here?" demanded Mr. Green as he entered the room carrying his toolbox. "I can hear you two all the way on the other side of the house!"

"She started it!" accused Diana.

"No I did not!" cried Cynthia. "You started it!"

"I don't care who started it, I'm ending it," said Mr. Green. "You're both too old for this and I'm not raising no football stars. Cut it out."

Diana stormed off to her room. Cynthia sat on the couch.

"Hey Mr. Freddie," said Matthias.

Mr. Green looked Matthias up and down. Then, he reached behind Matthias to pull his pants up.

"My pants are already up," said Matthias.

"That's a first," said Mr. Green. "I'm used to having to tell you that these button at your waist and not below your butt."

"Times have changed."

"Good," said Mr. Green with a triumphant nod. "I don't know why you wanted to walk around like that in the first place. I thought you were just being a rebellious kid but then you kept on doing it as an adult. And I know for a fact both your parents don't want you walking around like that because you're the closest thing I have to a son, and I wouldn't want my son walking around like that."

"I bet you they still match with his shoes though," snorted Cynthia.

"This is exactly why you need to keep your pants up," lectured Mr. Green. "My daughters have no business knowing what color a man's draws are or that they match with his shoes."

Cynthia snickered as Matthias sat beside her on the couch.

"Baby girl, I have officially finished building the shelves in your closet library thing," announced Mr. Green. "I hope you enjoy it."

"Thank you, Dad," said Althea with an excited smile.

The "closet library thing" was an extra room Althea had discovered behind her closet. She had her theories about what it used to be but could not find any proof to back them up.

Althea had chosen to turn the space into her own personal library. It would be a big help with storing all the books she had.

"You know she's never coming out of her room now, right?" said Cynthia. "You thought you barely saw her before? You're never seeing her now."

"Leave your sister alone," said Mr. Green. "Out of all the things your sister could be, a bookworm that stays in her room all day is the best-case scenario.

Althea excused herself to her room to change. It felt nice to call it 'her room' instead of 'her and Diana's room'.

Diana had taken over Cynthia and Gloria's old room after they had moved out. It was another thing that Cynthia and Diana had argued about over the past few months.

Althea changed clothes and admired her new space. Then she rejoined everyone in the living room.

Normally, she would spend the rest of her day curled up on the couch with a book. But her parents forbade her from that when they had company. Even if it was only Matthias.

"So, how's the job coming along?" asked Mr. Green.

"It's alright," said Matthias.

"Alright?" questioned Mr. Green. "Last time you said it was good."

"It's a good job but I don't want to be a mechanic for the rest of my life," said Matthias. "I've been thinking about going back to school."

"Really?" said Cynthia, surprised.

"I think that'd be good for you," said Mr. Green. "What are you looking at studying?"

"I was thinking maybe business," said Matthias.

"I think that's what Marlin got his degree in too."

Althea noticed Matthias frown a little. His relationship with his father was a tense one.

"You know, he also didn't go to school right away either."

"I know," said Matthias. "I was there."

"When he finally went to school, yeah. But we were all shocked that he didn't go right out of high school. Like he had offers to play in college and everything and he turned them all down to get married and be a garbageman. It was crazy!"

"What about you, Mr. Freddie?" asked Matthias, changing the subject. "What'd you study in school?"

"My degree is in kinesiology," said Mr. Green. "But I'll be honest. I wasn't focused on school at all until I got hurt. I was only there to play football and party."

"What made you get focused?"

"That's a man-to-man conversation," said Mr. Green with a wink. "We can't talk about that in a house full of women."

"Dad, your college years are not a secret," snorted Cynthia. "We all know what went down during that time."

"And just what do you know about my college years, young lady?" asked Mr. Green teasingly.

"I know you were out there being ratchet," teased Cynthia. "Poor Mama didn't make it pass freshman year because of you."

"Well, 'poor Mama' has never complained about that," said Mr. Green. "In fact, she seems very happy with her life to me."

Althea resisted shaking her head as she recalled the story of her dad's college years. The version the Green sisters heard as kids was that he started off as a promising athlete. In sophomore year, he started dating their mother and they got married in his junior year.

Toward the end of the season that year, a dirty hit permanently ended his football career. After that, he got serious about school, had Cynthia, got his degree, and settled down in Creeke as a teacher.

As the girls reached their parents' marrying ages, they filled in what their parents left out.

Their parents had gotten married at twenty and eighteen. They both came from religious families that believed in abstinence before marriage. So, they rushed into marriage so they could sleep together. Mrs. Green had dropped out because she got pregnant with Cynthia.

At seventeen, Althea could not imagine living her mother's life. She had worked too hard to get into a good school. There was no way she could throw it all away for a boy.

Not that boys mattered much to Althea.

None had ever shown any interest in her. Not the same way they had in Cynthia and especially Gloria.

Althea looked over at Matthias and Cynthia. Most people thought they would make a cute couple. But Althea knew better.

Matthias was a nice guy, but he was also a hothead. Cynthia was the oldest and most responsible of her sisters, but she was a brat when she did not get her way. And they both tended to be very unserious about serious things.

"When are you going to finish your last semester?" asked Matthias.

"I'm going back in the fall," said Cynthia.

"I think you should've just powered through on this last semester."

"Well, I didn't. I needed a break, my scholarship let me have one, so I took it."

"You could've took the break after you graduated."

"Oh well."

"Oh well," mimicked Matthias. "How you just going to 'oh well' your degree?"

"Because it's my degree to 'oh well'."

"I'm home!" called Mrs. Green as she entered the house.

"Hey Mama," said Mr. Green, strolling over to his wife. He kissed her and asked, "Do you regret your life with me?"

"Do I regret my life with you?" questioned Mrs. Green.

"Yeah."

"What kind of question is that?"

"I was just wondering. Your daughter claims I'm the reason you didn't make it pass freshman year of college."

"Did she lie?"

"Technically no."

"See?" said Cynthia, hugging her mother. "Mama agrees."

"I never said I was unhappy about not finishing though," said Mrs. Green.

"See?" said Mr. Green, adding himself to the hug. "Mama agrees."

"You two and your debates," laughed Mrs. Green. She walked over to Althea and kissed her on the forehead. "Why can't you ever be the out of control one for once?"

"The day that happens is the day pigs fly," said Cynthia.

"Hey Mrs. Athena," said Matthias.

"Pull your pants up," said Mrs. Green.

"They are up."

"That's a first," said Mrs. Green, surprised.

"That's what I said!" said Mr. Green.

"Where's Diana?" asked Mrs. Green.

"I'm right here," said Diana, bustling into the room. "And you won't believe the day I had!"

"The day she had," snorted Cynthia, rolling her eyes. "Let me tell you about what your daughter did today!"

"Girl, you just into it with everyone today, huh?" joked Mrs. Green with Cynthia.

As Cynthia and Diana filled Mrs. Green in on their latest argument, Althea went over to her father.

"Uncle Arnie said he's not coming tonight because he's got a lot of work to do still, and Aunt Ruthie is at the hospital still," said Althea. "But Mimi is still coming."

"That boy's always working," grumbled Mr. Green.

"He said he'll make it up to you another day."

"Alright," said Mr. Green, shrugging his shoulders. "Matt, you staying for dinner?"

"No," answered Matthias. "I just dropped by to say hi."

"Alright."

That evening, Althea's cousin, Naomi Green, joined them for dinner. Naomi brought her cousin, Angela Parker, with her. The Parkers were Aunt Ruth-Anne's people. But they were around so much that they were also pretty much family to the Greens.

"Auntie you did a good job hosting the Miss Teen Creeke pageant this year," said Naomi.

"Thanks," said Mrs. Green. "It's hard to believe it's already been twenty-five years since the last one. I'm glad they brought it back though."

"Why couldn't they bring it back last year?" griped Diana. "I could've easily swept that competition."

"Why'd they even stop doing the pageant in the first place?" asked Angela.

"Alright, so here's the story, right?" began Mrs. Green. "I was in that last pageant. But I ain't have no chance of winning since I was a fat little butterball. But no one, and I mean no one, was beating Soleya that year. She had the looks, the talent, the poise, the grace. She was *the* 'it' girl."

"She's still *the* 'it' girl now," said Diana. "I hope I still look that good when I'm old."

"Girl, first of all Soleya is only one year younger than me and I ain't old," said Mrs. Green. "But I agree that she still looks good and she's still just as kind and sweet as she was back then."

"So, what happened?" asked Cynthia. "How'd the pageant end up getting cancelled?"

"People started claiming it was rigged because Soleya won," said Mrs. Green, rolling her eyes. "They claimed Mayor Perry rigged it for her, but I'm telling y'all from someone who was there. That girl won fair and square."

"Well, her getting to crown Allison was such a cute moment," said Naomi. "The 'it' girl crowning the current 'it' girl."

"Now Allison has to have her own daughter and make it a family tradition," laughed Angela. "Why didn't you compete Althea?"

"I didn't want to," said Althea quietly.

"Well, I wish she had," huffed Mrs. Green. "Everyone else got to watch their babies compete except me!"

"Well, you know she's shy," said Diana.

"I don't know where she gets it from," said Mrs. Green. "I'm not shy and Freddie definitely isn't either."

"Hey!" whined Mr. Green, his mouth half-full of food. "What's that supposed to mean?"

"I heard once that some children adopt personalities completely opposite of their parents," said Naomi. "Maybe she's so shy because you two are so outgoing."

"Well, in Thea's case that's definitely true," said Cynthia. "She's always quiet, polite, and to herself with a book."

"First of all, we're polite too," said Mr. Green, pointing between himself and his wife.

"And there's nothing wrong with being to yourself," said Mrs. Green. "But you've got to know when to speak up and assert yourself sometimes. I used to tell your Aunt Marie the same thing when we were girls."

"Yet another example of somebody who's quiet because the rest of her family is loud," chuckled Cynthia.

"Girl, you ain't lying," said Angela. "But I will say, Aunt Marie asserts herself when she needs to. Maybe Althea will be the same way when she's grown."

"I hope so," said Mrs. Green. "And I also hope she'll make her mama happy and do the pageant next year."

"Speaking of next year, I heard they're thinking of bringing back the talent show next," said Naomi.

"Now that would be something," said Mr. Green.

"Me personally, I'm ready for that," said Naomi. "I've already got my stage name and everything. Mimi Renee."

"Where'd you get Renee from?" snorted Angela. "Your middle name is Leigh."

"Okay but Mimi Leigh sounds like a background singer name," said Naomi. "Mimi Renee sounds like I can *sang*. Which I can."

"Freddie did the talent show once," said Mrs. Green.

"You did?" asked Cynthia.

"It was a long time ago," said Mr. Green, blushing. "I was singing with Jeremy-Micah and Jacob."

"Since when do you sing?" snorted Diana.

"I'll have you know I can do a little something," protested Mr. Green.

"Emphasis on a little," said Cynthia.

"Whatever," said Mr. Green. "Y'all just playa hating. I only did it as a favor to Jeremy-Micah."

"Did you at least do good?" asked Diana.

Mrs. Green let out a laugh.

"I'll take that as a no," said Diana.

"It's not that," said Mrs. Green, still laughing. "Your father was the least thing wrong with that performance actually."

"What do you mean?" asked Cynthia.

"I know Uncle Mikey wasn't the problem," said Naomi. "He's a great singer."

Mrs. Green laughed harder.

"Him being a great singer was the problem," said Mr. Green.

"How?" asked Angela.

"Remember how him and Jacob almost got in a fight at Founder's Day?" asked Mr. Green. "The issue between them started from that talent show."

"They're beefing because of a talent show?" remarked Diana, scrunching up her face. "I've heard it all."

"I need the whole story on this too," said Angela. "First the pageant and now this. What was going on back in the day? I thought those were the good ol' days?"

"Basically, me and Jeremy-Micah were supposed to sing background for Jacob, right?" explained Mr. Green. "Well, the whole time leading up to the talent show, Jacob had been acting like he was this amazing singer like... like..."

"Like Uncle Torrey?" suggested Angela.

"Yeah," said Mr. Green. "But that boy had such a weak voice. And since Jeremy-Micah sings so loud, he basically had to sing at a whisper to even hear Jacob. But that Jacob Payne was just so rude and evil-acting the whole time in rehearsals that when it came time for us to perform, Jeremy-Micah just started blowing. All you could hear was him! He was singing so loud you would've thought he was the lead singer! It got to the point that Jacob tried to block everyone from seeing Jeremy-Micah by standing in front of him."

"No he didn't!" exclaimed Naomi.

"If I'm lying, I'm dying," said Mr. Green. "Once Jacob did that, Jeremy-Micah started singing louder. And I'm glad he did because I was laughing so hard I couldn't even sing. But the real show was after we got off the stage. Whew boy, we got back there and Jacob went *off*. It got so bad between them I had to pull Jeremy-Micah out the room before they started fighting!"

"So all this drama because Mr. Payne can't sing?" cried Diana.

"Mhmm," said Mr. Green. "And you know what the best part is?"

"What?" asked the girls.

"Your uncle got it all on tape."

"No way!" exclaimed Naomi. "Oh, I've got to see this!"

"Mhmm," said Mr. Green. "You know anywhere your daddy goes he's always got a camera with him."

"Oh yeah," said Naomi with a determined nod. "I'm finding this tape."

The rest of dinner was a lively one. Everyone traded stories while eating the delicious food Mrs. Green cooked. Eventually, the conversation turned to boys.

Diana gushed about Ralph. Cynthia, Angela, and Naomi dodged questions while also talking about other people's relationships. Everyone wondered which boyfriend number Gloria was on.

The only person who did not get brought up was Althea. And she did not mind at all. Because all she could think about was her new reading space waiting for her after dinner was over.

The next day, Diana went with Althea to work to visit Ralph. They had been dating for ten months.

Ralph had been in the same grade as Cynthia. After he graduated from college, he got hired full-time as a reporter at The Creeke Courier.

Diana used to visit the office during his first few weeks there. She had just graduated from high school and planned to go to cosmetology school next. Her eyes were set on Ralph from the moment she saw him.

Since then, Diana frequently visited the office. Her routine was always the same. She would greet Uncle Arnold, then go find Ralph.

"Hey Uncle Arnie!" said Diana.

"Hello sweetheart," said Uncle Arnold. "What's going on?"

"I just came to visit Ralphie, real quick before I head to work."

"Alright, but not too long," advised Uncle Arnold. "It's a busy day around here."

"Yes sir," said Diana.

Diana left the office. Uncle Arnold looked at Althea excitedly.

"I ran your article on Justin today," said Uncle Arnold. "Fantastic work!"

"Thank you," said Althea.

"Did you enjoy writing it?"

"Yes sir."

"Good."

Althea waited with anticipation. She hoped Uncle Arnold would next say he wanted her to write more in the sports section.

But the moment never happened. Instead, they both smiled at each other until she looked at the ground.

"You know, Derik's getting started on his article for the entertainment section today," said Uncle Arnold.

"Yes sir."

Althea waited for him to say more. When he did not, she looked at him. He was staring at her like he was waiting for her to say something.

"Yeah...," said Uncle Arnold, pursing his lips. "You're doing good. Keep it up. And remember your articles for the youth section are due by Thursday."

Althea left her uncle's office feeling disappointed. He had praised her article. But nothing had come of it.

She sat at her desk and got to work. It was not long until Derik found his way over to her.

"Hey, hey," said Derik cheerfully. "How you doing today?"

"I'm well," said Althea, trying to hide her disappointment.

"That's good," said Derik. "Hey! What'd Mr. Arnold think about your article on Justin?"

"He said it was fantastic."

"That's great! So, did you ask him about writing more for the sports section?"

"No."

"Why not? That would've been the perfect time to ask!"

Althea shrugged.

"You've got to stop being so shy," said Derik. "You'll never get what you want if you're too afraid to ask for it."

"Do you think we can talk about this later?" asked Althea, trying her best to hide her annoyance. "I've got some work to do."

"Alright," said Derik. "But I'm serious. If you want something, you've got to take it. Don't be afraid and don't wait on someone else to do it for you. Just take it for yourself."

Derik walked away, leaving Althea feeling worse than she had before. He was right. Althea could ask Uncle Arnold for her to do more.

But she did not know if that was the right thing to do. Althea believed her uncle would promote her when the time came.

And there was also the possibility that he would say no. Uncle Arnold was a nice man, but he did not play about his work. He was not afraid to deliver the death blow if he needed to. That was the worst thing that could happen to her.

Althea needed a moment to herself after work. So, she went to her favorite spot in town: the library.

Sometimes she went to the library knowing exactly what she wanted. Other times, she would just browse. Her latest visit was the latter type of day for her.

She talked to Mary Brown for a bit at the circulation desk. Sometimes, they traded books with each other. But Mary was leaving for music school in August, leaving Althea without a reading partner.

Althea perused the shelves, taking books she thought sounded interesting. Fantasy, science-fiction, poetry, romance; the genre did not matter to her.

She was looking at the autobiographies when she noticed one that caught her eye. It was one she had heard great things about. So, she reached for it.

Just as she grabbed it, so did another hand. Surprised, Althea looked at the other person holding the book.

"Oh," said Justin. He let the book go and said, "Hi."

"Hello," said Althea. She held the book out to him and asked, "Were you trying to take this?"

"Oh no, you can take it," said Justin.

"Are you sure?"

"Yeah, I'm sure. I read your article on me."

"Was it okay?"

"I thought so."

"That's good."

"Are you okay?"

"Yes. Why do you ask?"

"You just seem kind of down."

"It's... nothing. I just had a long day at work."

"Oh."

The conversation fell quiet. Althea could have said goodbye and kept browsing. But then something sprang to her mind, and it did not hurt to ask it.

"Can I ask you something?" asked Althea.

"Sure," said Justin.

"How are you always so confident on the field? It's like you're able to make decisions and not worry about it."

"Well, I kind of have to," said Justin, his face flushing a bit. "I'm not trying to get sacked. Especially not by some dude with a point to prove and an ego to match."

"I guess that makes sense," Althea chuckled.

"Also, I'm the QB," said Justin. "If I seem unsure, everyone else will too. Then we'll lose."

"That's true."

"To answer your question, I guess its just a mix of things. It's kind of like playing a character almost. I can pretend to be this cool quarterback on the field and then go back to being myself once it's over."

"But don't you ever get tired of doing that?"

"Yeah sometimes. But like I said, if I don't do it, we won't win. Plus, it's a lot easier because I like playing football. So, it's not like I'm completely pretending to be someone else."

"But don't you wish you didn't have to pretend? Don't you wish you could be yourself on the field?"

"Yeah, sometimes. But it's like my dad told me: no one will ever take you seriously if you refuse to ever speak up. So, I just have to push past what I think I want to get what I actually want."

"I see," said Althea. "Thanks Justin. That's all I wanted to know."

"No problem," said Justin. "I'll see you around."

Justin left. And he left Althea with a weird feeling. But it was not a bad feeling.

But what he left her with most was the question of what she wanted. She thought she wanted to do more at the paper. But she questioned if that was true because she kept coming up with reasons to not ask for it.

Althea made up her mind then. She would push past what she wanted to get what she wanted.

The next day Cynthia went with Althea to work. She said she had some business to discuss with Uncle Arnold.

"Well, this is a surprise," said Uncle Arnold when they arrived. "Maybe tomorrow Gloria will walk through the door with Thea."

"Ha!" snorted Cynthia. "As if!"

"How've you been?"

"Pretty good."

"You ready to go back to school?"

"No."

"Why not?"

"I want to enjoy my break."

"You sound just like your dad when he was in school," snorted Uncle Arnold. "Baby girl, how's your articles going for the youth section?"

"They're going well," answered Althea.

"You know your sister's a real talent here," said Uncle Arnold, beaming. "Did you read her article in the sports section yesterday?"

"I think I missed that one," said Cynthia.

"You sure did miss out," said Uncle Arnold. "She did a good job, and she said she enjoyed doing it. Right baby girl?"

"Yes sir," said Althea, flustered.

"I'm glad she enjoyed it," said Uncle Arnold. "I really want her to enjoy doing her work here."

"I do," said Althea. It was the perfect opportunity to ask.

But the words got stuck in her throat. And all these thoughts about what could go wrong started swirling in her head as Uncle Arnold stared at her.

Before she knew it, she was at her desk working on the youth section. And all she could do was kick herself for chickening out.

Matthias visited again that evening. He had been looking at some schools and wanted Cynthia's help with finding a good fit. And while Althea did not mind his visits, she hoped he would not stay long.

A lot of people always claimed Althea was too polite to everyone. Before, she had thought that was absurd. But her being polite was the exact reason she would not leave the couch.

It would be rude to not sit with a guest in her home. But she wanted said guest to leave so she could go to her room and mope over her missed opportunity. Even if it was only Matthias.

After a while, Matthias and Cynthia stopped to take a break.

"Cyn?" asked Matthias.

"Yeah?" answered Cynthia.

"Be real with me. Is college worth it?"

"I think it is."

"Yeah, but it's a lot of people out here that's been successful without it."

"There's just as many people who've been successful with it. It really all depends on what your goals are."

"What's your goals?"

"I'm still kind of figuring that out."

"Is that why you took a semester off?"

"Yeah, sort of."

"Sort of?"

Cynthia looked down.

"I'm just not sure what's next after graduation," sighed Cynthia. "I know what I want to do, but I don't know how to get there. Some of my classmates already have jobs lined up, while others are choosing to do more school. And everyone around here our age still lives with their parents and just seem like they're stuck here. And half of them went to college like me!"

"So?"

"So? What do you mean 'so'?"

"I mean 'so what'?" said Matthias. "Everyone is different. Just because everyone is still here doesn't mean you'll be."

"But what if I don't succeed? What if I end up like Gloria, going wherever the latest boyfriend takes me? Or like Diana, choosing to settle down before I've even gotten my chance to live life?"

"What's wrong with that?" asked Matthias. "They both seem happy to me."

"Exactly," said Cynthia. "Those things make them happy. But they wouldn't make me happy. I can't afford to let myself fall through the cracks and end up like them."

"So, your solution was to take a semester off from school?"

"I just needed time to think and plan," said Cynthia.

"You can't put off graduation forever," said Matthias.

"I know," sighed Cynthia.

"Dinner is ready," said Mr. Green, emerging from the kitchen. "It's not your mama's cooking but it is edible. Matt, you staying?"

"No," said Matthias. "I'll see y'all later."

After Matthias left, Mr. Green sat next to Cynthia.

"How's my lovely daughter doing today?" asked Mr. Green.

"I'm good," said Cynthia. "I went and talked with Uncle Arnie today, and he has agreed to do a makeup dinner at his house on Saturday."

"You didn't have to do that," said Mr. Green.

"Well, I wanted to."

"You know, you should take that initiative and use it to figure out what you're going to do after you graduate."

"Hey!" whined Cynthia. "Were you spying on us?"

"I don't have to spy," said Mr. Green. "This is my house and you're my daughter. Your business is my business. Besides, you guys were talking in the most public room in the house. It's not my fault I just happened to overhear."

"Mmhmm," said Cynthia.

"Listen," said Mr. Green. "Matt is right. You can't put off graduation forever. Eventually, you're going to have to enter the real world."

"I know," said Cynthia. "I just don't want to make a complete fool of myself when I do."

"There's nothing wrong with making a fool of yourself," said Mr. Green. "Everyone does at some point. What's important is that you learn from it, so you don't do it again the same way."

"Dad, you just don't understand."

"Sure, I do. I've been your age before. I've been where you are."

"But the world has changed since then."

"It hasn't changed that much," said Mr. Green. "You know after my football career got cut short, suddenly all the plans I'd made for my life had to change. My future became uncertain just like how your future seems uncertain now that you're about to graduate."

"I know."

"You think you do but you really don't," said Mr. Green. "When we were growing up, your uncle always knew what he wanted to do. He'd practically been born with a camera in his hand. But after I got hurt, I had to find what I wanted to do. And it took some time, and some trial and error. But what's important is that through it all I took life by the reins and kept getting back up when life knocked me down. And look at what I've gotten for it. A nice quiet life with a beautiful wife and four amazing daughters. So, don't be afraid to take life by the reins, Cynthia. Even if it leads you somewhere you didn't expect to go. Alright?"

"Alright," said Cynthia. "Thanks Dad."

"No problem," said Mr. Green hugging Cynthia. "And that goes for you too, Thea. If there's ever something you want to do in life, go after it."

"I'm home!" called Mrs. Green.

"It's about time!" teased Mr. Green, getting up to greet his wife. "The food's probably as cold as ice now."

"Thea," said Cynthia when they were alone. "Dad's right. We can't be afraid to take life by the reins."

Althea nodded her head, unsure of where her sister was going.

"I didn't feel very right telling you this because of how I was feeling myself about my life," said Cynthia. "But if we're going to take life by the reins then that means I should help you out too. Is there something Uncle Arnie wants you to do at the paper?"

"What do you mean?" asked Althea.

"What I mean is Uncle Arnie kept talking about how amazing you were doing when we were talking," said Cynthia. "And then he was saying stuff like he thinks you're way more capable of doing more than the youth section. I think he wants to give you a promotion. But he won't do it unless you ask."

"Why?" blurted Althea.

"I'll put it to you like this," said Cynthia. "One of my professors said he knew someone who didn't hire people unless they specifically said they wanted the job. The reason why was because he wanted the people to say that they actually wanted it. Maybe Uncle Arnie's doing the same thing. He's waiting for you to take charge and tell him what you want."

That settled it in Althea's mind. If Uncle Arnold wanted her to ask for a promotion, then that changed everything. She did not have to worry about him saying no.

The next day, Althea took a deep breath and walked into her uncle's office.

"Hello Uncle Arnie," said Althea.

"Hey baby girl," said Uncle Arnold. "What's up?"

"May I talk to you?"

"Always."

"Uh...," said Althea, feeling herself getting a bit nervous. "I um... I wanted to ask... if I could... write more... for the sports section. I understand if you say no, but I thought it might be worth a try to ask."

Uncle Arnold did not respond at first. Instead, his mouth grew into a gigantic grin. And there was a clear excitement in his eyes.

"Sure, I'll give you a crack at it."

Althea felt a huge wave of relief wash over her. And then she wondered why she had not asked earlier. It would have saved her a lot of time and heartache.

"What's up?" said Derik when he came to her desk.

"I asked Uncle Arnold about writing for the sports section," said Althea proudly.

"You did?" said Derik, surprised. "What'd he say?"

"He said he would give me a crack at it."

"Yes!" said Derik, pumping his fist triumphantly. "See? I told you he'd let you do it! This is great!"

Derik chattered on and on about how excited he was for her. She never remembered him having so much to say in all his life. It was usually the other Derek that went on and on.

But his excitement made her feel excited. She was glad to have finally overcome this obstacle. And she took that feeling home with her.

Her father was on the phone when she walked in the front door.

"Really?" said Mr. Green. "Here she comes through the door right now."

Althea was curious about the conversation that she apparently was the topic of. There were a few more "uh huhs" and "yeahs" before he hung up.

"That was your uncle," said Mr. Green with a proud smile. "He told me that you asked him for a promotion today. You know he's been waiting for months for you to do that?"

"He has?" asked Althea.

"Yeah," said Mr. Green. "He said he's been dropping hints, but he didn't want to push you until you were ready. I'm proud of you baby girl. Maybe one day we'll get you all the way out of your shell."

Saturday evening, the family went over to Uncle Arnold's for dinner. It was supposed to be a small family together. But it ended up turning into a celebration dinner for Althea.

Uncle Arnold was so proud of her that he made her the guest of honor. He gave a long speech about how excited he was that his little niece was finally starting to come out of her shell. Most of the family agreed.

Althea blushed from all the attention. Sometimes she wondered if her family thought her incapable of socializing at all. She could be persistent when she needed to be.

That reminded her of what Justin had told her. She realized then she already knew how he projected his confidence. And she knew how he felt when it was all over.

It *was* kind of like playing a character. The character was just a more exaggerated, more outgoing version of herself. But at the core, it was still her.

After dinner, Naomi gathered everyone together in the living room. She had found the infamous talent show recording and wanted to watch it with everyone.

It was definitely a memorable performance. And not in a good way. Just like Mr. Green said, the only person who could be heard was Mr. Jeremy-Micah.

Mr. Green was laughing in the background. And Mr. Payne kept looking back at Mr. Jeremy-Micah with annoyance.

"No, he didn't!" cried younger Uncle Arnold when younger Mr. Payne stood in front of younger Mr. Jeremy-Micah.

"That day was a hot mess," said Uncle Arnold.

"It sure was," agreed Aunt Ruth-Anne. "How you going to be jealous because my brother is more talented than you? That's why I'm glad Jeremy-Micah drowned him out."

The family kept laughing and poking fun at the tape. After a while, everyone started winding down.

Aunt Ruth-Anne pulled Althea to the side for a conversation.

"I just wanted you to know how proud we are of you," said Aunt Ruth-Anne. She handed a gift to Althea and said, "I bought this for you today."

It was a pen fashioned like a quill feather pen. And there was also a cute notebook to go with it.

"Thank you, Aunty," said Althea.

"You keep doing what you're doing," said Aunt Ruth-Anne. "And you keep being yourself no matter what anyone says."

"I will," said Althea.

"I hope so," said Aunt Ruth-Anne. "I remember when we were younger, everyone kept trying to force my sister to be more outgoing. But nothing anyone did worked. She wouldn't budge until she was ready to. I want you to have that same determination. No matter what anyone says, or tries to do, you continue being yourself."

"Yes ma'am," said Althea.

It made her happy to know how much support she had. And she was glad that she had pushed herself to get what she wanted. Althea planned to keep doing so, knowing one day that it would help her achieve all her dreams.

Benjamin Townsend

Benjamin never *ever* thought he would let Derek dress him. But that was exactly what he was doing.

Benjamin had been part of a reality show back in April. The cast would be filming the reunion on the first weekend in July.

He needed a memorable outfit for the occasion. And Derek was the only person he knew who made memorable outfits. So, he gathered some clothes and brought them to Derek's house.

Derek had been rapping along to Benjamin's song, "Home Team", as he worked. And he had not missed a word.

"Dang, you really know the lyrics to my stuff," said Benjamin.

"Why wouldn't I know the lyrics?" asked Derek. He motioned to the completed outfit and asked, "What do you think?"

"What in the world?" questioned Benjamin, looking at the outfit Derek had put together. "Boy, what is this?"

"What's wrong with it?"

"What isn't wrong with it? What even is the vision here?"

"Let me explain it to you."

Benjamin listened as his best friend explained how his creation was a good outfit. By the time Derek finished, Benjamin was fully convinced.

"Okay," said Benjamin. "I see it now."

"See?" said Derek triumphantly. "And y'all act like I can't dress. I told y'all I can make anything work."

"I mean, I *do* see your vision," said Benjamin. "But I can't wear this."

"Why not?" asked Derek disappointedly.

"Because what if I need to move quickly?"

"Move quickly?" repeated Derek. He mulled over the words, then said, "Well, in that case…"

As Derek put together a new outfit, Mr. Malcolm entered the room.

"Hey," said Mr. Malcolm. "Hey Benji."

"Hello," said Benjamin.

"What's up?" asked Derek.

"I got cookies."

"Nanna's?"

"Yup."

Mr. Malcolm put a bag of cookies on the nightstand and left the room.

"You can have some if you want," said Derek. "But don't eat too many though. One time Nanna made a whole batch of cookies and Dee-Three ate like half of them. He ended up throwing them up."

"Wow," said Benjamin.

"What do you think?" asked Derek, showing the new outfit.

"Much better," said Benjamin.

"This'll go great with that watch you got for your birthday," said Derek.

"I don't have it," remarked Benjamin bitterly.

"Where is it?"

"I don't know."

"You lost it?"

"Something like that."

"Bro, that was an expensive watch! How'd you lose something like that?"

"I don't want to talk about it."

Thinking about his watch made Benjamin mad all over again. And that was not the headspace he needed to be in going into that weekend.

The reunion would be a crucial moment in Benjamin's life. Not only because it would close a small chapter in his life, but also because he had a special job to do.

Drake Brown had come to Benjamin weeks earlier with an unbelievable idea. Benjamin still remembered it like it had just happened. He was clearing tables at Patty's when Drake approached him.

"Hey Benji," said Drake.

"What's up Drake?" said Benjamin, dapping Drake up. He had been surprised to see Drake there since he lived in the city.

"I saw you were a contestant on Rak's show."

"Yeah."

"And filming already ended?"

"We've still got the reunion coming up in the summer."

"Are you going to it?"

"Yeah."

"Good," said Drake. "I need your help to catch a thief."

"What?" said Benjamin confusedly.

"We're going to figure out who stole Rak's stuff."

"I think we should just stay out of that," said Benjamin.

"I was staying out of it until he started messing up my stuff," said Drake. "He and his boys showed up to the studio we were recording at looking for Vince again. Vince had to lock us in the studio until he was sure it was safe for us to leave. Now, he's postponed our recording sessions because he doesn't want to put us in a situation like that again. Rak is messing up my career and money, and if we don't find the thief, he's going to mess yours up too."

"But why do *we* have to do it?" questioned Benjamin.

"Because I'm on Vince's side of things and you're on Rak's at least up until this reunion. If we work together, we can figure out who the culprit is and put an end to all this."

"What if it's really Knokout who did it though?"

"He didn't."

"How do you know?"

"His story hasn't changed. And just from getting to know him personally, he doesn't seem like the kind of guy to steal from folks."

"Well, Rak's story hasn't changed either."

"Then the truth is somewhere in the middle. When's the reunion?"

"I don't know yet."

"Well, when you find out, let me know."

That conversation happened toward the end of May when the show started airing. It was nearing the end of June.

Most of the episodes were released on an independent streaming platform. Benjamin had avoided watching them.

But with the reunion approaching, he knew he had to get himself caught up. He had to have as much knowledge as he could going into it.

So, when he got home, he started at the beginning. The audition episode.

The auditions had been during spring break at a nightclub called Cinnamon. Benjamin had stood outside in line for hours on that warm Saturday.

But it did not bother him. He had been willing to go through anything to get his shot.

Benjamin had learned about the show on social media. KV had started his own label and wanted to sign his first two artists. The show was how he was going to select them.

There were as many people leaving as there were entering. And attitudes got worse as the temperature got hotter. It did not help that there was no food or water offered either.

At one point, some water boys pulled up selling water out of their truck. Benjamin wanted to buy one, but he was close to the door by that point.

After security patted him down, they directed Benjamin to go left. He found himself in a room filled with men of all ages.

"Dang," said the guy who entered behind him. "It's nothing but dudes up in here."

"Nah for real," agreed another guy. "Where the females at?"

"They're in another room," explained a third guy.

"Forget all that," griped another dude. "They got any food or water up in here?"

"Nah, I don't think so."

"Man, it's too hot for this! How they ain't got no water up in this joint?!"

The men ranted and raved. A big man holding a roll of tickets entered with two security guards and looked around.

"Hey, listen up!" hollered the man. "This how this going to go. Y'all get thirty seconds to impress me. If you fail, you're out."

"Impress you?!" cried a man. "Man, you ain't nothing but security!"

"And you ain't nothing but out!" snapped the man. He motioned for security to remove the man. After a small scuffle, the big man asked, "Anyone else?"

Nobody said anything.

"That's what I thought. Who's first?"

Impressing the big man was harder than Benjamin thought it would be. He and the two security guards voted based on who they liked. And they did not seem to have a criteria.

Some guys got thrown out based on their looks. Others for being boring. A few got aggressive and had to be forcibly removed like the first guy.

Then it was Benjamin's turn.

"Dang, you're short," said the big man. "I can look straight over your head, you so short."

Had he been anywhere else, Benjamin would have instantly fired off with a comeback. But he wanted to get on the show. So, he just ignored it and did a freestyle.

"You short but you got skills," said the big man. "Take this ticket and go where security tells you."

Security directed him to a space where sections were being used as a waiting area. He sat down and listened to the music.

It was a long waiting period. At one point, some of the others started talking about what happened on the girl's side.

"That one light-skinned security guard really thinks he something!" said one girl. "Like I ain't never seen a dude so thirsty in all my life!"

"No for real!" agreed another girl. "I thought we were going to be showing off our talents like rapping and singing. But all he wants to see us do is shake a little something!"

"No because them just walking in and immediately sending girls home because they weren't cute enough was crazy," said another girl. "Then he going to say we're not respectable females because no re-spectable female would be here after we said we weren't dancing for them."

"And then he talking about he make six figures and can buy our lives! You know that's a lie because those dusty shoes he had on from ten years ago and those cheap clothes told me he needed this job real bad!"

The girls cackled. After more waiting, the survivors had to sign release forms. After that, they lined up onstage and KV entered the building.

KV entering was where the episode started. Besides showing brief in-line interviews, none of the stuff with the security guards was shown.

The security guards turned out to be KV's entourage and extra security. Big man was Duke. Genie, which was short for Eugene, was the infamous light-skinned one. KV explained he sent them to weed out the weaklings before he got there.

The episode made the auditions seem like they went straight to the main stage. And it made the auditions look more fun than they were.

Benjamin watched his audition and was proud of himself. He had given his best up there after a long, hard day. And it had paid off.

At the end of the auditions, he made it into the top twenty contestants to be on the show. The only thing left after that had been to break the news to his parents.

Benjamin had done it at dinner that night.

"I've got something to tell you both," said Benjamin.

Everyone looked at him expectantly.

"I went to an audition," began Benjamin.

"An audition?" repeated Mrs. Townsend. "What for?"

"A reality show."

"A reality show?" questioned Mr. Townsend. "What reality show you trying to go on?"

"It's a... a music competition," stammered Benjamin.

"Like one of those TV talent shows?" asked Mr. Townsend.

"Sort of."

"Sort of?" said Mrs. Townsend skeptically. "What is 'sort of'?"

"It's a competition to get signed to a music label," explained Benjamin. "And I made it into the top twenty which means I passed the audition round to be on the show."

Benjamin waited for his parents to respond.

"Benjamin," began Mr. Townsend. Benjamin pursed his lips and sat back in his seat. He knew what was coming next. "We've already discussed this... thing... of you wanting to be a rap artist. It's not a stable career path. You need to focus on preparing to one day take over the family business."

"Running a restaurant isn't a stable career either," said Benjamin. "No career is stable."

"It's a whole lot more stable than a rap career is," said Mrs. Townsend. "Look at NikNak. He had a rap career and now look at what he's doing: running a restaurant. In fact, he's moving into franchising his restaurant now."

"Heck, look at all the Boyz," added Mr. Townsend. "King Roy owns a radio station, Tony-P does more songwriting than singing nowadays, Baby Luke has several different things he's doing, and the list goes on. You see how all these music artists have other things going on, Benji?"

"Yes sir," said Benjamin.

"You know why that is?" said Mr. Townsend. "Because the music isn't making the money you think it's making. But this house you're living in? That car you're driving? Those clothes you're wearing? This food you're eating? Patty's paid for all of that."

"I still think it's a good opportunity," muttered Benjamin.

"The boy is hard-headed," said Mr. Townsend.

"Just like his daddy," snorted Mrs. Townsend.

"More like his mama," countered Mr. Townsend.

Benjamin tried his best not to look disappointed. He had been rapping since he was thirteen years old.

But his parents always treated his rapping as a hobby he would grow out of instead of as his chosen career path.

After dinner, Benjamin went to his room to think. He felt seriously discouraged.

"Benji?" said Charmaine, slipping into his room.

"What?" answered Benjamin.

"Do you think you've got a chance of winning that competition?"

"Yeah."

"Then go for it."

"But Mom and Dad–!"

"Can just leave the restaurant to me," laughed Charmaine. "But if you don't take this chance, you might regret it later."

Benjamin felt a smile spread across his face. His sister had always been his number one supporter.

"Benji!" called Charmaine, bringing him back to the present. After watching the audition episode, Benjamin had gone to bed for work the next day. It was his turn to wait tables. When he approached his sister at the register, she said, "Those people sitting in the corner with Drake are here to see you."

"If they weren't trying to draw attention to themselves, they failed," snorted Benjamin, looking at the two figures dressed in black hoodies and sunglasses.

"For real," agreed Charmaine.

Benjamin approached the mysterious-looking group.

"What's up Drake?" said Benjamin, dapping Drake up. "Who are they?"

The man lowered his sunglasses. Benjamin instantly understood why they wore what they did.

"Hi," whispered Knokout. "Call me Vince."

"Alice," whispered DJ Mousie, also lowering her sunglasses.

"Hi," answered Benjamin, sitting next to Drake. "What's going on?"

"Drake told us you were working with us," explained Vincent. "So, we wanted to meet with you to bring you up to speed."

"What's happened?"

"I think I've figured out who the thief is," said Vincent. "All we've got to do is expose him."

"How are you going to do that?" asked Benjamin.

"At the reunion this weekend," explained Alice. "I'm going to be a special guest host since I'm Rak's cousin, and I'm bringing Vince as my surprise plus one."

"What do you need me to do?" questioned Benjamin.

"You're going to be our decoy," said Vincent. "We know who stole your watch."

"You do?" asked Benjamin. "How?"

"I had a little helper on the show," said Vincent, glancing at Alice. "Unfortunately, we couldn't stop him from stealing it without exposing that we were watching him. But we know who stole it and so does Rak."

"Wow," said Benjamin. "So, he's known the whole time who stole my watch and he didn't look out for me?"

"Not exactly," said Alice. "He knows what he was told about the watch. Trust me, it'll all make sense when we expose the thief."

"Who's the thief?"

"We can't tell you yet," said Vincent. "You might try to go after him, and we can't risk it."

"What exactly am I going to do?"

"I'm going to give you a chain to wear," said Vincent. "What you're going to do is when your watch gets brought up, you're going to 'go off' and leave the stage. You'll leave the chain in your dressing room then go back onstage without it. Then when our thief steals it, we'll expose him as a repeat thief."

"What if he doesn't take it?"

"Trust me. He'll take it."

"But how will that prove that he stole Rak's stuff too?" asked Benjamin.

"I've got that covered," said Vincent with a smirk.

After work, Benjamin settled in to watch the first episode. It opened with them pulling up to the house in two vans. He relived the nervous excitement he had felt in that moment.

Most of the women looked the same. Voluptuous bodies, brightly colored wigs, heavy makeup, skimpy clothes. The show gave heavy attention to one called Sweet Hunni.

Sweet Hunni was light-brown and had a black wig with bangs. She was twenty-one, a rapper, and a model. Benjamin had never seen her in anything though.

The camera focused heavily on her looks. But when Benjamin was there in person, he had immediately noticed another girl.

She was dark-brown, with black dreadlocks that hung near her cheeks. Her look had been more natural compared to the other girls. That's what made her stand out from the others.

Ra'Kaveon emerged from the house with Duke and Genie.

"Welcome," said Ra'Kaveon, throwing his arms up in greeting. "Who's ready for the first elimination?"

"Right now?" replied one of the girl contestants.

"Right now," said Ra'Kaveon. He pointed to the house behind him and said, "It's only ten beds in here. That means ten of y'all are about to get back on that van and go right back on home."

"Yo!" cackled Genie.

"Are you serious?!" cried another girl contestant.

"Yeah," answered Ra'Kaveon. "I'm looking for people that's willing to fight for everything they got out the gate. It's no handouts around here. So, if you want a bed in this house, you going have to fight for it."

"Say less," said another guy contestant, stepping forward and assuming a fighting stance. He challenged the other contestants, saying, "Who want it first?"

"Whoa, whoa!" laughed Ra'Kaveon. "I ain't mean *fighting* fighting. I meant y'all going to battle for it."

"Oh," said the guy contestant, falling back in line.

"I like your spirit though," said Ra'Kaveon. "Here's how we're going to do this. We're going to pair y'all up by drawing names and y'all going to battle off the dome for your spots. Winners get beds, losers get lost. Any questions?"

There were no questions. Benjamin had gone into game mode, tuning out the other contestants' rounds. It was not until he watched the episode that he heard for the first time what everyone else had performed.

Sweet Hunni had unsurprisingly sucked but still managed to win her round. The dark-skinned girl was Ebony. There was also a lot of emphasis put on a rapper named Grai. But the one to do the best by far was BigBucckz.

Benjamin was the last battle.

"Alright, we got Benji With Da Bad Attitude versus Skunk," said Ra'Kaveon.

The man that was willing to fight for his bed stepped up. Benjamin stepped up to meet him.

"Why y'all got me going against this little boy?" laughed Skunk. "Are you even old enough to be here?"

Benjamin did not respond. He silently waited for the battle to start.

"This is going to be a piece of cake," said Skunk confidently.

They flipped a coin to decide who would go first. Skunk won the toss.

They went three rounds. And nothing was off limits.

Skunk made fun of Benjamin's height, his stage name, his look, and more. But Benjamin came right back at him with shots at his stage name, how he looked like a skunk, and probably smelled like one too.

The battle ended. Benjamin and Skunk waited to find out who would move forward.

"I think Benji got that," said Ra'Kaveon. What y'all think?"

The entourage agreed.

"Alright, Benji's the winner," said Ra'Kaveon. "Skunk, that means you get lost."

"Man, this some bullcrap!" hollered Skunk. He swung at the camera and ranted, "Get that camera out my face! Brought me all the way out here just to waste my time!"

Benjamin chuckled rewatching Skunk's antics. Skunk had hollered, screamed, shown off his jewelry, thrown money at the camera, and even gotten into it with security. His last scene was him being carried away by his arms and legs and put into the van to go home.

It was hilariously obvious Skunk was trolling for camera time on the show. But in the moment, Benjamin had felt annoyed with Skunk. He had been ready to get in the house, but they could not go in until Skunk left.

The house was a normal two-story one located in a nice neighborhood. It had five bedrooms, a pool, a jacuzzi, and lots of space between it and the neighboring houses.

Benjamin went inside and chose a room on the first floor. As he was unpacking, he heard someone else enter the room.

"I'm rooming with you, little man."

"Don't call me that," snapped Benjamin, his back turned to the speaker.

"Dang boy. You sure wasn't raised right, that's for sure."

"Excuse me?!" cried Benjamin, wheeling around to face his accuser. But when he saw the speaker was older, he calmed down. "Oh. I'm sorry."

"Oh, you was raised right after all," said the man. "Benji, right? With Da Bad Attitude?"

"Yes sir," answered Benjamin.

"Forget all that 'sir' mess," said the man. "I ain't that old. Just call me Uncle Buck."

"Uncle Buck?" said Benjamin.

"Yup," answered Uncle Buck. "Uncle Charles Buck aka BigBucckz."

He extended a hand to Benjamin, which Benjamin took.

"Benjamin," said Benjamin. "Benji, for short."

"How old are you, Benji?"

"Eighteen."

"Dang, you're literally half my age."

After unpacking, the cast was summoned to the living room. Benjamin did not realize how much work went into a reality show until he saw it for himself.

There were lights and microphones everywhere. And there were a lot of people behind the cameras.

The security guards wore all black. But the uniforms were not uniform. And they all had on ski masks.

"Y'all are already starting off boring," said a producer. "Talk about something. Who y'all think is going to win?"

"I'm definitely winning," said Sweet Hunni.

The scene on the episode started with what she said after that.

"You guys shouldn't bother unpacking," said Sweet Hunni. "Because that top spot is as good as mine."

"You think so?" said another girl.

"Mhmm," said Sweet Hunni dismissively.

Sweet Hunni and the girl started arguing. Benjamin could tell then he was not going to like her. But he felt like he would like Uncle Buck despite their rocky start.

The episode ended with Ra'Kaveon explaining how the competition would work. He would be signing two artists to his new label, King Rak Records. Everyone would compete in a bunch of elimination challenges throughout the show.

Benjamin started the second episode which would cover their first challenge.

They had started the day being rudely awakened by Ra'Kaveon's entourage. They yelled, banged pots, and sprayed people with water guns.

Everyone gathered in the living room where Ra'Kaveon waited, fully dressed. Benjamin noticed how different everyone looked in their pajamas.

"Y'all look rough," joked Ra'Kaveon.

He and the entourage were the only ones to laugh.

"Welcome to day two," said Ra'Kaveon. "Yesterday, y'all proved y'all could hold y'all's own freestyling. Today, we're going to see how good your teamwork is. So, we're going to have a cypher battle. Y'all are going to be split into two teams of five and y'all got until three o'clock to prepare according to the concept we give y'all. The team with the weakest cypher will go home. Any questions?"

There were no questions. Benjamin was teamed up with Uncle Buck, Ebony, Sweet Hunni, and Grai. Their concept was Everything Gold.

They gathered in Sweet Hunni's room. Uncle Buck became the unofficial leader of their group.

He said he was big on knowing who he worked with. So, he made everyone tell their real names.

Charles Buck. Ebony Simmons. Roshonda Routledge. Jaden Gray. Benjamin Townsend.

Satisfied, Uncle Buck began strategizing. Grai dozed off to the side. Sweet Hunni messed with her hair in the mirror. Benjamin and Ebony waited patiently.

"Why don't I get to go first?" complained Sweet Hunni when Uncle Buck revealed his strategy. "Don't you want to start off with your best rapper?"

"We are," said Uncle Buck.

"Oh, so you're saying you're better than me?"

"I'm more experienced."

"Okay but we want to grab their attention immediately," said Sweet Hunni. "And I can do that."

Uncle Buck looked at Sweet Hunni thoughtfully.

"You're right," said Uncle Buck. "We'll make you last."

"Last?!"

"Think about it," said Uncle Buck. "You'll be the last thing they remember."

Sweet Hunni stared at Uncle Buck. Then she nodded.

"Ah," said Hunni, pointing at Uncle Buck. She pointed between their eyes and said, "So we're here, right?"

"Yeah, we're here," said Uncle Buck.

"Alright I got you," said Sweet Hunni with a smirk.

"I don't understand a single thing they're talking about," said Benjamin.

"It's because you're young," chuckled Ebony.

"You don't look much older than I am. How old are you?"

"Didn't your mama ever tell you it's rude to ask a woman her age?"

"Probably."

"And you just don't pay her no mind, huh?" laughed Ebony. "That's how I know you're young. But to answer your question I'm twenty-five."

They started talking after that.

Ebony was a singer. But she could rap too. She was hoping to get signed to advance her singing career.

The episode started with the scene right after their conversation. It showed both teams practicing and strategizing.

Then they went into the living room to perform their cyphers.

Team One's concept was Everything Silver. It seemed like a harder concept to pull off. But Benjamin thought they did okay.

However, his team was just much better. They all ran through their verses like it was nothing.

Uncle Buck started off with hard-hitting punchlines. Then, Ebony and Grai came with verses that were more chill like they were. Benjamin did his thing to bring the energy back up. And then it was time for Sweet Hunni's big finale.

Her rapping was mediocre. And she moved her body in a way that would have disgusted Benjamin's mother. But the reaction shot of Ra'Kaveon and his entourage showed they were all into it.

Once they finished, the two teams waited for the results.

"The winner is...," said Ra'Kaveon. "Team Two. Team One, it's time to get lost."

Benjamin and his team were still in the running.

The girl who had argued with Sweet Hunni the day before tried to start a fight with her. But security made sure the girl got nowhere near her.

Benjamin decided to stop there for the time being. Knowing what was coming in the next episode made him mad all over again.

The next day, Benjamin had his music going as he worked the cash register. His parents allowed him to play music as long as it wasn't anything distasteful.

Mariana Garza walked in. Ever since prom, Benjamin saw her differently.

It was like she was suddenly the prettiest girl in the world. And her bluntness had never bothered him as much as the others.

"Welcome to Patty's," said Benjamin with a smile. "How can I help you?"

"I want a grilled chicken sandwich with fries," said Mariana. "And I'll have a lemonade for my drink."

"Anything else?"

"No, that's it."

"Alright. I'll have your total for you."

Ebony's song started playing next. It was a slow, soulful song.

"What song is this?" asked Mariana. After Benjamin told her what it was, she said, "Hm. I like it."

After that, she moved to the side to wait for her food.

"I've never seen you smile that much with a customer before," whispered Mr. Townsend with a grin when Benjamin brought her order to the window.

"I was just showing good customer service," said Benjamin.

"Mhmm," chuckled Mr. Townsend. "Well, you keep it up. You're going to need those good customer service skills when you take over the restaurant."

Benjamin held in a groan. It frustrated him though that his parents did not take his music seriously. And sometimes that frustration got the better of him and made him lash out at others.

He was working on that especially since he wanted to make himself a more established artist. No one wanted to work with someone who was terrible to be around. That was something he learned firsthand on the show.

After work, he decided to power through episode three. It was the episode that made him the maddest.

"Welcome to day three," said Ra'Kaveon. "You five have proven yourselves as being able to spit off the dome and work well as a team. But it's more to being an artist than just being able to freestyle. Any artist that wants to join King Rak Records needs to have a strong pen game too. So, today you five will be going out to have some fun on the town. And make sure you're paying attention because when you come back, you're going to be writing a song based on your day. Whoever has the weakest pen game will be leaving the house. Any questions?"

They got one of Ra'Kaveon's previous songs to use as their beat and were taken to the park. Benjamin walked around trying to find something to use for inspiration.

The episode was pretty dry up until they got back to the house. They had to perform what they had decided to write about.

The skill levels were pretty much the same as they had been throughout the show. Uncle Buck wrote about being an oldhead. Grai wrote about relaxing, and Benjamin about being a kid again.

But the real highlight was between Ebony and Sweet Hunni. Sweet Hunni had written a rap about being the cutest wherever she went. And it was hot garbage.

Ebony had written this beautiful song about loving yourself. And the way she sang it amazed Benjamin. Even rewatching it, he was still amazed, and his jaw was still just as dropped.

But when it came time for elimination, the bottom two were Sweet Hunni and Ebony.

It had confused Benjamin. Sweet Hunni's material was terrible but Ebony did not deserve to be up for elimination. He thought it should have been between Sweet Hunni and Grai.

"Hunni, this wasn't your best work," said Ra'Kaveon. "But I can feel the passion you put into it. Ebony, you've got a great voice. In fact, it's so great that I'm concerned whether you'd be the right fit for the label. I feel like if I took you on, I wouldn't know what to do with you. That's why the person going home today is... Ebony."

Benjamin was shocked on the show. And rewatching it, he was livid. But the reason he was livid was because of what happened after elimination.

That night, Benjamin had sat in his room, processing what had just happened. Uncle Buck came in and asked him what was wrong.

"I just don't get it," said Benjamin. "I thought Ebony was better than Hunni. She's way more talented than her."

"Yeah," said Uncle Buck. "But the game doesn't revolve around talent. It revolves around what will make the most money. Talent is a bonus feature."

"I still don't get it."

"Here," said Uncle Buck, picking up a water bottle. "Think of this water as an artist."

"Okay."

"This is obviously better for you," said Uncle Buck, pointing to the water bottle. He placed it next to a soda bottle and said, "But if you gave most people the option to pick, what do you think they'll choose?"

"The soda," said Benjamin reluctantly.

"Exactly," said Uncle Buck. "Because it's more appealing now even though the water is the better choice in the long run. It's the same with entertainment. The talented people may be better in the long run and have better quality product. But the people who fit what audiences want now are who will get all the attention. And right now, Hunni fits what King Rak Records wants."

Uncle Buck said the last sentence with a snort causing Benjamin to wonder if there was a hidden meaning behind it. The unfairness kept him up that night.

He went to the kitchen to get some water around midnight. There was noise coming from the entertainment room.

Benjamin crept toward the room and found Sweet Hunni chilling with Ra'Kaveon and his entourage.

Sweet Hunni was playing a very personal drinking game with a shirtless, alcohol-covered Ra'Kaveon. The entourage sat around them cheering. Grai was also there too.

Benjamin realized then why Grai seemed familiar. He was also a member of Ra'Kaveon's entourage.

Suddenly, Benjamin understood perfectly what Uncle Buck had meant. Ra'Kaveon had already picked his winners.

And it made him mad.

That Friday, Benjamin went to get his hair retwisted at Miss Leya's Beauty and Barbershop. He was the only male on the salon's side.

Nisha had turned on the fourth episode, which had dropped earlier that day.

"Ooooh Benji, you're going to look so good," said Nisha as she retwisted his dreadlocks. "You make sure you shout me out so everyone can know who had you looking right."

"I'll try," chuckled Benjamin as he watched the show.

"Welcome to day four," said Ra'Kaveon. "It's only four of y'all left. Today, we're going to have a little fun. You four have been working hard and deserve to take a break from the rhymes. So, today we're going to host a King Rak Records house party because your public image is just as important as your art. The only rule is to have fun and be a good representative of the label. I'm going to have some secret judges amongst the guest. And whoever they say was the wackest person at the party will be leaving with the guests. So, have fun. Any questions?"

There were no questions.

Benjamin got ready for the party. But he had been off the whole day. He was still upset about Ebony's elimination.

He was even more upset that the show was basically rigged for Grai and Sweet Hunni to win. Benjamin could at least understand Grai winning. Grai was Ra'Kaveon's friend.

But Sweet Hunni confused him. As far as Benjamin knew, she and Ra'Kaveon met on the first day of filming. And she looked like every other chick on the cast besides Ebony.

He could not understand what made her so special.

The house party had a lot of people show up. Benjamin tried to have fun. But after a while, he went to be by himself.

What Benjamin remembered most about that day was his off-camera conversation with Uncle Buck. That talk had changed Benjamin's outlook not only on the show but the whole industry.

"You don't look like you're enjoying yourself," said Uncle Buck, his tone carrying a hint of warning.

"What's the point?" said Benjamin.

"The point is this is still an opportunity."

"An opportunity to be set up for failure?"

"Benjamin," said Uncle Buck sternly. It reminded Benjamin of the way his father would say his name when he was getting onto him. "The only way you'll fail is if you give up before the game is over."

"Well, it seems like the game has already been decided," spat Benjamin.

"Maybe it has," said Uncle Buck. "But just because you might not be the winner doesn't mean you can't still win."

"What do you mean?"

"You've got to learn how to benefit from every opportunity, even if it doesn't go how you want," advised Uncle Buck. "Look where you're at right now. You're on a show that people everywhere are going to watch. Even if you don't win, you can still get the people interested in you."

"I can?" asked Benjamin. "How?"

"That's up to you," said Uncle Buck. "Even if the game is already over before it's started, you should still stick around as long as possible. That's why you've got to keep trying."

He had to keep trying. The show had not aired that conversation between them, but Benjamin never forgot it. It was the fuel that he had needed to keep going on that show.

Benjamin got his head back in the game and returned to the party. He had fun as best as he could. And after the party ended, everyone went to bed.

Elimination was the next morning. The contestants had to clean up the house. By the time they finished, Ra'Kaveon showed up wearing sunglasses.

"Yesterday was a great time," said Ra'Kaveon. "I must've been going hard yesterday because I knocked out as soon as I hit the bed."

"Right?" laughed Sweet Hunni.

"So, somebody's getting lost today," said Ra'Kaveon. "And the party guests decided who that will be."

The four contestants waited to see who would leave.

"The person with the most votes...," said Ra'Kaveon. "Is Sweet Hunni."

"Why am I not surprised?" said Nisha. "Benji, you can tell me the truth. She was sleeping with him, wasn't she?"

"I can't say anything," said Benjamin.

"That's all the confirmation I need because it's so obvious," scoffed Nisha.

Benjamin understood Nisha's feelings perfectly. He himself had barely suppressed an eye-roll when Sweet Hunni was proclaimed the fan favorite. But he had to reluctantly admit, she had been the life of the party.

"The person with the second highest votes...," said Ra'Kaveon. "Is BigBucckz."

"Now that's my man right there," said Nisha triumphantly. "After you, of course."

"Benji, Grai," said Ra'Kaveon. "Whoever's name I don't call is who will be going home."

Benjamin knew he had messed up. Not only had he been standoffish most of the night, but Grai was also Ra'Kaveon's friend. He knew his time was up and began preparing to leave the show.

"The person with the third highest amount of votes," began Ra'Kaveon. He looked at the name for a long time, then said, "Benji."

Benjamin's mouth dropped.

"Why'd you look so surprised?" asked Nisha.

"I thought I was going home," answered Benjamin.

He had beaten Grai. The room was silent.

"Grai," said Ra'Kaveon. "You've... got to get lost."

"Dang," said Grai. "That's what's up."

Benjamin had been so confused about why Grai got sent home. But after watching the episode he realized what had happened.

Grai had gotten so drunk that he fell asleep in his room. He had slept through the whole party. So, he had no chance for anyone to see him and vote for him.

Grai sleeping through the party had kept Benjamin on the show. And it had given him a new energy.

With Grai eliminated that meant anyone could still win. That meant Benjamin still had a shot.

"Next week is the finale," said Nisha. "If you don't win and Hunni does, I know something."

"Yup," said Benjamin. "Next week the last episode airs, and the week after that is the reunion episode."

"Now, I can't wait for that," said Nisha.

"Neither can I," said Benjamin knowingly. "I have a feeling it's going to be unforgettable."

The reunion was that Saturday. They were filming it at Cinnamon.

Benjamin had decided to wear the original outfit Derek put together for him. There were only two things he planned to do at the reunion.

The first was to expose the thief. Vincent and Alice had that covered. They had given him a big, gold, diamond-encrusted letter-B chain to wear.

There was no way for anyone to miss him wearing it. And it looked too expensive for the thief to not want to steal it.

His second goal was to deal with Skunk. Skunk had gotten on social media talking a lot of smack about him right before the reunion.

Benjamin would have been annoyed. But his conversation with Uncle Buck at the house party had opened his eyes to what Skunk was doing.

Skunk was trying to make a viral moment for himself to get his name out there. His outburst on the first episode had gotten a little traction. So, Benjamin decided to give him what he wanted. Especially since it would benefit himself too.

Benjamin got to the reunion and was put in a dressing room by himself. Since Alice was a co-host, she was going around doing the pre-show interviews.

"We've got like two minutes before the cameras catch up with me," said Alice, flying into his dressing room. "I had to pay a security guard to fake some drama so I could ditch them real quick. You ready?"

"Yeah," answered Benjamin.

"You got the chain?"

"Yeah," said Benjamin. "Are we sure this will work?"

"It has to," said Alice. "Because if it doesn't we're all screwed."

There was a knock on the door and then the camera crew came in.

"Was everything okay?" asked Alice.

"Yeah," said the cameraman. "It turned out to be nothing. It'll be great trailer footage though."

"Okay," said Alice. "Sorry I ran off. I'm here to host not fight."

"It's all cool."

"Okay. We're ready to roll when you are."

"Rolling."

Benjamin conducted his pre-show interview with Alice. And he made sure to shout out Nisha and Derek for how they helped him out.

Then all there was left to do was wait for his turn to go onstage. When it was his time, he went and sat next to Uncle Buck.

The reunion host was DJ Yip-Yap, a popular DJ in the city. His real name was Chester, and he was in his early thirties. He was the most in tune with hip-hop culture in the city, and his opinion was highly valued by a lot of upcoming artists.

"Welcome to the reunion, Benji!" said DJ Yip-Yap. "How you doing?"

"I'm doing good," said Benjamin.

They talked a bit about how Benjamin had been after the show. Then they showed a montage of his good and bad moments in the house.

The one that got the most attention was a clip that would not air until the finale.

His watch had disappeared on the last day of the show. Benjamin was sure he had taken it off and left it in his room.

But when he went to retrieve it, it was gone. He had looked all over for it. But it was nowhere to be found.

Benjamin cringed watching himself rage through the house for his missing watch.

"Where is it?!" hollered Benjamin. "Where the heck is my watch?!"

Benjamin inhaled deeply. He was getting mad all over again reliving the moment.

"Yo, what's the problem?" asked Ra'Kaveon.

"Where's my watch?!" snapped Benjamin.

"What watch?"

"My gold watch!"

"Look, you need to calm down. You ain't going to keep screaming in my face."

Benjamin had lost it after that. Security had to lock him in his room to calm down. And that's where the clip ended.

"That was intense," said DJ Yip-Yap. "Benji, why'd you snap like that?"

"My watch was missing," answered Benjamin. "And it's still missing. Rak."

"What's up?" said Ra'Kaveon.

"What's up with my watch?"

"What do you mean?"

"Do you know what happened with my watch?"

Ra'Kaveon looked confused.

"Don't you have it?" asked Ra'Kaveon.

"No."

"You sure?"

"I'm sure," said Benjamin, starting to get annoyed. He did not understand why Ra'Kaveon thought he had his own watch.

"Are you trying to prank me or something?" asked Ra'Kaveon.

"Do I look like I'm playing a prank?"

"You should have your watch."

"Well, I don't."

Looking at Ra'Kaveon's confused face slowly irritated Benjamin. He felt like he was being played especially since Alice already told him Ra'Kaveon knew who had his watch.

"I don't know what to tell you...," said Ra'Kaveon. "I'll look into it."

"You were supposed to have been looked into it."

"Man, what you want me to do?"

"I want you to get me my watch."

"I'm not responsible for your watch. You need to keep track of your stuff."

"It went missing on *your* show. And you said you'd get it back. And I still don't have it."

"Well, I don't know what to tell you because you should have it. Anyways–!"

"Ain't no 'anyways'!" snapped Benjamin. "Where's my watch?!"

"Boy, how many times do I have to tell you I don't know where your watch is?!" snapped Ra'Kaveon. "Are you stupid or something?!"

"Who you talking to like that?!"

"Hold on Benji!" cried Alice. "No!"

Benjamin was not sure what happened. First, he was on his feet. Then, Alice was between him and Ra'Kaveon, yelling at him.

Then Benjamin was in a chokehold being carried off stage. He found himself in his room, angrily pacing back and forth.

"Put me back on stage!" hollered Benjamin. "That man is trying to play me! He knows where my watch is!"

A security guard entered the room. Once the door closed, he pulled down his ski mask.

"Alright, calm down," said Vincent.

"Nah!" bellowed Benjamin. "He knows something and he's trying to play me!"

"Benji!" snapped Vincent. "Calm the heck down and remember why we're here!"

Benjamin sat down. It took him a minute to realize he had unintentionally done his part of the plan. But instead of faking a reason to leave, he had gotten pulled offstage for real.

That helped him get refocused. He could not go back onstage until he calmed down.

So, he calmed down, took off the chain, and waited for the all-clear to go back out. After about fifteen minutes, Uncle Buck came to check on him.

"You sure are showing out today," said Uncle Buck.

"I just want my watch," said Benjamin.

"Well, trying to fight the host of the show isn't going to get it back."

"I know."

"If you're ready to go back out, we can go."

"Let's go."

They went back out onstage. While Benjamin was backstage, Grai had been brought out.

"What's up Benji?" said Grai.

"What's up?" answered Benjamin.

"You got an issue with Rak?" demanded Grai.

"And if I do?" replied Benjamin. He did not have an issue with Grai. But he was not going to let Grai try and punk him.

"Okay, hold on," said Alice, diffusing the situation. "We don't have to fight over a misunderstanding."

Benjamin and Grai both sat back, glaring at each other.

"This is your second time trying to fight me over this watch," said Ra'Kaveon. "How you going to try to fight me just because I don't know what happened to your watch?"

"You're right," said Benjamin. "My bad."

"Yeah, it is your bad," said Ra'Kaveon.

The reunion went on after that. Ebony was brought out next. Benjamin's mouth dropped when he saw her. She was bald.

Alright, I see you," complimented Alice. "This is cute."

"Thank you," said Ebony.

"So, Ebony," said DJ Yip-Yap. "You got eliminated at the songwriting challenge. A lot of viewers felt like you were cheated, and that Hunni should've went home instead. How do you feel?"

"It is what it is," said Ebony. "I brought my A-game but it wasn't what Rak was looking for."

"Do you think Hunni is a better writer than you?" asked DJ Yip-Yap.

"I'm not really focused on what the next person does," said Ebony. "I just focus on my craft and what I have going on."

"You notice how she ain't answer the question though?" snickered Sweet Hunni.

"I could've sworn I just did," said Ebony.

"It's a yes or no question," said Sweet Hunni. "It don't require all that explanation."

"Hunni, I don't have a problem with you," said Ebony.

"If you don't have a problem with me, then you could easily answer yes or no. You just don't want to answer because you're jealous."

"Jealous?!" cried Ebony.

"Jealous," said Sweet Hunni. "Look at you and look at me. I look bomb while you came in here baldheaded with frumpy church clothes. He don't want that!"

Ra'Kaveon's lowered his head. But he could not hide his moving shoulders.

"You got anything else to ask me?" asked Ebony, ignoring Sweet Hunni.

"No but I just want to say, I think you're super talented and I need you on a track," said Alice. "Come see me after the show."

"Okay, we'll talk," said Ebony.

Next came the five contestants eliminated in the cypher round. There were a few arguments, mostly with Sweet Hunni. But Benjamin was bored until the bottom ten came out.

Nine of them went to their seats. But Skunk stopped in the middle of the stage.

"So, I got a question," said Skunk. He pointed at Benjamin and asked, "Why y'all choose this baldheaded little boy over me?"

Benjamin laughed.

"Oh, you laughing?" asked Skunk, walking up on Benjamin. "But just earlier you was throwing tantrums over a watch. Where you get it from the dollar store? If you get your bread up, you wouldn't need to beg nobody to find your little watch. Here let me help you."

Skunk threw hundreds in the air and made it rain on Benjamin. Benjamin just kept laughing.

"You can keep that," said Skunk, taking his seat. "I know you need it since you're too broke to buy a new watch."

"You sure you don't need your rent money back?" questioned Benjamin.

"Nah, you can keep it," said Skunk. "That's just pocket change."

"You sure know how to make an impression," chuckled DJ Yip-Yap. "Why you don't like Benji?"

"Who said I didn't like Benji?" asked Skunk. "I like Benji."

"You like him but you just made it rain on him and called him all types of broke and baldheaded?" laughed DJ Yip-Yap.

"Aye look, if I ain't like him, I wouldn't have helped him out," said Skunk with a shrug.

"Benji, how do you feel about Skunk?" asked DJ Yip-Yap.

"All I'll say is one of us made it to the finale while the other ain't even make it into the house," said Benjamin. "And I'm keeping this money too."

"I would hope so since you're so broke," said Skunk. "And you getting in the house was a fluke. You can't beat me in no real battle."

"I already beat you," said Benjamin.

"I bet you can't do it again."

"I bet I can."

"Alright, come on," said Skunk. "I want a rematch. Right here, right now."

"A rematch?" snorted Benjamin. "The first whooping wasn't enough for you?"

"Oh, you got jokes, huh?" said Skunk. "You won't be laughing after I embarrass you in front of everyone."

"The only one getting embarrassed is you," said Benjamin.

The rematch went for three rounds. At one point, Duke left the stage and came back minutes later.

The rematch was declared a tie. And it took up so much time that the other nine contestants barely got to say anything.

"Man, you had a lot of baddies on this cast," said DJ Yip-Yap, looking around.

"Yeah man," said Ra'Kaveon.

"Was there any fun times we didn't see on the show?" teased DJ Yip-Yap.

Benjamin glanced at Sweet Hunni. There was not a hint of shame or embarrassment anywhere on her face.

"Man," laughed KV. "I'm pleading the fifth."

"Alright," laughed DJ Yip-Yap. "Ladies, if you ever get lonely, hit me up."

All the women laughed.

"With that being said, we're at the end of the reunion," said DJ Yip-Yap.

"Before we go, I brought a special guest," said Alice.

"A special guest?" asked Ra'Kaveon. "Who?"

"Let me go get him," said Alice.

Alice disappeared backstage. She returned with a man dressed in all black and a ski mask.

"Your special guest is security?" laughed Ra'Kaveon.

"Do I look like security to you?" asked Vincent, removing his ski mask.

Everyone's mouths dropped.

"Oh snap!" gasped Skunk.

"What the–!" cried Ra'Kaveon.

"What's up?" said Vincent. "You ready to stop acting like a little boy?"

"Don't act like you all tough!" spat Ra'Kaveon. "What you come around here for?"

"I came here to slay a thief since I'm a Thief Slayer," said Vincent.

"What's up then?!" challenged Ra'Kaveon.

"If y'all fight, it's one on one," said Uncle Buck.

"Man please," laughed Vincent. "I ain't come here to fight you!"

"Then what you here for?!" growled Ra'Kaveon. "And Mousie, you supposed to be my family but you setting me up?!"

"I am not!" snapped Alice. "Vince knows who stole from you and he can prove it!"

"Well duh!" said Ra'Kaveon. "He can prove it because he's the one who did it!"

"Boy, how many times I got to tell you to check your people around you?" snorted Vincent. "Maybe it'll get through your head if I put a name on it. Your thief you been looking so hard for is your right-hand man, Duke."

Benjamin watched as Duke's face became like stone.

"Man, you're a liar," said Ra'Kaveon.

"So Duke," said Vincent, ignoring Ra'Kaveon. "You can either confess or I can expose you. Which one you want to do?"

"You ain't exposing nothing over here!" hollered Duke angrily.

"Alright, you want to do this the hard way," sighed Vincent. "So Rak, remember when our stuff got mixed together at the music video? Who was watching our stuff?"

"Man, I don't got to answer you!" said Ra'Kaveon. "Duke already said he ain't do it, so I don't know why you're still here!"

"Because I'm about to prove that Duke is who's been stealing from you, idiot," said Vincent.

"Call me an idiot again!"

"Calm down idiot."

"You lucky my cousin's standing right next to you!"

"Anyways," said Vincent. "Like I was saying, Duke was the one watching our stuff since you don't want to answer. It was his job to keep our stuff straight and protected but somehow it all got mixed together. And Duke was also there that day we all hung out at your place when your stuff went missing. Now Rak, if I spent the whole day chilling with you, when did I have time to jack your stuff?"

"All I know is when you came over, my stuff was on my dresser," said Ra'Kaveon. "And when you left, my stuff was gone."

"Of course it was!" said Vincent. "I was the last one to leave. And then, you called me going off about your stuff being gone. And when I asked what you were talking about, you accused me of stealing it and started this whole mess."

"See, you just admitted it!" roared Ra'Kaveon. "My stuff disappeared after you left!"

"Like I just said, I was the last to leave. But that doesn't mean I took it."

"Well, that doesn't prove Duke did either."

"Alright, I got more," said Vincent. "Benji's watch went missing and turned up where he didn't put it right? Then it went missing a second time. But it got found that second time, right?"

Ra'Kaveon did not answer.

"It got found," said Vincent. "By Duke. Who told you that he would get it to Benji. But Benji clearly doesn't have it. And you don't have it. So, who has it? The last person with it was Duke."

"How do you know what we talked about?" accused Ra'Kaveon. "Who you been talking to?"

"Doesn't matter," said Vincent. "If you don't believe me, maybe you'll believe the footage from your own show. Roll the tape!"

The television showed raw footage of Duke going into Benjamin's room and taking the watch. Then it showed Duke putting the watch back during the commotion.

Then it showed him taking it a second time.

Ra'Kaveon was speechless.

"I'm not done," said Vincent. "There's one more theft Duke did. Tonight. Anyone notice anything different about Benji? Like a big missing chain?"

Ra'Kaveon's eyes shifted to Benjamin's neck.

"Where'd you leave your chain Benji?"

"My dressing room."

"I wonder if it's still there. Want to go check? Or should we just run Duke's pockets now?"

"I say we just run his pockets," said Benjamin. "Since he took my watch, I'm sure he probably took my chain too."

"And it's not in his bag because I took care of that," said Vincent. "The only place he could hide it was in his pocket."

"Don't listen to this clown," said Duke. "He's just trying to blame me for what he did!"

"Like I've been saying this whole time, why would I steal stuff that I already have?" said Vincent. "I have the same stuff you have. I made the same money you made. Ever since our split, I've made even more money. I don't need you or your stuff to make my own money. But Duke does. You're his only source of income. We just showed you proof that he did two of the thefts the exact same way. Is it so far-fetched to believe he didn't do the original one?"

"It doesn't make sense though," said Ra'Kaveon. "I've been good to Duke. He wouldn't do some mess like that to me."

"If you don't believe me after all this, I don't know what to tell you," said Vincent.

A commotion broke out.

Benjamin had been so tuned in to the drama, he had not noticed Uncle Buck had gotten up. Evidently, neither had Duke.

The two were tussling on the ground. When security pulled them apart, lying underneath them was Benjamin's chain.

"Look!" said Uncle Buck. "There's the chain right there! You really tried to steal my boy's chain?!"

"That's real broke behavior!" clowned Skunk. "How you going to rob a teenager at your big age? You mad he got it, and you don't?"

After that, there was nothing left for Duke to say. He became irate and was escorted from the building.

Ra'Kaveon looked really hurt. He looked at Vincent, who stared at him with a neutral face.

"So what now?" said Ra'Kaveon with a scowl. "You want a cookie or something because you proved it wasn't you?"

"Nah," said Vincent. "I got what I wanted."

"What you got your face all screwed up for then?"

"Because I'm trying to convince myself not to beat you up."

"Beat me up for what?"

"Boy, Zion got jumped and almost lost his job and his life behind you. And you've cost me a lot of money and opportunities. I want my round but I'm trying to be grown about this."

"Aye, cut the cameras," commanded Ra'Kaveon.

He and Vincent went backstage to talk in private.

"Are you okay?" asked Benjamin, checking on Uncle Buck.

"Yeah," said Uncle Buck. "I'm too old to be fighting, but sometimes you got to do what you got to do. That man wasn't going to let anyone get near his pocket unless he was caught off guard. So, I caught him off guard."

He returned the chain to Benjamin. After that, the show ended.

Vincent and Alice thanked Benjamin for his help and let him keep the chain. Ra'Kaveon did not apologize, but he did give Benjamin money to replace his watch. Benjamin left the reunion feeling like a winner.

The following Friday, the finale aired. It released later than usual, and as Benjamin watched he realized why. Everything was centered around Duke's thefts.

Benjamin felt confident in saying the relationship between Duke and Ra'Kaveon was over.

"Welcome to day five," said Ra'Kaveon. "Y'all had a good time yesterday?"

"Yeah," answered the contestants.

"Good, because we're getting back to work today," said Ra'Kaveon. "Tonight is the final challenge. I've got a booking at a club and y'all are going to be my opening act. Tomorrow I'll be picking who I sign. So, bring you're A-game. Any questions?"

After explaining the challenge, Ra'Kaveon introduced Alice as his special guest judge for the finale.

After Alice entered the house, there was a camera constantly following Duke. Benjamin assumed she paid a cameraman to do it, especially since she had influence as Ra'Kaveon's cousin.

The club performance had been Benjamin's favorite moment on the show. All the contestants had been brought back to avoid spoiling who was still on the show.

After they got back home from the club, the infamous watch saga kicked off. The show showed it all.

They showed the theft, Benjamin's rampage, and the aftermath of production having to shut down. Then it moved on to the final elimination, which was the next morning.

Benjamin watched the elimination, already knowing the outcome.

"Hunni," said Ra'Kaveon. "This week you've really shown me how much you want this."

Sweet Hunni smirked.

"BigBucckz," said Ra'Kaveon. "You've really been hanging in there and I respect that."

Uncle Buck nodded.

"Benji," said Ra'Kaveon. "You've got a lot of talent and you've got heart, but you're a firecracker. And that makes me wonder if I can really work with you, and if you're really going to trust me. Because if things don't go your way or if something goes wrong, are you going to go off on me like you did earlier?"

Benjamin had just stared at Ra'Kaveon. He was still mad about his watch.

"The first person that I'll be signing...," said Ra'Kaveon. "Is going to be the First Lady of Rak Records, Sweet Hunni."

Sweet Hunni celebrated. That time, Benjamin actually did roll his eyes on camera.

"The second person that will be signed to Rak Records...," said Ra'Kaveon.

"That's just wrong!" cried Charmaine when the name was announced.

"What?" asked Benjamin.

"You were better than both of them!" declared Charmaine.

"I'm definitely not better than BigBucckz," said Benjamin.

"Okay, but you definitely shouldn't have lost to no Sweet Hunni! She can't even rap!"

"Well, everything happens for a reason," said Benjamin as he watched his non-reaction to being eliminated from the show.

He had just shrugged and went to pack his stuff. At first, he was sad about not getting signed.

But after seeing how some of the industry worked, he figured it was better to be his own independent artist. That way, he could be in control of how his career went.

He would work hard to make sure it was a successful career too. But until then, he would have to make do as a cashier at his parents' restaurant.

The next day, he got up and went to work. When Patty's opened, and the first customer came in, he smiled.

"Welcome to Patty's," said Benjamin. "How can I help you?"

Derik Harrison

Derik Harrison was unsure how he ended up in his parent's bed. It was the third time that week.

Morning sunlight filtered into the room. His father held him close, and he felt his mother's presence on his other side. Derik had never known his father to hold him like that.

He wanted to cherish the moment because it might not happen again.

The alarm went off. Derik shut his eyes as his parents stirred from sleep. A quiet, disappointed sigh escaped his nose as they left him alone on the bed.

"Good morning, Marlin," said Mrs. Harrison sweetly.

"Yo," said Mr. Harrison gruffly.

"Did you sleep well?"

"Uh-huh."

"That's good," said Mrs. Harrison. She dropped her voice to a whisper and added, "Was he on the floor again?"

"Uh-huh."

"I wish there was something we could do for him," sighed Mrs. Harrison.

Mr. Harrison did not respond. Derik peeked his eyes open and saw his father ironing. His mother had gone into the bathroom.

He stared at his father's muscular back. Derik was still unsure how his father felt about him.

Mr. Harrison had told him that Derik was a part of his life. But that did not mean Mr. Harrison liked him.

Mr. Zackariah Graham visited that morning. He, Mr. Harrison, and Mr. Kasey had been friends for a long time.

The two of them sat in the kitchen eating breakfast. Derik sat in the living room, but he could hear their conversation.

"How much longer do you guys have to stay here?" asked Mr. Zackariah.

"I don't know," answered Mr. Harrison. "I don't know how long it's going to take to repair the house. It's costing me a lot of paper though, I know that much."

"Dang."

Derik felt bad. They were staying with his grandparents indefinitely. And it was all his fault.

He had accidentally set their house on fire when he tried to run away. It not only got him kidnapped but also cost his family a lot of money.

"I want to do something fun," said Mr. Zackariah. "Just the three of us like back in the day."

"What you want to do?" asked Mr. Harrison.

"There's this one place in the city that seemed kind of cool. It's this cigar bar and–!"

"No."

"Aw come on Marlin! You ain't even let me get the words out!"

"I don't smoke or drink so why would I want to go to a cigar bar?"

"Man, all you do is go to church, work, the gym, and home. You've got to have some fun and loosen up once in a while. You can't just hug the wall and mean-mug all your life like you used to do when we'd take you out partying with us."

"I'm not going to a cigar bar, and neither is Kasey."

"Well, I still want to do something fun," said Mr. Zackariah. There was a pause in the conversation before Mr. Zackariah exclaimed, "Man, this is some good food!"

Mr. Zackariah ate a few more bites before talking again.

"What's something you would like to do? Your interests are all over the place. You like sports and working out. But you're also heavy into fashion, especially shoes. Like I ain't never seen you in a bad pair of kicks. But you also like technology and all those gadgets."

"Just pick something."

"I'll have to figure something out," said Mr. Zackariah thoughtfully. "Of course, it'll have to wait till Kasey gets back."

Mr. Harrison did not respond.

"He sure is in a tough spot," sighed Mr. Zackariah. "I know he hates he had to go so far from Sami but he had to do what he had to do."

"Uh huh."

"I'm glad I didn't have to leave my family behind when I came back here," continued Mr. Zackariah. "Everybody was on board with coming here."

"What about your brother and sister?"

"It was like pulling teeth just to get them here for Jada's graduation," griped Mr. Zackariah. "I get Pops was hard on us coming up, but they act like he ain't never did nothing good for us at all. I'm not just going to abandon him just because we have a rough relationship."

Derik could understand how Mr. Zackariah felt. He had a rough relationship with his father too. But he would still be there for him if Mr. Harrison needed him.

"Like I had to give up my barbershop and everything," said Mr. Zackariah. "No offense, I like working in your shop."

"You don't have to explain," said Mr. Harrison. "I know what you mean. It's nice to not have to answer to nobody."

"Exactly," said Mr. Zackariah. "Of course, I'd never go behind your back or anything like that. But I might open my own shop in the city one day or something."

"Go for it. I've been thinking about opening a gym myself once we've got our house fixed."

"Finally," said Mr. Zackariah. "Isn't that something you've been wanting to do for a long time?"

"Yeah."

"Man, we've come a long way," said Mr. Zackariah reminiscently. "We used to get into so much trouble as kids. Now look at us. Successful family men. And Kasey will get there in no time especially since he's got us with him."

Mr. Harrison did not respond again.

"He was telling me the other day about his new job," said Mr. Zackariah. "He likes it but he misses Sami. He's been trying to figure out the right time to start telling Sami he loves him."

"Why?" asked Mr. Harrison.

"What you mean 'why'?" questioned Mr. Zackariah. "Don't you tell your kids you love them?"

"Do you?"

"All the time," answered Mr. Zackariah confidently. "Have you ever told yours?"

"No."

There was a pause, and then Mr. Zackariah asked, "Why not?"

"Just haven't."

"But you do though, right?"

Mr. Harrison did not answer.

"Marlin? Don't you love your kids?"

"Why are you asking me this?" questioned Mr. Harrison annoyedly.

"Because it shouldn't be that hard to answer," said Mr. Zackariah. "If someone asks me if I love my wife and kids, my answer is automatically yes. I don't play about them, and they know that. And you never have a problem saying the truth, so why is this any different?"

"Because is it really that big a deal what I say as long as their taken care of?"

"Heck yeah!" exclaimed Mr. Zackariah. "To this day, my pops still has not told me he loves me. I've told him but he hasn't told me. I'm in his house taking care of him, making sure he's straight, and he still hasn't told me that. Yeah, he made sure I was good, but do you know what hearing that from him would have done for me? I know how that jacked me up, so I make sure I always tell my kids. And you see how Kasey's parents did him. And think about your own relationship with your father. How did it make you feel when your father told you he loved you?"

"The first time he told me was this year," revealed Mr. Harrison.

"What's with the men in your family? Y'all hate love or something?"

"I just don't see no reason to say it."

"Well, how do you feel about your kids? At least tell me that."

"Matthias is psycho," said Mr. Harrison.

"Marlin," said Mr. Zackariah.

"He is," said Mr. Harrison. "Anyone that beats up and pulls a knife on their own brother is psycho. I'd never do that to Falcon no matter how much he pissed me off."

"To be fair, you and Malcolm are nine years apart in age," said Mr. Zackariah. "You practically helped raise him. Me and Trip are only three years apart and it went there a few times with us."

"Yeah, but not like Matthias and Deidrick," said Mr. Harrison. "Matthias was trying to kill that dummy. He's psycho."

"You can't go around calling your son a psycho," said Mr. Zackariah. "And why'd you call Deidrick a dummy?"

"Because he's a dummy," said Mr. Harrison. "I might have to end up boxing both of them. Matthias because he's a disrespectful psycho and Deidrick for being dumb."

"You think it'll come down to that? It never even got that far with you and your dad."

"It almost did," said Mr. Harrison. "We had a real bad argument and I rose up at him. Mom got between us and told us if we wanted to fight then we had to go through her. She was crying and everything. Not my finest moment."

"You're a bold man raising up at your old man like that," said Mr. Zackariah. "That man was a linebacker and a war vet."

"I was being stupid," said Mr. Harrison.

"You think Matt would do that too?"

"Like I said, he's psycho."

"Well... doesn't that make you psycho since you did it first?" joked Mr. Zackariah.

"Ha ha," said Mr. Harrison sarcastically.

"What about your other kids?" said Mr. Zackariah.

"Allison is smart," said Mr. Harrison. "Really smart. And she's not scared to tell you the truth either."

"It sounds like you don't like Matthias and Deidrick, but you like Allison. What about your son, Derik?"

"Derik is…," said Mr. Harrison. "Derik is soft."

Derik felt like his father had given him the meanest gut punch.

"Dang," said Mr. Zackariah. "You really don't like your sons at all."

"What do you mean?" asked Mr. Harrison.

"Matthias is psycho, Deidrick is a dummy, and Derik is soft while Allison is smart and honest," said Mr. Zackariah. "Honestly, that sounds kind of like my old man though. He came down hard on me and Trip, but Hannah was his sweet baby girl that could do no wrong."

"I…," uttered Mr. Harrison. "That's just what they are to me."

"But do you love them?"

Derik did not stick around to hear his father's answer. His father thought he was soft. And that hurt.

Derik decided to go hang out with his girlfriend, Danielle Lee. On the way there, he stopped at Brewer's to get her a gift. While there, he ran into his favorite teacher, Mrs. Gretchen Nelson-Brown.

"Hi Mrs. Nelson-Brown," said Derik.

"Oh, hi Derik," said Mrs. Nelson-Brown. "I hope you've been staying out of trouble this summer."

"I have," said Derik.

"Good. What you got there?"

"A gift for Danielle."

"Oh," said Mrs. Nelson-Brown, raising her eyebrows.

Derik knew Danielle did not like Mrs. Nelson-Brown, and she made it clear. However, Mrs. Nelson-Brown seemed to be indifferent toward Danielle. If she did dislike her, Derik could not tell.

"You're such a sweet boy," said Mrs. Nelson-Brown. "I'm sure she'll be very happy with the gift."

Derik left the conversation feeling annoyed. Everyone saw him as a soft and sweet boy. He hated it.

He decided not to get Danielle the gift. That afternoon, they cuddled in her room and watched a movie. Both of her parents were out.

There was a scene where a teenage couple was home alone. They started kissing. So, Derik kissed Danielle on the cheek.

Danielle giggled and kissed him back. Then, someone knocked on the door.

"Come in," said Danielle.

"Dani, I–!" said Mr. Lee as he entered the room. Noticing Derik, he stopped and said, "Oh."

"Hey Daddy," said Danielle.

"Hello sir," said Derik.

"Uh… hi," said Mr. Lee. "What's going on?"

"Nothing much," said Derik. "We're just watching a movie."

"Watching a movie," repeated Mr. Lee.

"What do you want, Daddy?" asked Danielle annoyedly.

"Uh… never mind," said Mr. Lee, leaving the room.

"Ugh!" griped Danielle. "He could've at least closed the door back!"

"It's fine," said Derik. "Leave it open."

"I want it closed!"

"I want it open."

"This is my room," said Danielle defiantly, sitting up.

"Are you really about to go to war over a door?" questioned Derik humorously.

"I'm not going to war over anything," said Danielle, getting up. She slammed her door shut and laid back down beside Derik.

Derik did not expect Mr. Lee to reopen the door. Nor did he expect him to get onto Danielle about slamming it.

Mr. Lee was very lenient with Danielle. That's why Derik always tried to balance him out by challenging her way of thinking and doing things.

He liked that Danielle was strong-minded, ambitious, and not afraid to speak her mind. But Danielle was also very spoiled and would do anything to get her way. Sometimes, Derik let her get her way, but most times, he did not.

"I'm heading out," said Derik.

"Why?" asked Danielle.

Derik wanted to say because her dad clearly wanted the door open. But he did not feel like fighting.

"I'm just heading out," said Derik.

"Alright then, fine," said Danielle.

They kissed goodbye. Derik came across Mr. Lee in the living room.

"Derik," said Mr. Lee.

"Yes sir?" said Derik.

"Do you think you guys could stay in the more common areas of the house from now on when you come over? Like the living room and the kitchen?"

"Okay."

"Thank you. Also you have a little uh... something on your cheek."

"Oh!" cried Derik, wiping his cheek. It was Danielle's lip gloss. "Uh, thanks."

He was able to get the lip gloss off his cheek easily. But the lip gloss on his shirt was another story.

When he got home, Granddad Derrick was reading in the living room.

"Hey Granddad," said Derik, trying to get past him quickly.

"Hello," said Granddad Derrick. He closed his book and asked, "What you trying to hide?"

"What?"

"You don't walk that fast normally."

"I uh..."

"Where you coming from?"

"Dani's," mumbled Derik.

Granddad Derrick frowned. Then he patted the couch next to him.

"I didn't do anything," said Derik.

"I didn't say you did," said Granddad Derrick. "You have lip gloss on your shirt."

"We we're just kissing and watching a movie," admitted Derik.

"From nothing to kissing," said Granddad Derrick. "That means it's time to talk about what comes after that."

"Granddad," whined Derik.

"Dee-Three," said Granddad Derrick seriously. "Are you sleeping with your girlfriend?"

"No!" said Derik, his cheeks reddening with embarrassment. "Can we not talk about this?"

"We've got to," said Granddad Derrick. "You're at the age your brothers started going wayward at and I don't want you following their same path. So, I've got to nip this in the bud now. You understand why it's important you wait, right?"

"Because you don't want to be a great-grandfather yet."

When his grandfather did not respond, Derik eyed him curiously. Granddad Derrick's jaw was clenched as he gazed at his hands.

"Granddad? Something wrong?"

"You've got to take this seriously."

"I am."

"You're not. I know you don't take my concerns seriously because their 'old-fashioned' but I know from experience what happens when you don't wait."

"You didn't wait?!" gasped Derik.

"I *did* wait," corrected Granddad Derrick. "But your grandmother didn't. Neither did your Uncle Damian. Or Mrs. Marianne and her husband. Or Falcon. Or your brothers. And all the trouble they had in their lives came from not waiting. Not waiting causes unnecessary drama. And that's just the natural side of things. The drama that comes from the spiritual side of not waiting is a whole entire mess on its own."

Derik did not know what to say. He just wanted the conversation to be over. So, he listened until his grandfather finished and then retreated to his room.

The next day, Derik went to the mall with his brothers and cousin, Marcellus Campbell. On the way there, he listened to a podcast episode with movie director, Morgan Abernathy, and his movie star wife, Irina Frazier.

"Give us a little of your background," said the host. "What were your childhoods like? Were you always interested in film and television as a career?"

"Ladies first," said Morgan.

"I come from a family of performers," said Irina. "My mama was an actress, and so was my grandma, and so were her parents. Like the history goes way back. But I was raised by my grandma in L.A. because my mama died when I was eleven."

"I'm sorry to hear that."

"Yeah," said Irina. "Even though my family was full of performers, they didn't make a lot of money. I mostly did plays at church and in school. Sometimes, my grandma would get roles in small movies but she pretty much gave up acting to raise me."

"Shoutout to her and all the other grandmas raising their grandbabies," said the host. "Morgan, what about you?"

"My father was a Reverend," said Morgan.

"So, you also grew up in the church?"

"Yup," said Morgan. "My father was strict too. I couldn't listen to nothing but gospel music. We didn't have a TV, and we didn't go see movies. In fact, I'm positive he never saw any of my films while he was alive."

"Doesn't that make you sad?"

"It is what it is," said Morgan. "My father was never a fan of my career choice. He didn't really mind when I was part of the special church productions as a kid. But once I told him I was going to college in L.A. to pursue a career in film, he wasn't thrilled at all."

"How'd you two meet?"

"We met on A'shyra," said Morgan. "That was my first feature. Super low-budget, independent, limited release. I was looking for an A'shyra that I could afford and Irina was acting in a play at our college at the time."

"Yeah, that's right," said Irina. "I was playing a supporting role and after one of the shows, this man comes up to me and asks me if I'd be interested in being in his movie."

"And you said yes, just like that?"

"Nope. At first, I thought it was a student film so I was like 'maybe'. Then when he said it was a professional film, my mind went to a certain genre and I was like 'No, I don't do that'. But then, he was like 'No, it's not that kind of film either' and he just started telling me about it. And after he got done I was like 'Okay, I'll do it'."

"So, you didn't even audition?"

"If you ask me, I didn't," laughed Irina. "But if you ask him, the play was the audition!"

"It was!" said Morgan. "Y'all just had to be there to see it! From the moment she hit the stage, I knew she was who I wanted for the role."

"So, how'd we go from making a movie to getting married?"

"How does any couple go from making a movie to getting married?" said Morgan.

"Um," said Irina. "I think you might need to try that again."

"You think so?"

"Yes sir."

"Okay. So I asked her out after we made a few more shorts together. We dated for a year then got married after she graduated."

"And?"

"What else is there baby? You want me to tell them we ain't sleep together till we got married?"

"Sometimes you're just too much, Morgan."

"So, you two have been married a long time then?" asked the host.

"Twenty-six years," said Morgan.

"And you guys seem to be very private about your family life. I don't think I've ever seen anything about your kids or anything. Assuming you have kids."

"You think we've been married twenty-six years without having any babies?" laughed Morgan. "Trust me, we have kids. But we want them to have as normal a life as possible, so we keep them out of the public eye."

"Well, y'all have done a good job," said the host. "We literally know nothing about your kids. We didn't even know y'all had them until now. But now, I want to talk about this Drake Malone 2 controversy."

"I feel like this shouldn't even be a controversy," said Irina. "You'd think I'd gotten booty butt naked and slept with Morgan on camera the way people are acting over that scene. I literally batted my eyelashes, unbuttoned one button on his shirt, and gave him two kisses on the cheek and one on the nose so Drake Malone could sneak into the facility. I don't know why people are so up in arms."

"Well, people are saying the scene was too much for their kids to be seeing."

"The movie was rated PG-13 for a reason," scoffed Irina. "People was getting beat up, shot, and all other types of violence in the movie but everybody's worried about a little kiss scene between me and my husband."

"Morgan, what do you think?"

"Man, I think everyone's just mad because my wife is hot," joked Morgan. "They think they know the type of person she is because of all these characters she plays, but they really don't know the actual her. Just like people think they know what type of person I am based off the movies I make, but they really don't know me at all. Because the people who know really us, know who the real director of that scene was."

"So, you both stand by the scene then?"

"We really weren't trying to do anything offensive," said Morgan. "I honestly just thought it would be a cute little cameo with my wife."

"And please name me one time I've ever gotten naked in anything I've done," said Irina. "I hate sex scenes and I've never done them, so for people to be this outraged is ridiculous."

"Well, let's talk about that," said the host. "It's no secret your best movies are the ones written for you by your husband. Why is that?"

"Because Morgan respects me as a wife and as a professional," said Irina. "He knows my boundaries and he's never tried to get me to change them. Even when we worked on A'shyra, he was that way."

"What about any other directors? Would you work with them?"

"Of course," said Irina. "But if they don't respect me, then I don't work with them."

"So, there's already some buzz about Drake Malone 2 being an award worthy movie," said the host. "Irina, I know you in particular want to win a Black Art Recognition Award. You were nominated at the first ceremony back in the nineties for Karla Klein."

"Yeah," said Irina. "And I lost. And you know, I've been nominated like seven more times and still never won, but I don't mind. I'm just glad we still have an award show that recognizes our achievements in entertainment. And the biggest reward for me is knowing my work touched someone's life. That's why I'm very particular about the roles I take and that's honestly why I love working with Morgan so much. Every role he's written for me allows me to show off our culture in a real and positive way. A'shyra was this young, beautiful, shy Black girl just trying to come into her own. Karla Klein is this strong, confident, smart spy."

"What's next for the Abernathy-Frazier duo?"

"I've got two films I want to do next," said Morgan.

"Is one of them Drake Malone 3?"

"I don't know," laughed Morgan. "You saw it took about twenty years just to get the sequel made. But no, one film is a based on a true story that happened in my hometown. The other is a dance film."

"A dance film?"

"There's this amazing ballerina who's been killing it for years. I want to do something with her in mind but it's still in the works."

"Oooh. I hope we get that film."

Deidrick whacked Derik on the arm.

"What?" said Derik annoyedly, taking his earbuds out.

"We're here," said Deidrick.

"I can see that."

"I'm going to the shoe store. You coming with me?"

"Fine."

Deidrick was looking for matching sneakers for him and his girlfriend, Esperanza Ortiz. He was a huge sneakerhead like their father.

"So, they have her size but not mine," griped Deidrick, holding the pink and white sneakers they wanted.

"Well... you do have big feet," said Derik.

"Are you finding everything okay?" asked the saleswoman. She was a buxom, tanned blonde. Her nametag read 'Carmen'.

"Do you have these in a size thirteen?" asked Deidrick.

"I can go check for you," said Carmen, slightly smirk as she walked away.

"Phew!" whistled Deidrick. He licked his lips and said, "She is *bad*."

"I guess," said Derik.

"You guess?" teased Deidrick. "I thought you liked older women."

"Dani is only a year older than me," said Derik, rolling his eyes.

"Yeah, well Carmen doesn't look that much older than me."

Carmen returned with a shoe box and handed it to Deidrick.

"Here you are," said Carmen.

"Thanks," said Deidrick.

"If you're ready to check out, I can help you at the register."

"Yeah, I think we're ready."

They followed Carmen to the register, who began ringing them up.

"If I'm being honest, this color will look really good on you," said Carmen.

"You think so?" said Deidrick.

"Oh yeah," said Carmen. "There's a sneaker ball happening at Club Paraiso tonight too. In case you're interested."

"I might be," said Deidrick. "Will you be there?"

"Maybe."

Deidrick smiled, and so did Carmen. Derik shook his head as they left the store.

"What you shaking your head for?" asked Deidrick.

"Why were you flirting with her?" asked Derik. "Aren't you and Esperanza dating?"

"Man, a little flirting never hurt nobody," said Deidrick, sucking his teeth. "You're acting like I tongued the lady down in the middle of the store or something."

Derik shook his head again.

They met up with Matthias. He wanted to go to a clothing store. Once Marcellus joined them, they set off for the store.

Derik followed Matthias to the men's section. He sifted through the shirts and spotted a shirt with a pharaoh on it.

"Don't you have a shirt like this?" asked Derik.

"I used to."

"You got rid of it?"

"Yeah."

"I thought that was your favorite shirt."

"I outgrew it."

Derik understood that. He saw an orange polo with navy sleeves. It was exactly like the first polo he had ever owned.

His family had said those shirts made him look like a prince. That's why he had liked them so much. He held the shirt to himself and studied his reflection.

Derik could almost see the old him. The boy with the shoulder-length black curly hair and innocent eyes. He could almost see that prince everyone else had seen.

"Don't tell me you're going back to those," laughed Matthias.

Derik blinked, and his old self was gone. The shoulder-length hair was a short blonde fade. His eyes were no longer innocent. And his kind smile looked disingenuous.

Seeing that polo in the store did something to Derik. It reminded him of his sixth-grade photo.

He hated that photo because it reminded him of who he used to be. A sweet, soft boy.

He was no longer himself. Derik had outgrown that shirt.

"No," said Derik, putting the shirt back on the rack. "I'm not."

"Good," said Matthias. "Those things are played out anyways."

They went back to Marcellus' house. Derik approached Marcellus, who was in the kitchen digging through the refrigerator.

"Cell, can I ask you something?" asked Derik.

"What's up?" answered Marcellus. He held up his beer and said, "If you're thinking of asking me for a sip of this, the answer is no. Deacon Playboy in there be done put me on a t-shirt."

"Matthias ain't my dad," grumbled Derik.

"Uncle Marlin would do me a lot worse," said Marcellus.

"I don't want none of your beer," said Derik annoyedly. "The one time you let me try some was enough to last a lifetime."

"Don't tell anyone I let you try some either," said Marcellus.

"I won't. Now can we focus on what I wanted to talk about?"

"What's up?"

"Am I soft?"

"Are you soft?"

"Dad said I was soft."

"Ha!" cackled Marcellus. "Uncle Marlin said that?!"

"You don't have to rub it in."

"I'm not!" said Marcellus, still laughing.

"What's so funny?" asked Matthias, entering the kitchen.

"Uncle Marlin called Derik soft," laughed Marcellus.

"And what'd you say to him?" questioned Matthias.

"I didn't say anything because he wasn't talking to me."

"Typical," scoffed Matthias. "He can't ever say stuff to your face."

"I don't know Playboy," disagreed Marcellus. "Uncle Marlin seems like he's pretty straightforward to me."

"Why are we even talking about him?" spat Matthias. "Do you think you're soft?"

"No," answered Derik.

"Then you're not soft," said Matthias. "Forget him and what he thinks."

Derik thought it was easy for Matthias to say that. Matthias and Mr. Harrison did not like each other. But Derik wanted his dad to like him.

He wanted his dad to love him. It mattered to him what Mr. Harrison thought of him. So, he could not just forget it.

They ended up in the living room watching the sports channel. Derik was absolutely useless with sports, so he did not add much to the conversation.

Then, the conversation turned to women.

"Man," said Marcellus, sucking his teeth. "Do y'all know I been with Beverly for two months and she still hasn't let me hit yet?"

"That's a new record for you," snorted Deidrick. "It usually doesn't take you this long."

"I know!" cried Marcellus. "I've tried testing the waters a few times and each time she shuts me down. She's talking about she's saving herself. Who she saving herself for?!"

"Maybe her husband?" said Matthias, rolling his eyes.

"Well, I ain't trying to become no husband no time soon," declared Marcellus. "This is why I stay single. I don't know how much longer I can go on like this. I ain't hit nothing since before we got together and I'm trying not to go crazy."

"Well man, it's like you always say," said Deidrick. "If she won't do it, find a girl who will."

"Nah," said Marcellus. "Bev is the baddest I've pulled yet. I ain't fumbling her."

"You better not," said Deidrick. "Because if you do, I'm going to be right there to scoop her up."

"Poor Espe," muttered Matthias.

"Ain't no 'Poor Espe'," said Deidrick. "She tried that good girl act with me too. All it took was one night of drinking and partying for her to throw all that right out the window. She practically threw me on the bed when we got home that night."

"Well, at least one of us got something," said Marcellus. "What about you Dee-Three? You got anything going with that Lee girl?"

"He better not be," warned Matthias with a stern look.

"Playboy, you were his age when you first got some," said Marcellus. "Why can't he do the same?"

"Because I had no business doing that at that age and he doesn't either."

"You're just mad because you ain't getting none now."

"By choice."

"Now here you go acting all high and mighty," teased Marcellus. "But I bet if Cynthia said she wanted to you'd be all for it."

"Look Cell," said Matthias. "You and Cornbread are grown. Whatever *wrong* choices y'all make is between you and The Big Guy. But Dee-Three is still a kid. So, let him be a kid."

"For all you know, he could've already started sleeping with the girl," said Marcellus. "It's better for us to know so we can guide him."

"Like how you guided us?" remarked Matthias.

"You're clean and you ain't got no kids, right?" said Marcellus. "So, I'd say I guided you pretty well. And it's not like I forced y'all to do it. Y'all came to me and asked me to help."

"Don't lump me in with him," said Deidrick. "I ain't complaining."

"Well, you should be," muttered Matthias.

"Why you always getting on me?" griped Deidrick.

"Because!" said Matthias.

He did not finish the sentence. But Derik noticed his brothers glaring at each other. It was like they were telepathically having the rest of their conversation.

"Playboy, you're tripping," said Marcellus. His mouth became a big proud grin, and he said, "Man I still remember my first time. I was fifteen. Pops had these magazines that I used to sneak and look at when he wasn't home. One day he caught me. You would've thought I scored the winning touchdown with how excited Pops was. He dapped me up and told me I was 'the man' now. Then he had the talk with me, bought me some protection, and showed me how to use it. After that, all I had to do was let him know when I planned to have a girl over and he'd make sure I had the house to myself."

"He let you bring girls home?" gasped Derik.

"Yeah," said Marcellus. "Pops is real chill, man. I remember on Playboy's eighteenth birthday, he took us to the booty club and–!"

"Don't bring that up!" griped Matthias.

"What?" said Marcellus. "You know you had fun that night. Don't try to act like you didn't."

"I've moved on from that phase in my life," said Matthias before getting up to go into the kitchen.

"So, you were fifteen when you first slept with a girl?" asked Derik.

"Yup," said Marcellus. "And Playboy and Cornbread were both sixteen. I set them up with my homegirls."

"His *older* homegirls," said Deidrick, matching Marcellus' big grin. He leaned back in his seat with his hands laced behind his head. "I felt like the man that night."

"Do all the men in our family lose their virginity during their teenage years?" questioned Derik.

"Not everybody," said Deidrick. "Granddad waited till marriage and so did Dad. Cousin Joe did too. It's really up to you what you do."

"He doesn't have a choice," said Matthias, returning with a glass of water. "You're waiting till you're grown and married. And if you don't I'll beat all of y'all up."

"Look Deacon Playboy," said Marcellus. "You can threaten us all you want. But at the end of the day, Dee-Three is going to do what he wants. I just want to make sure he doesn't make any bad mistakes and that he knows we've got his back."

Something happened on screen that returned the conversation to sports. Later, Uncle Quincy came home.

"Hey nephews," said Uncle Quincy. "How's it going?"

"Good," answered all of them.

"Lipstick," said Marcellus, motioning to his father's collar.

"I ain't worried about it," said Uncle Quincy. "Your mother doesn't care anyways."

"Alright," said Marcellus, shrugging his shoulders.

Matthias shook his head disapprovingly while Deidrick quietly chuckled.

"Nephew," said Uncle Quincy, addressing Derik with a big grin. "You still dating that Lee girl with the good hair?"

"Yes, I'm still dating Danielle," said Derik, making sure to call her by name.

"Good, good," said Uncle Quincy. "Nephew, you still dating that Spanish chick?"

"Sure am," said Deidrick.

"Nephew. You got anything going on?"

"Nah," said Matthias with some disinterest. "I'm just chilling."

"Hey, ain't nothing wrong with that," said Uncle Quincy. "Man, you boys sure pulled you some fine honeys. I'm proud of you boys."

"You ain't doing too bad yourself," said Marcellus, dapping his father up. "I hope I'm still pulling them like you are when I'm your age."

"You got to make it to my age first," laughed Uncle Quincy.

Derik did not say anything. He hoped he would be married and settled down with children by the time he reached Uncle Quincy's age. Not married and constantly cheating on his wife like his Uncle Quincy did.

"We're about to head out Uncle Quincy," said Matthias.

"Alright," said Uncle Quincy. "Y'all get home safe."

The Harrison boys left. Matthias and Derik chose to call it a night while Deidrick went out.

Derik was restless that night. Around four, he got up to get a glass of water.

While he was in the kitchen, he heard someone creep through the front door.

"Who's there?" whispered Derik, adding some bass to his voice.

"It's me," answered Deidrick. "What are you doing up so late?"

"I can't sleep. Where are you coming from?"

"The sneaker ball, remember?"

"It's after four in the morning."

"I went to a sort of afterparty."

"An afterparty?"

"Yeah."

Derik eyed Deidrick suspiciously.

"Did you have fun?" asked Derik.

"Man, I had a lot of fun," said Deidrick excitedly. "Man let me tell you something. Those people down at Paraiso love to dance. I ain't never danced so much in my life. And the baddies bro! They had so many baddies in there bro! I'm talking hourglass after hourglass!"

"Sounds like you had a lot of fun."

"Bro you don't even understand! It was like being in a whole new world! I might have to take you there when you're old enough."

"Okay," said Derik. "You know I got the talk from Granddad yesterday? He says I should wait."

"Well, of course he does, he's a pastor," said Deidrick.

"What do you think I should do?"

"I don't know," said Deidrick. "I get where Matty and Granddad are coming from, but me personally, I can't do it."

"You can't? Why not?"

"Because," said Deidrick. "The feeling I get from it is just so... like I feel like the man. After my first time, I gained so much respect from other men. They saw me as one of them."

"Really?"

"Yeah," said Deidrick. "But it really is up to you what you do. And anyone who's got anything to say about what you do can come see me about it."

"Thanks Cornbread," chuckled Derik.

That morning at church was a tough one. Derik fought hard to stay awake during service. But it was hard to do after the night he had.

He also noticed Uncle Malcolm and Derek were not there. They were attending church less and less. Derik was not really bothered by it, but Granddad Derrick and Nanna Kiana were another story.

"You look tired," said Antoine after service ended.

"I am tired," said Derik.

"You didn't get enough sleep?"

"No."

"Why not?"

"Just didn't."

"Okay then," said Antoine. "You want to hear the mix I've been working on?"

"Sure," said Derik.

"I'll send it to you," said Antoine. "Tell me what you think."

"Alright," said Derik. "Where's your sister?"

"She's off visiting her boyfriend Hosea at his church."

"When did Karla get a boyfriend?"

"They just started dating. Apparently, he's the pastor's son at the church Drake goes to."

"That's hilarious," said Derik. "Did Drake put them together?"

"You want to know what's crazy?" said Antoine. "They didn't meet through Drake at all. They met at the mall."

"That's crazy."

"Yeah."

"Well, what about you?" asked Derik. "It seems like all your siblings have got somebody except for you."

"Mary doesn't," said Antoine. "Layla doesn't."

"Layla is seven."

"So?" said Antoine. "She's still my sister and she doesn't have a boyfriend... that we know of. Andre doesn't have a girlfriend either. And Adrianna technically doesn't have a boyfriend anymore either."

"You know full well those two are basically still together."

"Look, I'm just telling you what she told us," said Antoine, throwing his hands up. "Besides, I don't think I'm even allowed to date yet."

"Why not? You're fifteen."

"You think that matters to my dad? The way he acted with Drake and Adrianna when they got in relationships, I don't think I even want to date while living with him."

"Good point," said Derik. It was time for him to leave, so he said, "I'll see you around."

Derik listened to Antoine's mix on the way home. Antoine had gotten into making music mixes a few months ago. His first ones had been a mess. But Derik could tell that he was improving with each new mix.

He had jokingly started calling Antoine "DJ Ant". Every time he said it, he thought of an ant DJ-ing with big headphones on. It made him laugh every time.

That evening, Uncle Malcolm and Derek came to the house for dinner. As soon as they came inside, Granddad Derrick and Nanna Kiana were on them.

"Falcon," said Granddad Derrick. "Why weren't you at church this morning?"

"I overslept," said Uncle Malcolm.

"You also overslept last week," said Granddad Derrick.

"And the week before that, you said you had a bad headache," said Nanna Kiana.

"Well, I did," said Uncle Malcolm.

"You sure there's not another reason why you keep missing church?" questioned Nanna Kiana.

Uncle Malcolm looked down guiltily.

"I expect to see you there next Sunday," said Granddad Derrick.

Derik knew Uncle Malcolm would never reveal why he was avoiding church. But he and Derek told each other everything. And Derek had no issue sharing what was troubling his father.

According to Derek, Uncle Malcolm had overheard someone at church badmouthing his parenting. That upset him, so he decided to stop coming.

Derek wanted to keep going to church. He did not care what others had to say about his relationship with his father. Even though they behaved more like brothers, he knew there were certain lines not to cross with his father.

But since his leg was broken, and his father was his ride, he had to wait until he could get back to driving himself.

At dinner, there were a lot of questions about Uncle Malcolm's girlfriend. He said they were not officially a couple yet. But his excitement when talking about her showed he hoped they would be soon.

"How do you feel about this Ms. Nita?" asked Derik when he and Derek were sitting on the porch.

"As long as my dad's happy, I'm happy," said Derek. "He deserves some happiness for once."

"He does," said Derik. He looked at Derek's leg and said, "That cast is coming off this month. You ready to start walking again?"

"Heck yeah," said Derek. "But I'm really ready to get back to dancing again."

"Do you think you'll still be able to?"

"I hope so."

Derik hoped so too. Especially because he felt guilty about Derek's leg getting broken in the first place.

Even though Derek told him not to blame himself, Derik could not help it. He believed if he had not run away, his cousin's leg would not have gotten broken.

Derik felt like he could never escape that experience. The nightmares he had from it were what kept driving him to his parents' room. He wondered if he would ever be able to move past it.

The next morning, Derik was once again in his parents' bed. His father stirred from sleep first but stayed in bed.

Then his heartbeat quickened.

"Why are you staring at me?" asked Mrs. Harrison

"Just was," said Mr. Harrison.

"You never look at me."

"You don't know what I do."

"You know, ever since you started spending more time with our nephew you've become more like your old self again."

"My old self?"

"When we were younger," clarified Mrs. Harrison. "Back when you were more outspoken and more obvious with how you felt. And always picking too like now."

"I was stupid back then."

"No more stupid than I was. I should've never trusted you with my purse. Why did you do that?"

"Because I didn't like how you were looking at me."

"How was I looking at you?"

"The same way you're looking at me now."

"Oh."

"I don't mind now though."

"When did you stop minding?"

"When I met your parents."

"When you met my parents?"

"That's the first time I realized I didn't mind."

"Then it could have been before that?"

"Maybe, but I didn't notice until then," said Mr. Harrison. "What are you doing tonight?"

"Why?"

"We're going on a date."

"A date? What made you want to take me on a date all of a sudden?"

"Allison suggested it."

"Oh," said Mrs. Harrison. After a few seconds, she giggled. "Why do you keep staring at me like that?"

Mr. Harrison did not say anything. But the way his heart was beating told Derik everything.

It was the same way his own heart was beating when he visited Danielle that afternoon. Mrs. Tasha Lee was there, but she left them alone in the living room. And Derik made sure they stayed in the living room like Mr. Lee asked.

He and Danielle were kissing. And things were starting to get intense. Derik knew he should stop before things went too far.

But he was too caught up in the moment to pull himself away.

"Oh!" said Mr. Lee. "Oh my!

The two pulled apart. Derik put his hands up like he had gotten caught doing something wrong.

Mr. Lee stood in the front doorway looking very embarrassed. His beige face had turned red. And he refused to make eye contact with them.

"This isn't exactly what I meant when I asked you guys to stay in the common areas," said Mr. Lee.

"We didn't do anything wrong," said Danielle annoyedly.

"Yeah but... this is a little much to walk in on, don't you think?"

"Dad, you're such a prude," complained Danielle.

"I just didn't expect to walk in on that, that's all," said Mr. Lee, retreating to his room.

"Oh my gosh," huffed Danielle, rolling her eyes.

"Why do you treat your dad like that?" asked Derik.

"Like what?" questioned Danielle.

"Like you just hate him."

"I do not hate my dad!" cried Danielle defensively. "I love my dad a lot!"

"I can't tell. You're always being mean to him and disrespecting him."

"No, I'm not."

"You're really going to sit there and try to tell me my own eyes are wrong?"

"I treat him the same way my mom does."

"That explains a lot."

"What are you trying to say?"

"That your mom is mean."

"My mom is not mean!"

"You told me yourself that she told you that sometimes you have to be mean to get what you want!"

"And she was right! The only times I get what I want is when I have to put my foot down."

"Well, you and your mom put your foot down for everything then. Because I'm telling you, you and your mom treat your dad very badly and he doesn't deserve that."

"You know what? Why don't we ask him what he thinks!"

Danielle got up and walked toward her parents' room. Derik followed behind her. He hoped to prove her wrong. But when they arrived at the room, they heard her parents talking inside.

"Why does he always have to be over here?" griped Mrs. Lee.

"He's her boyfriend," said Mr. Lee. "And I'd rather he'd be here in a place where we can keep track of them, then out there without supervision."

"She literally could've chosen anyone though. Why him?"

"I like Derik. I think he's a nice boy."

"Of course you do. You're just like everyone else in this town that thinks the Harrison family is so great. But I see through them and they're perfect little family act. They're no better than anyone else."

"They've never tried to be though."

"Oh yeah? They walk around here showing off their nice stuff and rubbing it in our faces that they can get what they want, when they want. They think they're all that just because they're family founded this town."

"You sound jealous of them."

"What do they have that I need to be jealous of? If you think I'm jealous of them, then you're dumber than I thought Arthur Lee. And your daughter made a dumb choice for a boyfriend and you can tell her I said so."

"I'm not telling her you said that."

"I'll tell her myself."

"For what?"

"Because she needs to know the truth. That's how my mama was with me."

"You hated your mom though. You said she treated you like competition and that your dad did nothing about it."

"So? At least she still told me the truth."

Danielle did not stick around for the rest. Derik followed her back to her room.

"She is so annoying!" griped Danielle.

"I don't care what she thinks," said Derik.

And he did not. Mrs. Lee had always been critical of his family. Nothing she said about him surprised him.

"She always does this though!" ranted Danielle. "She'll act like she's on my side and then always just switches up on me! Just like with cheer. I'm thinking she's supporting me and then come to find out she only sided with me because if Dad told me 'no', he'd start telling her 'no' too!"

"How'd you find that out?"

"She told me!"

Danielle sat on her bed and sighed frustratedly.

"For once, I would just like someone to have my back!" complained Danielle. "Is that too much to ask for?!"

"I have your back."

"No you don't. You always nitpick everything about me."

"I only tell you when you're wrong because I care about you."

"I must be wrong all the time then because you can't ever seem to find anything nice to say about me."

"Now you're just doing too much."

"I don't care!" snapped Danielle. "Just leave me alone and go home!"

Danielle shoved Derik out of the room and slammed the door in his face. He was not sure what to do. So, he went home.

His parents had already left for their date when he got home that evening. The afternoon with Danielle had left him with a lot to think about. He needed advice on how to deal with this kind of issue.

He, Allison, and Deidrick were chilling in the living room. Allison was a girl, and Deidrick had had plenty of girls. So, he figured if anyone could help him, it would be them.

"What should you do when your girlfriend feels like you don't have her back?" asked Derik.

"Tell her to stop putting herself in situations where no one likes her," snorted Allison.

"Queenie!" cried Derik.

"I'm just saying," said Allison. "It'd be one thing if it was just some regular girl. But this is Dani we're talking about. There's a reason no one likes her except you."

"You're too biased," said Derik annoyedly. "Cornbread, what do you think?"

"I don't know what you're asking him for," said Allison. "He runs through women like they're underwear. The only advice he can give you is how to lose one."

"Whatever Queenie," said Deidrick. "Dee-Three, all you have to do is make her feel safe with you. Just agree with everything she says, and all your problems will be solved."

"What if I don't agree with her though?"

"Then keep it to yourself. Whenever she says something you don't agree with, just nod. That way you're not saying you don't agree, but you look like you agree."

"What kind of mess is that?" cried Allison.

"That's real advice on how you keep a girlfriend," said Deidrick. "Of course, you wouldn't know that since you've never had a boyfriend."

"Well, if my boyfriend acts like that then I don't want him," declared Allison. "My man needs to be upfront with me."

"That's what you think you want," said Deidrick. "But wait till you get a boyfriend that's always disagreeing with you. You'll drop him in no time to go find a dude that agrees with you."

"No, I won't."

"You will. Trust me, you will."

"Whatever Cornbread. That advice is trash and you shouldn't follow it Dee-Three. You need to be upfront with her, but in a way that makes her feel comfortable. She'll appreciate that a lot more than you just going with whatever she says."

"What are you guys talking about?" asked Nanna Kiana, entering the room on her way to the kitchen.

"Relationships," said Allison. "Nanna, do you feel like Granddad has your back?"

"Has my back how?" asked Nanna Kiana.

"Just in general," said Allison. "Do you think if the whole town came at you, he'd have your back?"

"Been there, done that multiple times," said Nanna Kiana. "And he had my back every time. But it took a lot of trial and error to build up that level of trust between us."

"How did he get you to trust him like that?" asked Derik.

"He was honest with me," said Nanna Kiana. "But he wasn't mean about it."

"See?" cried Allison triumphantly. "I told you! Cornbread talking about the dude should just agree with everything a girl says to make her feel like you have her back."

"I've known some men to be that way," said Nanna Kiana with a frown. "Those were the guys that did and said whatever just to sleep with me. But they didn't really care about me. That's what made your grandfather different. He was honest with me because he cared about me. And he was gentle about it because he cared about my feelings."

"I rest my case," said Allison.

That night, Derik tossed and turned in his bed. There were so many things on his mind that he was having trouble sleeping. So, he got up and went to sit in the kitchen.

A few minutes later, Matthias came in behind him.

"What are you doing up?" asked Derik.

"I heard you get up, so I came to check on you," yawned Matthias. "I didn't want you going to the parents' room and getting the shock of your life."

"That's...," began Derik. "I could've gone without knowing that."

"Hey, I was just trying to save you from getting traumatized," chuckled Matthias.

"Matty," said Derik. "Do you think a guy who agrees with everything his girlfriend says is just trying to sleep with her?"

"Depends on the guy," said Matthias. "Some guys definitely. But some guys are just trying avoid fighting with their girl."

"But does that ever make the girl feel like you have her back?"

"Kind of," said Matthias. "A girl will never know if her dude truly values her until some real stuff goes down. And it's goes the other way too."

"I see," said Derik. "But what if I know I have her back, but she doesn't think I do?"

"Then you've got to figure out how to show her that you do."

"How?"

"That depends on the girl because every girl is different."

"What have you done?"

"To be honest, I haven't had a serious relationship," said Matthias.

"You haven't?" said Derik with surprise.

"Nope," said Matthias. "I won't lie to you Dee-Three. I'm not ashamed of the life I lived. Cell and Cornbread aren't lying about how I was or how much I enjoyed being like that. But after a while it gets old and leaves you feeling lost. So, I'm not really the best person to ask for relationship advice. But I will say this: if you can't ever be real with your girl, and you're always having to appease her, then she's probably not the one for you."

The next morning, Mrs. Harrison had cooked breakfast for the whole family. She was in a very happy mood.

By the time Derik got up for breakfast, most of the family had already eaten and left for the day. The only ones left were him and Allison.

"Hello Mother," said Allison when she entered the kitchen. "You want to talk about what I saw from my window last night when you and Dad got home?"

"What'd you see?" asked Mrs. Harrison, her cheeks darkening.

"I saw you acting in a *very* unladylike fashion," teased Allison.

"A-Allison!" cried Mrs. Harrison. "It's not nice to tease your mother! Besides I'm married! I did nothing wrong!"

"I just can't believe you and Dad gave the whole neighborhood a show like that," laughed Allison.

"You act like you've never seen two people kiss before," chided Mrs. Harrison. She added more quietly, "Besides, he started it."

"Oh really?" said Allison. "What happened?"

"We had a good date," said Mrs. Harrison. "And then he helped me out the car, and before we came in, he told me I looked nice."

"Well, that explains why you had him hemmed up against the car," laughed Allison. "He couldn't go nowhere even if he wanted to."

"Lord Allison, you make it sound like I did something inappropriate," griped Mrs. Harrison.

"So, if I pinned a boy down against my car and made out with him in front of the whole town, you wouldn't say nothing?" questioned Allison.

"The circumstances aren't the same," said Mrs. Harrison. "You're a single young lady. I'm a grown married woman."

"You were certainly acting very grown last night," cackled Allison.

Mrs. Harrison blushed very hard. Acting in an unladylike way publicly was embarrassing for her.

At one time, Derik had held that against her. He even accused her of caring more about her reputation than about them. It was something he regretted.

"Mother," said Derik.

"Yes?" said Mrs. Harrison, still blushing.

"I'm sorry."

"For what?"

"For what I said to you all those months ago. About Dad not loving you. And about you caring more about your reputation than about us. Can you forgive me?"

"Sweetheart," said Mrs. Harrison, stroking the same cheek she had slapped when he had insulted her. She kissed him on the forehead and said, "I forgave you a long time ago."

"Well, after last night, there's certainly no question about Dad loving you," said Allison.

"Oh my goodness!" said Mrs. Harrison, beginning to blush again. "Why do you have to tease me like this?!"

Derik could not disagree. He could never forget hearing the way Mr. Harrison's heart beat when he looked at Mrs. Harrison. What Derik wanted to know was if he had a similar affection toward his kids.

He was not sure if his grandfather could read his mind though. Because later that day, Granddad Derrick had all of them come together at the kitchen table.

"What's going on Dad?" asked Mr. Harrison.

"I wanted us to sit down and talk," said Granddad Derrick. "Something's been bothering me since you all have been here together, and I can't take it anymore."

"What?" asked Mr. Harrison.

"You and your sons don't get along," said Granddad Derrick. "I don't like that. I want us to try and fix that."

"I ain't got nothing to say to him," said Matthias.

"Matty," chastised Granddad Derrick.

"I ain't got nothing to say to him either," said Mr. Harrison.

"This is the problem right here," said Granddad Derrick. "If you two would just talk it out, you guys could probably move forward."

"He already knows what my issue is with him," said Matthias.

"And I already told him why I did what I did," said Mr. Harrison.

"Oh boy," sighed Granddad Derrick. "What about Cornbread? What's your problem with him?"

"He's a dummy," said Mr. Harrison.

"That's the issue right there," said Matthias. "He's disrespectful. My brother isn't a dummy."

"The same brother you choked out and tried to stab?" countered Mr. Harrison.

"That was years ago!" said Matthias, shooting from his chair. "You're bringing up stuff that's old, but you still suck as a father right now!"

"Matthias!" cried Granddad Derrick.

"What you standing up for?" asked Mr. Harrison, rising from his chair.

"What you trying to do?" challenged Matthias.

"What you trying to do?" said Mr. Harrison.

"Y'all ain't trying to do nothing," said Granddad Derrick. "Both of you sit down."

Mr. Harrison and Matthias glared at each other. Then, they both sat down.

"As long as you live under my roof, you live by my rules," said Granddad Derrick. "Rule number one is no fighting."

"Well as long as that psycho stays in his seat," said Mr. Harrison.

"See?" griped Matthias. "You always provoking me!"

"Stop it," said Granddad Derrick. "Marlin, these are your sons. You shouldn't be fighting with them. Matthias, this is your father. You need to show him some respect."

"Well, he needs to give me something to respect!" said Matthias.

"Matthias," said Granddad Derrick sternly. "You're in my house and you're talking about my son. If you don't respect him, then you're not respecting me. And you don't get to disrespect me in my own house."

Matthias sat back and crossed his arms.

"Marlin," began Granddad Derrick.

"I don't got nothing to say to them," said Mr. Harrison dismissively, looking harshly at his sons. "That one's a psycho, and that one's a dummy. There's no fixing that."

But Derik noticed when Mr. Harrison's eyes fell on him, they softened a bit.

"Boys, y'all can go," said Granddad Derrick with a sigh. "Marlin, you stay here so we can talk."

Derik went to his room. Matthias and Deidrick complained to each other about what went down, but Derik tuned them out. He wanted to know what his grandfather and father were talking about.

He could not hear the conversation, but he could hear the loudness of it. There were several times Mr. Harrison raised his voice. But Derik never heard Granddad Derrick raise his voice.

After a while the conversation ended, and the house grew quiet. There was no resolution to the matter. But Derik would never forget the way his father looked at him.

The next evening, Danielle asked Derik to go out with her. She seemed a lot better after their argument at her house. They ended up eating at Patty's. Throughout the whole evening, Danielle kept checking her phone.

At first, Derik paid it no mind. But the later it got, the more suspicious he became. Each time he offered to take her home, she would make an excuse.

"Dani, it's getting close to nine o'clock," said Derik. "I can't be out all night."

"But–!"

"No buts. I'm taking you home."

"Alright," grumbled Danielle.

When they got to her house, Mr. Lee was leaving the house. He saw them and marched over to Danielle.

"Where have you been?!" cried Mr. Lee. "I've been calling you and you didn't answer! I thought something had happened to you and I was about to go looking for you! Did you forget that we were having dinner with my family tonight?!"

"Ugh," uttered Danielle. "Daddy, I told you I didn't want to eat with those people."

"So, you just skipped it?!"

"Yeah," said Danielle, starting to walk away as if the conversation were over.

"Don't walk away from me when I'm talking to you!" commanded Mr. Lee.

"What else is there to talk about?" said Danielle, continuing to walk away.

"How about where you were all night?"

"I was with Derik."

"So, you skipped dinner to hang out with your boyfriend."

"Yeah?"

"And you just don't care that that hurt my feelings?"

"Daddy, it's just a dinner."

"No, it's not!" said Mr. Lee. "This was an opportunity for all of my family to be together with me and you, my own daughter, skipped it because you didn't want to be there! Do you know how that makes me feel? It makes me feel like you don't care about me!"

"Like *I* don't care about you?" repeated Danielle incredulously. She had made it onto the porch. But stopped and stared at her father. "Daddy, those people can just as easily go back to acting like you don't exist to them."

"They wouldn't do that."

"They did it before. What's stopping them from doing it again?"

"Because they care about me."

"Oh yeah," mocked Danielle. "They sure did care about you a whole lot. I mean it's not like they didn't leave you down the street on some random person's doorstep and didn't say nothing this whole time, right?"

"Stop it Danielle," said Mr. Lee. "I'm serious."

"I'm serious too," said Danielle, walking back toward her father. "Those people don't care about you for real and we'll see how long they keep pretending that they do."

"Everyone was right," said Mr. Lee. "You really are a terrible person."

"What?" snorted Danielle.

"This whole time I thought you were just being a teenager but no, you're really a terrible person," said Mr. Lee. "How can you be so mean?"

"I'm mean now because I told you the truth?"

"No, because you're selfish."

"I am not!"

"You are too!" said Mr. Lee. "You don't care about me. You only care about yourself!"

"Oh my gosh," snorted Danielle. "You are being so dramatic right now."

"Like you were when you got cut from cheerleading?" countered Mr. Lee, causing Danielle to stop smirking. "Cutting your friends off? Giving me the cold shoulder for most of the summer? Pitting your mother against me? That's not being dramatic?"

"No! Because that lady cut me because she doesn't like me and you let her!"

"And so, because you didn't get what you wanted, you decided to take it out on everyone else."

"Because it wasn't right!"

"You want to know what's not right, Dani? Treating me like trash when I've been nothing but good to you. I've given you everything you've ever wanted, and I've never been hard on you. And all I asked in return was one simple thing that you couldn't even be bothered to do. You claim my family doesn't care about me or love me but it's clear you don't either."

"That's not true! I–!"

"Just save it," said Mr. Lee. "There's nothing you can say to convince me otherwise. I really truly believed you were not as bad as people said you were. But I was wrong. You are a mean girl. And after what you pulled tonight, I'm done."

Mr. Lee went back inside the house, slamming the door behind him.

"Can you believe him?" complained Danielle. "Having the nerve to claim I don't love him!"

"Dani, some of those things you said to him were really mean," said Derik.

"So?" said Danielle. "He needs to wake up and realize the truth. If those people wanted him, they would've been came back for him."

"They just found out about him a few months ago."

"No, that lady knew," countered Danielle. "She knew the whole time and went on with her life like nothing happened. He just doesn't want to admit that lady didn't want him."

"Yeah, but you shouldn't throw it in his face like that."

"You're one to talk. Aren't you the same person that told your mama that your dad didn't love her?"

"This isn't about me."

"Yes, it is. Anytime I do something wrong you're quick to jump all over me about it, but when I do the same to you it's always, 'this isn't about me'. Why do you get to point out my stuff but I can't point out yours?"

Derik realized then he could not be a "just-go-along-with-her" type of guy. He could never support his girlfriend being so comfortable about being in the wrong.

So, he let her have it.

"Because I'm not the one skipping family dinners," countered Derik.

"Oh no, you just ran away and got yourself kidnapped instead," said Danielle mockingly.

"You're right, I did do that, and it almost got me killed. So, why do you think I'm being so hard on you about how you treat your dad?"

"Okay, but who are you to be hard on me though?"

"I'm your boyfriend!"

"You don't have to be."

"Oh really?"

"Really."

"So, what are you trying to say?"

"I'm trying to say you never have my back. You're always trying to boss me around and you never defend me. Just like last month at Founder's Day. You let all those girls gang up on me and you just stood there, saying nothing."

"Why are you bringing that up again?"

"Because it's an example. You're always doing that to me. I don't do that to you."

"Because what am I getting in the middle of girl drama for? What am I getting in the middle of your family drama for? None of that has nothing to do with me."

"Well, what about when everyone talks bad about me to you. You never stick up for me then."

"That's not true. I don't let people talk badly about you."

"I can't tell."

"Look Dani, you can't expect me to defend you when people are mad at you for how you treated them. At that point, it's between you and them."

"And that's fake."

"Then let it be fake," said Derik. "Like seriously Dani, I got a lot going on right now. I don't have time to put up with all your extra bullcrap too."

"So, what's up?" asked Danielle. "You trying to break up with me or something?"

"Like I said, I just got a lot going on right now and I don't got time for your bullcrap too."

"Well fine," said Danielle. "If you want to break up, then we'll break up."

"Fine," said Derik.

"Fine," said Danielle, crossing her arms. She looked him up and down and said, "You can go."

"Don't got to tell me twice," said Derik, getting back into his car.

As he drove off, he looked in the rearview mirror to see if she was watching him. But Danielle had already gone inside.

Derik felt nothing at first after breaking up with Danielle. But the next day, he felt like his world was over.

It did not help that he and his family had to go visit his Nanna's sisters – Aunt Nancy Keaton and Aunt Paulette Barnett – in the city that day. Derik wanted to be left alone so he could process the break-up alone.

Aunt Nancy's son, Joe Keaton, and his wife, Helen, had recently returned from their work overseas. They were going to visit to welcome them back. Cousin Joe would be barbecuing for them too.

Cousin Joe was a stout, bald man who was the same age as Mr. Harrison. He was very talkative like his mother, Aunt Nancy.

"Joe!" cried Uncle Malcolm when he saw his cousin. He ran and hugged him.

"Hi Falcon," said Cousin Joe. He looked at Mr. Harrison and said, "Hi Marlin."

"Hey," said Mr. Harrison.

Derik wondered if he was the only one who noticed that Cousin Joe was a lot more reserved than normal. He was usually much livelier.

After getting settled in, Cousin Joe recounted his experiences overseas to the family. But he barely said anything to Mr. Harrison. Derik thought it was odd since the two were said to be very close when they were young.

During the day, Cousin James got sent on a store run. Cousin Jordan was still recovering from being shot and could not go with him. So, Derik went with Cousin James in his place.

"Is your dad okay?" asked Derik when they were in the car.

"What do you mean?" asked James.

"He just doesn't seem like himself."

"He's probably just tired."

"And what about Jordan? He seems a lot quieter than normal too."

"He's been like that since he got home. I think we might need to get used to him being like that from now on."

Derik understood. He had gone through a similar process himself after escaping his kidnappers. It left him feeling unsure about the world and his safety. But it also made him not take his life for granted.

When they returned, Cousin Joe and Mr. Harrison were at the grill in the backyard. Derik started to bring them the stuff from the store but stopped when he heard their conversation.

"What's wrong with you?" said Mr. Harrison.

"Nothing," said Cousin Joe.

"Why've you been so quiet then?"

"Ain't got nothing to say."

Derik hid out of view. It was not his intention to eavesdrop. He just wanted to know what was wrong with Cousin Joe.

"Why are you acting like this?" asked Mr. Harrison.

"I'm just staying out your way," said Cousin Joe.

"Staying out my way? What you trying to say? That I don't like you or something?"

"If the shoe fits, wear it."

"Man, why you playing?"

Cousin Joe did not respond.

"Joe! Are you being serious right now?!"

"Like I said–!"

"I don't care about none of that!" hollered Mr. Harrison. "I can't believe you Joe! What you sitting up here lying on me for?!"

"How am I lying?"

"You claiming I don't like you! I ain't never said that!"

"You ain't have to say it. I could see it in the way you act toward me."

"How do I act toward you?! I ain't never treated you badly! I'm thinking you just got a lot going on but no! You just straight up avoiding me and claiming I don't like you!"

The conversation grew quiet.

"Is that why you left for the army without telling me?" asked Mr. Harrison.

"Why would I waste my time telling you?" said Cousin Joe. "It was clear to me you didn't want me around anyways! Every time I called you, you acted like it was such a pain to talk to me!"

"Boy, I ought to smack you!" griped Mr. Harrison. "I ain't never treated you like that! You're my cousin for crying out loud!"

"You might not have said it, but you didn't have to," said Cousin Joe. "You didn't like talking to me. You probably only dealt with me because I *was* your cousin. I'm sure you were glad when I left."

"Who would be glad about that?" said Mr. Harrison. "You just disappear on me and I called Aunt Nancy to check on you because I thought something had happened to you. Imagine my surprise when she told me you left for the army, and she thought I'd been known you were leaving because everyone else knew! And now you're telling me you left without saying something because you think I don't like you!"

"Well look, the truth is out now!"

"I can't believe you did this Joe!"

"Did what?! I'm perfectly fine with us not talking or being friends!"

"Stop saying that!" commanded Mr. Harrison. "We are cousins! If you think I'd ever treat you bad then you're crazy!"

Derik decided to interrupt the conversation. He brought them the items they needed, then retreated to the house to find James.

"I know what's wrong," said Derik. "Your dad thinks my dad doesn't like him."

"I see," said James. "That explains a lot. I know it'd make me very sad to even think that one of my cousins thought I hated them."

"You're such a big softie, James," said Derik.

"So?" countered James. "Y'all are important to me. Just like Cousin Marlin was important to my dad. Why you think his feelings are so hurt?"

Derik could understand how Cousin Joe felt despite his teasing. He knew well the betrayal-like feeling Cousin Joe felt.

It was the same way he felt about Mr. Harrison. And it was all because Mr. Harrison was never clear about how he felt.

At some point in the day, it became clear that Mr. Harrison and Cousin Joe had made up. Derik had missed the conversation, but he saw the outcome.

Cousin Joe was acting more like himself again. But he still held some reservations around Mr. Harrison. Derik wondered if they would ever again be as close as they were once said to be.

And he wondered if he would ever be able to be that close with his father.

That Saturday started out as an uneventful one. Derek had gotten his cast removed and the family was gathering to celebrate. He still had physical therapy to get through. But at least the cast was finally off.

Derik was inside the closet looking for something nice to wear for the occasion. He was still reeling from the break-up. But he would do his best to not be negative.

Deidrick was lounging on his bed, scrolling through his phone. Then Mr. Harrison and Uncle Malcolm came into the room.

"We need to talk to you," said Uncle Malcolm. "You need to break the news to the family."

"Can't this wait?" griped Deidrick. Derik noticed him glance at the closet where he was.

"It can't," said Mr. Harrison.

"But–!"

"You've held off on this long enough," interrupted Mr. Harrison.

"Yeah," agreed Uncle Malcolm. "Your grandfather knows something's up, but we've been trying to let you tell when you're ready. But it's getting close to the end of July, and Sharon could have that baby any day now. You need to tell everyone that it might be yours."

"Unc!" cried Deidrick.

"What?" said Uncle Malcolm.

The closet door opened. Derik was not sure how because he did not remember pushing it.

"Aw shoot," said Uncle Malcolm. "Dee-Three..."

Derik ran. He let his feet carry him wherever they would carry him.

He thought if he let them lead the way, they would carry him away from what he had just heard.

His feet carried him to the creek. After that, he could not run anymore. He sank down under a tree and buried his head in his knees.

Derik was not sure how long he sat there. But he wished the footsteps coming to check on him would go away.

"Hey grandson," said Nanna Kiana.

"I don't want to talk right now," said Derik in the most respectful way he could muster.

"I know how you feel," said Nanna Kiana, standing beside Derik. "Trust me, *I know.*"

"How could he do this?"

"He's hardheaded," said Nanna Kiana. "I tried to warn him, but he just won't listen. Unfortunately, he'll have to learn the hard way."

"Of all the people he could've chose, why her?"

"If you ask me, it shouldn't have been anyone at all."

Hearing Nanna Kiana say that brought to mind what Granddad Derrick had told him during "the talk". How not waiting caused unnecessary drama.

Deidrick had caused him unnecessary drama.

If Derik had not made up his mind before about waiting, he made it up then.

"I just can't believe this," said Derik.

"I know," said Nanna Kiana. "And it's okay to feel upset about it. But as some point, you're going to have to get up from there."

Derik did not want to move. There was too much happening at once.

Recovering from getting kidnapped, processing his break-up, and a baby from his brother through his kidnapper! It was just too much.

But Derik knew Nanna Kiana was right. He could not stay down at the creek forever. So, he got up and went home with her.

As they arrived at the house, they noticed a new car in the driveway. It was Deidrick's girlfriend, Esperanza Ortiz.

"Hey Espe," said Nanna Kiana. "What are you doing all the way out here?"

"I uh... I need to speak with Deidrick," said Esperanza. "Is he inside?"

"Yeah, he's inside," sighed Nanna Kiana. "He's got the house in an uproar though."

"What's the matter?"

"Well, we just found out he's got a baby on the way," said Nanna Kiana.

Esperanza's brown eyes went wide.

"I'm pretty sure it was from before you two got together though," added Nanna Kiana quickly.

"Can you tell him to come out here please?" asked Esperanza.

"Sure."

"A baby?!" ranted Allison when they entered the house. "Do you realize how this could affect Granddad and Nanna?! They could get sat down again! And this time for good!"

"I ain't mean for this to happen!" argued Deidrick.

"You never mean for anything to happen!" snapped Allison. "You never keep your word! You never think about anyone but yourself! You never do anything right! Never, never, never!"

"Oh yeah, say how you really feel!"

"I am!"

"Both of you, stop!" commanded Granddad Derrick.

"No because if I had done this, I'd get thrown out on the street with nobody to turn to!" declared Allison. "But nobody has nothing to say when it's him!"

"You would not be thrown out on the street," said Granddad Derrick. "And quit hollering at me before I get my belt!"

"Hmph!" muttered Allison, plopping down on the couch.

"Cornbread," said Nanna Kiana. "Esperanza's outside to see you."

"What's she doing around here?!" griped Deidrick. He went outside to see her. Derik remained by the door while Matthias moved near the window to watch.

"What you doing here?" asked Deidrick.

"I'm here because I want to know why I have people telling me that they saw my man hugged up on the dance floor down at Paraiso with a whole bunch of women," accused Esperanza.

"Baby," said Deidrick.

"Don't 'baby' me," snapped Esperanza. "Because these same people told me you left the club with one of those girls! And now I'm hearing you got a baby on the way?! While we're supposed to be in a relationship?!"

"Dee-Three, close that door and stop being nosy," commanded Granddad Derrick.

"You know, you and your sons are a little too calm about this," said Nanna Kiana. "How long have y'all known about this?"

"Since January," answered Mr. Harrison.

"And you said nothing to me?" questioned Mrs. Harrison.

"It wasn't for me to tell."

"I didn't know for sure," said Granddad Derrick. "But I figured it out because everyone was being too suspicious."

"I was the first person he told," said Uncle Malcolm. "He wanted advice on what to do."

"AW HECK NAW!" hollered Deidrick loud enough to be heard through the window.

"What's going on out there?" asked Granddad Derrick.

"They're arguing," said Matthias. He continued watching, then reported, "She drove away crying."

Deidrick stormed into the house, and everyone looked at him expectantly.

"What?" said Deidrick.

"What we're y'all arguing about?" asked Nanna Kiana.

"Nothing," mumbled Deidrick, sitting down.

"A girl doesn't make a half-hour drive alone for nothing," observed Nanna Kiana. "What'd she want?"

Deidrick mumbled a reply.

"What'd you say?" asked Malcolm.

"She told me she's pregnant," repeated Deidrick. "And she broke up with me."

"This is too much," said Mrs. Harrison, leaving the room.

"Esperanza's pregnant?" said Granddad Derrick. "I thought she was waiting till marriage."

"Evidently, Cornbread managed to talk her out of that," scoffed Allison. "Out here just ruining lives one girl at a time!"

"Why don't you shut up!" snapped Deidrick.

"Make me!" argued Allison.

"Allison, go check on your mother," ordered Granddad Derrick.

Allison shot Deidrick an angry glare before leaving the room.

"So, Esperanza's pregnant?" asked Granddad Derrick.

"That's what she says," said Deidrick. "But I don't know how. We only did it one time!"

"That's all it takes sometimes," said Uncle Malcolm. "How you got two girls pregnant at the same time?"

"I didn't mean to do this!" said Deidrick. He looked at Derik and said, "I'm sorry!"

Derik shook his head and walked away. So much had happened in the past few days.

But Derik knew one thing for sure. No one would be able to call him a soft and sweet boy anymore. Being sweet and soft and emotional had gotten him where he was.

He decided it was time to become a man. Real men lived life un-apologetically on their own terms. And Derik decided he would start doing that.

PART 2:

IN THE LAST DAYS OF ADOLESCENCE

Samiel Dow Jr.

It had been one year since Kasey left. His job contract had been extended through the year, so he did not return at the end of summer as originally planned. And it had taken Samiel a long time to get over that.

Kasey had called frequently of course. But it was not the same as having him there physically. He had missed all the holidays, Samiel's nineteenth birthday, and Samiel starting college. Samiel had been so upset with Kasey that half the time he would not even answer the phone.

He could not believe that Kasey would break his word like that. Kasey was supposed to be back by the end of the previous summer. Instead, he was returning at the beginning of the current summer. Although Samiel tried to remain angry with him, the anger slowly went away when he knew for sure Kasey was coming back.

The day before Kasey's return, Samiel chilled with his boys at Derek's house. Benjamin was on lunch break from work, while Derek had the day off from his job at Flowerbud's. He had been working there for a few months. Samiel himself was working for Mr. Payne as his assistant, but he felt in his gut that his time there was quickly coming to an end.

"Kasey is coming back tomorrow," said Samiel.

"That's great!" exclaimed Benjamin.

"He said he's got a surprise for me," continued Samiel. "I wonder what it is."

"A woman," said Derek.

"A woman?" repeated Samiel.

"Mhmm," answered Derek. "My dad pulled that same thing on me last summer. Told me he had a surprise for me and bam! It's Ms. Nita who he'd been seeing for about a few months at that point."

"You think she's the one for him?" asked Benjamin.

"I don't know," said Derek. "She's cool though."

"A woman...," said Samiel. "The only woman he likes though is Samantha... What if she's the surprise?"

"Your birth mom?" questioned Benjamin. "How would you feel about that?"

"I don't know," said Samiel. "I'm open to meeting her. But the real question is, is she open to meeting me?"

"Well, if she isn't then she can go right back to where she came from because nobody was thinking about her in the first place," remarked Derek.

"Don't say that!" whined Samiel. "I want us to like each other!"

"I'm just saying," said Derek. "Don't get your hopes up too high because she might suck."

"Dude!" cried Benjamin. "Don't listen to him Sami. If Mr. Kasey likes her so much, then she must be a great person. And if she's coming here then she must want to meet you."

"Or she might want to score a payday," countered Derek.

"Will you shut up?" chastised Benjamin. "We're supposed to be encouraging him."

"I'm just being honest," said Derek with a shrug. "He needs to be prepared for anything just in case."

Derek's words had not helped ease Samiel's concerns. In fact, Derek himself had become more pessimistic over the past year. The best way Samiel could describe Derek's change was like going from a sweet, friendly puppy to a grouchy, guard dog. Samiel knew the biggest cause of Derek's change in personality was his leg. Although his leg had fully healed, Derek could not pursue dance professionally anymore. It was something that had affected Derek deeply. And although Samiel tried to be understanding, sometimes Derek said and did things that made Samiel want to smack him upside his head.

But even still, he knew Derek was right. Derek was still his best friend and still cared about him, after all. Samiel had to prepare and consider that Samantha might come with an ulterior motive. He just was not sure what that ulterior motive could be. That evening, Samiel decided to call Kasey and find out if Samantha was coming.

"Hello?" said Kasey.

"Hey!" said Samiel. "You still coming tomorrow?"

"Of course!" said Kasey. "I ain't seen you all year!"

"Well, you could've if you came home like you were supposed to."

"You're right, that's my bad. But I'm coming tomorrow for real."

"And is your surprise... a woman?"

There was a short pause before Kasey answered.

"I guess the cat's out the bag," said Kasey. "Yeah, my surprise is a woman. I'm bringing Samantha back with me. She's ready to meet you."

Samiel was stunned. His biological mother *was* coming to Creeke to meet him. And he was totally unprepared.

"How long is she staying?" asked Samiel. "And where is she going to stay?"

"Relax," said Kasey. "We booked a room in the city. She's only staying for a week."

Samantha would only be there for a week. Samiel wondered how much he could learn about her in only a week. He wondered if he would be able to tell what her motives were in that amount of time.

"We'll be down there tomorrow afternoon," said Kasey. "We can't wait to see you."

"I can't wait to see you too," said Samiel with a smile.

The next day, Samiel was full of nerves. He had enlisted his sisters in straightening up the house. However, Samiel was so nervous that he kept going over the same spots. His sisters had given up and decided to watch by the window for Kasey.

"Sami," said Latasia annoyedly. "The house is clean. You don't have to go over it again."

"I'm sorry," said Samiel. "I just want everything to be right."

"Will you stop worrying so much?" said Latasia. "Everything will be fine."

"They're here!" announced Kameryn.

"Already?!" cried Samiel. "Uh... I... I need to go... do... do... something!"

"Lord, have mercy," sighed Latasia as Samiel fled to his room.

He paced around trying to clear his thoughts. After taking some time to compose himself, he peeked out the window. Kasey's hair had gone from an afro to a bald fade. And he was helping Samantha from the car. She was slender and fashionably dressed. They came in the house and Samiel could hear them exchanging greetings with everyone.

"Sami," said Mrs. Dow, peeking into the room. "Kasey and Samantha are here."

"I know," answered Samiel.

"What's the matter?" asked Mrs. Dow, entering and closing the door behind her.

"Nothing," said Samiel, trying to appear cool and calm.

"Sami, I know how you are when you get nervous. What's wrong?"

"Nothing! I just... want to know what she's like, that's all."

"Well, the only way to find out is to go and meet her," encouraged Mrs. Dow.

Samiel wrung his hands.

"Sami, there's nothing to be nervous about," said Mrs. Dow. "Trust me when I say that if your father and I felt even the slightest bit off about these two meeting you, they would've never been able to come anywhere near you. And I also believe Kasey wouldn't have brought Samantha here if he felt like she didn't have good intentions toward you either."

"Okay," said Samiel. He took a deep breath and followed his mom to the kitchen to meet his other mom.

The first thing he noticed about Kasey was that he wore name-brand clothes. A year ago, Kasey's wardrobe consisted entirely of cheap faded t-shirts and worn frayed jeans. And Kasey looked a lot happier and thicker than he had the previous year. It was like he was almost a new person.

"Ah, there he is!" said Mr. Dow.

"There's my boy!" exclaimed Kasey, pulling Samiel into a hug. "Oh, I missed you so much!"

"I missed you too," said Samiel. "I almost didn't recognize you."

"I haven't changed that much," said Kasey. He excitedly and proudly motioned to Samantha. "Sami, this is Sammie. Sammie, this is our boy."

Samiel looked at Samantha. She was pretty and her smile lit up her face. He felt a sense of pride knowing that both his mothers were pretty. Seeing her was like finding the missing piece to a puzzle he had been trying to solve his whole life.

"Hi," said Samiel.

"Hi," said Samantha. "Can I give you a hug?"

"Uh, sure," said Samiel.

Samantha hugged Samiel. It was a warm embrace full of love and kindness. And she smelled really nice too.

"We'll give you two some time to talk," said Mrs. Dow, pushing the two men out of the room.

Samiel and Samantha sat across from each other at the kitchen table. They studied each other, waiting for the other to speak first.

"So," said Samantha.

"So," repeated Samiel.

"How have you been?"

"I've been good. You?"

"I've been good."

The two sat in awkward silence, unsure of what to say next. Samiel wanted to know so much about her. But most importantly, he wanted to know why she had given him up in the first place.

"What should I call you?" asked Samiel.

"What do you mean?" asked Samantha.

"I call Kasey 'Kasey' because he doesn't want to be called Mr. Ferguson," said Samiel. "And he won't let me call him Mr. Kasey either because he says it makes it sound like we're not related. He said Uncle Kasey sounds too confusing because he's my dad but he also said not to call him 'Dad' because I already have a dad."

"Hmm," said Samantha. "I don't know. I would say Sammie, but you're also Sami so that won't work. I guess I'm fine with Samantha, but when we're around other grown folks, Ms. Samantha."

"Okay," said Samiel. "How about we start from the beginning."

"Okay...," said Samantha hesitantly. "How much did Kasey tell you?"

Samiel summarized everything Kasey had told him.

"Yeah, that's about right," said Samantha. "I guess I just need to fill in my side."

"I'd like to hear it."

"Yeah," said Samantha. "I'm not from this area. I was born and raised in Atlanta. I was just going to school out here. I stayed over the summer to take a summer class and that's how I met Kasey. I didn't know Kasey had gotten arrested until his friend Marlin told me. So, I went back home and found out I was pregnant. I was going into my senior year, and I was too scared to tell my parents. So, when I came back for school, I made excuses not to go home and had you by myself. I didn't tell them until much later, and my mom said they'd always suspected it because I was gaining weight during the summer and then never came back home until the next summer."

Samantha paused as her eyes started watering.

"It was a hard decision giving you up because I wanted to keep you," continued Samantha. "But I was worried my parents would put us out, so I gave you up. I thought about you every day, hoping I'd made the right decision, hoping I hadn't given you to someone who wasn't doing right by you. So, when Kasey called me and told me about you, and how you were doing, and how we could meet you when you turned eighteen, I was excited. But then last year came and I got scared again."

Samiel handed Samantha a napkin so she could wipe her face.

"Thank you," said Samantha. "Honestly, I thought you were going to hate me."

"Same!" exclaimed Samiel. "I was nervous that you would hate me for coming back into your life after you gave me away."

"What?!" cried Samantha. "I could never hate my baby!"

"And I don't hate you either," said Samiel tenderly. "What about your parents? How'd they react to the news?"

"They were disappointed of course. But they were even more disappointed that they never got to meet you. They always talked about hoping to get to meet their only grandbaby one day."

"Are they still alive?"

"Yes. But I didn't want to drag them all the way out here and everything be a hot mess"

"Oh. Well, I'd like to meet them."

"Oh, they definitely want to meet you too."

After that, the conversation only got better. Samiel and Samantha spent so much time talking that before they knew it, it was time for her to go. She and Kasey had to go check into their room. But he promised the three of them would spend time together all throughout the week. Once they left, Samiel's parents asked him what he thought.

"I think she's great," said Samiel.

"See?" said Mrs. Dow. "I told you there was nothing to be worried about."

"I agree," said Mr. Dow. "I officially approve of Samantha."

Samiel felt happy. Samantha was better than he could have ever imagined. And he could not wait to spend more time getting to know her.

That evening, Samiel met up with his boys at Patty's. He was super excited to tell them everything about Samantha. They listened intently as Samiel spilled the whole story about his day with her, being sure not to leave out a single detail.

"So, things went okay with her then?" asked Benjamin.

"Things went great," said Samiel. "She's really cool."

"Uh huh," uttered Derek. "How long is she staying for?"

"A week."

"Only a week?" questioned Derek.

"Yeah," said Samiel. "What's wrong with that?"

"Nothing," said Derek. "I just thought she'd stay a lot longer than that."

"Well, she can always come back to visit again," said Benjamin.

"Yeah," said Samiel. "Tomorrow me and Kasey are going to show her around the city."

"Cool," said Derek.

"You don't have to seem so excited," said Samiel sarcastically.

"Look, as long as you're happy, I'm happy," said Derek.

"Well, you could do a better job at showing it."

"Whatever Sami."

Andre and Drake walked into Patty's. Samiel felt his stomach knot up. He had not seen Andre since winter break, and it had been even longer since he had last seen Drake. The last thing he heard about Drake was that he had married Tamela a few months prior.

At first, Samiel was sad that he had not even known about the wedding or been invited to it. But then he discovered there had not been a wedding at all. Drake and Tamela had gotten married at a courthouse with only their families present. Unfortunately, since there was no wedding for Samiel to not be invited to, he was unsure of where his relationship with Drake stood.

"Yo Browns, let me holler at y'all for a minute!" said Derek, imitating his Uncle Marlin. Samiel noticed how he seemed to brighten up when the topic turned from Samantha to something else.

"Oh my gosh, you sound like your uncle," cackled Andre.

"What's going on?" greeted Derek. "Queenie told me you got some great news last week."

"I wouldn't exactly call it great, but it has made my life make a lot more sense," said Andre. "Apparently, I have ADHD."

"Really?" exclaimed Benjamin, his eyes growing wide.

"Uh huh."

"How'd you find that out?" asked Derek.

"I did so bad at school this past year that I almost lost my scholarship!" said Andre. "That was the last straw for my mom, so she took me to get tested. Apparently, she's *been* suspecting I had it, but my dad wouldn't let her get me checked out."

"And how'd he take the news?"

"Well," said Andre, slightly wincing. "He didn't seem as surprised as I thought he would've been. I'm hoping he was just in denial this whole time and not the alternative."

"What's the alternative?"

"Being a bully," said Andre distantly.

"Nah," said Derek. "Mr. Brown is a lot of things, but he isn't a bully."

"Yeah, I agree with Derek," said Benjamin. "Your dad wouldn't treat you badly on purpose. He was probably in denial just like you said."

"Probably," said Andre in a hopeful tone.

"So, how long are we going to talk before you two speak to each other?" asked Derek, pointing between Andre and Samiel.

"I just didn't have nothing to add," said Samiel. "Hey."

"Hey," answered Andre.

Samiel was a lot clearer about his relationship with Andre. They were back on friendly terms, but their friendship was not the same as before. It was something Samiel regretted and probably would regret for the rest of his life.

"And what about you, Mr. Dragon?" said Derek. "Standing back there being all quiet. How's married life treating you?"

"Ha," laughed Drake. "It's still the best decision I've ever made. You should try it someday."

"Got to land a wife first," joked Derek.

"You'll land her," said Andre with a smirk. "Trust us you will land her with no trouble at all."

"Shoot," said Derek. "I'm trying to get like y'all first. I need a nice paying job like Drake."

"You need to go back to school," said Drake.

"School wasn't for me," said Derek quietly. "That's why I left."

"That's alright," said Andre. "Do you still want to learn how to skateboard?"

"Of course!" said Derek. "You make it look so cool!"

"It's fun."

"I don't have all night you know," said Drake to Andre.

"Alright," said Andre, rolling his eyes. "Hit me up Derek and we'll figure something out."

"Alright," said Derek.

Drake and Andre walked away.

"Dude, they basically just told you Adrianna's still into you," said Benjamin. "You going to get back together with her?"

"Not right now," said Derek. "I've still got some things to sort out with myself."

"Makes sense," said Benjamin. "But you do still like her?"

"Yeah," said Derek. He looked at Samiel and asked, "So, you and Andre are good now?"

"We've been cool for a while now," said Samiel.

"What about you and Drake?"

"It is what it is," said Samiel glumly. "I want to fix things, but I don't know how."

"Just go talk to him," said Derek. "That was your whole issue with Andre, remember? You caused all that drama because you just wouldn't talk to him."

"Please don't remind me," groaned Samiel.

He wished he could go back and stop himself from acting out of jealousy. But he could not. All he could do was figure out a way forward. So, he decided to take Derek's advice and talk with Drake once and for all.

"Drake," said Samiel, approaching Drake. "Can I talk to you?

"Sure," said Drake.

"Look," said Samiel, a little nervous. "I know what I did to Andre wasn't cool. And I understand if you don't want to be friends after it. But I just wanted to say I was sorry for disrespecting your brother like that, and I hope you can forgive me."

"Um...," said Drake. "I mean thanks for apologizing. But we've been moved on from that."

It took Samiel a few seconds to process what he had just heard.

"So, you mean I've been feeling bad over this for nothing?" cried Samiel. "I thought our friendship was over!"

"I mean I was upset that you did that to Andre," said Drake. "But he said you apologized, so we all moved on and let it go."

Samiel did not know what to say. But he was glad that he had finally gotten some clarity. He was ready to put the whole situation behind him forever.

The next day, Samiel went with Kasey and Samantha to explore the city. They ended up walking around downtown, visiting different stores and attractions.

"I wanted to ask you both something," said Samantha. "What do you think about me moving out here?"

"Really?" cried Samiel excitedly.

"Don't you think you're moving a little too fast?" questioned Kasey, shocking both Samiel and Samantha.

"No, I don't," said Samantha, slightly hurt. "There's nothing keeping me in my hometown, and I want to be closer to Sami so we can continue building our relationship."

"What about your parents?"

"What about them? They're grown and can take care of themselves."

"So, you just want to pick up and move, just like that?" said Kasey, snapping his fingers.

"Yes," said Samantha annoyedly. "Honestly, I thought you'd like the idea since it meant I'd be closer to you too."

"I'm not against it," said Kasey, his face reddening. "I just wanted to make sure you thought it through. This isn't like Atlanta."

"I know that," griped Samantha. "And there's nothing to think about. I want to be near my child and be in his life. Did you think about it when you came back here?"

"It was different with me," argued Kasey. "I just had a car and some clothes. You have a whole condo full of stuff and a job. You can't just pick up and move on a whim."

"It's not on a whim!" snapped Samantha. "I have a good reason for wanting to move here! Plus, you'd have a place to stay permanently!"

"Oh, so that's what this is about," said Kasey accusingly. "You think I need a handout from you or something?"

"No, that's not what I'm saying," huffed Samantha. "I'm just saying if I moved here, I can be near Sami and make things easier for you."

"What you trying to make things easier for me for?" asked Kasey. "I'm not your man."

"Because you're the one that wanted to take a break, not me!" argued Samantha.

"Oh, so what, this is your scheme to get back together with me?" said Kasey.

"It's not a scheme! It was just a suggestion!"

"So, if I said I wanted us to get back together right now, you'd say no?"

"Kasey."

"Answer the question."

"I'm not answering that ridiculous question."

"Fine. I already know your answer anyways."

"Then why'd you ask then?"

"Because I'm just trying to figure out why you want me so badly. I ain't got nothing. I mean I know I'm good-looking but it's all these rich, successful guys out here you can be with. Why you trying to be with me?"

"For starters, you're my child's father," said Samantha. "And we've been on and off for years."

"I just don't understand why your standards are so low that you want to spend the rest of your life with me."

"My standards are not low!"

"They must be if you're trying to be with me. I don't know how long it's going to take me to get on my feet."

"All that matters to me is that you want to get on your feet and that you're trying. Why don't you want me to be with you through that?"

"Because I ain't got nothing for you. What I look like being laid up under you and not able to do nothing for you?"

"You could love me."

"Can you pay a bill with love? Can you put food on the table with love? Can you buy your girl anything she wants with love? Can you take care of a kid with love?"

"First of all, I am not having any more kids," said Samantha. "And I don't need your money to make me happy. Having you around will make me happy."

"Yeah but for how long?" scoffed Kasey. "Sooner or later you're going to want me to step up and take care of you and I just ain't in the position to do that yet."

"Kasey, you just spent a whole year sleeping in my guest room!" cried Samantha. "Did I ask you for one thing during that whole time?"

"No."

"Exactly. Have I ever asked you for anything all the other times you stayed with me over the past eight years?"

"No but–!"

"But nothing," interrupted Samantha. "Just having you there was and is enough for me."

"Well, it ain't enough for me. You're buying me clothes, fattening me up, gave me a kid, and I can't give you anything in return. That's not good enough for me."

Kasey continued walking without them.

"Am I wrong?" asked Samantha.

"No, I don't think so," said Samiel. "I'd like it if you moved here."

"See?" cried Samantha. "At least someone gets it!"

"Why didn't you answer his question about getting back together?"

"Because he already knows my answer like he said. If it were up to me, we would be together for good. But he doesn't think he's good enough for me and that's why he keeps breaking things off."

The ride back to Creeke was quiet. They were supposed to go bowling the next day, but Samiel questioned whether that would still happen.

"How was your day?" asked Mrs. Dow when Samiel entered the house.

"Interesting," answered Samiel.

"Interesting?"

"Kasey and Samantha got in an argument."

"An argument? What about?"

"She wants to move here and be a family but Kasey's not where he wants to be at in life."

"Ah," said Mrs. Dow with understanding.

"I'd like it if Samantha moved here."

"Yeah, it'd be nice. Go ahead and go get ready for dinner."

Samiel did as he was told. Even though he was an adult, it did not feel like much difference had happened. His parents still treated him the same as they did when he was a kid.

At dinner, Kameryn shared about her day at work. She was a cashier at Brewer's with Latasia. Kameryn went on and on about all the difficult customers she had to deal with. Samiel wished difficult customers were the issue at his job.

The issue at his job was his boss. Working for Mr. Payne had turned out to be a stressful experience. Mr. Payne always wanted Samiel to do a bunch of work, was always conveniently late with Samiel's paychecks, and was stingy with the hours. Only the exact time spent at his office counted as time at work. He refused to round up to the nearest hour but had no problem rounding down.

Samiel was beginning to get fed up with Mr. Payne and considered quitting. Mr. Payne was a cheapskate and just a general pain in Samiel's neck. He would rather deal with Kameryn's difficult customers than deal with Mr. Payne.

As he was preparing for bed, Samiel received a message from Mr. Payne saying he had to come to work the next day. This infuriated Samiel. He had deliberately taken the week off to spend time with Samantha.

He reviewed his time off request and discovered only one day had been approved. This was his last straw. Samiel responded to the text saying that he would not only not return the next day, but that he quit for good. It felt like such a weight off his shoulders not having to deal with that man anymore.

The next day, Kasey decided to have man-bonding time. He and Samantha were not speaking, so she had gone to do more exploring on her own. Kasey and Samiel went to the barbershop where they met up with Mr. Harrison. Derek met them there. When he saw his uncle, he took off running toward him.

"Uncle Marlin!" hollered Derek, clamping on to his uncle from behind.

"Derek!" griped Mr. Harrison. "Why the heck would you jump on my back like that?!"

"I was just trying to give you a hug."

Mr. Harrison grumbled something to himself, but he did not shove Derek off. In fact, he waited until Derek was ready to let him go.

"Hey Marlin," said Kasey, dapping Mr. Harrison up. "Is Zack here yet?"

There was no need for Mr. Harrison to answer because Mr. Zackariah came through the door with his twenty-year-old son, Tyler.

"Hey, hey!" hollered Mr. Zackariah. "What is up with the fellas today?"

"We're going to do something with just us men," said Kasey.

"Finally!" said Mr. Zackariah. "I've been wanting to do something but you weren't here."

"Well, now I'm back. So, let's do something."

"Great!" said Mr. Zackariah excitedly. "What are we doing?"

"How about we go bowling?" suggested Kasey.

"I like that!" agreed Mr. Zackariah. "What you think Marlin?"

"I think I want to crack your skulls together," said Mr. Harrison.

"Then that settles it," said Mr. Zackariah. "We're going bowling."

They got two lanes at the bowling alley. One for the older men, and one for the younger. Mr. Zackariah and Tyler ended up completely demolishing everyone else. After two games, everyone was ready to call it quits.

"You guys sure you don't want to go again?" asked Kasey.

"I mean we're just trying to have mercy on you," said Mr. Zackariah, giving Tyler a proud shake on the shoulders.

"I'm not playing again," said Mr. Harrison. He eyed Kasey and asked, "Why are we really here?"

"We're bowling," said Kasey.

"When Samantha's in town?"

"Dang Marlin," griped Kasey. "I can't want to hang out with my boys?"

Mr. Harrison crossed his arms and glared at Kasey.

"Man, why you always got to get tough with people?" complained Kasey. "You always riding my back about something. You don't see Zack doing me like that."

"I was wondering why you suddenly wanted to hang out," admitted Mr. Zackariah. "But I wasn't going to complain about it. I've been trying to get us to do something together for a minute now."

"Well, if you must know," said Kasey annoyedly. "Me and Sammie had a fight."

"What about?" asked Mr. Zackariah.

"She wants to move out here."

"What's wrong with that?"

"I'm not ready for that yet!" ranted Kasey. "I'm still trying to get myself together!"

"Uh Kasey, I don't know if you've noticed, but you're halfway through your forties," said Mr. Zackariah.

"First of all, we were literally born the same year," said Kasey. "I was just born at the beginning of the year, while you were born at the end."

"My point is you're not getting any younger," said Mr. Zackariah. "You better snatch Samantha up while y'all still got time."

"That's easy for you to say," said Kasey. "You're married and got money. I don't got nothing."

"Man, when me and Fina got together we was both struggling," said Mr. Zackariah. "But we stuck it out together because we loved each other. And even though he'll never say it, Marlin loves him some Soleya.

Ain't no way you build and rebuild a woman a house, a hair salon, and constantly buying her stuff and you don't love her."

"Bro, Marlin is a literal ATM," said Kasey. "He gives her everything she wants just like that. I can't do that yet."

"You just going to let him call you an ATM?" instigated Mr. Zackariah.

"I'd say he's more like a vending machine," whispered Derek to Samiel, causing Samiel to chuckle. "Auntie Leya can take her pick of what she wants from him, and he'll give it to her no questions asked."

Tyler asked them why they were laughing. They shared the joke with him, and he smiled.

"Here she go now calling me," said Kasey.

"Answer it," said Mr. Harrison.

"I ain't answering her," said Kasey.

"Boy, you going to fumble a good thing if you don't answer that phone," warned Mr. Zackariah.

Kasey waited until the last ring to answer it. He walked away to privately have his conversation. Mr. Harrison walked over to Derek and put him in a loose chokehold.

"So, I'm a vending machine huh?" said Mr. Harrison.

"Dang!" cried Derek. "How'd you hear me?!"

"You suck at whispering."

Kasey came back with a neutral face.

"It's been real," said Kasey. "Sami, you ready to roll?"

"Uh, okay," said Samiel.

"Tired of getting whooped on?" joked Mr. Zackariah.

"You wish," snorted Kasey.

They all walked out of the bowling alley together. Samiel was shocked to see Samantha standing outside, waiting by Kasey's car.

"When'd you get here?" asked Samiel.

"Not too long along," said Samantha. "I took a cab."

"You must be the mysterious Samantha I've heard so much about," said Mr. Zackariah. "I'm Zack, Kasey's best friend. This is my son, Tyler."

Tyler waved.

"Nice to meet you both," said Samantha. She looked at Mr. Harrison and said, "Nice to see you again, Marlin."

"Yo," said Mr. Harrison casually. He motioned to Derek and said, "This is my nephew, Derek."

"Hi," said Derek curtly. Samiel did not like the tone of voice Derek used.

"Hello," said Samantha.

"If I'd known you were coming here, we could've played one more game," said Samiel disappointedly.

"That's alright," said Samantha. "I think I've had enough activity for one day anyways."

Everyone made small talk and then went their separate ways. Samiel rode with Kasey and Samantha back to their hotel room.

"You could've at least called me to come pick you up," said Kasey, after riding in silence for a while.

"Why?" asked Samantha. "I'm a grown woman. I can handle myself."

"I don't get you, Sammie," snorted Kasey. "You claim you want me around, but then you go and do stuff on your own without me. Which is it?"

"Why would I take you with me when you're being such a child?" said Samantha.

"I'm being a child?" cried Kasey.

"Yes!" said Samantha. "We're supposed to be here spending the week together with our child. But you're mad at me because I want to move here to be together and spend time with our child. You see how backwards and childish that sounds?"

"I already told you I don't care about you moving here."

"No, you just care that I don't need you to do it."

"Why you got to be so disrespectful?"

"I'm just being honest. That's why you're mad."

"I'm not mad but you're starting to make me mad."

"You're not mad but you haven't spoken to me all day? Did I miss something here?"

"What is your problem?"

"My problem is you want everything to be your way. But guess what Kasey? Everything is not going to be your way. I have no problem letting you figure things out on your own. But telling me I have low standards and ignoring me because you don't agree with me is not going to fly with me."

"Well, you making big decisions for both of us without consulting me is not going to fly with me either."

"Then, I guess we're flying in two different directions."

"I guess so."

Samiel felt sad hearing the conversation. The week was not supposed to turn out badly. They were supposed to be spending time together, making new memories as a family. He wanted to say something to get them back focused on why they were there. But Samiel felt like no matter what he said, only Kasey and Samantha could fix what was happening between them.

When Samiel got home, he called Derek. He wanted to talk about what had happened earlier at the bowling alley.

"What's up?" asked Derek.

"What's up with you?" replied Samiel.

"What?" answered Derek.

"Why did you act like that with Samantha today?"

"Because I don't trust her. Why is she really here?"

"To get to know me?"

"Well, she wasn't around all day."

"That's because she and Kasey are into it right now."

"So, then who is she actually here for? You or him? Because an argument with him shouldn't mean she stops spending time with you."

"Look," said Samiel sternly. "You have no reason to act like that towards her. You're more upset about her not being there today than I am and I'm her son!"

"You just met her," said Derek. "If she loved you so much, and wondered about you so much, why miss out on any opportunity she has to spend time with you? Why stay away for so long and not come back last year when Kasey did?"

"Because she wasn't ready yet!"

"Why even give you away in the first place if she cared so much?"

"Bro what?! You know full well she wasn't ready for a kid, so she did what she thought was best for me! Come on now!"

"How do you know that's the truth? How do you know she just didn't want you in the first place?"

"How do you know it's a lie?!"

"Because I've seen it happen too many times! These women will have these babies and give them away claiming they did what was best for their kid, but really they just never wanted the baby in the first place! They never think or care about how it would make their child feel to know their mother didn't want them and that's wrong! She claims she wanted to do what was best for you but didn't come running back for you the first chance she could? It doesn't make sense!"

"*She* is my mother," said Samiel. "And I believe everything that she's told me. And as my best friend, you can either support me or you can get lost."

"Oh, so you'd choose her over me when I'm the one that's been here for you all this time?"

"The whole time she's been here you've been her biggest critic," countered Samiel. "You act like you're the son that got left behind or something!"

It was not until he said it that Samiel finally understood why Derek had been acting rudely toward Samantha.

"Oh, I get it now," said Samiel.

"Finally!" said Derek. "So, you get where I'm coming from right?"

"Yeah," said Samiel. "But you're still wrong."

"How am I wrong?!"

"Because Samantha is not like your mother."

Derek went quiet. Samiel knew he had hit the nail on the head.

"I don't have a mother," said Derek.

"Yeah, you do," said Samiel. "Her name is Monique, she had you at seventeen, and she left you behind with your dad, and never came back. But Samantha had me at twenty-one. She didn't have anybody, and she was scared, and that's why she gave me away. Those are not the same situation."

"That doesn't matter."

"It does too. Samantha is not the same as Monique. I'm sorry that Monique never came back for you, but you can't hold that against Samantha!"

"Whatever Sami," said Derek. "I'm done talking about this. Clearly, you've picked your side."

"I'm not on anyone's side," said Samiel.

"Whatever you say," said Derek before hanging up.

"Sami?" said Mr. Dow, knocking on his door. "Is everything alright? It sounded like you were arguing."

"I'm fine, Dad," said Samiel. "It's just been a long day."

"Want to talk about it?"

Samiel wanted to say no. But he knew his dad would not accept that as an answer.

"This week just isn't going how it's supposed to go," said Samiel.

"Oh," said Mr. Dow. "Your mom did say that Kasey and Samantha were arguing."

"They are," said Samiel. "All because Kasey feels like his life isn't together for us to be a family. But me and Samantha don't care about that. We just want to spend time with him."

"I can see how that would be frustrating," said Mr. Dow. "But once you become a full-grown man with your own family, you'll understand exactly how Kasey feels. There's nothing worse as a man than not being able to take care of the people you care about how you want to. Especially when you know it's your fault why you're in that position in the first place."

"Well, what are we supposed to do?" asked Samiel. "Samantha's leaving at the end of the week, and they aren't talking. We haven't gotten to spend that much time together because of this."

"You've just got to let them work it out," said Mr. Dow.

The next day, Samiel decided to stay home. He secretly hoped not being with Kasey and Samantha would force them to refocus and make up. But he knew that was very unlikely.

"You're not doing anything with Kasey and Samantha today?" asked Mrs. Dow.

"No," said Samiel. "They're still fighting."

"That's too bad," said Mrs. Dow.

"Why don't we do something today?" suggested Samiel.

"Us?" said Mrs. Dow. "What are we going to do?"

"What do you want to do?"

"Well, I was planning to clean the house today."

"...Can we do something else?"

"No, I need to get this done," said Mrs. Dow. "You can help me out by sweeping the floor and washing the dishes."

Doing housework was not how Samiel had planned to spend the week or his summer. But he did it. Then, he went and lay on his bed. He watched his ceiling fan spin round and round. That was how his life felt at the moment. Kasey and Samantha just going in circles, blaming each other for why they were not together. And it was costing poor Samiel the already limited time he had to spend with them.

Samiel did not know how long he watched that ceiling fan. Nor did he remember much of what else he spent the day doing. He was honestly bored for most of it. Derek stopped by on his way home from work, wanting to talk about their argument from the previous night.

"I thought about what you said," said Derek. "You were right. I'm sorry."

"It's alright," said Samiel. "I'm starting to wonder if maybe you were a little right too."

"What do you mean?"

"I haven't heard from either of them since this morning."

"Did you try calling them back?"

"No."

"Maybe you should."

"What's the point? They're so distracted with what they've got going on that it feels like they've forgotten all about me."

"I might have a way to fix that. If you'll let me, of course."

"What are you going to do?"

"Ask them to come over for dinner."

Samiel did as Derek suggested. Then, they got to work on making a dinner. Since it was short notice, the best they could do was sloppy joes with French fries.

"Are you sure this will work?" questioned Samiel.

"Just trust me," said Derek.

Kasey and Samantha arrived around five that evening. It was clear they were still mad at each other.

"Hi Sami," said Samantha, giving him a hug.

"What's up with my boy, today?" said Kasey, patting Samiel on the back.

"We put together a dinner for you today," said Samiel. "It's nothing fancy.

"Hi," said Derek, properly introducing himself to Samantha. "Nice to see you again. I'm sorry that I wasn't more friendly the other day. I'm not usually like that."

"No hard feelings," said Samantha. "What'd you guys make?"

"Sloppy joe and French fries," said Samiel.

A small chuckle escaped both Kasey and Samantha. Then, they looked at each other icily and settled back down.

"What's so funny?" asked Samiel.

"Nothing," said Kasey.

"Um... before we eat there's something I wanted to talk to you both about," said Derek. Samiel looked at Derek curiously, wondering what he was up to.

"What's up?" said Kasey.

"So," said Derek, sitting down across from them. "Sami kind of feels abandoned by you guys."

Samiel's jaw dropped. He had not asked or expected Derek to say that. And judging by the looks on Kasey and Samantha's faces, they were just as shocked.

"Sami, why didn't you tell us you were feeling like that?" demanded Kasey.

"I...," said Samiel, feeling put on the spot. He glared at Derek, saying, "I just meant you guys constantly fighting was taking away from our time together.

Kasey and Samantha looked at each other guiltily.

"Dang," said Kasey. "We really haven't spent much time together this week have we?"

"It's alright," said Samiel.

"No, it's not," said Samantha. "We're supposed to be here for you and we've spent most of the time arguing. You had to resort to sloppy joes and French fries just to get us back together."

Kasey snorted. And then, Samantha started laughing too.

"What's so funny?" asked Samiel.

"This was what we ate on our first date," laughed Samantha. "Remember you made this for me?"

"Yeah," said Kasey. "I didn't have any money."

"Neither did I," said Samantha. She sighed contently and said, "I was so happy on that date. You made me laugh so much."

"We had a pretty good time together, didn't we?" said Kasey.

"We did," said Samantha. "You know, we didn't need money to enjoy each other's company back then. All we needed was each other."

"Yeah, but we were young and broke back then," said Kasey. "We're older now. We should be able to do a lot more than sloppy joes and fries."

"Sloppy joes and fries that our son made us," said Samantha. "I'd rather be here eating this meal that was made with love and brings back good memories, than be at some fancy restaurant worrying about how much everything on the menu costs."

Kasey did not say anything.

"How about this?" said Samantha. "How about we put everything to the side and just focus on Sami for the rest of the week?"

"No," said Kasey. "There's nothing to put to the side. If you want to move out here, then go ahead and move out here. I'm not against it."

"You sure?"

"I'm sure."

As Samantha and Kasey began talking again, Derek and Samiel moved off to the side.

"Looks like our work here is done," said Derek.

"Oh, I'm totally getting you for that," said Samiel.

"Go ahead," said Derek, lifting his head. "Chop me."

Samiel chopped Derek in the neck, causing them both to laugh.

It seemed like the rest of the week passed by too quickly. Samantha was leaving just as fast as she came. As Samiel watched her walk into the airport after hugging them goodbye, he felt tired of watching people leave his life. He hoped that one day he would be able to have his whole family together forever.

Latasia Williams

Latasia was glad to finally graduate from high school. Her first goal of the summer was to compete in Miss Teen Creeke. Mr. Dow had secured a job, so she and Kameryn could compete without worrying about spending money the family might need. On the first day of summer break, they went to the recreation center to register. They were in line behind Althea.

"Are you doing the pageant, Althea?" asked Latasia.

"Yes," said Althea. "My mom was adamant I do it this year."

"Do you want to do the pageant?"

"I don't mind."

Tamara got in line behind Latasia. It surprised Latasia that Tamara was entering the pageant, considering her mother's recent passing. Mrs. Frances had died a few days after their graduation. Some town elders said she had lived long enough to ensure her daughters would be okay without her.

Latasia believed it too. Tamela would soon start her job as a teacher at Creeke Elementary, while Tamara would be starting college soon. She knew not to ask Tamara if she was sure about competing so soon after her mother's death. Granny Elaine had passed away in October, and Latasia hated how much people had questioned her desire to do something so soon after her death.

"How many girls do you think are signing up for this?" asked Latasia.

"Shoot, probably the whole town," answered Tamara. "Mom was mad I didn't do the pageant last year because I was so focused on her. So, this year I'm going to do it for her."

"I'm sure she would be proud of you."

"Yeah. Honestly, I just needed to get out of that house. I'm going crazy thinking about how Tamela is going to handle all those bills."

"I'm sure Drake will help," said Latasia. "Especially with that good job he's got."

"A good job that's nowhere close to what he wants to do," said Tamara quietly. "And I don't think he planned to marry Tam this soon either. I think he wanted to be more established first."

"Well, that's okay," said Latasia. "This just means they can grow together."

"Yeah," sighed Tamara. "He's hoping one day they can have the wedding she's dreamed of instead of the one they had."

"What's wrong with a courthouse wedding?" asked Latasia playfully. "My parents got married in a courthouse."

"It's not what she dreamed of, even if she won't say so. And poor Drake had to put his whole life on hold to help us out. Maybe I should hold off on school so I can stay and help."

"You know Tamela doesn't want you to do that. And neither would Mrs. Reesy."

"You're right," sighed Tamara. "I can hear them both now. 'Don't put off living your life just because of us'."

"Exactly," said Latasia. "You're going to do this pageant, one of us is going to win, and then you're going off to college."

"Okay," said Tamara with a laugh.

Allison was the one handling registration. It was one of her duties as the current Miss Teen Creeke. There were different registrations for the pageant, the talent show, the Founder's Day choir, and the Founder's Day play. The choir registration was mostly filled with the Brown family's names, and the play registration was filled with many names too. Latasia signed up for the pageant and considered signing up for the play.

"If you do the play, you can't do the pageant," said Allison, as Latasia started to write her name on the play sign-up sheet.

"Why not?" asked Latasia.

"The rules say if you do any artistic activities for Founder's Day, you can't do the pageant and the talent show. So, if you do the play, the choir, or dance, you can't do the other stuff. Also, if you've ever done any professional artistic work and gotten paid for it, you can't do the talent show either."

"Those weren't the rules last year."

"Well, last year Mr. Payne wasn't sponsoring the pageant and talent show," said Allison, rolling her eyes. "He's doing entirely too much if you ask me, but it's his money, so it's his rules."

"Well, that sucks," said Latasia.

After Latasia and Kameryn signed up for the pageant, they stuck around for a bit to talk with the other girls. A small commotion broke out in the line. The girls looked to see that Adrianna and Mariella were making a fuss.

"What's going on?" asked Kameryn.

"I don't know," said Latasia. "Hey! What's going on?"

"What's going on is they changed the rules on us!" cried Adrianna. "They're telling us we can't compete this year!"

"Oh yeah," said Latasia. "Isn't it crazy?"

"I find it funny how the rules only really seem to affect our family though!" ranted Mariella. "Mr. Payne is behind this! I know he is! He's just trying to cheat so Prissy to win!"

"You think so?" asked Latasia.

"Why else would he change the rules?" said Mariella. "He's overly competitive and he doesn't play fair. We all know this."

"There might be another reason why he's doing this," said Althea quietly.

"Another reason?" questioned Adrianna. "Like what?"

"He might be doing this to get revenge on your uncle. They performed in a talent show together once. Mr. Jeremy-Micah upstaged him."

"So, that's it!" exclaimed Mariella. "He's just mad because he has no talent, and he wants to take it out on us!"

"Maybe we can still do the talent show," said Adrianna.

"Unfortunately, you can't," said Allison. "The rules are the same for the talent show."

"You're lying!" cried Adrianna.

"Trust me, I wish I was."

"This is ridiculous!" ranted Mariella as she and Adrianna left.

"Uh oh," said Allison. "Mariella forgot to write her name down for the choir."

Latasia thought it was a shame that Mr. Payne had changed so much just because he was funding everything. And it was even more shameful he did it so his daughter could win. All Latasia knew was that she would give it her best shot. She just hoped Mr. Payne did not try to stack any more odds against them.

"Where'd you two go?" asked Mrs. Dow when Latasia and Kameryn got home.

"We registered for the Miss Teen Creeke pageant," said Latasia.

Mrs. Dow smiled. But Latasia noticed it was a very tight smile.

"Mom, what's wrong?" asked Latasia. "We thought you'd be excited about this."

"I am excited," said Mrs. Dow, holding her giant, tight smile. "But I wish you guys had made this decision when registration first opened. Now you're going to have less time to prepare."

"That's not a big deal," said Kameryn. "Right?"

"It's a huge deal," said Mrs. Dow, her smile relaxing into its normal state. "They're things to buy. You've got to learn how to walk, how to interview. This isn't something you can just do last minute."

"I thought pageants were supposed to be fun," remarked Kameryn.

"They are fun," said Mrs. Dow. "But they're also hard work. If you're going to do this then you've got to be serious."

"I'm serious," said Latasia. "This is my last chance to compete in Miss Teen Creeke and I want to take it."

"I'm serious too," said Kameryn.

And they were serious. That evening, they attended the pageant interest.

"Hey," said Nicole, coming to sit next to Latasia.

"Hey stranger," said Latasia. "I see your boyfriend likes to keep you locked away from the rest of the world."

"No, he doesn't," chuckled Nicole.

"Well, ever since y'all started dating, you've been M.I.A."

"It's not on purpose," said Nicole. "You'll see when you start dating."

Nicole had been dating Derik for a few weeks. It was not clear how the relationship started, but the two were definitely an item by the graduation. Latasia suspected Nicole had liked Derik for some time, and took her chance when it was clear he and Danielle were finished.

"Mhmm," said Latasia. "What's your brother think about the relationship?"

"Are you kidding me?" chuckled Nicole. "I think he's the only person more hype about it than I am."

"Seriously?" asked Latasia. "Shouldn't you be the most excited about it?"

"I mean, I guess," said Nicole. "It's still early in our relationship so maybe we just need time for our feelings to grow stronger."

More girls filtered into the room. Priscella walked in looking annoyed, and Danielle walked in right behind her.

"What's wrong with her?" asked Latasia, focusing on Priscella.

"I don't know," said Nicole. "I know I wouldn't be looking like that if my dad basically rigged everything for me to win."

Latasia agreed. Although the pageant was in Priscella's favor, Latasia still wanted to do it. There was still a chance that she could win, and she did not want to miss it.

When it came to Danielle, Latasia had not seen much of her during senior year. What little she did see of her, Danielle always seemed to be by herself. She never seemed to have any friends with her, and she had not wreaked havoc like she had the years before. Danielle had just been... there.

Principal Lee had also been a lot different during their senior year. He was more authoritative, less cheerful, and less forgiving towards misbehaving students. If anything, he had been more like Danielle than Danielle had been herself. The personality switches had shocked Latasia, leaving her to wonder if the two were connected somehow. But it was hard for Latasia to feel bad for Danielle. She thought Danielle had gotten what she deserved for treating everyone else badly.

The interest meeting started. Mrs. Harrison, her sister Mrs. Soriah Campbell, and Allison led it. Latasia stared at the crown on Allison's head, hoping that her head would be the next one to wear it.

"Good evening, young ladies," said Mrs. Harrison. "I want to thank you all for joining us for the Miss Teen Creeke pageant interest meeting. I'm sure almost all of you are familiar with who we are and also competed last year. But just to be sure, I am Mrs. Soleya Harrison. I am a previous Miss Teen Creeke winner. I'll allow my co-presenters to introduce themselves."

"Hello," said Mrs. Campbell. "I am Mrs. Soriah Campbell. I'm Mrs. Harrison's older sister but we all know this. I also competed in Miss Teen Creeke every year I was eligible. I never won but I did enjoy every experience I had. And I hope that all of you will enjoy this wonderful experience regardless of who wins. Allison."

"Y'all know who I am," said Allison. After receiving a stern look from her mother, Allison stood up and sighed. "I'm Allison Harrison, and I am the current Miss Teen Creeke. All of you already saw me when you registered for the pageant. And I'm excited for the opportunity to crown the queen coming after me."

"Thank you, Allison," said Mrs. Harrison. "We don't plan to hold you long. We just want to go over how the pageant will work, what will be different from last year, and what will be expected from you all. First is the goal of Miss Teen Creeke."

Latasia watched as the presentation moved to the next slide. It was a short paragraph on the pageant's history and values.

"Miss Teen Creeke was started with the purpose of encouraging Creeke's young ladies to develop into respectable women," said Mrs. Harrison. "This pageant aims to do that through service and scholarship."

The presentation moved to the next slide, detailing the meanings of service and scholarship.

"That leads us into the first changes from last year's pageant," said Mrs. Harrison. "In previous pageants, we used to do what was known as service day. The goal of service day is to encourage you all to come out and support the community that has supported you and your growth into young women. We did not have a service day last year because we did not want to be too overly ambitious with the pageant's return. But this year we will be bringing it back. Service Day this year will consist of helping to set up for Founder's Day. Mrs. Soriah will tell you about the scholarship aspect."

"Thank you," said Mrs. Campbell. "Scholarship is meant to encourage you all to not only take your academic careers seriously, but also to encourage you to go beyond just what you learn in the classroom. There is always an opportunity to learn from everything you go through in life. We hope this pageant will help you learn skills and abilities that you can use in real life. Another change to this year's pageant is the awarding of a scholarship in the amount of two-thousand dollars. This scholarship is only eligible for those who are college-bound this upcoming school year, and you must complete an application and essay to be considered for it. Your application and essay are required to be completed in person at the recreation center to avoid cheating. Application day will be this Saturday. Only those with valid reasons for not being able to attend will have an opportunity to complete the application and essay on another day. Next, Allison will tell you about the pageant breakdown and important dates."

The next slide described how the pageant would work. It would follow the same format as the previous pageant and award the same prizes as last year. Everyone had to submit biographies by the day of the final rehearsal.

"As you can see," said Allison, moving to the next slide with the dates. "The pageant is in two weeks on Founder's Day. Registration will close this Friday when the recreation center closes at ten at night. And trust me when I say registration will close *at* ten. As stated earlier, application day is this Saturday at the recreation center. There is no specific time to come do it, but the deadline is *at* ten when the recreation center closes. Therefore, do not come at two minutes before ten trying to apply because whatever you have written down at ten is what will be submitted. The week of the pageant we will have two practices, and then a final rehearsal the day before. The important thing about the pageant is to have fun and make good memories."

"That's right," said Mrs. Harrison. "We want this to be a fun experience for all of you. So, with that being said, this concludes our meeting. If you have any questions, please let us know."

Latasia thought doing the pageant would be a fun, easy-going thing as one last hurrah for her teenage years. She was wrong. From the moment they had signed up for the pageant, Mrs. Dow took it upon herself to train her daughters.

Latasia and Kameryn had to learn how to walk, talk, and dress like true pageant girls. And they only had two weeks to do it. After training for a week, Latasia questioned whether she had made the right decision. She started believing it would have been easier to let Priscella win it like Mr. Payne wanted.

But that Friday, Priscella visited Latasia and changed her view on everything. It surprised Latasia to see Priscella at her house. Although they were no longer at odds, they were not exactly back to being the best of friends. Priscella had developed her own new friend group, proving she did not need Latasia, Nicole, or Danielle.

"I need your help," said Priscella.

"With what?" asked Latasia.

"I'm trying to get my dad to change the rules for the pageant."

"How am I supposed to help you with that?"

"One of the rules is if you've done any professional art stuff you can't compete, right?"

"Yeah."

"So, if I can prove I did something professional I can't compete. Then my dad will have to change the rules because he wants me to compete."

"Why though? You're pretty much set up to win the whole thing."

"I don't want to win that way," said Priscella. "My parents always cheat to get ahead and I don't like that. I never have."

"Okay... but again, how am I supposed to help you with that?"

"Well, I was looking all over the house for something, and I couldn't find anything. So, I'm thinking he might have hidden it in his office. I need you to help me look."

"You want me to help you break into your dad's office?"

"We're not breaking in," said Priscella. "I have the key."

"But why do you want my help though?" asked Latasia. "Why can't you just go look through his office yourself? Or ask your friends for help?"

"His office is too big for only one person to search through it. Jada is busy helping with her grandfather and the Garza sisters have choir rehearsal. I need help going through everything. Please help me."

Latasia considered what Priscella said. It would help her chances of winning if she helped Priscella.

"Alright, I'll help you," said Latasia.

"Great!" said Priscella gleefully. "Meet me at my dad's office tonight."

That evening, Latasia took Nicole with her to meet up with Priscella. Latasia was unsure of what Mr. Payne did exactly. She remembered hearing once that he owned a few properties that generated money for him. All she knew for sure was that he was nowhere near broke.

"What are we looking for in here?" asked Nicole.

"Any proof that I've ever done any modeling," said Priscella.

"Why would it be here?" asked Latasia.

"Because I couldn't find anything at home," said Priscella. "My parents are very sneaky so they could've hidden the proof somewhere I wouldn't find it."

"How do you know there's even any proof to find?" asked Nicole "How do you know if you've even ever done modeling?"

"It could've been when I was a little girl," explained Priscella. "My dad used to model when he was younger, so he could've tried to get me into it at one point too."

"What was he modeling for because I ain't ever seen him in nothing," snorted Nicole.

"Just local stuff in the city. That's how he met my mom."

"And what was she modeling for?"

"She wasn't. She was the photographer's assistant. They said it was love at first sight."

"More like they both saw dollar signs from all the scams they could run together," whispered Nicole to Latasia, causing the latter to giggle.

The girls searched all throughout Mr. Payne's office. The search was unsuccessful, and the only place left to look was his desk. Priscella tried to open the drawer, but it would not budge.

"It's locked," said Priscella. "And I don't have the key."

"No problem," said Nicole, removing a bobby pin from her hair. She began using it to try and pick the lock.

"You've been spending entirely too much time around your boyfriend," said Latasia.

"Having bobby pins on him saved his life," said Nicole. "So, now I keep some on me too in case I ever need to save my life."

When they got the drawer open, all they found were business papers and copies of the Founder's Day registration sheets. Latasia snorted at Mr. Payne's arrogance to make final copies of the registration sheets when registration was still open for a few more hours. He was so sure no one else would register for anything.

"There's nothing here," sighed Priscella.

"I think it's safe to say there's no proof," said Nicole.

"There's got to be," said Priscella. "It's just not here."

"Do you remember doing anything professional?" asked Latasia.

"No."

"Then you probably didn't," said Latasia. "I don't think your dad would be dumb enough to make rules that would screw him over too."

"True," agreed Nicole. "He only makes rules that screw everyone else over."

"What am I going to do?" griped Priscella.

"Lose," said Nicole.

"At this point, she might be the only person competing," said Latasia. "Even if she threw the competition, she'd still win."

"Darn it," sighed Priscella frustratedly.

Latasia looked at the registration sheets. On the choir sheet, she read Samiel's name and the names of the Brown and Parker family members. But she quickly noticed one name was missing.

"Maybe there is something we can do," said Latasia, showing the sheet to Nicole and Priscella. "Look. Mariella never signed up for the choir."

"So?" said Priscella.

"She technically never signed up to sing with the choir," said Latasia. "So, she's still able to compete in the pageant and talent show."

"And she's a Brown," said Nicole, catching on to Latasia's thinking. "They're the best singers in this town."

"Okay?" said Priscella, tilting her head a little. "What's that got to do with changing the rules?"

"We don't have to change them," said Latasia. "We just have to go around them."

"And then your dad doesn't get what he wants," said Nicole.

Latasia did not want to waste any time. Registration would close in less than an hour when the recreation center closed. She and Nicole raced over to the church to convince Mariella to go along with their plan.

"You want me to what?" questioned Mariella after Latasia and Nicole finished explaining.

"Not sing with the choir," explained Latasia.

"Why would I do that when I've been coming to all the rehearsals?"

"Because you never signed up for the choir."

"Yes, I did."

"No, you stormed out, remember?" said Latasia. "Allison even said you forgot to write your name down."

"So, my name's not on the sign-up sheet?" asked Mariella.

"Nope," said Latasia.

"And the rules say only people who are participating in artistic productions for Founder's Day can't compete in the pageant and talent show," said Nicole. "Since you technically never signed up for anything…"

"I can compete," said Mariella, her brown eyes brightening with realization.

"Mariella," said Mrs. Marie Garza, coming into the foyer. "Come on honey. We're about to get started again."

"Mamá," said Mariella. "Latasia and Nicole just told me I have a chance to compete in the talent show and pageant."

"What?" said Mrs. Garza. "How? I thought Jacob changed the rules."

"They said I never signed up for the choir," said Mariella. "Apparently, I forgot to write my name down."

"She did," said Latasia, chiming in. "Today's the last day for registration and it's closing soon. We were hoping she could sign up and stop Mr. Payne from cheating so Prissy can win."

"Mamá, can I?" asked Mariella. "I know I'm supposed to sing with the rest of the family but…"

"Go ahead," said Mrs. Garza without hesitation.

"Really?" gasped Mariella, surprised.

"Really," said Mrs. Garza. "I've never liked Jacob. I hope you whip his butt and give him everything he deserves. It's time he gets a taste of his own medicine."

Mrs. Garza's harsh words surprised Latasia. She was used to Mrs. Garza being a nice, sweet lady who kept to herself and never said a bad word about anyone. But the more Latasia thought about it, the more she realized she should not have been surprised. Especially because Mrs. Garza was still, after all, a Brown.

"What's taking so long?" asked Mr. Jeremy-Micah, coming to join them. "Your brothers are getting antsy. Torrey looks ready to come up out his shoes."

"Mariella is about to go sign up for the pageant and talent show," explained Mrs. Garza. "I'll explain it all later, but she's got a chance to stop Jacob from cheating."

"You do?" asked Mr. Jeremy-Micah, a big grin spreading across his face. "You better win too. I mean stomp that negro out, niecey. Show him that liars and cheaters never prosper."

"Yes sir," said Mariella with a giggle. And then the girls were off.

They got to the recreation center two minutes before closing. The girls dropped Mariella off at the entrance, who raced inside to register.

"I hope this works," said Nicole. "This is our last chance at stopping Mr. Payne's cheating."

A few minutes later, Mariella came outside. She got in the car with a huge smile on her face.

"Did we make it?" asked Latasia.

"Sure did," said Mariella triumphantly. "Mr. Payne is going down."

Saturday morning, Latasia went to the recreation center to fill out her scholarship application. Danielle was also there, but Latasia tried not to let that rattle her. Filling out the application was the easy part. The essay portion was the tricky part. There was only one question: *How will receiving this scholarship help you achieve your collegiate goals?*

Latasia tried to think of a creative way to say it would help pay for school. The essay had to be at least one page and Latasia had the unfortunate curse of small handwriting. But even worse, she could not focus with Danielle sitting only a few feet away, scribbling out her own reason for needing the scholarship.

She wondered what Danielle could possibly say to make herself look good enough to get the scholarship. But then Latasia wondered what she could say about herself. There was no doubt about her leadership capabilities, but Danielle was just as strong a leader.

Latasia had done cheer, but so had Danielle. She had been a founding member of the Little Sister Society, but she did not know if that would be enough. It seemed like everything Latasia could say about herself, Danielle could too, or it did not seem good enough. They had been friends for so long and had done everything together. But even after separating herself from Danielle and working to not be like her, Latasia still felt like she was fighting to keep up with her.

Danielle stood up and submitted her application and essay. She had already finished, while Latasia had yet to write something besides her name. It felt almost pointless to try at that point. But she had to write something.

Latasia started by restating the prompt. Then, she thought about what her goals in college would be. Whenever her mother talked about her college years, she always talked about how much she had learned and grown. So, that's what Latasia wrote about.

She wrote about the grades she wanted to aim for and what she wanted to get out of her college experience. And she wrote about what she wanted to do after college. Latasia wanted to do something to help kids who had been in her position: left without anyone in the world and relying on the kindness of strangers.

To emphasize her goals, Latasia had to talk about what losing her parents at such a young age was like. Unfortunately, since she did not remember much about them, all she could write about was wondering what they would have been like. But she also had the chance to write about what being adopted had done for her life.

She remembered when she first came to the Dows. Being with people she did not know had been scary for her and caused her to be very shy. But over time as she got more comfortable with them, she came out of her shell and became more like herself. By the time she finished, she had written more than the required page and had put her all into it. Latasia turned the application in, hoping it would be enough to secure her the scholarship.

The week leading up to the pageant had been stressful. There were physical aspects such as what Latasia would say and what she would wear that had to be taken care of. Latasia decided to re-wear her green prom dress as her evening wear. And she practiced for her interview and onstage questioning so much that she did not know what else she could do to prepare herself.

The real battle was in Latasia's mind. During group rehearsals, she saw how well the other girls did. And she began to wonder if she really stood a chance against them. Especially Danielle, who seemed to be a strong contender to win if Priscella's plan worked.

By the time Founder's Day arrived, Latasia was ready to get the whole thing over with. But as the day went on, she grew more excited for the actual time of the pageant. Participating in Service Day was a treat because Latasia always liked helping out in the community. And the interview portion was not that bad, and she thought she did a good job.

Then Founder's Day commenced. The choir sounded amazing, the dancers performed Mikayla's choreography well, and the play was even better than the previous year. Brianne Lewis was the standout, portraying various women in Creeke's history. Her portrayal of Pastor Derrick's grandmother, Laverne Creeke, brought him to tears.

But what Latasia was really looking forward to was the talent show.

The talent show was after Pastor Derrick's speech. It did not last long because there were not that many acts. But Latasia's main focus was on whether their plan would work. When it was Priscella's turn, she sang normally. She, like Latasia and Nicole, was counting on Mariella to pull out all the stops in her act.

And Mariella did not disappoint. When she came on stage, Latasia took in the confused look on Mr. Payne's face. He kept going through his clipboard, trying to find her name on the choir sheet. Meanwhile, Mariella did what her family did best.

Mariella had a nice soprano voice like her mother, but her range was not as wide as her older sister's. However, that did not mean Mariella was not by any means skilled. She poured everything she had into her song.

The applause was thunderous when she finished. And Mr. Payne looked highly upset. It was clear he had realized that Mariella could compete, and he was absolutely enraged when she won.

Then came time for the pageant.

"Good evening and welcome to the Miss Teen Creeke pageant," said Pastor Hall. "Before we start, I'd like to open with a word of prayer."

Pastor Hall prayed. And then he introduced Brianne as the emcee for the evening. She would be taking over for Mrs. Green since Althea was competing.

"Our emcee this evening will be Miss Brianne Lewis, daughter of Troy and Tavia Lewis," read Pastor Hall. "Brianne just recently graduated with her Bachelor of Arts in Theatre, which if I might add, was displayed very well at this afternoon's Founder's Day play. And I also like to add that she is my favorite niece."

Brianne welcomed everyone to the pageant and then began introducing the contestants. Latasia was the last contestant, number eight. She waited for her turn to go onstage. Then, it came.

"Hey!" said Latasia, being sure to show as much personality as possible. The lights were so bright that she could not see the audience. And that to her was a good thing. "My name is Latasia Laminah Williams. My parents are Samuel Dow Sr. and Christine Dow. And I am your contestant number eight."

Latasia completed her walk around the stage as Brianne read her biography. Then, she exited the stage to prepare for casual wear. She could hear the crowd cheering loudly for Allison as she came onstage.

Casual wear was anything but casual as far as Latasia could see. She had seen what most of the girls normally wore and it was not what they were wearing for the pageant. Most of them, including her, wore their less fancy church clothes. Althea was the only person wearing her normal, everyday clothes, in that case, a blue flower-print dress.

Then, there was evening wear. Most of the girls, like Latasia, wore their prom dresses. Latasia was mentally preparing herself for her onstage question.

"What's the biggest challenge you faced this past year and how did you overcome it?" asked Brianne to Nicole, who was the first contestant.

Everyone knew Tamara would have the best answer. There was nothing more challenging than dealing with the loss of a parent. And the other girls' challenges seemed so small compared to hers.

Nicole talked about balancing her work and extracurricular schedules. It took everything in Latasia not to laugh at Kameryn describing learning how to drive. Latasia had gone along for a ride once and decided very quickly she would not do that again. Althea gave a good answer about how she had to work hard to be taken seriously as a journalist because of her quiet personality. Priscella's answer was not that great, but she also seemed like she had been barely trying the whole time.

The answer that shocked Latasia the most was Danielle's. Danielle talked about realizing she had not been a good person and working on being better. Latasia did not know what to make of it. She could have said it to win the pageant. Or she could have been sincere.

Latasia chose to answer the question by talking about her time as cheer captain. Her second year had actually been more challenging than her first because she no longer had anything to prove. She had earned everyone's respect during her first captain year. It was challenging not to get complacent and to keep pushing herself to do more than necessary.

After the question came time for Allison's final walk as queen. Then, it would be time for the results. Latasia had enjoyed the pageant and was ready to see how much her hard work had paid off. All the girls lined up onstage and Brianne explained the various prizes and scoring.

"First we have people's choice," said Brianne. "This award will go to the contestant most voted for by the audience. And the People's Choice Award goes to... contestant number four, Miss Tamara Kane!"

Everyone cheered because Tamara truly deserved it. She had every reason to act out but instead had been the kind, sweet, no-nonsense girl she had always been.

"Next is our Miss Congeniality Award. This award was determined by the contestants based off who they felt was the nicest and most helpful during this process. Miss Congeniality goes to... contestant number seven, Miss Charmaine Townsend!"

Then it was time for the Scholarship Award. Latasia felt her stomach tighten as she waited to find out who would win.

"Our next award will be our Scholarship Award. This is a scholarship awarded in the amount of two-thousand dollars to a college-bound contestant. Contestants submitted an application and an essay, and a recipient was chosen after careful judging. The recipient of this award is..."

It seemed as if the world had gone quiet. Everyone cheered and clapped, but all Latasia could do was wonder if her ears had stopped working. Then she was standing up front, holding a big check with her name on it, and smiling for the camera. She had won the scholarship.

It took everything in her not to cry. She still had to hold it together for the announcement of Miss Teen Creeke. If she had been able to win the scholarship, then she definitely stood a chance to win the whole thing.

"Second runner up for Miss Teen Creeke will receive a medal and a cash prize of one-hundred dollars. Second runner up is... contestant number four, Miss Tamara Kane!"

Tamara was shocked to have won more than one award. And after she was presented with her award, it was time for the moment everyone was waiting for.

"Our final awards of the night are first runner up and Miss Teen Creeke. First runner up will receive a medal and a cash prize of five-hundred dollars. Miss Teen Creeke will receive a crown, a sash, and a cash prize of one-thousand dollars. I will now announce the two finalists for the crown. The finalists for Miss Teen Creeke are... Miss Danielle Lee and Miss Althea Green."

It was strange. Latasia did not feel disappointed to have not made it into the finalists. She also did not even care that Danielle had made it into the finalists. All Latasia could think about was how grateful she was to have won the scholarship. Having that was honestly more satisfying than having the crown.

"The next name I call will be Miss Teen Creeke. This year's Miss Teen Creeke is... Miss... Althea Green!"

A collective of loud screaming erupted through the auditorium. There was no doubt that it was Althea's very loud, very shocked family, losing their minds over the fact that she had won. Latasia hugged Althea, whose mouth was also wide with shock. Allison could not move fast enough to place the crown on her head.

As Latasia watched her friend be crowned, she snuck a peek at Danielle. She expected Danielle to look upset or even be throwing a fit. But Danielle genuinely looked happy for Althea. Latasia did not know what to make of it.

After everything was over, Latasia reflected on the whole experience. And she realized the underlying cause of her stress the whole time was wanting to beat Danielle. She wanted to prove that she was nothing like her and maybe even better than her. But in the end, Danielle had come out on top over Latasia. Latasia had won the scholarship, but Danielle was the first runner-up. If Althea forfeited the crown for whatever reason, Danielle would be Miss Teen Creeke.

Danielle had managed to win everybody's hearts. And Latasia once again felt like she was trying to keep up with her. Even with all the work she had done to try and not be like Danielle, she realized she still had a long way to go. So, she decided to try something else. Latasia decided to just live her life and be herself.

Althea Green

Althea found that being Miss Teen Creeke was hard work. There was always some event she had to attend or some group she had to talk to. When she signed up for the pageant, she had not expected to actually win. And based on her family's reactions, they had not expected it either. For the whole week after the pageant, it was all they could talk about.

"I still can't believe you won," said Mrs. Green the following Saturday after the pageant. "This just makes me so happy."

"I'm even more happy Prissy didn't win," said Diana.

"Did you see her face when she didn't win anything?" laughed Cynthia. "I don't think I've ever seen anyone in my life so excited to lose."

"Well, I'll tell you one thing," said Mrs. Green. "I hope that Jacob Payne learned a valuable lesson about trying to cheat his way to the top."

"You know that boy ain't learned jack," snorted Mr. Green.

"Just a sin and a shame," said Mrs. Green, shaking her head. She looked at Althea and grinned. "But that ain't got nothing to do with me because my baby is Miss Teen Creeke!"

"This year our little Althea was *it*," cheered Cynthia.

"Oh, if only your sister could've been here to see it," sighed Mrs. Green. "I just don't understand why she can't even bother to visit at least once a year. She could at least come for special occasions!"

"That's just how Glo is," said Cynthia, shrugging her shoulders.

"All I know is she better show up when we start getting married," said Diana.

"Speaking of getting married, don't forget we're all going to Bud and Greta's wedding next weekend," said Mrs. Green. "And we're all invited to the reception at the Vaughn estate."

"This is so wonderful for her," said Cynthia. "Going from being left at the altar to marrying into a rich family."

"Mhmm," agreed Mrs. Green. "Maybe The Lord will bless me by marrying you all to rich men too since he's in the neighborhood."

"Well, Ralphie's already starting to do good for himself," bragged Diana. "He recently rented an apartment in the city."

"Ralphie's leaving Creeke?!" cried Mrs. Green.

"He's just moving down the road," said Diana. "He'll still be working at the paper and the grocery store. He was just ready to move out of his parents' house. Now, don't tell him, but I'm planning a surprise housewarming party for him."

"And just where is this surprise party going to be?" asked Mr. Green suspiciously. "Because usually housewarmings are held at said house. And there's no way you should have access to Ralphie's house."

"Dad relax," huffed Diana. "I've got his family in on it. It'll be at his parents' house."

"Alright," said Mr. Green, still eyeing Diana.

Althea tuned out like always when her family started talking about romance. She was not against romance and finding love someday. It was just that men were the least of her priorities, especially with her new position as Miss Teen Creeke. But she did hope that one day she would find the right man for her.

That Monday, Althea had an event to attend at the library. It was an initiative event to inspire students to read while they were out of school. Althea would give a speech on the importance of reading. Then, she would help pass out reading lists one could earn prizes for every five books they read on it.

Even if Althea was not Miss Teen Creeke, she still would have spoken at the event if asked. Her love for reading alone would have been enough to encourage others to read. She enjoyed events like the reading initiative because they aligned with her interests. Events like the women's leadership brunch she had later that week sometimes made her wish someone else had won.

Althea arrived at the library already glammed up in her queen attire. Unfortunately, she did not have enough time to browse beforehand, so she sat in her seat waiting for the event to start. Then, Justin walked in.

Althea had not seen Justin since the previous summer. While she was finishing up her final year of high school, he was off experiencing his first year of college. And he looked even better than he had before. He seemed more manly and grown up.

His face lit up when he saw her. Althea did not know why but seeing him happy to see her made her blush. It felt like the world slowed down as he came over to her. He sat beside her, and they exchanged pleasantries.

"Are you speaking at this event too?" asked Justin.

"Yes," answered Althea. "You are too?"

"Yeah," said Justin. "I guess it's because I'm playing college football, even though I wasn't on the field much this past year..."

"That's okay," said Althea.

"I feel like we haven't seen much of each other lately," said Justin. "How have you been?"

"I've been well. You?"

"I've been good. Are you enjoying being Miss Teen Creeke?"

"It's a position that requires a lot of dedication," said Althea, trying not to say anything negative about her position. She did not dislike being Miss Teen Creeke. It was just that it required a lot from her.

"I'll bet," said Justin with a small laugh.

The event was preparing to start.

"There's something I'd like to talk to you about," said Justin. "Can we have lunch tomorrow?"

"Okay," said Althea.

Justin gave a speech about how reading books is his favorite pastime after getting off the field. Then, Althea followed up with how reading helped one to develop intelligence and learn new things. Overall, she found it to be a fun and satisfying experience. After the event ended, she returned home happy to finally be able to go back to her normal self.

"Hey girl!" called Allison when Althea exited her car. Allison ran across the street to meet her. The Harrisons were finally back in their house after it had been restored from its fire damage. "Where are you coming from looking all cute?"

"An event at the library," answered Althea.

"Ah, the summer reading initiative," said Allison knowingly as she followed Althea into the house. "Honestly, that was probably my favorite event to speak at."

"Really?"

"Yup," said Allison. "That's not to say the other events were bad. The library one was just fun."

"It was," said Althea. "I didn't expect Miss Teen Creeke to be so much work though."

"Mhmm," agreed Allison. "Girl, why you think I was so happy to put that crown on your head?"

"How did you manage it all?"

"I just did it," said Allison, shrugging. "Honestly, getting to go away for school was amazing because it's like a nice long break after working hard all summer. My mother said when she was Miss Teen Creeke, she had to do stuff throughout the entire year she was queen."

Althea shivered at the thought of having to do twelve months' worth of events and appearances. Just doing a few weeks' worth had been a lot.

"Just know when you get back from school next summer, these people are going to put you to *work*," cautioned Allison. "They're going to squeeze everything they can get out of you."

"Thanks for the warning," said Althea.

Althea met Justin for lunch the next day at Patty's. Benjamin was working the cash register that day. However, it seemed that within the past year, his dedication to his family's business had declined. Sometimes, it almost felt like he would rather be anywhere else.

Justin began ordering first. After about the first five words, Benjamin interrupted him.

"Could you speak up?" requested Benjamin. "I can barely hear you."

Althea felt herself grow annoyed. It was a knee-jerk reaction because the same thing happened to her often. Hearing those words or anything similar automatically irked her.

"A chicken sandwich please!" said Justin annoyedly. Althea was surprised by the added bass and volume in his voice.

"That's more like it," said Benjamin.

Benjamin finished taking their order. They found a table to sit at, and Althea waited curiously to find out what Justin wanted to speak about.

"I really hate when people cut me off to tell me to speak up," said Justin. "It's so annoying."

"I know," agreed Althea. "There was something you wanted to talk about?"

"Yes," said Justin. "I'm planning to hold a field day for the kids next week. I was wondering if you would be willing to come?"

"As myself or as the queen?" asked Althea.

"Aren't they the same?" questioned Justin.

"Uh...," muttered Althea.

Justin raised a good point. Her reign had just started and already she was separating herself from the pageant queen image. When really, she was most likely chosen because she suited what everyone wanted Miss Teen Creeke to be.

"I was just asking because I think being in a dress at a field day would be kind of impractical," said Althea.

"Of course," said Justin. "I didn't mean for you to come dressed like that anyways..."

Justin averted his eyes from hers, his face beginning to blush. Althea found it quite cute, even though she knew the feeling itself was not a great one.

"So, will this be something similar to the camp you did last year?" asked Althea.

"Yeah," said Justin. "I wanted to do something that was more inclusive this year. Last year, I think because it was a football camp was why I only had mostly boys show up. And a lot of their parents were very annoying to deal with. They all had that football star mentality."

Althea understood well what Justin meant by "football star mentality". Those were people who were overzealous for success to the point that it took away from the fun of just playing. Her father often said he was not raising football stars to keep his players from growing egos. He also used it to remind his daughters that they should get along and have each other's backs.

"I want to do something that can participate in," continued Justin.

Althea liked that Justin cared so much about the community. And she liked that he was so driven to give the community things to come together for.

"I would love to come to field day," said Althea. "If you need me to do anything to help, just let me know."

"Thanks Althea," said Justin, smiling.

She liked seeing Justin smile. It was always so genuine and nice-looking.

Friday would be a long day for Althea. She had the women's leadership brunch that morning and Ralph's surprise party that evening. Mrs. Campbell was hosting the women's leadership brunch. Attending the brunch itself was not a problem. The problem was Althea had to speak about leadership.

Althea had never been the leader of anything. Although she had become more confident in asking for what she wanted, she was by no means a leader. She was used to letting other people make decisions and then deciding whether to go along with them or not. The only reason she was even speaking at the brunch was because she was Miss Teen Creeke. Other speakers included Mrs. Harrison, First Lady Hall, and Mrs. Townsend. Those were women Althea considered real leaders, and she felt like an imposter among them.

The brunch was held at the recreation center. It was beautifully decorated and many women attended, including Althea's mother and sisters. They were seated with Mrs. Ernestine Allen, First Lady Hall's mother.

"Hello Mrs. Ernestine," greeted Mrs. Green. "How are you today?"

"I'm doing good, Athena," said Mrs. Ernestine. "How are you all today?"

"We're doing good," said Mrs. Green. "My baby is speaking today and I'm so excited!"

"Girl, I know how you feel," giggled Mrs. Ernestine. "Lana has done a whole bunch of speaking engagements but I still get excited all over again like it's her first one."

"Mhmm," agreed Mrs. Green. She looked around and said, "No granddaughters today?"

"Nope," said Mrs. Ernestine. "Karla's at home with Layla, Mary had work, and Adrianna just ain't want to get out the bed."

"Oh Lord," laughed Mrs. Green.

"I'm kind of glad they're not here though," said Mrs. Ernestine. She screwed up her face and said, "Apparently that Sophia is supposed to be coming here."

"Oh boy," groaned Mrs. Green. "Why does she have to come?"

"Girl, I wish I knew. All I know is she better not say nothing to me because I don't have nothing nice to say to her."

The "Sophia" in question was Lady Sophia Perry. She was the mother of Mrs. Campbell and Mrs. Harrison. And she was a very unpopular figure in the town along with her husband, Mayor Bernard Perry. What made Lady Sophia so unlikeable was that she tried to act like she was better than everyone because she had married well.

But most of the elderly women remembered Lady Sophia's humble beginnings. They remembered how her father had run off on her pregnant mother with another woman. And they remembered how Lady Sophia's mother had been a maid barely making ends meet. That last point was why Mrs. Ernestine disliked Lady Sophia so much. Mrs. Ernestine had worked as a maid for the Perrys for decades and had been replaced with a younger woman without warning.

What was most scandalous about Lady Sophia was her shamelessly marrying her daughters off to the highest bidders. Many wondered how Mrs. Campbell and Mrs. Harrison had turned out so sweet compared to their rotten parents. But the truth was that Mrs. Campbell, for all her sweetness, was very passive. Mrs. Harrison was also passive to an extent, but there were times when she put her foot down.

However, the rumor that Lady Sophia would be at the brunch remained just that. The brunch was a nice, inspiring event. Each speaker encouraged the women with some variation of not being afraid to take charge without compromising their values. Then, it was Althea's turn to speak.

Althea had been unsure of what to say. So, she and her mother had come up with a pre-written speech she could read. Her speech was about how great leaders first had to be led. She talked about the importance of learning how to take direction helped when one was finally in a position to give direction. And she talked about the importance of learning the difference between good and bad leadership.

Everyone applauded when she finished. Althea was grateful for the opportunity to give such an inspiring speech, but she would be even more grateful to go back to being her normal self. Although she tried to mesh the two images of herself in her mind, she could not. Regular Althea was a bookworm, a journalist, and a sports fan. Nobody special. Miss Teen Creeke was who mothers pointed out to their daughters as who they should aspire to be.

While Althea did not mind being a source of inspiration, what bothered her was that it was not necessarily *her* doing the inspiration. It was the position itself that was inspiring. Any girl could fill that spot, and it would be seen the same way. Miss Teen Creeke was like a character she was playing, and she would be recast with a new girl in a year.

That afternoon, Althea, Cynthia, and Mikayla helped Diana prepare for Ralph's surprise housewarming party. Diana directed the girls to and fro on how she wanted things to be. It would not be a huge extravaganza, but Diana still wanted it to look like effort was put into it.

I'll tell you one thing friend," said Mikayla. "My brother better appreciate all this hard work I'm doing for him."

"Mmhmm," agreed Diana. "He better since I'm trying to make this perfect for him."

Diana had worked everything out to ensure Ralph would be at the party. She got his parents to come up with a reason for him to go to their house rather than going straight home. They had recently hired Samiel, so he, Latasia, and Kameryn would handle the store while they attended the party. And she convinced Uncle Arnold to close the paper on time for once so they could ensure Ralph would not be stuck at work late.

By the time six o'clock rolled around, everyone was in place waiting for Ralph to arrive.

"He's coming!" said Mikayla. "Everyone get ready!"

Everyone got quiet as they waited for Ralph to walk in.

"What's with all the cars outside?" muttered Ralph. "And why couldn't they just do this themselves? I was ready to go home!"

"SURPRISE!" yelled everyone, turning on the lights.

"AAHH!" yelped Ralph, clutching at his chest with surprise. When he recovered from shock, he asked, "What is all this?"

"This is your surprise housewarming party!" announced Diana, hugging Ralph. "I put it together for you."

"You did all this for me?" asked Ralph. "Oh wow! Thanks! I don't know what to say!"

The party went on successfully. Everyone had a good time, and towards the end of the night, Ralph gathered everyone for a speech.

"I want to say thank you all for coming," said Ralph. "This has been a wonderful evening. Baby, you kind of put me on the spot here. And to thank you, I'm going to put you on the spot."

"What are you talking about, Ralphie?" laughed Diana nervously.

"Diana Rubylynn Green," said Ralph, taking Diana's hands in his. "We've been dating for two years and I think it's time we take things to the next level."

Ralph got down on one knee.

"Oh my gosh!" gasped Diana, her hands flying to her mouth.

"Baby," said Ralph. "I was planning to do this when I had the ring on me, but just know I do already have it. Will you become my Mrs. Brewer?"

Diana stared at Ralph, her hands still covering her mouth.

"For once, the girl is speechless," joked Mrs. Green.

"Diana," whispered Mr. Green. "Diana! Answer the poor boy!"

Diana started bouncing excitedly as tears fell down her face. She threw herself on top of Ralph, knocking him to the floor and covering his face in kisses.

"I think that means 'yes'," said Mr. Green. "Welcome to the family son!"

"I'm getting married!" announced Diana enthusiastically. "I'm really getting married!"

It was the perfect ending to a great evening.

The next day, the Green family traveled to the city for Bud and Greta's wedding. Although Mr. Bud wanted a small wedding, his family decided to give him one that was very lavish. They also took care of accommodations for Ms. Greta's parents so that she could only focus on enjoying her day.

The actual wedding was held at a church twice the size of Creeke's church. Mr. Bud and Ms. Greta had decided on yellow and silver as their wedding colors. Ms. Greta had the same bridesmaids that her sister had plus Mr. Bud's sister, Jana. However, unlike at her sister's wedding where Ms. Greta walked down the aisle alone, Mrs. Nelson-Brown walked down the aisle with Mr. Bud's best man.

Mr. Bud's best man was interesting. Most of his groomsmen were cousins from both sides of his family. But his best man was his first cousin, Will Vaughn, from his father's side. He looked like a regular White man with curly gray-red hair and green eyes. But when he smiled, one noticed he had worn a silver grill for the wedding.

The wedding went normally for the most part. There was only one part that was kind of funny, which was the part where they asked for objections.

"Do you Greta Ella Nelson, take this man to be your lawfully wedded husband?"

"I do," said Ms. Greta.

"Do you, Bud Vaughn, take this woman to be your lawfully wedded
wife?"

It seemed everyone in the room stared at Mr. Bud with bated breath.

"I do," said Mr. Bud.

"HALLELUJAH!" shouted Mrs. Myrtle Nelson, shooting from her
chair. Mr. Gerald Nelson nodded approvingly before pulling his wife
back into her seat.

After that, everything went according to plan.

"Wasn't that such a nice ceremony?" asked Diana as they left the
church. "And to think that'll be me up there at the altar soon. And
you're going to be my maid of honor, Thea."

Diana grabbed Althea by the hands and swung her around in circles
as she sang bridal music.

"Do you think Glo will come home for the wedding?" asked Althea.

"She better," huffed Diana. "What kind of sister would miss their
own sister's wedding?"

"When's the last time you talked to her?"

"I don't even know. You know she goes wherever the wind takes her
and tells us all about it when she remembers we exist."

Although she would never dare to say it, Althea could relate to Diana's annoyance. The last time any of them saw Gloria was four years
ago when she left town a few months after graduating high school. She
had missed all her sisters' graduations and only called once every few
months. And each time she called she never stayed long on the phone
and always had some new guy on her arm.

"Now we've just got to find you somebody," said Diana.

"I don't think I'm ready for a relationship right now," said Althea.

"Althea!" whined Diana. "Cynthia's clearly not looking right now,
and who knows if Gloria will ever settle down with anyone. You've got
to find someone. I can't be the only one of us who gets a happily ever
after."

"If I'm meant to have someone, it'll happen when it happens."

"Ugh," grumbled Diana.

The wedding reception was held at a beautiful garden venue. Mr. Bud's family spared no expense on the wedding, the venue, or the food. He walked around with Mr. Will, thanking everyone for coming.

"Oh my gosh!" gasped Diana. She pointed and gleefully asked, "Is that Myrna Watson?"

"Good Lord, I think it is!" cried Mrs. Green.

Myrna Watson was something like a local celebrity in the city. Her first brush with fame had been an unfortunate one. During her freshman year of high school, she had been the first and only Black girl to attend the Willard Academy For Girls in the seventies. When she enrolled in the school, it caused it to be officially desegregated. Although her father had been a doctor and her mother a nurse, and they could easily afford the tuition, many of the students, faculty, and parents felt that she did not belong there.

She had only been at the school for a semester. After winning the election to become her class's secretary, she was jumped after school and Willard did nothing to punish her attackers. That led to her being pulled from the school and the school refusing to acknowledge her ever being one of their students.

However, her second brush with fame was due to her luxury boutique. Every woman especially wanted a Myrna Watson handbag. She was starting to franchise the business and it was even rumored that a biopic about her life was in the works. Myrna Watson's story was an inspiration, especially to Diana who loved all things fashion and cosmetics.

"Hi Green family!" said Mr. Bud excitedly when he arrived at their table. "Thank you guys so much for coming!"

"You talk like such a white boy," joked Mr. Will, causing everyone to stare at him.

"This is my cousin, Will," said Mr. Bud, blushing.

"What up, what up?" greeted Mr. Will. "Y'all be sure to have a good time. And don't be afraid to make more than one plate. We ain't trying to take no leftovers home!"

"Bud!" said Mrs. Green. "Is that Myrna Watson?"

"Yes," said Mr. Bud. "She's our godmother."

"Myrna Watson is your godmother?!" cried Diana.

"Yes," said Mr. Bud casually.

"That's so cool!"

"I guess," said Mr. Bud, shrugging his shoulders.

"Why you being all casual about it?" said Mr. Will jokingly.

"He's always like that," said Mr. Green.

"Don't I know it," said Mr. Will.

"Thanks again for coming," said Mr. Bud quickly. He grabbed Mr. Will's hand and dragged him away, saying, "Come on, Will."

"Now ain't that something?" said Mr. Green. "The Black one acts like a White man, and the White one acts like a Black man."

"And you can tell that's really just how they are too," laughed Mrs. Green.

"Is it just me or was he looking at me a little too much?" asked Cynthia.

"He probably thought you were cute," joked Diana. "That might be your rich husband right there."

"He is like Daddy's age," said Cynthia. "That is too old for my taste."

"Normally, I'd take offense but you're right," said Mr. Green. "That man is too old. And so is that one, and that one, and that one–!"

"Lord, now look what you did," said Cynthia to Diana. "You done got him started."

A while later, Mrs. Greta came by the table.

"There's our lovely bride!" said Mrs. Green. "So, what's your new last name?"

"Mrs. Nelson-Vaughn," said Mrs. Greta. "I've got too many accomplishments under the Nelson name to just throw it away now."

"True," said Mrs. Green. "We met your husband's cousin."

"Oh Lord," chuckled Mrs. Greta. "Yeah, Will has a strong personality. But he's not a bad guy and that's Bud's favorite cousin."

"And that's really just how he is and that's okay," stated Mr. Green. "He just needs to keep his eyes off my daughter."

"Oop!" said Mrs. Greta. "Alright Dad, you better be a protector. Y'all saw how my daddy basically chucked me at Bud. Pastor ain't even get the words all the way out and he already handing me off."

"That was funny," said Mrs. Green. "And the way your mama hollered when Bud said 'I do'."

"Oh Lord, don't remind me," groaned Mrs. Greta. "I can't take those two nowhere. Listen, I can't stay over here too long but thank you guys for coming. Make sure to enjoy yourselves."

The rest of the wedding reception was a fun night.

The following Monday, Althea knew from the moment she woke up that something was wrong. Her nose was stuffy, and her throat was sore. But Justin's field day was that day, and she wanted to be there. So, she decided to push through.

"You don't look so good," said Diana when Althea entered the kitchen.

"I think it might be allergies," said Althea.

"No, you look really sick," said Diana. "I don't think you should go anywhere."

"I'm fine," said Althea.

"You ready to roll, baby girl?" said Mr. Green. He was going with her to the field day.

"Dad, doesn't Thea look sick?" asked Diana.

"You do look a little flushed," said Mr. Green. "Are you feeling alright?"

"I'm fine," said Althea. "I think it might be allergies."

"Allergies huh?" said Mr. Green, putting a hand on Althea's forehead. "I've never heard of allergies causing fevers before. Diana, get me the thermometer."

Diana did as her father asked. A few minutes later, the thermometer confirmed what Althea was dreading. She was sick with a fever.

"Yeah, you're not going anywhere," said Mr. Green.

"See?" said Diana. "I knew you were sick."

"But I told Justin I'd be there," said Althea distressfully. "I can't back out now."

"Well, baby girl, you may not want to be sick, but your body is definitely not feeling well," said Mr. Green. "You stay home and get some rest. Justin will understand."

Althea felt bad. She had told Justin that she would be at his event. Instead, she was stuck at home on bed rest with Diana and Cynthia taking care of her. They gave her soup and put cold compresses on Althea's head to lower the fever.

"Cheer up Thea," encouraged Cynthia. "It's not like you'll be sick forever."

"I just don't like not being able to keep my word," said Althea.

"Well, you can't help that you got sick," said Diana.

"But it's not fair to Justin that I'm not there."

"It would've been more unfair to Justin if you were there and ended up falling out or something," said Diana. "Listen Thea. That event went on without you and life is the same way. Don't try to be everything for everybody, especially when you're not in a state to show up for yourself first."

Althea did not want to listen, but she knew Diana was right. Diana never had an issue saying no. And she probably never felt like an imposter, taking up a spot that someone else should have had. No, Diana made her presence known and made it known she belonged whether one agreed or not.

And Cynthia was a natural leader. She always managed to take charge of a situation and make leading look easy. Althea wished she could be more like her sisters. Maybe then she would see herself as Miss Teen Creeke and not just a girl filling the role.

Things at home were pretty calm until Mrs. Green came home.

"What's wrong with my baby?" asked Mrs. Green, bustling into the room. "Your sisters said you have a fever."

"She does!" said Diana. "And she's talking about she needs to be at Justin's field day event. I told her she wasn't going anywhere."

"Your sister's right, honey," said Mrs. Green. "You don't look good at all. I'm going to call your aunt to come check you out."

"You don't have to do that," said Althea. "I don't want to bother her."

"Girl, are you kidding me?" said Mrs. Green. "If your aunt finds out I didn't call her when she's a whole nurse, she'll have a fit."

Fifteen minutes later, Althea was being looked at by her Aunt Ruth-Anne. Aunt Ruth-Anne diagnosed her with a cold and said she would be good in about a week. She told Althea it was best to stay home and get some rest.

Later that day, Justin came by to check on her. It was clear he had come straight from field day because he looked and smelled like outside. But Althea did not mind. She kind of liked the way it smelled on him.

"I heard you weren't feeling well," said Justin. "I just wanted to make sure you were okay."

"I'm sorry, Justin," said Althea. "I know you wanted me there today."

"That's alright," said Justin. "Your health is more important."

"Yeah, but I know it would've been great for you to have Miss Teen Creeke there."

"Miss Teen Creeke is just a title," said Justin, taking Althea's hand. "Just like being quarterback is just a title. You're the person holding the title. Having you there would've been great, but making sure you're okay is more important."

Althea shivered when Justin touched her hand and looked at her tenderly. She was not sure if it was because she was sick or something else. But she did know she liked the way it made her feel. Not to mention, she could not help but notice how cute he looked when he did it.

Benjamin Townsend

Benjamin was working harder than ever to make his music more known. A year after competing on Ra'Kaveon's show, he had made some career progress, but success was still far away. If he wanted to get there, he had to keep going. So, on a Friday night in early July, Benjamin was heading to a performance. He sat in the back of Derek's jeep, making yet another promotional video to get people to come out and support him.

"I'm going to be at Club Cinnamon tonight," said Benjamin. "Pull up on me."

"Pull up on me," said Derek, mimicking his voice. He turned his music back up, revealing the song as "My Dawg", the latest collaboration between Ra'Kaveon and Vincent. The two had repaired their friendship but had agreed to continue pursuing their own solo music careers.

"Hey," said Benjamin. "I ain't your cousin. Don't be mocking me."

"Sir, you are in my vehicle," said Derek. "We are riding up here to support you. So, if I want to tease you about what you said, I can do that."

"Can you believe this man?" asked Benjamin to Samiel.

"I'm not getting in that," laughed Samiel. "What time are you performing again?"

"Eleven," said Benjamin.

"Dang, that's late," said Samiel.

"That's actually really early," said Derek. "You're opening up for Sweet Hunni, right?"

"Yeah," said Benjamin.

As much as he disliked Sweet Hunni, Benjamin had to respect her rise in popularity within a year. He had learned that the most popular hits were those that women liked and would sing along to. And Sweet Hunni's music hit that sweet spot very easily. She and Grai had both signed to King Rak Records and their music was everywhere. Uncle Buck had rejected the deal, choosing to stay independent for creative control.

Sweet Hunni and Grai were not the only successes from the show though. Ebony had collaborated with Alice on her Love Me Back Remix and was gaining traction in the R&B genre. And Benjamin himself was experiencing minor success due to his collaborations with Skunk.

Benjamin and Skunk worked well together and made money together. But after a year of collaborating with different artists, he knew the difference between a partnership and a friendship. He and Skunk were in a mutual partnership. What he had with Uncle Buck was a genuine friendship.

"I'm good to stay at your place tonight, right?" asked Samiel to Derek.

"Of course," answered Derek. "You know my dad doesn't care. You can stay at my place too Benji if you need to."

"That's alright," said Benjamin. 'I'm opening the restaurant tomorrow so I'll just go home."

Although Benjamin focused heavily on his music, he was still expected to work at Patty's during the summer. It was almost like a culture shock returning home after being away at college for a year. He had done so much work musically while away at school, that it almost felt like going backward returning to work at his parents' restaurant. And it was more difficult juggling the two than he expected. So, Benjamin put most of his energy towards his music.

People were just starting to arrive at Cinnamon when Benjamin got there. The line was starting to get long. But thankfully, Benjamin and his boys did not have to wait in line.

"Watch your step!" warned Derek when Benjamin exited the truck.

Benjamin looked down to see he was about to step into a muddy puddle.

"Boy, I just saved your whole life," laughed Derek. "Especially with them white shoes on."

Benjamin could hear the music from inside as they neared the club. He sent off a text to Skunk and rapped along to the lyrics as they approached. By the time they reached the door, Skunk was outside waiting to take them in.

"What's up?" said Skunk. He turned to the security guard and said, "They're with me."

"What's up?" said Benjamin.

"What's going on?" answered the security guard. "Let me pat y'all down real quick."

"Alright," answered Benjamin.

Once they passed security, Benjamin and his friends entered the party. It was mostly empty but as the night went on, more people showed up. They spent most of the night in Skunk's section, waiting to perform. Skunk, as was always the case with him, started flashing all his valuables and his money.

"We got Skunk and Benji in the building!" announced the DJ. "Y'all make sure y'all show them some love!"

The crowd cheered as the DJ started playing their most popular collaboration, "Spray Em Down". Skunk became animated, making sure to showcase just how proud of the song he was.

"You better be careful flashing all that money before someone in here robs you!" hollered a woman's voice. Benjamin looked over to see Sweet Hunni walking up to them.

"What's up Hunni!" greeted Skunk, giving her a hug.

"What's up!" said Sweet Hunni. She looked at Benjamin and said, "You going to act like you don't know me, Benji?"

Benjamin relented and gave Sweet Hunni a hug. She joined them for a while before moving on to her own section. By the time eleven o'clock hit, everyone was amped up and ready for the performances to start. The DJ announced Benjamin and Skunk as the opening act. They went onstage and performed two songs.

What Benjamin loved most about performing was the energy. He loved the energy that he and the crowd traded with each other. After the performance ended, Benjamin and his friends stayed through Sweet Hunni's performance. Even though Benjamin felt she still needed improving, he could admit that she had improved. He was proud that she at least could remain on beat throughout the whole song.

By the time Benjamin got home, it was almost three in the morning. He crept to his room, trying to avoid the floorboards that creaked extra loud. It felt like he had just laid down when he heard Charmaine telling him it was time to get up.

"Benji," said Charmaine. "Get up. It's time for work."

"Okay," murmured Benjamin. He looked at the clock, which read seven o'clock, and figured he could sneak in five more minutes of sleep. When he opened his eyes again, the clock was seventeen minutes past eleven. Benjamin flew from his bed, crying out, "Shoot! No, no, no!"

Time seemed to move faster than usual. Benjamin normally could get himself ready in about fifteen minutes. But that day, it seemed like it took an eternity to get ready. By the time he arrived at Patty's, it was almost noon.

"Hey," said Benjamin, greeting his very annoyed-looking sister who stood at the counter.

"Don't 'hey' me," snapped Charmaine. "You were supposed to open today!"

"I had a long night," muttered Benjamin annoyedly.

"Yeah, I noticed. You came sneaking in the house at three in the morning!"

"Why are you all up in my business?" griped Benjamin. "And what were you doing up that late anyways?"

"I wasn't until you woke me up with all the noise you were making!" ranted Charmaine. "You need to be glad I got up and came in to cover for you since you wouldn't get out the bed."

"Yeah whatever," snorted Benjamin.

"Alright," said Charmaine. "Next time, I'll let you take the heat from Mom and Dad for oversleeping."

"Whatever Charmaine," said Benjamin, rolling his eyes.

Things had been like that since he had returned home from college. There was always something to argue about with one of his family members about his music. It was annoying, but Benjamin had to put up with it until he could prove he could have a successful, sustaining career in music. After the small argument with Charmaine, the day went pretty normally. She left when he would have if he had been on time, so he stayed until closing.

"Benjamin," said Mr. Townsend when the restaurant was closed.

"Sir?" answered Benjamin.

"Come here."

Mr. Townsend motioned for Benjamin to join him at a table. Benjamin did so and waited for his father to speak.

"Where were you this morning?" asked Mr. Townsend.

"What do you mean?" asked Benjamin.

"What I mean is I make the schedule," said Mr. Townsend. "So, I know which child is supposed to help open on which days. Where were you this morning?"

"I overslept," said Benjamin.

"Mmhmm," uttered Mr. Townsend. "Look, me and your mother decided to let you do your music thing because you're a grown man now. But part of being a grown man is handling your business. You're the oldest. You're supposed to be looking out for your sister and setting an example for her, not making things harder for her. You understand?"

"Yes sir," said Benjamin.

"You need to shape up. Next time your sister comes in here covering for you, I'm going to send her right back home and just dock your pay."

"Yes sir."

"And next time you decide to stay out all night without letting anybody know where you're at, just stay where you're at. Because you're not coming in my house at all hours of the night and expecting things to be all peachy keen."

"Yes sir."

Benjamin was not sure if his father had forgotten about his performance the night before. But he was positive he had told everyone where he would be. It did not matter though. As long as Benjamin stayed on top of things from then on, he was sure he could pursue his music without much pushback.

The following weekend, Benjamin had a performance lined up at a different club. However, the performance never happened. He and Skunk had arranged to get paid upfront. But when they showed up to collect, the promoter kept giving them the runaround, claiming he would have their money ready after the show.

"Look, we're supposed to get paid up front," said Skunk. "If you don't have our money right now, you don't get a performance from us."

"Bro, you're always flexing money and jewelry everywhere you go," argued the promoter. "You're telling me you can't wait until after the show to get this little bit of money?"

"If it such a little bit of money, why you can't give it to us now?"

Skunk and the promoter went back and forth until Skunk decided there would be no show. He and Benjamin left and ended up at some diner.

"This is crazy," said Skunk. "That man really tried to play us!"

"What if he was serious about having our money after the show?" questioned Benjamin.

"Nah, I've been through this enough times to know if they don't got it when you ask for it, they ain't never going to have it. And I don't perform for free."

Benjamin took two big lessons away from that night. The first was knowing his worth and not working for free. And the second was sticking to his worth and not allowing himself to get played.

The next day, Benjamin showed up for work on time. However, he was tired. And that caused him to mess up some orders, and he even had an attitude with some of the customers that had attitudes with him. Benjamin was working hard to be nicer at work, but that day he just was not feeling it. During his lunch break, his mother approached him.

"Benji, I've been getting some complaints about your attitude," said Mrs. Townsend. "You can't have a bad attitude with the customers."

"Well, maybe they shouldn't have an attitude with me," said Benjamin.

"No sir," said Mrs. Townsend sternly. "You know that's not how we do business. You've got to maintain a good attitude with the customers no matter how they act. I don't want anymore complaints about you today, understand?"

Benjamin was annoyed. It was already bad enough that his parents were making him divide his time between Patty's and his music career. But it was even more annoying that they kept scheduling him for the most inconvenient shifts and expected him to be perfect at his job. After work, Benjamin went to hang out with his friends at the park. He needed people to vent to who would not try and make him the villain in his own story.

"Am I wrong?" asked Benjamin after venting.

"Kind of," said Derek. "You've got to be nice to customers."

"Yeah," said Samiel. "You shouldn't give them a bunch of attitude. That makes the business look bad."

"Oh please," said Benjamin. "You two work customer service for a few months and think y'all know something. I've done customer service for four years. Those people are annoying."

"You asked us if you were wrong," said Derek. "Don't get mad at us because it's not the answer you wanted."

"Whatever," huffed Benjamin. "Believe what you want. I don't care at this point."

"There's no need to get upset with us," said Derek. "You did it."

"I'm not upset, I'm irritated," said Benjamin. "I feel like I'm the only person who has my back at this point."

"Benji, you know we've always got your back," said Samiel.

"Well, you both have a funny way of showing it," griped Benjamin. "Why should I have to give up my music just because they want me to run their restaurant?"

"Well, sometimes sacrifices have to be made," said Derek.

"So, you're saying I should just give up on everything I've worked hard for?"

"You just might have to."

"That's not fair!"

"That's life."

"What do you think Sami because clearly he's not thinking straight."

"I–!" began Samiel.

"I'm not thinking straight?" repeated Derek. "Benji, you have a good business being handed down to you and you don't want it because you want to take a chance on being a rapper. Which one of us here isn't thinking straight?"

"Businesses can fail too," said Benjamin. "And yes, I do want to take a chance on my music career because that's what I want to do with my life. If you don't like it or support it, then you can just shut up."

"Don't got to tell me twice," said Derek before leaving. "I'll catch y'all later."

"What the heck is his problem?!" ranted Benjamin.

"What's been his problem for the past year?" sighed Samiel.

"Well, that's not my fault and he shouldn't take it out on us like it is!"

"Yeah, but imagine how it makes him feel to hear you complain about being annoyed with people not supporting your dreams when he literally can't chase his anymore."

"He needs to toughen up! I'm not going to shut up just to spare his feelings!"

"Both of y'all just need to relax," sighed Samiel. "I just want to know why you can't do both? Why not do music and run the business?"

"I don't want to do both," said Benjamin.

"But why not? That's more money."

"You just don't get it Sami. I have no interest in running that business. I have no interest in making food and dealing with annoying customers. Do you get it now?"

"Yeah," said Samiel, nodding slowly. "You need more sleep. That's the problem."

Benjamin resisted the urge to scream. It felt like everyone was reducing everything he wanted to him being an ungrateful brat. He was grateful for what his parents had accomplished and done for him. But it felt like no one understood that he wanted to go on and make his own accomplishments. Everyone wanted him to take a path he had no interest in taking.

He felt alone.

Over the next few weeks, Benjamin's performance at work got worse and worse. He was putting more focus on his music and doing the bare minimum at Patty's. Benjamin felt like the only way he would be able to get everyone to understand his view was to work even harder to be successful. By the beginning of August, most of his energy was focused on his career.

He had been doing performances everywhere. It got to the point where he was skipping church and was constantly tired at work. But Benjamin believed if he could just show his parents some proof that he could be successful, they would start supporting him.

However, his parents seemed to go in the opposite direction. One day, his father sat him down for another meeting.

"I told you to shape up," said Mr. Townsend. "Did I not?"

"Yes sir," answered Benjamin.

"Then why haven't you?" questioned Mr. Townsend. "You've been late to work, you've been messing up orders, getting into it with us, just being irritating all the time. What is the problem?"

"Nothing," said Benjamin. "I've just got a lot going on."

"Yeah," scoffed Mr. Townsend. "Maybe too much going on. Benjamin, you've got to make a decision."

"What?"

"You've been slacking."

"Well Dad, if you'd stop scheduling me for morning shifts literally right after I have performances the night before I'd probably do better at work."

"No sir, do not try and make this my fault. You need to stop accepting performances when you know you have work the next day."

"I schedule those performances long before you schedule me for work."

"Well, then you might want to cut back on them."

"How am I supposed to get myself out there if I can't perform?"

"That's not my problem. The only performance I care about is the one you give as my employee. And right now, it's piss poor."

"I'm convinced you're purposely trying to sabotage me at this point," accused Benjamin. "You keep scheduling me for bad shifts, then complain about how I'm doing when I'm literally worn out! That's not fair and you know it."

"Sabotage you?! Boy, sabotage would've been kicking you out at midnight on your eighteenth birthday with no warning like your grandfather did me! All I'm asking you to do is show up to work on time and act like you're part of this darn family! I don't give two craps about whatever else you got going on outside of that!"

"I know you don't," said Benjamin. "You've made that perfectly clear."

"Don't take that tone of voice with me, young man," warned Mr. Townsend.

"Look Dad, it's perfectly clear at this point that you and mom don't support my music. That's fine. But I'm not going to stop trying. All I'm asking you to do is work with me so we both get what we want."

Mr. Townsend stared at Benjamin, then sat back and crossed his arms.

"I don't have to do crap," said Mr. Townsend. "Especially not after you just sat here and disrespected me. You've been disrespecting me all summer and I don't like it. I'm the boss and I'm the father. You will shape up or you will ship out. Those are your options. The conversation is over."

Mr. Townsend walked away, leaving Benjamin feeling very annoyed. But he was not surprised at all. Usually, whenever one of the Townsend siblings got into it with their parents, they would go to the other to talk about it. So, Benjamin went to Charmaine to talk about what had happened with Mr. Townsend. He went through the whole story, being sure to include every detail.

"They don't support me at all," said Benjamin when he finished.

"At this point, I don't blame them," said Charmaine.

Benjamin froze. He had just spent all that time confiding to Charmaine and that was her reply.

"Why would you say that?" said Benjamin.

"Because you're out here chasing your dream and we're having to pick up your slack!" snapped Charmaine. "So, yes, I don't blame them for not supporting you because you're not supporting us. All you care about is yourself!"

"That's not true and you know it!" argued Benjamin.

"Yes, it is! For the past year, you've had tunnel vision for your music and that's it!"

"So, I'm the bad guy for being focused on my future?"

"Your music has *all* of your attention! You don't give us or the restaurant anything but bad attitude and piss poor effort! And the crazy part is, Mom and Dad still hope you'll take over the restaurant when they retire! Meanwhile I'm the one that's actually here helping them run it! I'm the one actually interested in taking it over from them, I'm the one actually learning the business and getting a business degree, and they still don't take me seriously at all!"

"Have you told them you want to run the business?"

"What's the point when they're so bent on giving it to you?! Get out of my room! I'm over talking about this!"

Charmaine threw Benjamin out of her room and slammed the door behind him. Benjamin could not believe it. His whole family had turned on him. The only supporter he had amongst them was his sister and she had turned on him too.

Benjamin did not know how to feel. But he knew he could not stop. He had worked too hard to get to where he was just to give it all up. And yet, he felt lost on what to do next. So, he decided to talk to someone he knew would legitimately hear him out and help him.

"Hello?" said Uncle Buck.

"Hi," said Benjamin. "Is this a bad time?"

"Nope. What's going on?"

"I need some advice."

"What's up?"

Benjamin told Uncle Buck everything that had happened.

"None of my family supports my music," said Benjamin. "They all just want me to give up and help run the family restaurant."

"They're probably just scared you're going to fail. Entertainment is a very unstable career, and it can leave people broken down in more ways than one."

"But this is what I want to do."

"I get that. But you can't bite the hand that feeds you while you're trying to get there. I'm going to be honest Benji, based on what you've told me, you've been acting a little like a brat."

"I'm not trying to," said Benjamin. "I'm just trying to stay focused."

"But you're hurting your family in the process. There's no point in aiming for the top if you don't have anyone to celebrate with you when you get there."

"What do you think I should do?" asked Benjamin.

"You've got to make a decision," said Uncle Buck.

"That's the same thing my dad said," sighed Benjamin.

"Then he's a smart man and you should listen to him more," advised Uncle Buck. "You've got to choose what's more important to you. Your music or your family?"

"Both of them are important to me. There's no way I can pick between them."

"With the way you're going about things now, you'll end up losing one of them forever if you don't start making some changes."

Benjamin did not want to admit that Uncle Buck was right. But he knew he was. He just wished there was some way he could get his family on board with him.

Benjamin was scheduled to do another booking that weekend, but he had a bad feeling about it. He felt he should not go but could not think of any reason not to. The booking would be like most of his other ones. It was at a club, Skunk would flex, and then they would perform. Everything would go how it always went. That was the only thing that Benjamin did not like about music. Sometimes, things started to become monotonous, and he would have to switch it up.

When Benjamin got to the club, he noticed it seemed a lot less secure, and it was in a rough part of the city. Inside was small and the crowd seemed sketchy. But he had been paid to perform, so he would forge ahead and perform.

That night, Skunk showed off a lot more than usual. Benjamin was unsure why he did so, but he was not surprised. He knew that Skunk liked to be the center of attention, and showing off was his way of generating hype. When it got close to the time for them to perform, they went backstage to get ready.

That's when everything went wrong.

One moment, he and Skunk were walking through the barely lit hallway. The next, Skunk was being attacked by a group of men. During the commotion, Benjamin got knocked to the ground. He went to stand back up and got knocked back down. Then, there was a gun in his face.

"Give me all your money!" demanded the robber.

Benjamin froze. Skunk was curled up on the ground beneath a barrage of fists and feet, while the robbers were snatching his chains off and going through his pockets. Fear ran through him as his whole life flashed before his eyes. All he could think about was his parents and sister, and how for the past few months he had spent most of his time fighting with them. Their last memories of him would be them arguing about his music.

"I said give me your money!" yelled the robber, kicking Benjamin in the chest.

Benjamin wheezed while he tried to find his wallet. By the time security came, the robbers had taken their money and fled. Skunk laughed as if it were just another day for him.

"That's the best they could do?" laughed Skunk. "They ain't even do nothing for real! I ain't even leaking!"

Benjamin could not perform after that. He was so scared to go to his car alone that security had to escort him. As he drove home, the shock of the moment slowly wore off.

He had been robbed at gunpoint. Laughter filled the car. It was his laughter. Benjamin laughed until his laughter turned to tears. That's when he understood just how terrified he had been.

In the days following the incident, Benjamin received calls from various people checking on him including Skunk, Uncle Buck, and Ebony, to name a few. Skunk took to social media to show how unaffected he was by the incident. Since he had been in similar situations before, he was pretty much unscathed by it. And when he started talking about their next booking, Benjamin knew he had to make a decision.

"Skunk, I don't think I'm going to do any more bookings for a while," said Benjamin over the phone.

"Come on Benji," said Skunk. "You can't let one little robbery stop you from getting to the bag. I thought you were tougher than that."

"Look, I'm just doing what's best for me right now," said Benjamin. "I'm going on a break."

And that's just what Benjamin intended to do. The experience had caused him to reevaluate what was important to him. He could have lost his life over money. He could have died at odds with his family. Benjamin did not want that. So, he decided to choose his family over his music.

Benjamin had not told his family what happened at the club. But he suspected they knew since it had become a small viral story for a day. What was important to him was that they knew how sorry he was. So, at their next family dinner, he apologized and promised to do better as an employee and a son. He also made it known that he would be taking a break from his music to help out at Patty's. His parents were ecstatic to hear that.

When it was all said and done, Benjamin wondered if he had made the right decision.

Derik Harrison

When Derik looked at the scars on his back, they reminded him of the time he got kidnapped. He remembered how his first failed escape attempt ended with one of his kidnappers, Hakeem, dragging him back inside the trailer by his hair. Hakeem had pulled his hair so hard that he pulled it out of Derik's head. That was the main reason Derik refused to ever have long hair again.

Derik also remembered how Hakeem beat him with the buckle end of a leather belt to punish him for trying to escape. That was where the scars came from. After that, Hakeem had offered him a cigarette, which Derik had taken out of fear of what would happen if he had not.

Whenever he thought of Hakeem, all he heard was that gruff, evil voice calling him "Little Man". And then he would have to remind himself that all his kidnappers – Hakeem, Malik, and Sharon – were locked away, awaiting trial.

That's what he was doing when Allison started yelling for him. Derik blinked and he was back in his room. He pulled his shirt on over his shoulders and down over his scars.

"Are you ready?" questioned Allison.

"Ready for what?" answered Derik.

"To go see Vonnie," said Allison, referring to Deidrick's one-year-old son, Devon Pierce.

"What am I going to see him for?" remarked Derik. "He's not my child."

"Cornbread said the same thing," snorted Allison. "And yet here we are. Auntie and Unky."

"Unfortunately," grumbled Derik.

"What'd you say?"

"Devon is not my child so why should I have to see him?"

"Because he's your nephew."

"He's Cornbread's responsibility, not mine."

"Well Cornbread's too busy playing house with *Carmen* and her kids," griped Allison mockingly. "He doesn't even bother with Vonnie."

"Well, that's his business, not mine."

"It's just wrong," said Allison. "First, he leads on Nisha for three years. Then he gets three women pregnant at the same time. Then the babies come and instead of stepping up for all three, he decides to lay up with Carmen, taking care of Car'drick and her other son that isn't his, while completely ignoring Vonnie and Bianca. It's just wrong."

"That ain't got nothing to do with me," said Derik.

"It does too," countered Allison. "You treat Vonnie differently from Bianca and Car'drick. It seems like Matty and I are the only ones who care about Vonnie. Say I'm wrong."

"Whatever Queenie," said Derik, rolling his eyes.

"Just terrible," scoffed Allison. "You and Cornbread both are just terrible."

Derik grimaced as his sister walked away, knowing she was right. He did act differently toward his nephew Devon, and although he knew it was wrong, he could not help it. Devon looked too much like Sharon, and the mere sight of him reminded Derik of the kidnapping.

Since Sharon was in prison, Devon had been placed with her parents. The rest of the Harrison family visited him regularly, but Derik refused to set foot in that house. Matthias particularly had become attached to all three of Deidrick's kids. Derik thought it was ironic because Matthias was adamant that he did not want any kids of his own.

Instead of going to see Devon, Derik went to lunch with Nicole. They had been dating for three months. At the beginning of the summer, the sparks were crazy between them. But as summer neared its end, it seemed like their relationship did too.

What Derik liked about Nicole was that she was a total sweetheart. She was always a shoulder to lean on and he did not have to constantly challenge everything he did like with Danielle. In a lot of ways, Nicole reminded Derik of her brother Ralph.

But that was also what was killing their relationship. Nicole was great at listening, but not that great at sharing. The few times he tried to have deeper conversations with her, she let him do all the talking and kept her thoughts to herself. It was so unlike his relationship with Danielle, who always said how she felt and challenged him as much as he did her.

Nicole also tended to get jealous very easily. And she had her friends too involved in their business. The one time they argued, Latasia looked at him crazy for a whole week. Nobody ever knew when he and Danielle had a fight.

What annoyed him most about Nicole was her lack of ambition. She had goals, but she always treated them like they were far off in the future. And if something seemed too hard to achieve, she would give up. Danielle fought for what she wanted.

And that was Derik's main problem with Nicole. She was not Danielle. Even though he had been the one to break up with her, he had not expected them to stay broken up. Derik had only really done it to teach her a lesson.

But in typical Danielle fashion, she turned things around on him and never came back to him. So, he tried Marcellus' approach of getting with another girl. And he regretted it. He regretted it even more because he knew Nicole was not the one for him, but he did not want to hurt her feelings.

However, he knew breaking up with her was better than leading her on. The day before, he had asked Derek for advice on how to break up with a girl and still remain friends. He wanted to do things right since his breakup with Danielle had been a fiery one. Derik recalled the conversation he had with his cousin.

They had been in his room watching a movie. At some point, Derik had dozed off. When he opened his eyes, it had taken him a few moments to register that he was still in Derek's room. Derek was next to him scrolling on his phone, and smiled at him when he noticed Derik was awake.

"Enjoy your nap?" asked Derek.

Derik realized he was lying against his cousin's shoulder and quickly scooted away.

"When did I fall asleep?" asked Derik.

"About halfway through the movie. I didn't notice till you started using my shoulder as a pillow."

"Why you ain't push me off?"

"Why would I do that?"

"Because what man lays up under another man?"

"Boy, you're my cousin," snorted Derek. "I don't care about you napping on my shoulder. Just as long as you don't start drooling all over me. If you do that, I'll have to chop you in your throat."

"Alright, kung-fu master," teased Derik, rolling his eyes. "I need to talk to you."

"What's up?"

"I need advice on how to break up with Nicole."

"You need advice... on how to break up... with your girlfriend?"

"Yes," said Derik. "I don't want it to be a big thing like with Danielle. I want us to stay friends."

"You plan to break up with your girlfriend and think y'all will stay friends?"

"You did it with your girlfriend."

"First of all, Adrianna broke up with me," corrected Derek. "And we only broke up out of necessity. There was an understanding that it was only temporary."

"How long is temporary? It's been over a year."

"It's however long it needs to be. The point is the situations aren't the same."

"Look, are you going to help me or not?"

Derek stared at Derik for a long time. Then, he sighed.

"Alright, pay attention," said Derek.

Derik and Nicole had lunch at the Flowerbud's food truck, where Derek worked that day. That way if things took a bad turn, Derek could swoop in to save his cousin. Derik picked a table in the shade, so they would not be under the hot sun. He knew how attitudes could flare up when amped up by intense heat.

"Nicki," said Derik when they were settled at a table.

"Yeah?" replied Nicole.

"I've got to talk to you."

"Okay."

"I don't know how to say this but...," started Derik. He trailed off and made the mistake of looking her in the eye. Nicole was listening intently like always. But her eyes told it all. She knew where he was going. "Nicki, I don't think we're meant for each other."

Nicole did not say anything at first. She nodded and took a bite of her sandwich.

"So, which one of us is going to tell Ralphie?" asked Nicole nonchalantly.

"What?" said Derik, a little shocked.

"What?" asked Nicole confusedly.

"I just told you we're breaking up and you're just like 'okay... anyways...'."

"Well Derik, to be honest... I already knew we weren't going to last."

"Seriously?"

"I'm serious. This turned into a fun summer fling. Except it became less fun as the summer went on."

"What do you mean by that?"

"What I mean is you suck at hiding how you feel," said Nicole. "I know you're not over Danielle. I was testing the waters to see if I had a real chance with you and the answer is a big, fat no."

"I uh...," said Derik, unsure what to say next. Even though he did not want to admit it, he knew Nicole was right.

"No need to say anything," said Nicole. "We can go back to being friends. But one of us is going to have to tell Ralphie."

"I'll tell him," said Derik. "But if you knew I wasn't over Danielle, why stay with me?"

"I don't know," said Nicole. "I guess I just figured you'd get over her eventually. But you never did."

"How's my favorite future brother-in-law?" asked Ralph when Derik went to work the next day.

"Uh about that...," said Derik. "Me and Nicki broke up."

Ralph stopped smiling.

"When?!"

"Uh, yesterday."

"Yesterday?!" cried Ralph. "What happened?!"

"We just decided it was best to go back to being friends."

"This is...," said Ralph. "This just ruined my day."

"Sorry?"

"Man, I was hoping y'all would last forever," sighed Ralph.

Derik did not know how to respond.

"I guess it is what it is," said Ralph, coming to terms with the breakup. "Mr. Arnold wants to see you. He said he had a special assignment for you."

Derik went to Mr. Arnold's office.

"Hello sir," said Derik. "Ralphie said you wanted to see me."

"Yes," said Mr. Arnold. "I have an assignment for you. I'm sure you're aware that Mayor Perry is the longest-serving mayor in this town."

Derik nodded, resisting the urge to say "unfortunately".

"I want to run a special interest piece about him and why he's been able to last so long," said Mr. Arnold. "Normally, I wouldn't assign something like this to family members because of conflict of interest. However, Ralphie and I are very busy with other sections of the paper, and Althea has her Miss Teen Creeke responsibilities. That leaves you. I trust that you will give me unbiased work."

"Yes sir," said Derik. "You can count on me."

Derik could have set up an interview with Mayor Perry to get his story. But he did not trust that Mayor Perry would tell the truth. He needed to do his own research to corroborate whatever Mayor Perry told him. First, he checked the public library newspaper archives. But all they had was information he already knew. The dates Mayor Perry served as mayor and the fact that after a while he ran unopposed. Derik wanted more.

He wanted to know how Mayor Perry had gained his wealth. And he wanted to know how he managed to keep getting re-elected by a town that mostly disliked him. What he wanted most was the full truth.

He started interviewing residents on their views on Mayor Perry. What he discovered was eye-opening. While a lot of the residents disliked Mayor Perry personally, they saw all that he accomplished as inspiring. Many continued to vote for him because he was a successful, smart Black man they could aspire to be like.

The residents' perspectives helped Derik understand how Mayor Perry maintained his position as mayor. His next step was to get Mayor Perry's side of things. But he would not just take what the man said. He would have to get creative.

"Mother, your parents have a library in their home, right?" asked Derik when he visited her at her salon.

"Yes," said Mrs. Harrison.

"Do you think it would have things like family history in it?"

"I'm not sure," said Mrs. Harrison thoughtfully. "Daddy was very particular about his library."

"Do you think he'd let me see it if I asked?"

"It would certainly be a first if he did," said Mrs. Harrison with a small sigh. She had not spoken with her parents in over a year, and it was something Derik knew made her sad. Mrs. Harrison had always wanted her parents' approval, but she could never get it no matter what she accomplished.

Derik, however, did not care if the Perrys liked him. That's why he had no qualms about devising a plan to infiltrate their house. And the best part about it was, it would not be anything illegal. All he had to do was tell Mayor Perry the truth, and say he wanted to stay the night, and he was in.

"You're staying with us overnight?" questioned Lady Sophia when he arrived at their home that Friday.

"Yes," answered Derik.

"Why?"

"I'm doing a special report over Mayor Perry."

"And that requires you to stay with us?"

"Yes."

Lady Sophia looked at him suspiciously. She was no doubt beautiful in her youth, as she was still good-looking at her current age. And Derik could see that his mother heavily resembled her, while Aunt Soriah took more after Mayor Perry. But despite her good looks, Lady Sophia was a very mean-spirited woman. Derik wondered if he could uncover why that was while he was there.

"I guess," said Lady Sophia unconvinced. She summoned the head butler and said, "Jack will show you to your room. And it better look the same way it does now when you leave."

"Of course," said Derik.

"This way sir," said Jack. Derik followed him through the house to the guest room. As they walked, Jack talked about how he had not seen Derik since he was a little kid.

But throughout the whole thing, something about Jack's face kept bothering him. He was not sure if maybe it was the angle, but he swore Jack's face seemed eerily familiar. Except it was not Jack's exact face that he was remembering. It was strange.

Derik got himself settled in and then he got to work. The library was more like a study, and it was located on the first floor. As he began to search through it, it became clear what he was looking for would not be there.

However, Mayor Perry had plenty of interesting reading material. There were many books about being a leader, politics, and royalty. But the one that caught Derik's attention was an old book about primogeniture. He remembered Allison saying Mayor Perry planned to leave everything to Marcellus, his oldest male heir. She wondered if that had any bearing on Lady Sophia trying to convince her to marry to "support the family".

"What are you doing in here?" demanded Lady Sophia.

"I was just looking through the library," said Derik.

"You don't just go snooping around in other people's houses!"

"I was just looking for something to read."

"All of you children are the same," complained Lady Sophia. "You're all disrespectful and all have a mouth on you. All of you, just like your mother."

"Do you know anything about primogeniture?" asked Derik.

"What?" questioned Lady Sophia.

"Primogeniture," repeated Derik. "The practice of leaving an inheritance to the oldest male heir."

"I know what it is," said Lady Sophia, rolling her eyes and waving her hand dismissively.

"I was just wondering," said Derik. "I heard Mayor Perry was doing something like that. Doesn't that mean you won't get anything?"

"Who are you to be in my business?!"

"I was just curious."

"Well, I think it's time you stop being curious! Get out of this room! Right now!"

"Is that why you want Allison to marry well?" asked Derik as she shooed him from the room.

"I don't have to explain myself to you!"

"I'm just curious because I want to know how that would work. How does Allison marrying well benefit you?

"Again, I don't have to explain myself to you."

Derik stopped pressing after that. He had come there looking for information to support whatever Mayor Perry told him in their interview. Instead, he felt he was on the verge of discovering something deeper.

When he had his interview with Mayor Perry, Derik tried his best to get all the information he could. Mayor Perry claimed his wealth came from his car dealerships and his investments. As far as his time as mayor, he said that nobody opposed him because nobody could do a better job than him. He was very confident, but Derik could see he was also very conceited.

In the middle of the night, Derik was having trouble sleeping. So, he decided to go exploring. It was easy for him to explain why Mayor Perry would do something like primogeniture. Mayor Perry was all about himself and considered himself royalty, so he copied what royalty did. But there were so many questions that Derik had.

He wondered why Mayor Perry remained with Lady Sophia. Historically when a wife did not provide a male heir, the man got rid of her. And yet, Mayor Perry had not done that. That had allowed Lady Sophia to orchestrate her own marriage schemes for her daughters.

Derik also wondered why Mr. Jack was still employed. They had no problem firing Mrs. Ernestine and replacing her with someone younger. But Mr. Jack was still there. And he could not understand why Mr. Jack's face bothered him.

On his way to the library, Derik decided to stop in his mother's old room. All her accomplishments were available for all to see. Her portrait smiled down at him. The green dress she wore in it created a striking contrast against her dark-brown skin. She would have been around the same age he was when it was painted.

Aunt Soriah's room was a little barer. She did not have as many accomplishments as Mrs. Harrison. And her portrait was not as interesting to look at, due mostly to her medium-brown skin nearly blending in with her dress.

Derik was almost to the library when he came across a photo of Mayor Perry. It was a side profile from when he was a bit younger. That's when Derik saw it. He wondered how he had not seen it sooner. The answer to all his questions was literally on the side of Mayor Perry's head. But Derik decided to wait until he had more solid proof before he acted on anything.

The next day, Derik returned to his mother with a new list of questions.

"Mother, how far apart are your father and Mr. Jack in age?" asked Derik.

"I think four years," said Mrs. Harrison.

"And Mr. Jack grew up here in Creeke, right?"

"Yes."

"How long has he been working for your father?"

"Since before I was born," said Mrs. Harrison. "I'm pretty sure he was the first person Daddy hired. Why all the sudden interest in Mr. Jack?"

"I just wanted to know more about him. Has your father ever had any affairs?"

"I don't think that's any of your business," said Mrs. Harrison sternly. "And I hope you're not planning to write anything defamatory about my father in your article on him. I thought it was supposed to be celebrating his accomplishments."

"It's talking about his journey and accomplishments," corrected Derik. "But I was just curious because I wanted to know why he stayed married to your mother. It doesn't line up with anything that he's trying to copy from royalty."

"What are you saying?"

"There are things about your parents that don't make sense," said Derik. "Your father is trying to live like royalty, and yet he keeps his wife who didn't give him a male heir, and he keeps an old butler even though he's been known to replace people for younger people. That makes me wonder what they have on him."

"I don't know what they have on him, but I do know what I have on you," said Mrs. Harrison. "And that's being your mother. I suggest you stop meddling in other people's affairs and stick to what you're supposed to be doing."

After that, Derik hit a wall. And the only way to break the wall was to get somebody to break and start revealing information. So, Derik would have to play his hand a bit and force a break.

But before he could do that, he had to focus on his own affairs as his mother said. Derik finished his article and turned it in for review. Then, he went down to the creek to relax for a bit. There were a few people having a good time when he got there. And one of them was Danielle.

She was sitting in one of the chairs by the water, lost in thought. And she was looking as good as she always did. Derik licked his lips as he approached her.

"Well, well, well," said Derik. "If it ain't Miss Danielle Lee."

"Oh boy," snorted Danielle when she saw him. "Won't your girlfriend get mad seeing you talking to me?"

"I ain't got a girlfriend."

"Oh really?" said Danielle. "When'd that happen?"

"A few days ago."

"Tough."

"Eh, it was for the best. I couldn't help but notice you sitting here all alone, looking good like you usually do."

"Oh my gosh!" laughed Danielle. "You just got out of a relationship and you're already flirting with someone else?"

"To be fair, it wasn't that serious of a relationship. Not like ours was."

"What are you trying to say?"

"I was just wondering if you'd let me take you on a date some time."

Danielle eyed Derik with a smirk on her face. Then she started laughing.

"You know what?" said Danielle, still laughing. "Sure. You can take me on a date."

"Cool," said Derik. "You won't be disappointed."

Derik learned that while he was staying with the Perrys, Deidrick had had his own little drama going on. Typically, whenever he had a visit with one of his kids, he would do so at Granddad Derrick and Nanna Kiana's house. However, that weekend, he chose to have Bianca visit him at the apartment he shared with Carmen. That ended up being a huge mistake. Esperanza and Carmen had gotten into it because Esperanza felt like Carmen was being disrespectful to her.

"And I'll bet you just loved watching them fight over you," said Matthias sarcastically when he and Deidrick visited him. Matthias had moved to an apartment in the city with his best friend, Alexander Brown.

"Hey man, I can't help it that I've got females ready to brawl over me," said Deidrick.

"These aren't just females, Cornbread," said Matthias. "These are the mothers of your children. You shouldn't be encouraging all this drama between them. You should be trying to make it to where all your children can get along and be siblings."

"I'm not doing anything," said Deidrick. "I tried to have Bianca and Car'drick together. It's not my fault they're mamis can't get along."

"It kind of is your fault though," said Matthias. "You cheated on Espe with Carmen. That's why they don't like each other."

"That's all in the past," said Deidrick.

"Look, I just think you could be doing a better job of keeping the peace for your kids," said Matthias.

"Alright Dad, whatever you say," said Deidrick, leaving the room.

"Good grief," muttered Matthias.

"I think it's ironic how you don't want kids, but you care more about Cornbread's kids than he does," said Derik.

"They're still my niece and nephews," said Matthias. "Someone's got to care about them."

"True," said Derik. "Can I ask you something?"

"Go ahead."

"Do you have one that you like more than the others?"

"Like do I have a favorite among his kids?"

"Yeah?"

"No," said Matthias. "I treat them all the same."

"There isn't one you're always more excited to see?"

"Nope."

"What about one you don't like? Is there one you like less than the others?"

"If I don't have a favorite, what makes you think I have a least favorite?"

"I was just asking."

"Well, I don't."

Derik wished he could have been the same way. He wished he could treat all of Deidrick's kids the same and not care who their mothers were. But that was not the case. And with the revelation Derik believed he had at the Perrys', he wondered if it was generational through his mother's family.

He unfortunately was less enthusiastic about seeing Devon. And depending on the parent, there was a point when he and all his siblings had felt like the least favorite. Mrs. Harrison was clearly not the favorite because she had a more independent spirit. If Derik was right in what he had perceived, then it went back further. The only way to find out though was to finally get a definite answer. So, that Tuesday, he went back to see Mayor Perry.

"I see you published your special piece on me in the paper," said Mayor Perry. "I think it came out great."

"Thank you," said Derik.

"So, what did you want to see me about today?"

"I'd like to make some changes to your will," said Derik. He knew the only way to get information from Mayor Perry was to speak his language.

"Excuse me?" said Mayor Perry.

"I'd like to make some changes to your will," said Derik. "Unless of course you want everyone to know your secret."

"What secret?"

"How about the fact that you're not an only child like everyone believes?"

Mayor Perry's smirk dropped. His eyes became serious as he stared at Derik.

"The resemblance is just faint enough that you won't see it right away," said Derik coyly. "But if you look close enough from the side you start to see it. Then you start to put pieces together. Different last names from different mothers. Four-year age difference. Maybe he doesn't know who he is. Or maybe he knows not to bite the hand that's been feeding him all this time."

It was Derik's turn to smirk. Based on Mayor Perry's reaction his theory had been correct.

"But I'm not being fed by that hand," said Derik. "I haven't told anyone of course. He doesn't even know that I know. And it'll stay that way if you cooperate."

"If I cooperate?" repeated Mayor Perry.

"Yes," said Derik.

Again, Mayor Perry stared at Derik. Then, he called Mr. Jack into the study.

"Sir?" said Mr. Jack.

"Have a seat, Jack," said Mayor Perry. "I need to talk to you about something."

"Have I done something wrong, sir?"

"No," said Mayor Perry. He motioned to Derik and said, "You know Derik?"

"Yes sir," said Mr. Jack with a smile.

"He's trying to blackmail me with some information about you."

"Me?!" cried Mr. Jack. "Sir, I–!"

"Calm down," said Mayor Perry. Mr. Jack sat back nervously. "Now Jack, during all the years you've worked for me, I've taken good care of you."

"I know, Sir," said Mr. Jack. "And I've never complained! I've–!"

"I know," interrupted Mayor Perry. "But still, you must wonder why I've done all of this for you."

Mr. Jack sat listening intently. Derik also waited, wondering if Mayor Perry would really go there.

"Remember when you told me about your father?" said Mayor Perry. "How he visited you when you were young, but you don't remember for sure who he was?"

"Yes sir," said Mr. Jack quietly.

"Well, I know who he was."

"You do?!" gasped Mr. Jack. "You know who my father is?!"

"Was," corrected Mayor Perry. "He's dead."

Mr. Jack stared with silent anticipation.

"Your father was my father."

Mr. Jack blinked. Then he sunk in his chair.

"Sir, if this is your idea of a joke it's not very funny," said Mr. Jack sulkily.

"I'm not lying," said Mayor Perry. "We had the same father. His dying wish was that I look out for you."

Derik could not believe it. Mayor Perry had really said it. Mr. Jack was his younger brother whom he was taking care of. That explained why he had kept Mr. Jack around for so many years.

"The three of us are the only ones who know about this," said Mayor Perry. "Derik wants to reveal this to everyone because he wants something from me. Jack, you've always been the most loyal to me here in this house. And I hope I can count on that loyalty now more than ever. Because if this information is ever made public by anyone other than me, I will no longer be able to take care of you."

"You mean no one can know about this?" whispered Mr. Jack.

"No one but the men in this room," said Mayor Perry. "I promised our father I'd take care of you and I've done that. And as long as you keep this to yourself, I will continue to."

"Yes sir," said Mr. Jack. "Should I still call you sir?"

"Yes Jack," said Mayor Perry. "It'll help with avoiding confusion. You can go back to work."

"Yes sir," said Mr. Jack, exiting the room with a dazed expression.

"You know what, I'll give it to you," said Mayor Perry, looking at Derik curiously. "You are your mother's son. But she's a lot better at manipulating than you are. Did you really think that would work?"

Mayor Perry laughed.

"You can't out-hustle a hustler," said Mayor Perry. "You'll have to do a lot better than that to get me to change my will. And if anything, you've given Jack even more of a reason to be loyal to me."

Mayor Perry continued laughing as Derik left. But Derik was not disappointed because he had gotten what he came for. On his way out, he found Mr. Jack arranging the dining room.

"Mr. Jack?" said Derik. "Are you okay?"

"I'm great," said Mr. Jack. "I never thought my father was Bernard's father. My mama always told me my father was dead."

"What if Mayor Perry doesn't keep his word though?" asked Derik. "What if he gets rid of you?"

"He won't," said Mr. Jack with a wink. He dropped his voice to a whisper and said, "I have my own little insurance to make sure that doesn't happen."

Derik's eyes widened. He realized then that everyone in the Perry household was a schemer. It seemed like the only way to be to survive in that place.

After meeting with Mayor Perry, Derik returned home. He knew he should keep what he learned to himself. But he felt it was right that his mother knew the truth.

"Mother, I've got to tell you something and you can't tell anyone," said Derik.

"What is it?" asked Mrs. Harrison.

"You've got to promise not to say anything to anyone," said Derik. "Mr. Jack's whole life depends on this."

"If it's that important, should you be telling me?"

"Yes. Do you promise?"

"It depends on what it is."

"Mr. Jack is your uncle. He's your father's brother."

"That would explain a lot. How'd you find this out?"

"I asked Mayor Perry."

"And he just told you, just like that?"

"Well, not exactly. I tried to blackmail him with the information."

"Tried?"

"I didn't succeed. He spun it and told Jack himself."

"Oh," said Mrs. Harrison. "I can't even say anything because I've blackmailed him too. I succeeded though."

"He told me," said Derik. "Now, do you promise not to tell anyone?"

"I'm telling your Aunt Soriah, but other than that, I won't say any-thing."

"I guess that's fair."

"What were you trying to get from him?"

"I told him I wanted to change his will," said Derik. "But honestly, I just want the truth about everything. I want to know why he wants to leave everything to Cell. And I want to know why your mother keeps trying to marry the girls off to rich men."

"I can't explain Daddy but I know Mother married us off the way she did because of Daddy leaving everything to Marcellus. Your Uncle Quincy had a promising career at the time, and now he's a successful real estate agent."

"And you?"

"I married your father because I loved him. But Daddy also saw it as an opportunity to get in good with your grandfather."

"And Allison?"

Mrs. Harrison frowned. It was clear she knew the answer but did not want to say it.

"Mother?" said Derik.

"Mother believes...," began Mrs. Harrison. "Mother believes that if she can get Allison to marry well, then I can use that money to take care of her. It's the same reason she used to convince your aunt to stay with your uncle after he started cheating."

"That's...," said Derik. "You wouldn't do that though. Right?"

"I've asked myself that question," admitted Mrs. Harrison. "But the truth is I don't know. She's still my mother after all. And if she needs help, then I'm going to help her."

"Even if it means forcing Allison to marry a man for money?"

"I'm not going that far," said Mrs. Harrison. "Allison can marry whatever man she wants, and she can do whatever she wants with her life. All I'm saying is, I won't let my mother struggle if I can make sure she doesn't have to."

That Friday, Derik and Danielle went out to eat in the city.

"How's life been?" asked Derik.

"It's been life," said Danielle.

"Oh," said Derik. "How are things with your dad?"

"Things are... things."

"Things?" repeated Derik.

"Yeah...," said Danielle quietly.

"Does he still talk to his family?"

"Yeah."

"Do you still dislike his mom?"

"She's alright," said Danielle. "I still think she should've come back earlier though."

"Hm."

"What about you?" asked Danielle. "How have things been in your life?"

"Things have been... things."

"Hm."

Things got quiet between them.

"So, what happened between you and Nicki?" asked Danielle.

"Nothing," said Derik. "We just thought we worked better as friends."

"So, y'all are still friends?"

"Yeah."

"Hmm."

"Is that a problem?"

"No, I just... things between y'all are for sure over?"

"Things never really even got started. It was more like a fling than a relationship."

"Oh?"

Derik looked at Danielle.

"I'll be honest," said Derik. "When we broke up, I didn't think we'd stay broken up."

"What'd you think was going to happen?" asked Danielle.

"I thought you'd realize I was right and come back to me."

"See, that's where you messed up," laughed Danielle. "I don't chase guys. Guys chase me."

"What guys were chasing you?" questioned Derik.

"That's none of your business because you're not my man," said Danielle.

"Oh really?" snorted Derik. When Danielle shrugged, Derik said, "What if I wanted to change that?"

"I wouldn't mind," said Danielle. "But I think you'd see very quickly I'm not the same girl I was last year."

"That's alright, because I'm not the same boy I was last year."

By the middle of August, Derik had gotten back together with Danielle. And their relationship was going a lot smoother than the first time around. There was not as much friction or as many arguments.

However, Derik was experiencing a different problem dating Danielle. And that problem was he was young and getting ready to go to college. He was not sure if he wanted to be in a committed relationship while he was at school. While he liked Danielle, he wondered whether she would still be the one once he got around college women.

The only person he knew who had experience with this kind of thing was Deidrick. However, Deidrick did not have the best dating track record and still seemed to be searching for the one. Deidrick did, however, seem to be happy with Carmen. Derik, like most of his family, did not like her because she was divisive. But no matter what anyone said to him, Deidrick did not care. He was all about Carmen.

One Saturday, Derik got a call from Deidrick.

"Hello?" said Derik.

"Bro, I need a favor," said Deidrick.

"What?" questioned Derik.

"I need you to go pick up Vonnie for me."

It took Derik a second to process what he had just been asked to do.

"You want me... to go over there?"

"Matty was supposed scoop him but something came up, and Queenie's at work. You're the only one I can ask."

"Why can't you do it?"

"Bro, I'm doing something right now. Please do this for me. I'll owe you one."

Derik reluctantly agreed to do it. He sat in the Pierces' driveway for a long time, building himself up to go in there. And when he finally did, the Pierces were shocked to see him. They had a mix of pity, fear, and shame in their eyes.

Derik knew it was not their fault for what their daughter did to him. But his heart would not get with the program. And that feeling intensified when he laid eyes on Devon. All he felt was apathetic looking at the baby that had been forced into his life.

He wondered if that was how his father felt when he looked at them. Mr. Harrison had not wanted any kids, and he had always been emotionally distant as a father. Derik wondered if his father felt nothing toward them because he had no emotional connection to them like Derik had no emotional connection to Devon.

After picking up Devon, Derik tried calling Deidrick so he would know what to do with him. But Deidrick did not answer. After a few more tries, he gave up and called Matthias.

"Hello?" said Matthias.

"Do you know where Cornbread is?" asked Derik. "I can't get in touch with him, and I have his baby."

"I know," said Matthias. "I'm with him right now. Something happened."

"What?" asked Derik. "Is he okay?"

"He's f –! CORNBREAD NO!"

"I DON'T CARE!" hollered Deidrick in the background. "THIS IS WHAT SHE DESERVES!"

"I got to go," said Matthias quickly. "Take care of Vonnie till we get there."

Matthias hung up. Derik did not know what to do. He did not know how to take care of a baby and everyone who did was unavailable. So, he called the one person he hoped could help.

"Hello?" said Marcellus.

"I need help," said Derik. "Do you know anything about taking care of a baby?"

"Uh... no...," said Marcellus. "Why do you need help with a baby? You got a baby?"

"I have Cornbread's baby and he wants me to hang onto him until he gets back."

"Bring him over here then, I guess."

Derik took Devon to Marcellus' house. And while Marcellus was absolutely hopeless as a caretaker, he was at least nurturing. He played with Devon and did his best to keep him happy. Derik wondered why he was the only one who could not feel anything toward Devon. Thankfully, Devon did not require much while in the care of Marcellus.

"Seems like he likes you," said Derik.

"I guess," said Marcellus as he rocked Devon in his arms. "This isn't so hard. I could do this."

"Did you think you couldn't?"

"Honestly man, I don't know," said Marcellus. "Ever since I hit my mid-twenties, I've just been feeling like I'm slowing down."

"Slowing down?"

"I don't know how to explain it," said Marcellus. "I've just had a lot to think about this past year. Me, losing my job was a mess. But now I'm like do I even want to go back to doing that or do I want to do something different. Especially now that I'm with Beverly. She's got her nice job at the bank while I feel like I'm just sitting around doing nothing. I don't like that. And then I just like being with her. It's like no other girl interests me anymore. She could be the one for me for real."

"Does she know about your inheritance?" asked Derik.

"I haven't told her yet," said Marcellus. "I don't want her to be with me because of the money I'm supposed to get."

"You want her to like you for you."

"I guess you can say it like that."

"Have you ever thought about what you'd do with the money?"

"Not really."

"Are you going to share it with us or keep it for yourself?" joked Derik.

"It seems like everyone's already decided they're getting a cut of it," said Marcellus, his face darkening. "Sometimes I feel like that's all the family sees me as. Their ticket to Pawpaw's money."

"Pawpaw?"

"Pawpaw Bernard."

"You call him Pawpaw?"

"Yeah. Don't you?"

"No. I call him Mayor Perry."

"What?" snorted Marcellus. "Why?"

"That man isn't my grandfather," said Derik. "I don't like him."

"To each his own," said Marcellus with a shrug.

"Have you ever been with a girl but wondered if things would last?"

"Yeah."

"What did you do?"

"Well, I was in my younger years, so I went exploring."

"Was it worth it?"

"Never."

"Oh."

Matthias returned with Deidrick that night. Deidrick went straight into the kitchen and returned with a beer.

"You want your baby?" asked Derik.

"Yeah, give him here," said Deidrick.

He balanced Devon on his leg with one hand while using the other to drink his beer. It was such an interesting visual that Derik took a picture.

"You look like crap," said Marcellus. "What happened?"

"Carmen cheated on me bro!" hollered Deidrick, causing Devon to cry. Matthias took the baby from his brother and started soothing him.

"She cheated on you?" answered Marcellus.

"Yeah! With her ex! I walked in on them bro! She had him in my bed bro!"

"Dang," said Marcellus. "That's messed up."

"Yeah bro," said Deidrick. "But that's alright. I taught them both a lesson."

"What'd you do?"

"I beat that man up!" said Deidrick proudly. "And since she want to play with me, I took all the stuff I bought her. And whatever I couldn't take, I made sure she couldn't have it either."

"You tore her place up?" asked Marcellus.

"Bro, she needs to be glad that's all I did," said Deidrick. "Mr. Nice Guy over here kept trying to stop me."

"Because you shouldn't be tearing up the place where your kid stays," said Matthias.

"You should sue her for full custody of your kid," said Marcellus.

"And put all that extra work on myself to feed him?" snorted Deidrick. "She can keep that brat."

"He's not a brat," said Matthias sharply.

"I'm just saying, she might fill his head with lies and turn him against you," said Marcellus.

"I don't care what she does," said Deidrick. He leaned his head back against the couch and said, "I'm the best daddy in the world to these brats and one day they'll all be thanking me."

Something in Derik shivered at Deidrick's words. They sounded like something his father would say. It was strange. Matthias was closer to Mr. Harrison in personality, yet he was a better father figure than Deidrick and Mr. Harrison. Meanwhile, Deidrick was almost the opposite of Mr. Harrison in personality but was turning out to be a similar type of father. Derik wondered how he would turn out. He wondered if he would be like Mr. Harrison or completely opposite, or maybe even somewhere in the middle.

By the end of summer, Derik was perplexed. He had discovered a generational curse, gotten his girlfriend back, and even gotten a better understanding of his father. But all his emotions felt off.

Derik felt very all over the place. And it was starting to show in his relationship. He and Danielle had only been dating for a short time, but he felt not fully committed to the relationship. There were many things he needed to figure out, and he did not know if being in a relationship was right for him then.

At the same time, he did not want to run the risk of losing Danielle again. He had foolishly allowed her to walk away once and he did not want to do so again. But it seemed like there was a hidden side to him that wanted to see what he could get away with with her.

Danielle had changed but not completely. She was not as mean or ruthless as she was before. But the traits he liked about her seemed to have gotten stronger. Her confidence was higher, her ambition was stronger, and her honesty was not brutal anymore. To him, it seemed like Danielle had really worked hard to grow from who she was before.

But sometimes the old Danielle would still show up, like the week before he left for school. The two of them had gone shopping for college supplies and had stopped to get lunch. While they were eating, Derik was caught off guard by a girl wearing the shortest shorts he had ever seen. And his eyes followed her as she walked past them.

"Really?" asked Danielle. "Just right in my face, huh?"

"What?" said Derik with a smirk. He recognized this as an opportunity to mess with Danielle and took it. "I stare at you the same way."

"Is that supposed to make me feel better?"

"Did it?"

"No. You just admitted to checking out other girls."

"I'm a writer. It's my job to observe."

"And what about that girl did you observe that would help you in your writing?"

"You'll find out when you read it."

"Why did you even bother getting back together with me?"

"Because I wanted to give us another shot."

"That's what you said. But you don't act like you're serious about me."

"All because I stared at another girl for a few seconds?"

"Yeah. You're not as emotionally connected like you were when we first dated. It's like you're just with me until someone better comes along."

"If that were the case, I'd just be single."

"Well, if you keep it up you will be."

"If that's how you feel then I'll go get that girl's number."

"If you want to chase after other girls go ahead. But don't expect me to be here waiting for you when you come back."

Derik got up and walked away. He was not really going to get the girl's number. He just wanted to prove a point to Danielle that she could not control him and what he chose to do. But Danielle apparently had a point to prove to him too because when he came back, she was gone.

PART 3:

IN THE LAST DAYS OF INNOCENCE

Samiel Dow Jr.

It felt like Samiel had just graduated from high school. And yet, he was already twenty years old and graduating from college. He was receiving his associate's degree. After that, he would attend university to get his bachelor's degree in psychology. Then after that, he would be a full-fledged adult.

He remembered how unsure he felt graduating from high school, and he felt even more unsure graduating from community college. But the good thing was he had his whole family around him to support him. Samantha had bought a condo in the city and Kasey was living with her in his own separate room. They had resumed dating, and Samantha hoped there would be no more breakups.

Samantha was also helping Kasey get his record expunged. He had not been able to do it because he could not afford it. But he finally caved and let Samantha handle it because he wanted access to better jobs. Samiel was glad to have them both in his life and was glad they had worked out their differences. He had decided to attend university in the city to stay close to everyone.

Samantha had gone to visit her parents in Atlanta. And she was bringing them back to Creeke for the graduation. It would be Samiel's first time ever meeting them. But he was not as nervous as he was when he met Samantha. She told him her parents were more than ready to meet and get to know him, and he was too.

He wondered what they were like. If they were sweet grandparents that would spoil him like Granny Elaine and Granddaddy Henry used to. Or if they would be more strict and stern grandparents like Papa Lawrence and Grandma Eula.

Samiel low-key wished they would be like his maternal grandparents. But he would not complain if they were like his paternal grandparents.

All that truly mattered to him was that they were kind and accepting of him.

The day before Samantha and her parents were due to fly in, Samiel hung out with his boys. Benjamin was halfway to earning his degree in communications. Derek, however, had decided to not return to college and continued working at Flowerbud's.

"What's it been like working at Flowerbud's?" asked Samiel. "You've already been there a year."

"It's been cool," said Derek. "He hired Prissy. He's hoping he'll be able to hire more people one day. Mrs. G also comes and helps sometimes."

"She really hit the jackpot with him," laughed Benjamin. "He comes from a rich family, he's got his own business, and he's a nice person."

"Mrs. G isn't like that," said Derek. "And neither is Mr. B. They really do love each other. And he never brags about being from a rich family."

"He probably doesn't even think about it to brag about it," snorted Samiel.

"Y'all leave Mr. B alone," chided Derek. "His cousin Mr. Will is always down here teasing him."

"I swear his cousin only comes down here because he's trying to find himself a Black queen," laughed Samiel.

"Maybe," said Derek. "All the men in that family love our women. But Mr. Will's a cool guy."

"Speaking of love," said Benjamin. "What's up with you and Adrianna? You guys going to get back together yet?"

"I don't know," said Derek with a shrug. "She's going to the same college Andre goes to. She made it on the dance team there."

"That's not surprising," said Benjamin. "She was captain of the dance team here this past year."

"Yeah," said Derek.

"You sure you don't want to see where things are at with her?" asked Benjamin. "It's a lot of guys at college for a girl to choose from."

"I'm alright," said Derek. "I'm really just focusing on me right now."

Samiel could tell Derek still had a hard time talking about dance. Losing that as a career option had left his best friend in a confusing place. He himself was in a similar confusing place. Choosing psychology as a major was due to needing to declare a major for university. But the truth was, Samiel was still unsure about his future and what he wanted to do. His only hope was that he would have it figured out by his next graduation.

The next day, Samiel and Kasey spent the whole morning cleaning up the condo. Samantha and her parents would be flying in that afternoon, and Kasey wanted the place ready for them. One thing Samiel had come to learn about Kasey was that he was a meticulous cleaner. He liked things organized a certain way, even if they did not make sense to anyone but him.

"I finished making the beds," said Samiel, coming out of the room Samantha's parents would sleep in.

"Alright," said Kasey. He assigned Samiel to sweep the floors next and went to inspect. "Boy, you call this making a bed?"

"Yes?"

"My parents would've whooped you for this," laughed Kasey. "Let me fix this for you."

That was another thing Samiel had learned about Kasey over time. Whenever Samiel did something poorly, Kasey would tell how his parents would have disciplined him for it. The more Samiel heard about Kasey's childhood, the more he disliked Kasey's parents. They always seemed harsh and critical based on how Kasey described them. Samiel hoped Samantha's parents were not like that. She always spoke highly of them, but Samiel figured it was because they were her parents. So, he decided to get a second opinion on them.

"What are Samantha's parents like?" asked Samiel when Kasey came back into the living room.

"They're... like her honestly," answered Kasey. "Unfortunately, I didn't make the greatest first impression when I met them but it is what it is."

"What happened?"

"The fight," said Kasey.

"The really bad one you got locked up for?"

"Yeah. They don't think I'm the right guy for her."

"You didn't think you were the right guy for her either."

"That's different. I didn't want us in a relationship until I got myself together. They just don't want us together at all."

"Are you going to be alright while they're staying here?"

"I'm going to have to. I ain't got nowhere else to go."

Kasey's cell phone rang. It was Samantha, calling to let him know they had landed and were on the way from the airport.

"And the fun begins," sighed Kasey. "One thing before they get here."

"Shoot," said Samiel.

"You're going to have to call me Mr. Kasey, and if I say something to you, you're going to have to say, 'yes sir'," said Kasey annoyedly. "The same goes for Sammie. Her parents are super old-school and I'm not about to fight with them over how you address us."

"Okay," said Samiel.

"You can't say okay or yes or yeah either," said Kasey. "Start practicing now."

"Yes sir...," said Samiel awkwardly. It felt weird calling Kasey 'sir'. Especially because Kasey hated to be referred to as 'sir' because his parents would smack him whenever he did not say 'sir' or 'ma'am'.

Samiel decided not to bring up Samantha's parents after that. But it was like trying to avoid a huge elephant in the room. The fact of the matter was her parents were on their way. And Samiel felt like he was entering a tense situation where he would have to take sides. He hoped it would not come to that.

Almost an hour later, Samantha and her parents arrived at the condo. Samiel and Kasey waited near the door, ready to greet them. Or at least, Samiel was waiting to greet them. Kasey seemed like he was posted up, waiting for a fight to start.

The first person through the door was Samantha. Samiel thought she was rushing to hug them after being gone for two weeks. Instead, she flung her suitcase to the side and rushed past his open arms, to the bathroom.

"Sorry!" called Samantha through the door. "I had to go! I was *not* using that airport bathroom!"

"Where's your parents?" asked Kasey.

"Getting the bags! I told them you'd get them but you know how they are!"

"I do," grumbled Kasey. He motioned for Samiel to follow him and said, "Come on."

Samiel followed Kasey outside to the driveway. The woman saw them first.

"Oh Lord!" cried Mrs. Wallace, clutching her chest. "Kasey, why would you sneak up on us like that?! Lord, you look so different I almost didn't recognize you!"

"Hello, Mrs. Wallace," said Kasey.

"You sure have been eating good," joked Mrs. Wallace. "You done put on a little weight since the last time I saw you. Hasn't he, Dennis?"

"I guess," said Mr. Wallace. "You just going to watch me work or you going to help me with these bags?"

"That's what I came out here to do, sir," said Kasey.

"Uh huh," uttered Mr. Wallace. Samiel could already tell Mr. Wallace would be hard to get along with.

"And who is this nice young man you have with you?" asked Mrs. Wallace, noticing Samiel.

"That's Sami, your grandson," said Kasey nonchalantly while carrying the suitcases to the house.

The Wallaces stared at Samiel.

"This is Sami?" whispered Mrs. Wallace. She touched Samiel's shoulder, almost like she did not believe he was in front of her.

Then, Mrs. Wallace started crying.

"Are you okay?" asked Samiel worriedly.

"I'm fine," said Mrs. Wallace, wiping her face. "I'm just so happy. We've been waiting for this day for a long time."

Mrs. Wallace hugged Samiel. Then Mr. Wallace shook Samiel's hand excitedly.

"Good to meet you, son," said Mr. Wallace, pumping Samiel's hand. The change in his demeanor had taken Samiel by surprise. "I can see now you got all my good looks."

"Yes sir," said Samiel.

"We've heard so much about you from Samantha," said Mrs. Wallace. "But she didn't tell us how handsome you were."

"Thank you," said Samiel, blushing.

"My name is Janice, I'm your grandmother," said Mrs. Wallace. "You can call me Mawmaw. This is your grandfather, Dennis."

"You can call me Pawpaw," said Mr. Wallace proudly.

"Oka-!" said Samiel, before catching himself. "Yes ma'am, yes sir."

"I can see you were raised right," said Mrs. Wallace. "Such a respectful, handsome young man. If only we'd been around to be part of raising you."

Samiel walked the Wallaces into the condo. They commented on how nicely decorated and clean it was and tried to give Samantha all the credit. Samantha, however, made it clear that Kasey was responsible for how clean it was. And they were both equally responsible for decorating it.

Throughout the day, Samiel better understood why Kasey was ambivalent about the Wallaces. They were nice people, but they also clearly did not think much of Kasey. Especially Mr. Wallace. He constantly gave Kasey disapproving looks, which made it hard for Samiel to connect with him.

"Tomorrow, we're going to visit Sami's parents," said Samantha.

"I thought you were Sami's parents," said Mrs. Wallace. She phrased it like a joke, but it was one Samiel did not appreciate.

"His *adoptive* parents," said Samantha, shooting Samiel an apologetic look.

"I just call them his parents," said Kasey. "They raised him after all. And that's who he calls Mom and Dad."

"I know that," said Mrs. Wallace. "I was just making a joke."

"Mama, I don't think you should make those type of jokes."

"You two have no sense of humor," said Mrs. Wallace, shaking her head.

"So Kasey," said Mr. Wallace. "You said you have a job at a factory now?"

"Yes sir," said Kasey. "We'll drive past it on our way to Creeke tomorrow."

"Hm," said Mr. Wallace, with a seemingly approving nod. It was the first sign of approval he had shown Kasey all evening.

"So, what do your adoptive parents do?" asked Mrs. Wallace.

"My dad used to be a police officer," said Samiel.

"Used to be?" questioned Mr. Wallace. "Did he retire?"

"The department closed down," explained Samiel.

"It closed?" repeated Mr. Wallace. "I didn't know police departments could close."

"Well, ours did."

"Interesting," said Mrs. Wallace. "And your adoptive mother? What does she do?"

"She's the vice principal of our high school," said Samiel.

"Vice principal!" said Mrs. Wallace, astonished. "No wonder you're so well-behaved. Being raised by a cop and a vice principal. You know we used to be teachers."

"You did?" asked Samiel.

"Mhmm," said Mrs. Wallace. "I taught English and Dennis taught History."

"You like history?" asked Samiel.

"Love history," said Mr. Wallace. "You can't understand the present if you don't understand how we got here. History also helps you identify how things are more likely to turn out."

He looked at Kasey when he said the last sentence. Kasey shrugged and nodded. As it got closer to the time for Samiel to go home, Kasey seemed to withdraw more and more from the conversation.

"I should get going before it gets too dark," said Samiel. "It was nice meeting you both."

"It was nice meeting you too," said Mrs. Wallace. "I hope we get to spend more time together this weekend."

"We will," said Samiel. "I'll see you both tomorrow."

"I'll walk you out," said Kasey.

Neither Kasey nor Samiel said anything until they had reached Samiel's car.

"You didn't say very much back there," said Samiel. "Are you okay?"

"I'm cool," said Kasey. "I was just chilling."

"They seem like nice people."

"Never said they weren't."

There was a pause in the conversation. Samiel hesitated to get in the car. He had more that he wanted to say about the Wallaces, but he was not sure if he should say it.

"What's up?" asked Kasey.

"I just...," said Samiel. "I want to like them."

"But?"

"But... they keep saying slick stuff."

"Yeah, they're like that," said Kasey.

"Why though?"

"Mr. Wallace is just being a dad," said Kasey. "He's just wants to be sure I'm not a crackhead that's going to ruin his daughter's life."

"You're not though."

"We know that. Sammie knows that. But they're not convinced yet."

"But what about Mrs. Wallace?"

"I think she's just disappointed she missed out on your life honestly," said Kasey. "She probably blames me for that too."

"How's that your fault though?"

"Got her daughter pregnant, was locked up during the birth, made it to where we couldn't have no contact with you for eighteen years."

"All that matters is you're here now. All of you."

"Again, we're not tripping. They just need time to come to terms with everything. Don't worry about them saying slick stuff. It ain't hurting no one's feelings. Just focus on getting to know them."

The next day Kasey, Samantha, and the Wallaces came to the Dow household. Mr. and Mrs. Dow welcomed everyone with open arms and did their best to provide a comfortable atmosphere. Things started out great as everyone got to know everyone.

"You were a beauty queen?" asked Mrs. Wallace, looking at Mrs. Dow's old picture on the wall.

"Yes ma'am," said Mrs. Dow. "I was crowned Miss Teen Creeke when I was eighteen."

"I always wanted to do a beauty contest," said Mrs. Wallace. "I tried to get Samantha to do them, but she wanted to play basketball instead."

"I didn't know you played basketball," said Mrs. Dow to Samantha.

"Girl, I tried," laughed Samantha. "I spent more time on the bench than I did the court. I would've been better off being a cheerleader."

"Cheer is not for the weak," said Mrs. Dow. "Lala will tell you. Ain't that right, Lala?"

"Yes," said Latasia. "I have no regrets about not doing it in college."

"Were both your daughters were cheerleaders?" asked Mrs. Wallace.

"Only Latasia," explained Mrs. Dow. "Kameryn is more into doing art."

"These girls nowadays have so much free time," said Mrs. Wallace. "When I was there age all I did was cook, clean, sew, and do chores. Wasn't no cheerleading or drawing or none of that."

Latasia and Kameryn glanced at each other. Kasey had given them the same warning about the Wallaces being old-school that he had given Samiel. Therefore, they were instructed not to speak unless they had been spoken to. It was weird for all three of them to abide by these new rules. Their parents encouraged them to respectfully ask questions. Just sitting there not saying anything and letting anyone talk any old kind of way about them was not what they were used to.

"So, Samuel," said Mr. Wallace to Mr. Dow. "You were a police offi-cer?"

"Yes sir," said Mr. Dow.

"And now what do you do?"

"I'm a Deputy City Marshal in the city."

"Does that pay the same?"

"Just about."

"Hm. Didn't you want to find something that paid more though?"

"Don't most people?" said Mr. Dow with a smile and a slight nod.

Mr. Wallace suggested other positions Mr. Dow could have taken. He even suggested Mr. Dow might have gone back to school or even learned a trade. And with each suggestion, Mr. Dow's slight nods be-came more pronounced and his smile became wider and wider.

Mrs. Dow had prepared a nice lunch for everyone to eat. While they were eating they got on the topic of Samantha settling out there.

"Are the schools out here nice?" asked Mrs. Wallace.

"Some of them," said Mrs. Dow. "Where are you working Saman-tha?"

"Preston High School," said Samantha.

Everyone snorted and rolled their eyes.

"What's wrong?" asked Mrs. Wallace.

"Nothing," said Mr. Dow. "Preston is Creeke High School's rival school."

"Oh," laughed Mr. Wallace. "So, you're working for the enemy."

"I guess so," laughed Samantha.

"Well Sammie, maybe you could become a vice principal like Chris-tine. She seems to be living a pretty nice live. Nice husband, nice kids, nice house. And she looks about the same age as you even though she's about a dozen years older."

Samantha gave her mother a very tight smile. As the afternoon went on, Samiel and his childhood became the topic of conversation. Every so often, the Wallaces would comment on how they wished they could have been around to witness some of the events described. Around four in the afternoon, Kasey, Samantha, and the Wallaces departed. It was very quiet for a while until Samiel's sisters gathered in his room to talk about how things went.

"Sami, how well do you like these people?" asked Latasia.

"I think they're pretty okay," said Samiel.

"Okay, then I won't say anything," said Latasia.

"What do you want to say?"

"No, I'm not going to say nothing."

"Just say it, Lala."

"You sure?"

"Latasia."

"Alright," said Latasia with a shrug. "You asked."

"What's the problem?" asked Samiel.

"I just want to know what Mrs. Wallace meant by we have so much free time?" questioned Latasia.

"Right?" agreed Kameryn. "She made it sound like we don't do nothing."

"I'm sure she didn't mean it like that," said Samiel.

"Well until I get some clarity, that's how I'm taking it," said Latasia. "And then Mr. Wallace sitting up acting like he's better than Dad. Talking about what he should and shouldn't have done. Who is he?"

"For real though," agreed Kameryn. "At least Dad has a job."

"I think you guys are taking what they said the wrong way," said Samiel.

"Well, then they need to fix how they say stuff," said Latasia. "Maybe then, it won't get taken the wrong way."

Following that conversation, Samiel went into the living room where he found his father pacing.

"Your daughters are upset with the Wallaces," said Samiel.

"They're not the only ones," said Mr. Dow. "Your mama didn't like being used as point of comparison for Samantha. Especially that dozen years older comment."

"This is a mess," said Samiel. "Dad, what should I do?"

"About what?"

"The Wallaces. They're rubbing everyone the wrong way."

"I can't disagree with that," said Mr. Dow, scratching his chin. "They certainly seem to be the nosy type, that's for sure."

"I want us all to be able to get along," said Samiel. "I want to be able to have my whole family in one place and there not be an issue."

"Well, sometimes that's just not possible," said Mr. Dow. "Sometimes people just don't get along and there's nothing you can do about it except let things be."

"But I feel like in this case, everyone can get along," said Samiel. "Kasey said he thinks they're just acting this way because they're disappointed about missing so much of my life and they're still coming to terms with it."

"Maybe," said Mr. Dow. "And unfortunately, they're taking their disappointment out on us."

"There's got to be something we can do."

"Maybe try talking to them about how they're making you feel?" suggested Mr. Dow. "Don't expect too much though. Once people get past a certain age, they get set in their ways. It's rare that they'd be willing to make a change."

"I've got to at least try," said Samiel. "Or else, I'll never be able to have my whole family together at once."

"Alright then," said Mr. Dow. "But I suggest you take some backup. Like your grandparents. They're on level with the Wallaces so if things get out of hand, they can step in and handle it."

"Okay Dad," said Samiel. "Thanks."

"No problem," said Mr. Dow. "I honestly hope it works. It would be a shame for you to have to pick between your families. That's not what your mother and I want, and that's not what Kasey and Samantha want either."

"Well, then let's hope this works," said Samiel.

The next day, Samiel and his grandparents met with Samantha and her parents at Patty's. He had chosen Patty's because he knew a plate of good food could help diffuse a situation. While they waited for the Wallaces, Samiel filled his grandparents in on everything that had happened.

"Well, I can't wait to meet these people who just have so much to say," said Grandma Eula.

"I don't want an argument, Grandma," said Samiel. "I want us to get along."

"Sami, when you get our age, you'll understand that sometimes things have to get worse before they can get better," said Papa Lawrence. "We might have to have it out with these people before we can get them to get along."

"Well, if you guys have it out, can it be after we eat?" asked Samiel. He had ordered a Sami Special for the first time in a long time. With how nervous he was, he needed something to lift his spirits.

The Wallaces arrived before his food did. There were greetings and introductions given, and then Samiel got to the point.

"Pawpaw, Mawmaw," began Samiel. "I wanted to talk to you about your trip so far."

"I think it's been lovely," said Mrs. Wallace. "Don't you agree, Dennis?"

"Uh huh," said Mr. Wallace.

"It has been good for the most part," said Samiel. "But there are some things that's happened that I still wanted to talk about."

"What's happened?" asked Mr. Wallace with concern.

"What's happened is you disrespected my son in his house," said Papa Lawrence, unable to contain himself any longer.

"Excuse me?" cried Mrs. Wallace.

"You heard what my husband said," said Grandma Eula. "I heard you both have had a lot to say to everyone."

"Hold on," said Mr. Wallace. "What are you two talking about? We haven't said nothing bad about nobody."

"Well...," said Samantha, wincing. "There have been some moments where you both put your foots in your mouths."

"Feet in your mouth," corrected Mrs. Wallace.

"Same thing," said Samantha.

"No, its not the same thing," said Mrs. Wallace. "Foots is not a word."

"Mama, the point is you and Dad have said some kind of rude stuff."

"What did we say?" asked Mrs. Wallace confusedly. "I thought we were all getting along."

"Well, comparing me to Christine wasn't nice to either of us," said Samantha. "And I didn't appreciate that joke you made about me being Sami's mother over her. We're both his mothers, but she raised him."

"I wasn't trying to be mean," said Mrs. Wallace defensively. "I was just saying you could be a little more like her when it came to your career."

"I heard you had a lot to say about my son's job," said Papa Lawrence to Mr. Wallace. "How you think he could've done a lot better."

"I didn't say it like that," said Mr. Wallace. "I was honestly just theorizing about what other positions he could've gotten."

"My sisters also felt like you were saying they didn't do anything," said Samiel.

"I wasn't saying that at all," said Mrs. Wallace. "I was actually impressed with how much they got to do and was just talking about how different things were from when I was their age. Eula, was it? I'm sure you know what I mean. You know your granddaughters have a lot more options available to them than we had."

"They do...," said Grandma Eula reluctantly. "I couldn't do half the stuff they get to do nowadays."

"Exactly," said Mrs. Wallace. "That's all I meant."

"It seems like everything we've said has been taken out of context," said Mr. Wallace. "I can't help but wonder if it's because we're secretly not welcome around here."

"No, it's because you both keep putting your foots in your mouths," said Samantha.

"Feet," said Mrs. Wallace.

"However," continued Samantha. "There is one thing that can't be misconstrued and it's how you've both been treating Kasey."

"How have we been treating Kasey?" questioned Mr. Wallace.

"Like you don't like him," said Samantha. "Now look, he knows he made a huge mess of things back in the day. But that Kasey back then, is not the same Kasey today. Today's Kasey has worked hard to turn his life around and is trying. Whether you like it or not, I love him and I plan to be with him for the rest of our lives. So, if you want to be around for my life and Sami's life, then you have to accept that."

Mr. and Mrs. Wallace looked at each other.

"They're speechless now," said Papa Lawrence, amused.

"I want you both to be part of my life and part of the family," said Samiel. "Everything else I can accept as being a misunderstanding. But I really want you guys to get along with Mr. Kasey, because he's important to me too, and he's not going anywhere."

"Since when do you call him, 'Mr.' Kasey?" snorted Grandma Eula. "I thought he hated that."

"It's a long story Grandma," whispered Samiel.

"I'll admit I've had some reservations about Kasey," said Mr. Wallace. "But from what I've seen he does seem to be doing better than from the first time I met him."

"We just want to be sure that he'll do right by you," said Mrs. Wallace.

"He will," said Samantha. "Just give him a real chance."

"I hope we can put this all behind us and start over," said Samiel.

"There's no need to start over," said Mr. Wallace. "We'll just move forward."

"That's right," said Mrs. Wallace. "We came out here for you baby. So, we'll do whatever it takes to make this work. Because we're not going anywhere."

The rest of the week went smoothly. At graduation, there was no big celebration like when Samiel graduated from high school. Everyone cheered for him when his name was called and then they went home to have a nice family dinner. At one point, Samiel found Kasey sitting outside on the porch.

"What you doing out here?" asked Samiel.

"I just like sitting on the porch," said Kasey. "You know I'm real proud of you."

"Thanks," said Samiel.

"Yes sir," said Kasey. "You've made me a real proud father today. I want you to know that. And I want you to know that I love you."

"I love you too," said Samiel.

"And I love both of you," said Samantha, peeking her head outside the door. "Christine sent me to tell you that the food was ready."

"Alright," said Kasey. "Let's go eat."

The three of them joined the rest of the family at the table. As Samiel looked around at everyone eating, all he could feel was thankful. He finally had his whole family together, and everything seemed like it would be alright.

Althea Green

It had been five years since Althea last saw her sister Gloria. At that time, Althea was fourteen and going into high school, while Gloria was a freshly graduated eighteen escaping Creeke. Over the years, Gloria would occasionally call and say she was doing alright. But she had not set foot in Creeke since she had left.

Althea had not expected her sister to be in the same town where she was going to college. Diana had eagerly told her that, hoping Althea would pressure Gloria into coming home for the wedding.

It was the middle of May. Althea had just turned nineteen three days after Diana had turned twenty-one. Yet she felt rather silly standing on Gloria's doorstep, nervous to knock on her own sister's door. But it was only because she did not know what to expect. She wondered whether Gloria was the spunky older sister she remembered or if she had changed. And if Gloria had changed, Althea wondered if it was for better or worse. After pondering it for some time, she gathered her nerve and finally knocked.

"Thea!" squealed Gloria when she opened the door. She threw her arms around Althea and hugged her close. "Oh, I haven't seen you in so long! Come in, come in, come in!"

Althea relaxed as Gloria pulled her inside. Her sister had not changed one bit in personality or even in looks. Her golden-brown skin glistened, her hair was beautifully styled in a pixie cut, and her plump lips were covered in gloss.

Althea marveled at her sister's apartment as Gloria led her to the couch, where some snacks waited for them.

"How's everybody doing?" asked Gloria.

"Good," said Althea. "Did Diana tell you I was coming?"

"Yeah," said Gloria. "Along with an earful about how I *better* be at her wedding next month. As if I would miss something important like that."

Althea decided not to point out that Gloria had missed all her sisters' graduations.

"I can't believe you've been here this whole time and I didn't know," said Gloria. "What have you been doing with yourself these days?"

"I've been going to school and working at Uncle Arnie's newspaper," answered Althea. "This is a nice place you have here."

"You like it?" said Gloria, beaming with pride. "I decorated it myself. Mama would be so proud."

"Is it expensive?"

"I don't have to worry about the cost. I've got someone who handles that for me."

Althea could have feigned surprise. But Gloria having "someone" was not surprising. Even back in Creeke, Gloria always had a "someone" spending all his money on her.

"This is why I love you," said Gloria.

"What?" asked Althea.

"You never react to anything I tell you," chuckled Gloria. "Cyn would've tore my head off claiming I was a harlot."

"Are you?"

"Do I look like a harlot to you?" questioned Gloria with her signature mischievous smile.

Althea tried her best not to smile so she would not encourage her sister's antics, but it was hard. Gloria was mischievous like their father and he always joked God made her look the most like him because of it. But for all her mischief, Gloria was also a caring and loyal person. Just like their father.

"Is that how did you ended up living here?" asked Althea. "Because of your man?"

"Isn't it always?" said Gloria, playfully rolling her eyes. "I'm just glad this one isn't married."

"This one?" remarked Althea, raising her eyebrows.

"It was an accident!" griped Gloria. "He said he was single and not looking for anything serious, and you know I don't deal with anyone who's taken, so I thought we were good. Next thing I know I've got an angry wife and her homegirls beating on my door! Girl, I had to sneak out the back window of my own place! My homegirl goes to school here, so I was able to stay with her till I got my own place. And then I met my boo."

"Who is he?" asked Althea.

"A banker," said Gloria. "I met him while running at the park. Apparently, I caught his attention when I ran past him. The joker almost got himself shot too because he followed me to get my number. It's a good thing he was cute."

"Do you like him?" asked Althea.

"He's alright," said Gloria dismissively. Her brown eyes glowed excitedly as she asked Althea, "But what about you? You got a special someone?"

"No," answered Althea.

"Oh, well we're going to get that fixed tonight," said Gloria. "I'm going out to a party tonight and you're coming with me!"

"A party?" questioned Althea.

"Yeah," said Gloria. She looked at Althea skeptically and added, "You *have* been to a party here before, right?"

"No?"

"Althea!" whined Gloria. "You're in college! These are the years when you should be living it up! You can't spend your whole life with your nose in a book!"

"Why not?"

"Oh my gosh!" huffed Gloria. "You are coming out with me tonight and we are getting you a man!"

Althea resigned herself to her fate after that. She knew it was futile to go against her sisters when they were set on something. Gloria curled Althea's hair and applied makeup to her face. But she and Althea compromised on the outfit when Althea saw what her sister wanted her to wear.

"I don't want to wear that," said Althea, looking at the outfit her sister was holding. It was small, tight, and showed too much skin for Althea's liking.

"Why not?" asked Gloria. "It just like the one I have on."

Althea gave her sister a stern look. Gloria gave her a jumpsuit to wear instead. It was still tight but at least Althea did not have to show as much skin. She imagined what the rest of her family would think if they saw what she had on.

The party was being held at a venue off campus. When they got inside a guy handed Althea and Gloria each a pair of beads. He told them a prize would be given to the girl with the most beads at the end of the night. Althea blushed uncomfortably as he placed his hand on her lower back to guide her into the party.

Althea followed Gloria and her friends to the dance floor, wanting to stay near her sister. She stood awkwardly, watching as they collected beads from various guys. Her first straw was when a guy brushed past her a little too closely, and her second was when a guy smacked her behind.

But Althea's final straw was when a guy grabbed her to dance with him. She tore away from him and escaped to the wall, where a few other girls sat. Althea wanted to leave and hoped something would end the party early so she could escape.

Then someone waved and sat next to her. At first, Althea tried to ignore him, having reached her limit of patience with men for the night. But when he waved again and called her name, Althea turned to him wondering what man in that dreadful place could possibly know her.

"Justin!" exclaimed Althea when she saw who it was. "It was so dark I didn't recognize you!"

"That's alright," said Justin. "What are you doing here?"

"I'm here with my sister. You?"

"Some friends wanted to go out. Honestly, I'd rather be at home."

"Me too. I had planned on finishing my book after visiting Gloria, but she decided she wanted to go out."

"Aw man!" said Justin when Althea told him the book's title. "That book has a good twist too!"

"I know!"

"How do you know?"

"I think I've read more than enough books to know when a good twist is coming."

"True," said Justin. "I think the supermarket still has it in stock."

"But I already own it."

"Who said anything about buying it?"

It was the plan of escape Althea needed.

"I need to let my sister know where I'm going."

"No problem."

Althea inhaled and dove back into the wild frenzy of dancers, looking for her sister. Gloria was collecting her latest set of beads when she saw Althea.

"There you are!" said Gloria. "You just disappeared on me!"

"Gloria!" said Althea. "I ran into a friend and we want to leave! I don't want to leave you here alone though!"

"A friend?!"

Althea motioned to Justin, who had followed her. Gloria's eyes widened and her mouth became a grin.

"Oh okay!" said Gloria. She shooed Althea with her hands, saying, "Go, go! I can handle myself and I've still got my girls with me! And here, take the key so you can get in!"

Althea left with Justin. They went to the supermarket and walked around while Althea finished her book. She felt a lot more comfortable being with him than she was at that party. After that, he dropped her off at Gloria's apartment.

"Thanks Justin," said Althea when they were on the doorstep. "I really did not want to be at that party."

"Neither did I," said Justin.

"You even still have your beads," giggled Althea.

"That's because I hid out as soon as we got there," laughed Justin. It had been some time since she last heard that cute little laugh. He took the beads off and handed them to Althea. "I'll give them to you. You're the only girl I had fun with tonight anyways."

Althea blushed. That always happened throughout the school year the few times she ran into Justin. He never failed to make her blush.

Gloria returned home a few hours later. She had not won the prize, but she did not care. What had her happy and excited was that Althea had left the party early with Justin.

"I can't believe you left the party with a guy!" said Gloria excitedly. "And a football player at that! Oh my gosh, wait till Cyn hears about this! I can't believe it! What'd you two do?!"

"We went to the supermarket so I could finish my book."

"Seriously Thea?!" cried Gloria. "You pull a guy and you take him to go read a book?!"

"It was his idea."

"Oh my gosh," snorted Gloria. "You would find the bookworm at the party."

Gloria griped and complained for a little while longer before going to bed. But Althea did not care. Her sister had had fun her way, and Althea had fun her way. What stuck in her mind most was how she felt when Justin said she had been the only girl he had fun with that night. It was the same warm, fuzzy feeling she got the previous summer when he came to check on her. She looked at the beads and blushed all over again.

The next day, Althea bid Gloria goodbye and reminded her about Diana's wedding. Gloria rolled her eyes and said she would be there. Diana had originally wanted the wedding to be the day after her twenty-first birthday. Ralph had encouraged her to space the two days apart. It had ended up being the right call because Diana would have been too exhausted from celebrating to get married the next day.

Althea returned to Creeke, glad that the school year was over. Nothing excited her more about the summer than the approaching end of her time as Miss Teen Creeke. While she was honored to have held the position, it required a lot of her time and energy, and she was ready to move on. Unfortunately, she would still be fulfilling queen duties up until the crown was literally placed on the next winner's head.

The townsfolk had wasted no time putting their reigning queen to work after she returned. Her next appearance would be the upcoming day at the library's annual reading initiative. It had been moved to May and would be the same as the previous year.

The next day, Althea arrived early at the library. She gave herself enough time to browse as Regular Althea to get into a good frame of mind before going into queen mode. While she browsed the fantasy books, she reached for one and grabbed it at the same time as someone else. Althea looked at the person reaching for the book and felt her face grow hot.

"Hey," said Justin, his face brightening when he saw her. "We're you trying to get this?"

"You can take it," answered Althea.

"Okay," said Justin. "I'm supposed to be speaking at the event later, but I wanted to look around to clear my mind."

"You're speaking too?"

"Yeah. They asked you to do this too?"

"Yes."

"It's last year all over again," laughed Justin.

The whole day after that was weird. All Althea could think about was how she looked, how she sounded, and whether Justin was looking at her. Throughout the school year, she had grown a lot in confidence and had become more comfortable with telling people no. But whenever she looked at Justin, all she could think about was how she would say yes to anything he asked her to do.

That's when it hit her. And she could not believe it could be possible. She had never cared about boys before. But all that had changed with Justin.

She needed someone to confide in and get advice from. It could not be any of the women in her family because they would get too excited and carried away. Her father was also out of the question because he would either be highly unserious or overly serious. Althea needed someone she could trust to be honest and focused.

"Allison," said Althea. She had invited her friend to her house after the reading initiative was over.

"Yeah?" answered Allison.

"Have you ever liked a boy before?"

Allison did not answer right away. But Althea noticed her face start to blush.

"Allison?"

"Yeah, I have."

"What's it like?"

"I don't know," said Allison, blushing harder. "One day I looked at him and thought he looked kind of cute and wondered how I'd never noticed before. And then I freaked out because I couldn't believe I thought that."

Althea knew then what she felt was real. She liked Justin. And she could not believe it.

"Did you ever tell him you liked him?" asked Althea.

"Heck nah!" cried Allison.

"Why not?"

"Because what if he doesn't like me back? Then things will be awkward, and he might not want to be friends anymore..."

"Will?" repeated Althea. "As in, you still like him?"

Allison did not answer, but her blushing told Althea all she needed to know.

"Why are you asking me all this anyways?" questioned Allison. "Do you like someone?"

"I... uh," stammered Althea, starting to blush herself.

"You do, don't you? Who is it?"

There was a knock on the door. Althea got up to answer it and found Justin on the other side.

"Hi!" said Justin. He glanced down at her shirt and his smile became more pronounced.

Althea looked at the random t-shirt she had put on. It was a vintage-style shirt with various pictures of Justin in action on the field and his name in big block letters. She had gotten it from a vendor at one of the games.

"Uh...," muttered Althea, her cheeks becoming hot with embarrassment. Of all the shirts for him to see her in she could not believe it was that one. "I uh... I got this at the game..."

"Oh," said Justin. "I have a hat that goes great with that. I don't know if you'd want it though since it's not your team."

"Oh."

"Uh... anyways. I came by because I accidentally took one of your books by mistake."

Justin handed her the library book he was referring to. Althea chose to look at it instead of Justin, fearing her face would become even redder.

"Thanks," said Althea.

"Hi Justin," said Allison, appearing behind Althea. "I'm here too."

"Hi," said Justin. "What are you doing here?"

"I'm always here," said Allison. "I live across the street, remember?"

"Right," said Justin.

"You know, it was great to get to see you play in some of the games this year," said Allison. "I'm sure you'll be the star quarterback that everyone's looking at in no time."

"I uh...," said Justin, laughing nervously. "Thanks I guess. I got to go. I just wanted to give you that. Let me know if you want the hat."

"Okay," said Althea. She willed herself to look at Justin. He smiled at her, and she smiled back. "Thanks again."

After Justin left, Allison looked at Althea knowingly.

"It's him, isn't it?"

Althea did not answer. Instead, she blushed.

"I won't tell anyone," said Allison. "But I will say, a boy doesn't just come all the way across town just to return a library book to anyone. And their hats are sacred to them. Like you'd have to pry them from their dead, cold hands as they're holding them onto their heads. Ask me how I know."

"You think he likes me back?" asked Althea, feeling a flutter in herself.

"Mhmm," affirmed Allison.

The idea made Althea happy. She would like nothing more than for the feelings between her and Justin to be mutual.

As time went on, Althea found that a lot of her thoughts centered on Justin. Everything she wore was carefully chosen with the hope he might see her in it and think she was cute. Each book she read was one she thought he might also like and that they could discuss together. She even found herself watching his football highlights. By the beginning of June, Althea knew what she felt was very real.

Diana's wedding was the first weekend of June. And then Founder's Day was two weekends after that. Althea was excited for both. She would be the maid of honor at her sister's wedding and then would finally crown the next girl after her. While Althea was excited to be done with Miss Teen Creeke, she was a little sad about her time coming to an end. Compared to the previous summer, she had become a bit more comfortable in the role, and she felt less like she was playing a character. It was becoming easier to see her regular self and her queen self as the same person.

That was most evident in her role as Diana's maid of honor. Diana, being Diana, wanted everything to be perfect. And while she zealously pursued the perfect wedding, Althea was able to be more realistic. The way Althea took charge felt more like something Miss Teen Creeke would do rather than what Althea would do. Except, Althea was more comfortable taking charge after dealing with a difficult college roommate.

By the time the wedding rolled around, Althea was more than equipped to do her part to lessen the stress of the day. It was about as stressful as expected. To her credit, Diana had not been as dramatic as her family had expected her to be. Instead, all of the stress was centered around whether Gloria would show up. Diana had prepared for Gloria to be a bridesmaid, but she had planned in case Gloria did not show up.

The wedding would be at five in the afternoon at the church. Diana had put off getting ready as long as possible so that she could watch for when Gloria arrived. She spent most of the time sitting on the porch, watching for Gloria. Althea and Cynthia joined her, but by three-thirty, everyone was getting worried.

"I don't know how much longer we can wait," said Cynthia. "We have to be at the church at five and she's still not here."

"That's alright," sighed Diana. "She ain't coming."

"That Gloria," scoffed Cynthia. "She had one darn job!"

It suddenly became very windy, and a huge flock of birds flew overhead. Diana waited a few more minutes, then sighed and began going inside. Althea watched with a heavy heart as her sister headed for the door. However, just as she started to close the door behind her, a car pulled in front of the house. A dark-brown man walked to the passenger side and helped a golden-brown woman out.

"Thank you honey. Go on ahead to the church, I'll meet you over there."

The woman approached the porch, her heels clicking rhythmically against the pavement. Her red dress clung to her in a way that covered what was necessary but still accentuated what was hidden. Under the brim of her hat, only her painted red lips could be seen. But for Althea and her sisters, there was no mistaking who this woman was.

"Well, look who finally decided to show her face," snorted Diana.

"What?" whined Gloria. "I got here as fast as I could."

"Seriously?!" cried Diana. "The wedding starts in an hour and we've been waiting on you all day!"

"Well, this is some way to treat me after we ain't seen each other in all these years!" griped Gloria.

"Well girl, it's only been one, two, three, four, five years!" fussed Diana, counting the numbers off on her fingers. "At this point, we weren't sure if you would show up at all like usual!"

"Now don't do that!" countered Gloria, pointing her finger at Diana. "Don't do that! You know full well I wouldn't miss my own sister's wedding!"

"You missed our graduations!" argued Diana and Cynthia.

"Well, how do you like that?" complained Gloria. "I come down here for what I think is a happy occasion just to get attacked! Why can't y'all be more like Thea? You don't see her complaining!"

"She may not be saying nothing, but she sure is thinking it!" said Cynthia.

Althea quickly averted her eyes. She hated that her sisters always knew what she was thinking even without her saying anything.

"And who is this man you brought with you?" questioned Diana.

"That's my boo," said Gloria, smirking. "He's a military man."

"That ain't the same boo you left town with," said Diana while Althea silently noted he was also not the banker Gloria had been seeing just weeks prior either.

"Well sweetheart, that was five years ago," said Gloria. "A lot can change in five years. Now are we going to stand out here all day fussing, or are y'all going to get me in my dress so we can go get you married?"

"You look pretty ready to me," said Diana.

"This was my just-in-case-I'm-late dress. But I'm not."

"Sometimes I just can't stand you," said Diana, rolling her eyes.

"I love you and I'm happy to see you too, you little bridezilla," teased Gloria. "I'm happy to see all my sisters again."

The wedding went well after that. Althea walked down the aisle with Matthias, who Ralph had asked him to be his best man. Diana and Ralph seemed very happy, and Althea had to fight back tears to not mess up her makeup. Mrs. Green, however, could not help but cry.

Althea also noticed that Justin was at the wedding with his family, and they were also at the reception. At the reception, Althea ended up seated next to Gloria. When everyone else went to the dance floor, Althea decided to get the details on Gloria's latest boyfriend.

"What happened to the banker?" asked Althea.

"He had to go!" answered Gloria. "He thought just because he was spending money on me that he could tell me what to do! Can you believe that?! He was trying to tell me where I could go and who I could hang out with! Then when I kicked him to the curb, he going to talk about some I owe him for all the money he spent on me! I told him I don't owe him nothing, so he said he was taking everything that he paid for! The joke was on him though because I paid for that apartment and everything in it. He was just paying the rent. I guess he thought since he was spending his money on me that I ain't have my own. And this body is reserved for the man that I marry. Is it so hard to find a guy who wants more than that and that respects that? Listen Althea, always have you a little something set off to the side for yourself just in case. Because these men will try to use their wallets to control you, and you don't want to be stuck with a man like that."

Althea nodded as she listened to her sister's tangent. Gloria mentioned she was considering moving back closer to home. A slow song started playing, and Althea could see Justin sitting across the room. She thought about everything she had learned from her sisters in the past few years. To not be afraid to take risks, to fight for her happiness, and to not compromise herself for a man. And she was still Miss Teen Creeke for two more weeks. Miss Teen Creeke was not afraid to take charge.

And neither was Althea.

"Gloria?" said Althea, interrupting her sister. "I'm sorry to cut you off but do you mind if I go dance?"

"Dance with who?" asked Gloria. "This is a slow song."

"I know," said Althea. ""There's someone I'd like to dance with."

"Oh?" gasped Gloria with a smile. "Don't let me hold you up then. Go get your man, girl!"

Althea thanked Gloria and went over to Justin.

"Justin," said Althea when she reached him. "Would you like to dance with me?"

"Uh…," said Justin, his cheeks growing dark. "Actually, I want you to dance with me."

It was Althea's turn to blush as she took Justin's outstretched hand. He led her to the dance floor and they began dancing with each other. She had allowed herself to be bold up to that point. So, she decided to take it all the way.

"Justin, I need to tell you something," said Althea nervously.

"What is it?" asked Justin.

It took all of Althea's strength to push past everything in her telling her to not say anything.

"I like you," said Althea quietly.

Justin did not say anything at first. That made Althea nervous. He leaned in near her ear and whispered.

"I like you too."

Althea could not believe it. She felt a sense of relief and happiness wash over her. And as she and Justin continued dancing, she laid her head on his chest, happy with life and with herself.

Latasia Williams

Founder's Day was facing a serious dilemma, and it was all Mr. Payne's fault. He had decided not to renew his sponsorship of the day's events. Officially, he claimed it was because his company was not in a position to sponsor. But everyone knew it was because he had not gotten his way with the pageant and talent show the previous year.

Losing Mr. Payne as a sponsor was a huge blow to the financial capabilities of Founder's Day. Many feared Founder's Day would be canceled completely. But that was not an option for Latasia. So, she called an emergency Little Sister Society meeting.

The Little Sister Society had not been as active as in high school. Most of the girls were away at college, but they remained passionate about helping their community when necessary.

"We've got to do something," said Latasia. "There's no way we can let Founder's Day just not happen."

"What can we do?" asked Kameryn. "We're just girls."

"No, you're just a girl," teased Latasia. "The rest of us are grown women now."

"Hey!" whined Kameryn. "I'm seventeen and I'm going into my senior year! I'm not a little girl!"

"No, you're not Lil Bit," said Allison. "But your sister's right. We're grown women now. We can take action ourselves."

"I agree," said Nicole. "What ideas do we got?"

"The two biggest things affected are the pageant and the talent show because those need a venue and paid volunteers to make happen," said Allison. "Mr. Payne's sponsorship last year covered those costs which is why he had the final say on how those events went."

"So, what if we just didn't have those then?" asked Tamara.

"I would prefer not to hold onto the Miss Teen Creeke crown any longer than necessary," said Althea. "I think another girl should have a chance to wear it after my term is complete."

"Plus, the bright side of not having Mr. Payne sponsoring the talent show is that my family can compete again," said Adrianna. "Although pulling that loophole with Mariella last year was genius. That was a well-deserved win."

"Okay, so we want to have the pageant and the talent show but should be prepared in case we can't," said Allison.

"My family has always catered Founder's Day, and we plan to do so again this year," said Charmaine. "Food will never be an issue."

"What if we did individual sponsorships?" suggested Jada. "Like having families give sponsorships too?"

"Most families don't contribute," said Allison annoyedly. "In fact, I'm pretty sure my family is the only family contributor to Founder's Day."

"Your mom's family could honestly finance the whole day on their own," said Nicole.

"The only way they're pitching in is if they can write it off of their taxes," scoffed Allison. "Every day I wonder more and more how my mother and aunt came from those people."

"How did Founder's Day go when there wasn't a pageant and talent show?" asked Jada.

"Think of a big family reunion at the rec center but with a sermon thrown in," said Latasia. "What makes the pageant and talent show so special is that it gives us younger folks something to participate in that we don't have to audition for."

"Yeah," said Allison. She pondered momentarily and then said, "Do you think we could do them without money?"

"I don't know a single person on this earth who is willing to do any-thing for free," said Tamara.

"You're right," said Allison. "It was just a thought."

The meeting ended without any clear objective. They wanted to do something to help. But the reality was Founder's Day could not happen without money. Latasia was disappointed that she could not do more to help.

That evening, Latasia helped her mom cook dinner.

"Mom," said Latasia. "Do you think they'll have to cancel Founder's Day this year?"

"Founder's Day is definitely happening," said Mrs. Dow. "But the pageant and talent show are another story."

"This is just so wrong," griped Latasia. "How could he just pull his sponsorship just because Prissy threw the pageant last year?"

"I won't pretend like Mr. Payne is a saint," said Mrs. Dow. "But believe me when I tell you no one will miss his sponsorship. The way he acted last year is totally worth losing out on what he would've paid for if it means we won't have to deal with him again."

"I guess you're right," said Latasia.

A special announcement was made at church the next day. The church would host the upcoming Founder's Day. However, the pageant and talent show would be replaced with a special Founder's Day service. Volunteer positions would be unpaid, unlike in previous years. Latasia did not care though. She was willing to do her part to ensure Founder's Day still happened, no matter how it happened.

"It's better than nothing," said Latasia to Nicole after church ended.

"Right?" agreed Nicole. "But I have a sneaky suspicion I know who was behind this."

"Who?"

"A certain pastor's stepdaughter and a certain pastor's granddaughter."

"Now that you say it, I believe it."

"I wonder how this will go though," said Nicole. "I don't think the church has ever hosted Founder's Day before."

"They used to according to my grandparents," said Latasia. "But at some point, they decided to separate it and make it its own thing outside of the church."

"Interesting," said Nicole.

The volunteers attended an interest meeting that Monday. Latasia and her whole family were there. At the meeting, they received their assignments, partners, and instructions on how the day would work. Latasia was assigned to help with food by making some pies for the event. Although Patty's and Flowerbud's would be providing catering, the church also wanted to help by providing their own food. Her partner was Danielle, and she did not know how to feel about that. They had not seen each other in a year because they went to separate colleges. And they obviously were not friends or even cordial.

Tuesday morning, Latasia went to work hoping to get some advice from Nicole. She was working at Brewer's for another summer.

"I can't believe they paired me with her," said Latasia when she and Nicole were opening the store. "I swear somebody did this on purpose."

"Maybe," said Nicole. "Thankfully it won't be for too long."

"Yeah," agreed Latasia. "Hopefully, she'll just cooperate and not cause any issues."

"No, for real," said Nicole. "We're too old for all that drama now."

"Can she even bake?" asked Latasia. "I'm not being shady. I really just don't know."

"Honestly, I don't know," said Nicole. "I've never seen her cook anything."

"This just becomes more and more of a hot mess," griped Latasia. "First, I got to work with this girl, and I don't know how she's coming. And then, we don't even know if she can actually cook."

"All I can say is I wish you the best," said Nicole.

After work, Latasia would meet with Danielle at Flowerbud's. Flowerbud's had been successful enough that they were able to move into a building. It was small and located in a shopping center, but it was a huge step for Mr. Bud and his restaurant.

Priscella worked the cash register that day, while Derek was in the back helping Mr. Bud cook the food. Mrs. Greta technically was not employed by Flowerbud's, so she could not be behind the counter. But she did help make sure the atmosphere there stayed a positive one. And

Latasia could also not help but notice how Mrs. Greta and Coach Nelson-Brown seemed to be glowing lately.

Danielle walked into Flowerbud's and Latasia almost did not recognize her. She looked like she was full of light as she came over to Latasia.

"Hi," said Danielle.

"Hi," said Latasia.

"I'm going to get something and then we can talk."

"Okay."

Latasia watched as Danielle got in line. Priscella was the cashier. As she watched the two interact, Latasia wondered if things were just as awkward between them. She ended up getting in line too to also get herself something.

"Hello," said Priscella. "How can I help you?"

Latasia put in her order, and then asked, "Did she give you any problems?"

"Nope," said Priscella. "She just ordered her food and sat down."

"She didn't say anything slick?"

"Nope."

Latasia was surprised. The Danielle she was used to always took opportunities to take little shots at others. She returned to the table wondering what Danielle's game was.

"So," said Danielle when Latasia sat down. "We have to make three pies. I was thinking we'd either make three of the same pies or three different pies. What do you think?"

Latasia was speechless. The Danielle she knew never asked what others thought of her plans. She just did it and expected you to go along with it.

"Let's make three of the same pies," said Latasia.

"Okay. Do you want to make them from scratch or do store-bought ones that we just put in the oven?"

"What do you want to do?"

"I kind of want to make them from scratch. I was hoping we could make sweet potato pies. Is that good with you?"

"Sure."

"Okay. Are you free Thursday? Because we can go get the stuff then."

"Yeah, I'm free."

"Great. I'll see you then."

And she was gone. The whole interaction threw Latasia for a loop. It was weird sitting with Danielle and not feeling like she had to argue and fight with her.

"How'd it go?" asked Nicole the next day at work.

"It was weird," said Latasia.

"Weird?"

"Yeah. She didn't try to boss me around like she used to. She even asked for my opinion and took it seriously."

"Are you sure that was Dani?" questioned Nicole. "Maybe she has a nice twin out here that we don't know about."

"Oh my gosh," said Latasia. "The last thing we need is two of her running around."

Latasia and Nicole laughed.

"I say don't let your guard down yet," said Nicole. "Especially because this is Dani we're talking about."

"True," agreed Latasia. "I'm going to keep my eye on her. We're supposed to be coming here tomorrow to get stuff to make sweet potato pies. I would just have you set aside some stuff but I don't know what to get."

"That's alright," said Nicole. "Miki will be here tomorrow so she can help."

The next day, Latasia met Danielle at Brewer's. They went through the store, picking out everything they would need to make the pies. Things were going fine until they were looking for pie crusts. While they were trying to figure out which one to get, Mikayla approached them.

"I hope you plan on buying all that," said Mikayla.

"Duh," said Danielle, rolling her eyes.

"Don't 'duh' me," snapped Mikayla. "I haven't forgotten about how you tried to rob us blind."

"That was two years ago!"

"All I know is I better see you at the checkout line. And you better not have anything in your purse either."

"Oh no, I planned to stuff three whole pie crusts in my purse," said Danielle sarcastically.

Mikayla gave one last side-eye to Danielle before walking away.

"Oh my gosh!" griped Danielle. "You make one mistake as a teenager and people hold it against you for the rest of your life!"

Latasia was unsure if Danielle was talking to her or ranting to herself. So, she did not respond. But it was interesting to see that some of the old Danielle still remained in her. She had not completely changed.

Latasia did not know why but she found that strangely comforting. While the old Danielle had been a horrible person, the overly positive Danielle that Latasia had been with the past few days seemed unsettling. The one ranting to herself while picking out pie crusts suited her best.

It reminded Latasia of how Danielle used to be back before middle school. Danielle had always been the type to take the lead and speak her mind. And she would make a sarcastic remark occasionally, but she had still been a friend. When they got to middle school, she started being nastier towards them. Back then, Latasia wondered what had caused Danielle to change so much. After their day at Brewer's, she wondered what had caused Danielle to change back and why it had taken so long.

Founder's Day would be that Sunday. That Saturday, Latasia and Danielle got to work on their pies. They were cooking at Latasia's house while her family was out doing their parts to help set up for Founder's Day. Danielle had a recipe she wanted to follow, but it became clear neither she nor Latasia were as skilled as they thought they were.

"I didn't realize this would be this hard," said Latasia.

"This is the time when you'd need a mother's help," said Danielle.

Latasia did not say anything. Although Danielle herself had not said anything about it, it was no secret she and her mother were not on good terms. And Danielle's relationship with her father was also in a rough spot. Since neither had a mother to call on then, Latasia decided to turn to the next best thing.

"I'm phoning a friend," said Latasia.

"Who?" asked Danielle.

"Someone that knows what they're doing."

Latasia called Nicole for help. And when Nicole came, she was not alone. She had brought Priscella with her.

"Lord, look at you," chuckled Nicole. "You covered in flour!"

"Am I really?" asked Latasia.

"Mmhmm," uttered Nicole.

"I heard you needed help baking some pies," said Priscella gleefully.

"Yeah, we need a lot of help," laughed Latasia.

"Who's we?" asked Priscella.

"Me and Dani."

Priscella stopped smiling. Her eyelids drooped and her face contorted to show her displeasure at the mention of Danielle's name.

"I didn't know she was here," said Priscella.

"She's my partner for Founder's Day," said Latasia. "Didn't Nicki tell you?"

"She just said you needed help baking pies," said Priscella, glaring at Nicole.

"In my defense, I thought you both were baking separately and would just combine what you made at Founder's Day," said Nicole, throwing her hands up.

"Prissy, we really need your help," said Latasia. "You're the only one who knows what she's doing making a pie from scratch."

"Why didn't you just get premade pies to stick in the oven?" asked Nicole.

"We wanted to do it from scratch," said Latasia. "Prissy, will you help us? Please?"

Priscella released a sigh and entered the house. She said nothing to Danielle and gave all her instructions to Latasia and Nicole. With her help the girls were able to get all three pies done and in the oven.

They sat in the living room, waiting for the pies to finish baking. Aside from the television, there was a tense, awkward silence in the air. It was the first time all four girls had deliberately been together in two years. Latasia thought about saying something to lighten up the mood, but Danielle beat her to it.

"Can you mute that?" asked Danielle. "I have something to say."

Latasia obliged and the girls all looked at Danielle curiously.

"Um," began Danielle. Latasia noticed that whatever she had to say made her nervous. Danielle continued, saying, "Look. We've had a lot of drama between us during the past few years. And I know most of it was my fault. I just want to say I'm sorry."

"For?" said Priscella.

"For?" repeated Danielle.

"I want to hear what you're sorry for."

There was a short lull in the conversation. Priscella had retorted so quickly that Latasia had not even had time to process that Danielle had apologized to them. And she could tell that Danielle had not expected it either.

"I'm sorry for everything," said Danielle.

"Be specific," said Priscella.

"Prissy," said Nicole.

"No, I want to hear her admit to everything she did wrong," said Priscella. "She literally ruined all of our friendships with each other. She's the reason I didn't have any friends for a while. I missed out on a whole year of cheer trying to have her back. And in return she called me stupid and tried to replace me like I meant nothing to her after all that time we were supposedly friends. So, I'm going to need a little more than an 'I'm sorry'."

Latasia could not argue with Priscella. Danielle had done a lot of damage during their middle and high school years. Simply saying "I'm sorry" felt hollow when stacked up against everything Danielle had done throughout the years.

"Look, you don't have to believe me," said Danielle defensively. "But I know that when I say I'm sorry, I mean it."

"Why now?" demanded Priscella. "Why are you so sorry now?"

"Because I've had time to think about what I did," said Danielle. "I was wrong."

"That's it?" questioned Priscella. "You just suddenly had time to think about it? Why didn't you think about it back then?"

Latasia could see Danielle was getting frustrated. Part of her wanted to leave it alone and just let Danielle get the heat that she deserved. But another part of her wanted them to take advantage of Danielle being apologetic and reach an actual resolution to the situation. Especially because there was no way of knowing if Danielle would ever apologize again.

"Why'd you even do all of that in the first place?" asked Latasia. It was the one thing she never understood. "Like we were your friends. And then all of a sudden we hit middle school and you just acted like we were beneath you. You were bossing us around and then in high school, you just acted like you were that girl. And then you got to replacing us and cutting us off. Like what happened to even cause all that?"

Danielle looked as if she did not want to answer. But with the others looking at her, she had no choice but to.

"My mom told me that I had to stay one step ahead of everyone," said Danielle. "She told me that if I wanted to be somebody in this world, then I would have to fight for what I deserved. That meant not trusting anyone, making sure I was always the one in control, and being ready to cut off the people I thought I didn't need anymore. When she saw me being the leader of our group, she was proud of me, so I kept it up."

Danielle stopped for a moment, then kept going.

"But over these past two years, I've realized her way of life is terrible," said Danielle. "Doing things her way made me to be lonely and miserable. And when I thought about how I got there, the only person I could blame was myself. So, that's why I'm sorry. That's why me and her are into it right now. She thinks I'm calling her a bad mother when all I'm saying is I want to do things differently and not be miserable anymore."

"I mean if the shoe fits…," mumbled Nicole, causing Latasia to elbow her.

"You know what?" said Latasia. "I accept your apology, and I forgive you. Because I think all of us here can agree that we had to face those same things with ourselves. I know I did."

"Yeah, I did too," said Nicole. "We all had our part to play in the drama and we all had to take the blame for it. So, I accept your apology and forgive you too."

Everyone looked at Priscella. She looked like she did not want to accept the apology. And then, she exhaled.

"You know, you really hurt my feelings when you treated me like that," said Priscella. "But I know what it's like to want to be different from your parents because you know they're wrong. And I also had to work hard to get people to trust me and be my friend because of what we did. So, I'll accept your apology too. I just hope you really mean it."

"I do," said Danielle. "I can't take back everything I did. And I know everyone won't be as forgiving as you guys. But I hope you guys will let me show you that I can do better."

"I think we can all agree to give you a second chance," said Latasia. "It's only fair since we were all given second chances."

The oven chimed. And as Danielle went to check on the pies, Latasia recalled what Tamara had told them two years ago. She hated to admit Tamara was right, but she had no choice. Danielle had apologized and just like that everything seemed to be all good. It made Latasia wonder if Danielle was sincere or just trying to get people back on her side. But all she could do was accept that it would have to be left up to time to reveal the truth.

Founder's Day ended up going very well. And it felt even more special and more like a community event having it happen through the church. It felt right having it there because the church was at the center – the very heart – of the town.

Latasia and Danielle's pies did okay. But they were nothing compared to the ones Mr. Bud and Priscella baked through Flowerbud's.

However, Latasia's family got as much of her pie as they did Flowerbud's.

Another family that tried their pies was a couple of visitors to Creeke. An Asian family asked for some slices of pie and made small talk with Danielle. She seemed very happy and open to talk with them. Then, Mr. Lee came and got his own slice of pie.

"I hope you two knew what you were doing when you made this," joked Mr. Lee.

"Dad, if I wanted to poison you, I wouldn't do it with a pie I made for the whole town," said Danielle.

Latasia snorted, remembering the infamous fight at Founder's Day two years prior between Mr. Payne and the Browns over cookies. That reminded her of the argument she had had with Danielle right before that incident. It was amazing how much had changed since then.

"Dani, sometimes I just don't know what to do with you," said Mr. Lee, taking a bite of the pie. "It's good."

"Duh," said Danielle. "We made it."

"You could just say thank you."

"Thank you," said Danielle quietly.

"You would say it all quietly after being all loud and proud about how you made it," snorted Mr. Lee.

"Look, I said thank you," said Danielle annoyedly. "Take it or leave it."

"I'll take the thank you and leave you with the attitude," said Mr. Lee. "And I suggest you have it fixed by the time you get home, young lady."

After that, Mr. Lee left to enjoy Founder's Day. Danielle looked disappointed and breathed a frustrated sigh.

"Hey," said Latasia. "I don't know what's going on between you and your dad, but I will say this: he's definitely nothing like your mom."

"I know," said Danielle. "It's just going to take us time to have a good relationship again. I really hurt his feelings, and he still doesn't trust me because of it."

"It'll get there," encouraged Latasia. "Don't give up."

After Founder's Day ended, Latasia sat in her room thinking about everything that had happened. She had managed to not only forgive Danielle but also even was potentially starting back towards being friends again. It was incredible. But as Latasia thought about it, she pictured the four of them as they used to be. Four little girls holding hands, happy to be friends. And she wondered if they would one day get back to that again.

Benjamin Townsend

Benjamin had not made any of his own new music in the last year. The most he had done was a handful of features on other artists' tracks at his university. And he had spent more time helping others film their music videos than making his own. After finishing his sophomore year, Benjamin had come home to quietly work at Patty's.

He felt empty and unfulfilled.

On a late July Thursday, it was Benjamin's turn to work the cash register. When he was younger, he hated working the register. But at twenty, he had grown indifferent to it. Sometimes, he even wondered if he would be stuck as a cashier at Patty's forever.

Usually, when he had thoughts like that, he would sigh and say it was better than nothing. But he also thought if he had to be at Patty's forever, he would rather do so as the head of marketing than as a cashier. That was one positive about majoring in communications: he had learned some great marketing tips. Combining that with his first-hand experience making music videos provided him the one bright spot in his dull life.

That Thursday, business was slow. Benjamin had his music going, blasting Uncle Buck's latest project. He would be performing in the city that weekend and Benjamin planned to go support him.

Charmaine came into work as her usual cheerful self. If life had been unkind to Benjamin, it had been the opposite to his sister. She came back from university more cheerful and livelier than before. And university had added more fuel to her burning ambition to one day take over Patty's.

"Did you hear the big news?" asked Charmaine.

"What?" said Benjamin.

"Mrs. Gretchen and Mrs. Greta are pregnant!" said Charmaine excitedly.

"At the same time?"

"Yes!"

"They do know they don't have to do everything together, right?"

"Benji, can't you just be happy for them?" griped Charmaine.

"I am happy for them! I was just making a joke."

"Whatever Benji," said Charmaine as she went to start her work.

There was a sort of bittersweet feeling in Benjamin's spirit. Everyone was getting what they wanted. Except him. He felt like he was the only person who understood how he felt. All the work he put in to make his music career take off, and all he had to show for it was a part-time job at Patty's.

Later that day, Drake came to Patty's. He wanted something to eat for himself, his wife, and his sister-in-law. But while he was ordering he took a good look at Benjamin.

"You look kind of down," said Drake. "Something wrong?"

"It's nothing," said Benjamin. "I was just thinking about my music."

"It's been a minute since you put something out."

"You're one to talk," said Benjamin. "Two years ago, we were doing big things. I was getting my name out there and you were singing backup for Vince. Now look at us."

"I don't know," said Drake. "I like where I'm at in life. I'm married, I live in a nice house, I've got a good job. That's not an easy feat at my age in this economy."

"But don't you ever wonder how things would've been different if you had continued with your music?"

"Not really. I'm fine with just singing at church. I have no regrets about the path I chose."

"Well, I wish I could say the same. I just feel so... out of place."

"That's not always a bad thing. Feeling out of place is a sign of growth."

"How are you so calm about this?"

"Because three years ago I was where you were. The best advice I can give you is don't be afraid to leave your comfort zone no matter how rough it might get."

Drake left after he got his food. But his words of advice stayed with Benjamin. If feeling out of place was a sign of growth, then Benjamin wanted to know what he was growing towards.

Benjamin was lying on the beach, enjoying feeling the sun's rays on his skin. The only sound he could hear was the water flowing to and away from the sand. It was peaceful and relaxing.

Then, he heard the opening lyrics to "Home Team".

Benjamin smiled hearing the lyrics to his song. It made him glad to know that his music was being heard by people. He opened his mouth to rap along to the song.

Nothing came out.

He sat up and tried again. Again, nothing came out. Not a note, a crack, or even a wheeze of air. It was like he had no voice at all. Benjamin put his hand to his throat and massaged it, wondering where his voice was. Looking around, he tried to see where he had left his voice. He did not remember when he took it out, but he had to have left it somewhere nearby. As he searched, he heard more lyrics of his song.

He lifted his sunglasses and looked around for the source of his music. Standing upshore was someone in a black hoodie. They bobbed their head to the beat of Benjamin's song and moved their hands around almost like they were rapping the song. Then Benjamin realized they *were* rapping the song. And the voice coming out was his voice.

He was not sure how someone else had gotten his voice. But he knew he needed to get it back. Benjamin started running toward the person. The person in return ran from him.

The person was fast. And throughout the chase, they kept rapping Benjamin's lyrics. Benjamin felt himself growing annoyed. Not only was he running too slow to catch the person, but the person had his voice. They both ran through the city's streets, and people complimented the person on his skills.

But it was Benjamin's voice, it was Benjamin's song, those were Benjamin's skills. The person had stolen them. And now they ran through the streets taking credit for all of Benjamin's hard work. Before Benjamin knew it, they were running through the streets of Creeke. Then they were at Patty's.

"Welcome to Patty's," said Charmaine with a big smile. "How can I help you?"

Benjamin tried to yell that the person had stolen his voice. But nothing came out. The person had not stopped rapping either. Charmaine nodded, acting like she was taking the person's order.

Benjamin calmed down. He figured maybe Charmaine was stalling for him to take his voice back, and he was missing the chance. So, he crept up to the person. And right when he tried to snatch them up, the person sidestepped him and ran out the door.

Benjamin tried to chase the person. But something took hold of his arm.

"Benjamin!" said Mr. Townsend.

Benjamin turned around to look at his father. But it was not the father he was used to seeing. It was the younger version of Mr. Townsend he had seen in pictures. The chubbier one that used to have dreadlocks that had inspired Benjamin to grow his own as a kid.

"How many times do I have to tell you that's not how we treat customers?" snapped Mr. Townsend.

Benjamin tried to explain what was happening, but he still had no voice. And the person was getting farther away with every passing second. He tried to pull away from his father, but Mr. Townsend's grip was too strong.

"That's not how we treat customers!" said Mr. Townsend. He kept repeating it, expecting Benjamin to repeat it with him.

Benjamin tried to scream his frustration. But while his head shook, and his body ached with rage, no sound came out. Eventually, he gave up trying to get free and listened to his father continue to repeat himself.

Mrs. Townsend came out of the kitchen. She also was her younger self, sporting the mushroom haircut she had worn in her twenties instead of the dreadlocks she wore as his mother.

"You need to listen to your father," said Mrs. Townsend, wagging her finger in Benjamin's face. "One day you're taking over this restaurant. And we worked too hard to let you destroy our dream."

Benjamin listened as his parents nagged at him. Then they chained him to the counter behind the cash register.

"It's okay, Benji," said Charmaine. "Maybe one day they'll leave the restaurant to me and set you free."

The three of them kept repeating those same lines. Benjamin resigned himself to his fate, accepting he would never get his voice back. He would be stuck behind the counter forever, wasting his life and never achieving anything.

The lights flickered and the sky outside darkened. Wind swirled around outside the door, howling to be let inside. It created such a ruckus that the doors could no longer stand it and yielded to the violent wind. Napkins and cups flew around the restaurant. Benjamin looked up to see the person standing in the doorway.

The person walked up to the counter with their face covered with a ski mask. Benjamin tried to look into the eyes of the person who had stolen his voice and his life. But there were no eyes to look into.

The person mocked him with his own voice, spewing Benjamin's lyrics at him. Throwing it in his face that he could no longer rap those songs. Then they tilted their head, almost like they were questioning him.

Benjamin shook his head. He did not know what the person wanted. All he wanted was his voice back. If he had his voice back, he could at least run the cash register. It was not the worst fate to be resigned to. At least he could say he tried with a music career.

The person picked up the cash register and smashed it to the ground. Benjamin stared in horror. Then he flew into a rage. That cash register had been there since his parents had first opened Patty's. They had worked hard to build their business, and the person was destroying it.

Benjamin tried his hardest to force sound out of himself. Something that would show the person he meant business and wanted it to leave.

But there was no point. Nothing came out. The person tilted their head again in that same questioning manner and rapped more lyrics.

Benjamin pulled at the chains holding him against the counter. All he could think was how he wished his parents had not held him back like that. If he had his hands, he could get his voice back. And he could teach that person a lesson about messing with the Townsends' business.

He pulled so hard that the chain on his right wrist broke from the counter. Benjamin took advantage of the sudden freedom and ripped the ski mask from the person's face. What he saw horrified him. The figure was gray and had no eyes. It was like looking at death in the face.

Benjamin screamed. And his scream filled the room. But it didn't come from him. It came from the person. He stopped screaming and stared.

"How did you do that?" asked Benjamin. His mouth said the words, but the voice came from the person's mouth. "How are you doing that?"

The person tilted their head.

"What?" asked Benjamin. He felt like a ventriloquist, saying the word himself but having the voice come out of the person's mouth. "Why are you tilting your head like that?"

The person pointed at Benjamin. Then it pointed at its throat and then at Benjamin's throat.

"My throat?" asked Benjamin. "What about my throat?"

The person walked into the kitchen and returned with a knife. It began cutting its throat open. Benjamin could not look away. He was too in awe of what he was seeing.

The person reached inside and pulled something out. It looked like a piece of candy.

"What is that?" asked Benjamin. But he realized what it was when he heard the words come from it. It was his voice. The person held it out to Benjamin.

"Why did you steal my voice in the first place?" demanded Benjamin. "It's mine."

The person shook their head. It shoved the voice into Benjamin's mouth. Benjamin felt it go down his esophagus and then rest comfortably in his throat. He had his voice back.

"Who are you?" questioned Benjamin. "And how did you get my voice?"

Benjamin blinked. One moment, he was looking at the figure. The next he was looking at himself behind the counter. And his body had no eyes.

"Where are my eyes?!" cried Benjamin, his hands flying to his face in panic.

Then they dropped to his side, his whole body going limp. His voice did something weird. It became scratchy, as if it had not been used in a long time, and was being dusted off for the first time in ages.

"I... am... your... voice... You... stopped... using... me..."

Benjamin was in disbelief. The person that looked like death was his voice. That meant the person was a part of him. Or maybe even was him.

"If you're my voice, why did you break our cash register? I would never ruin my family's business!"

"They... trapped... me..."

"They trapped you?"

"You... stopped... using... me... They... trapped... me..."

Benjamin had had enough. Nothing was making sense anymore. He took his eyes back from his voice, put them back in his own head, and then opened them.

He was lying in his bed, drenched in sweat. It was six o'clock on a Friday morning. It had all been one big, weird dream. And as he tried to think about it, all he could remember was his voice saying it was trapped by his parents.

Benjamin had spent all day at work trying to make sense of his dream. While a lot of it had been weird, there was one thing his mind kept going to. His voice had said it was trapped by his parents. He wondered if that was how he really felt inside. Part of the reason he had not

made any new music was because of the fallout with his family the previous year. Pursuing music had almost taken him away from his family in
more ways than one. But ever since he stopped pursuing it, he felt there
was a void in his life.

Leaving music had been hard at first. It had felt like he was ripping a
crucial part of his identity off from himself. But he had promised to be
a better son and be more attentive and involved with his family. So, he
slowly lessened his focus on music. He did a few features occasionally,
but as time passed, Benjamin felt numb to his situation.

Sometimes, he would feel the ache of wanting to return to music.
And it was those times when he felt the worst. He would get irritated
with how everyone got to pursue their passions except him. It felt unfair
to have what he wanted pushed aside. But then, those aches would pass,
and he would refocus on the bigger picture: spending time with his family and finishing school.

He was already halfway through university. There were two years left
before he could claim his degree. His freshman year had been spent trying to get his music known on campus. Sophomore year, focused more
on enjoying the campus and participating more as a student.

As far as his family went, he had much more time to spend with
them. He was there for things he would have missed due to possible performances. And working in the restaurant was not and had never been
a terrible experience. One thing he discovered that he liked about working there was that he liked being able to help people.

He had always been able to take consolation in these small victories.
But the dream had changed things for him. Instead of seeing Patty's as
his family's greatest achievement, he saw it as a prison holding him back.
His family was no longer his family but instead were jailors keeping him
trapped. His desire to be helpful to others had been overridden by his
desire for what he wanted for himself.

Benjamin felt confused. All his hard work to forget music had come
undone by that stupid dream. He could not forget the glee he felt when
he thought someone was listening to his music. It was the same glee he
felt when he realized his listener base was growing. But he also felt that

same glee when he helped serve others at the restaurant. That feeling of knowing he had helped someone have a good day, even if it was as simple as getting someone's order right, was also hard to shake.

He wished he could somehow mash the two into one feeling. A singular feeling of satisfaction of helping make someone's day better, while also pursuing what made him feel satisfied. Benjamin knew it was possible because music made him feel that way. But he wanted it to be possible in a way that did not turn him against his family and vice versa.

That evening was Uncle Buck's concert. Uncle Buck was the only person from the show that Benjamin regularly talked to. While he had kept in contact with Skunk, Skunk had continued making music without him. Uncle Buck was invested in Benjamin as a person. He was always checking on Benjamin and always giving him good advice for everything.

Benjamin had planned to just attend the show and go back home. But Uncle Buck had spotted him from the stage and made sure to have someone bring him to his dressing room. So, after the show ended, Benjamin sat backstage, waiting for Uncle Buck.

"How you been?" asked Uncle Buck when he entered the room.

"I've been alright," said Benjamin. He did not want to unload on Uncle Buck, especially after the amazing performance he had just had.

"Just alright?" questioned Uncle Buck.

"I've just had some things going on, but it's not important right now," said Benjamin.

"What's been going on?"

Benjamin hesitated to say anything. But after a few moments of Uncle Buck's expectant gaze, Benjamin decided to open up. He explained about the dream and the feelings he had been feeling.

"Sounds like you're homesick," said Uncle Buck.

"Homesick?" asked Benjamin. "How can I be homesick when I'm at home?"

"Let me rephrase it. You're sick of home."

"I...," said Benjamin, before trailing off.

"Just be honest with yourself," said Uncle Buck. "You know full well running your parents' restaurant is not what you want to do with your life."

"I don't mind helping though."

"There's a difference between helping and making it your whole life."

"What should I do then?"

"You've got to find your purpose again," advised Uncle Buck. "Find what made you love music in the first place. Ask yourself why music is important to you? What do you want to accomplish with it?"

Benjamin decided to take Uncle Buck's advice and rediscover his love for music. The farthest back he could remember enjoying music was when his parents would play their old-school jams. Then there were the songs he would hear on Sundays at church. He loved hearing the choir sing the different notes and parts and hearing the harmonies.

What made him want to make his own music was a mixture of things. The first was participating in his first Youth Sunday at church when he was seven and remembering how much fun it was. The second was when he and his friends would have rap battles and freestyles at school. By the time he was thirteen, he knew music was what he wanted to do.

Age thirteen was also when he made his first song. Benjamin re-watched his first-ever music video and immediately laughed at how amateurish it was. The lyrics were garbage, the editing was a mess, and the sound production was horrible. He had not done a good job enunciating his words at all. And his attempts to look hard by not wearing a shirt and borrowing his father's chain were hilarious.

But despite how cringe-worthy it was, Benjamin also saw how happy he was in the video. He remembered how much work he had put into making that video, and what he had learned to better himself. The whole video had been shot by himself using his phone and propping it up on different things to get the angles he wanted. His lyrics reflected his thirteen-year-old life, and he had made that beat himself.

Before he knew it, Benjamin had rewatched all his music videos. He saw the progress and improvements he had made over the years. And he saw the drive that had developed along with it. By the time he reached the last video, all he could do was wonder when he had lost his drive. The fire inside of him was relit after watching the progression of his career. Benjamin knew then that he had to get back to what he loved to do. A lot of momentum was lost from taking a year off, so he would have to work twice as hard to get himself caught back up.

The good news was that working hard was what Benjamin did best. But the challenge would be getting his family on board. Charmaine would easily support him because she had always been supportive and honest with him. His parents would take some convincing. So, Benjamin knew he would have to give them some solid evidence that he could succeed with a music career.

Benjamin got to work immediately, deciding to start with the lyrics first. He decided to use his dream as inspiration for his comeback song. It was the spark that had gotten him back to work, and it also reflected how he was currently feeling about his life.

A few days later, Benjamin met up with Alexander Brown. Like most of the Brown family, Alexander was heavy into music. But unlike most of his family members, Alexander preferred to work behind the scenes. He worked as a cafeteria worker at Creeke Middle School for his day job, but his passion was producing music. Alexander had produced plenty of tracks for local artists in the city. However, he had yet to catch his big break.

Benjamin wanted to work with Alexander for a few reasons. The first was because he was familiar with Alexander's work and knew how talented he was. Reason two was because Alexander was from Creeke, and Benjamin wanted to support his people. His final reason was because Alexander was a Brown, and the Browns strove for excellence in music.

"What's going on, Benji?" said Alexander, dapping him up when they met up.

"What's up Alex," said Benjamin. "I wanted to talk to you about this new song I'm working on that I want you to produce."

"Oh, you finally want me to produce something for you?" joked Alexander. "I was wondering when you'd finally make your way around to me."

"It's because you cost money, man," laughed Benjamin. "And now I got the money. I'm calling this project Nightmare Fuel."

"Nightmare Fuel...?" repeated Alexander skeptically.

"Yeah," said Benjamin. "It's about reclaiming your power and using it to escape your nightmares."

"I might need to hear the lyrics," said Alexander, still skeptical. "I'm trying to be more careful about the projects I attach myself to."

"I get it," said Benjamin. "But I know once you hear it, you'll know exactly where I'm going with this."

"I hope so," said Alexander. "Because I'm always willing to put on for my people. But my people got to give me something I'm willing to put on for."

"I've got the lyrics with me," said Benjamin. "It's more like a first draft, but at least it'll give you an idea of what I'm going for."

"Let me hear it."

Benjamin played his recording of him rapping the lyrics for Alexander.

"Mhmm," uttered Alexander, nodding his head. "Alright. Let me cook up something for you and get back to you in a few days. If you like it, we'll go from there."

"I'm sure I'll like whatever you do."

After the meeting, Benjamin asked Derek and Samiel to meet up with him. All of them were off that day, which was a rare convenience since they were all working adults. Benjamin missed when they could just meet up on a whim like when they were teenagers.

"I need some help," said Benjamin.

"What's wrong?" asked Derek.

"Nothing's wrong," said Benjamin. "I've decided to get back to doing music."

"You're finally getting back to it?" asked Samiel excitedly. "That's great! You've just seemed so off this past year when you weren't doing it."

Benjamin felt a pang of sadness hearing Samiel say that. He was not the only one who had felt how off he had been over the past year. Even the people around him had felt it.

"Yeah," said Benjamin. "I want to get back to what I'm best at. I need you guys to help me figure out how to tell my parents."

"Oh," said Derek. "That's a tough one. The best advice I can give you is to just tell them."

"Yeah, I agree," said Samiel. "But also be respectful when you do it. They'll probably take it a lot easier that way versus you just being like 'I'm going to be a rapper and there's nothing you can do about it'. Also do it when food is involved. People are a lot less likely to argue when they've eaten."

"True," said Benjamin.

"So, you already working on something or...?" asked Derek.

"I'm definitely already working on something," said Benjamin. "I'm hoping Alex will produce it."

"Man, if he does, that's going to be an instant classic," said Derek. "That's going to be like 'Home Team' levels of good."

"It'll be better than 'Home Team'," declared Benjamin. "I want to make sure I'm always improving."

"Most definitely," said Samiel.

Benjamin had gotten things set in motion. But it was time to face his biggest hurdle. That evening at dinner, Benjamin decided to go ahead and get it over with. His family was mid-bite when he kicked off the conversation.

"I've got something to tell everyone," said Benjamin.

"What is it?" asked Mrs. Townsend.

Benjamin paused before answering. It struck him how over two years ago, he was in this same situation. Telling his family about the next move he was making in his music career. But the difference was, two years later, he wanted to support his family just as much as he wanted their support. Two years later, it was no longer all about him and what he wanted. Preserving the legacy his parents had built was just as important to him.

"I've decided to return to making music," said Benjamin.

He had said it. Benjamin prepared himself for the lecture his parents were sure to give. But instead of arguing like he had two years ago, he would just listen.

"I say go for it," said Mr. Townsend.

"What?" said Benjamin with surprise. "Seriously?"

"Seriously," said Mr. Townsend. "You know, we've always wanted what was best for you and we thought music was too risky of a move for you to make. But over the past year, you've been around here wilting like a dying plant. And I don't know about you, but I'd rather have a son that's passionate about something than one forcing himself into something he doesn't connect with. So, go ahead. Make your music."

"And it better be good too," said Mrs. Townsend. "If you're going to pursue this music thing, you're going to do it right. You're going to make good music, you're going to learn how to sell good music, and you're going to learn how not to get screwed out of your money."

"Oh yeah, that last part is an absolute must-know," said Mr. Townsend. "Thankfully, we can teach you everything we know about running a business."

"And who knows," said Mrs. Townsend, hopefully. "Maybe you'll decide to run more than one business one day."

"Maybe," said Benjamin. "But I think Charmaine would be better suited to running the business side of the restaurant."

"I like that idea," said Charmaine.

"Yeah, but that's all in the future," said Mr. Townsend. "You need to focus on the present. And your present right now is convincing us that you can really do this as a career."

"I'm already cooking something up," said Benjamin, rubbing his hands together.

"I figured as much," said Mrs. Townsend. "But I just want to make it clear that that degree needs to be just as important."

"Yes ma'am," said Benjamin. "It will be."

After dinner, Mr. Townsend asked Benjamin to take a ride with him. They rode around for a bit before Mr. Townsend started talking.

"There's something else I want to tell you," said Mr. Townsend. "Something only between us men."

"Okay," said Benjamin.

"Benjamin," said Mr. Townsend. "I'm really proud of you."

"What for?" asked Benjamin.

"Because you have fought me tooth and nail on this music thing," said Mr. Townsend. "And through it all you've never lost your determination. That alone tells me that you can really do this. I'm really proud to see the man you're becoming."

"Thanks Dad," said Benjamin.

"I just want you to know I never purposefully tried to stand in your way," said Mr. Townsend. "I just–!"

"I know," said Benjamin. "You don't have to explain anything. You weren't completely wrong either."

"What do you mean?"

"What I mean is, I don't have any interest in running the restaurant. But I do like serving people and making their day. And I do want to make sure that what you and Mom worked so hard to build keeps going even after you're gone. That's why after I graduate, I want to help with the marketing and communications for the restaurant. That way I can still do my part and it'll be something I like."

"Dang," said Mr. Townsend. "You really have grown up on me."

A few days later, Benjamin rode around with Alexander in his truck. Alexander had created some beats for Benjamin and wanted to preview them for him.

"Let me know what you think," said Alexander, as he started the first one. It blasted through the car speakers and Benjamin was instantly in love.

"Whew!" exclaimed Benjamin as he bounced along to the beat. "Dang! That's it! That's exactly what I want!"

"You sure?" said Alexander. "Maybe you should hear the other ones first before you decide."

Benjamin listened to the other beats. All of them were good, but he knew the first one was it. The two coordinated a schedule for putting the song together, discussed payment, and everything was set. "Nightmare Fuel" was officially going to be his next song.

Benjamin felt proud of himself. He felt like he was becoming himself again. Like he had reclaimed his voice. And he knew that as he continued toward his future, he would find a balance in life that would satisfy him. But until then, he went to work and got behind the counter, clearing his throat to ensure his voice was still there. When the first customer walked in, he gave them a smile.

"Welcome to Patty's. How can I help you today?"

Derik Harrison

Derik's first year of college had been a wild one. He had partied and flirted with his fair share of girls. But he knew he was not looking for anything serious. However, the school year ended with him staying an extra week in Los Angeles. And it was all because of his girlfriend, Odette Rosalind Abernathy. She preferred to be called Rose, but he had the special privilege of being the only one to call her Rosie.

They had met in a theatre introduction class. He took it as an elective, while she was took it as the next step in her quest to become a renowned actress. Their paths had crossed when they had been paired on an assignment.

Derik had wanted to experience college life without being tied down to anyone. But Odette had managed to break through what he wanted and secure her spot as his lady.

Odette, just like his previous two girlfriends, was a year older than him. And she was the perfect mixture of what he had liked about Danielle and Nicole. She was strong-minded, ambitious, honest, sweet, and attentive. The only things about her that were potentially negative were that she was spoiled and sheltered.

But those negatives were barely negatives to Derik. Odette was spoiled because she was the daughter of a movie director and a movie star. She was used to a certain lifestyle and getting what she wanted without much pushback. Yet, she was never demanding about getting her way like Danielle used to be. There just never was a reason for her not to get her way because she could afford everything she wanted.

Her famous parents were also the reason she was so sheltered. The Abernathys had gone to great lengths to keep Odette and her siblings out of the spotlight. They wanted their children to be humble and grateful and live as normal and private lives as possible.

However, a normal and private life was the opposite of what Odette wanted. Odette wanted to be an actress like the many in her family had been before her. She had been in church and school plays since she was a little girl, but as a grown woman, she could pursue the bigger career she wanted.

But all of that would come down the line. For the moment, Derik was on his way to meet her family for the first time after a few months of dating. Derik wanted to make a good impression and have a great experience.

The journey to Odette's family was a long one, mostly caused by lots of waiting. By mid-afternoon, they were finally on their way to where her family was.

"We're going to meet my parents out on the yacht," said Odette.

"Yacht?!" cried Derik. "Your family has a yacht?!"

"Yeah?" said Odette confusedly.

"Oh wow! I've never been on a yacht before!"

"Oh."

It was like stepping into a whole new world. And Derik was excited to experience every part of it. When they arrived at the yacht, the first thing they saw was a man standing on the top deck in an open white button-down shirt, a sailor cap, and a bright blue Speedo.

"Ahoy!" called the man.

"Oh my gosh!" cried Odette, covering her face in embarrassment.

"Who is that?" asked Derik.

"That's my dad," groaned Odette. "I can't believe this."

Derik followed Odette onto the yacht. A woman stood by the railing, looking out over the water.

"Mom, why would you let Dad stand on the top deck with no clothes on?" whined Odette, marching over to the woman.

The woman turned around. It was *the* Irina Frazier.

"Is he naked for real?" questioned Mrs. Irina.

"He has a speedo on."

"Oh. Well, you know your father is a wild child. I can't control what that man does."

"This is so embarrassing," said Odette.

"Well sweetheart, just be glad you weren't alive for the time he actually *was* naked," said Mrs. Irina. She motioned to Derik and asked, "Who's this?"

"This is my boyfriend Derik," said Odette. "Derik, this is my mom."

Derik stared. He was meeting *the* Irina Frazier. *The* woman of every Black man's dreams was his girlfriend's mother.

"Oh, this is the boyfriend I've heard so much about," said Mrs. Irina. "You didn't mention how cute he was."

Derik could not speak. *The* Irina Frazier thought he was cute.

"Mom," whined Odette.

"Honey, you always get so easily worked up over everything," said Mrs. Irina. She held out a hand to Derik and said, "Hi Derik. I'm Mrs. Irina Abernathy."

Derik stared at the hand. *The* Irina Frazier was offering him her hand.

"It's okay, you can take it," giggled Mrs. Irina. "I don't bite."

Derik slowly shook her hand. Then he processed what she said.

"D...did you say Mrs. Irina *Abernathy*?" asked Derik.

"Yes," said Mrs. Irina. "That's my legal married name. In my normal life, I'm Irina Abernathy. Wife, mother, hoodrat."

"You are not a hoodrat," said Odette sharply.

"Some of my social media comments beg to differ," said Mrs. Irina. "But I don't care. I'm not ashamed to say I grew up in the hood out here. Anyone who knows me, knows that. But yeah, like I said, in real life I'm Irina Abernathy. Irina Frazier is the movie star. I try to keep them separate, because Irina Abernathy isn't as media trained as Irina Frazier."

"Ah," said Derik in awe. "I'm Derik."

"Nice to meet you," said Mrs. Irina. "You go to school with my daughter?"

"Yes ma'am."

"How old are you?"

"Eighteen. I turn nineteen in November."

"Interesting. Where are you from?"

"You've never heard of it."

"Try me."

"I'm from this town called Creeke."

"Oh, the town down the road from where Morgan's from."

"Yes ma'am," said Derik, his cheeks flushing. He had forgotten Morgan Abernathy was from the city.

"I've always been curious what it's like there," said Mrs. Irina. "I wanted to see it when we last visited because I had heard it was an all-Black town, but Morgan said there wasn't anything really worth seeing."

"It's definitely a lot smaller than the city, and way smaller than here," said Derik. "But it's not a bad place to live."

"So, then you like it there?"

"Yes ma'am."

"That's good. I've met a lot of people who hate their hometowns. I hope you enjoy your time while you're out here with us."

"I plan to," said Derik.

Odette took him to the other side of the yacht where a chubby man and a blonde girl relaxed. Derik had seen the guy at a few of the parties near campus.

"Hey Rose," said the man. "I see you made it back from school okay."

"I mean, it *is* just down the road," said Odette. She motioned to Derik and said, "This is my brother, Siegfried. Sieg, this is my boyfriend Derik."

"Yooooo, what's up, my man!" hollered Siegfried. He dapped Derik up and said, "I'm Siegfried but you can call me Sieg. As long as you don't break my sister's heart I'll be your big bro."

"What happens if I break her heart?" questioned Derik defiantly.

"Do yourself a favor and never find out," laughed Siegfried warningly. He motioned to the girl he was with and said, "That's my girl Becky."

"Nice to meet you," said Becky.

After meeting Siegfried and Becky, Derik and Odette found a corner of the yacht to settle into.

"This is so nice," said Derik.

"You've really never been on one before?" asked Odette.

"No."

"That's crazy. My dad loves sailing."

"Wow," said Derik. "Maybe he can give my best friend some tips. He's leaving me to join the navy after he graduates this year."

Derik was still shocked by Antoine's decision to join the navy. His music mixing skills had improved tremendously and he even took some DJ-ing classes in the city. Even though Derik would miss him, he knew Antoine was doing what was best for himself.

"You have another brother and sister, right?" asked Derik. "Where are they?"

"Camille lives in my dad's hometown," explained Odette. "Morgan's at home."

Derik noticed Odette avert her eyes when she mentioned her brother Morgan. At that moment, Morgan Abernathy came into the area where they were.

"Dad, I can't believe you!" complained Odette. "Why would you go up there with no clothes on?"

"No clothes on?" repeated Mr. Abernathy. He looked down at himself and said, "Last time I checked I had a swimsuit on. And I could've sworn I had a sailor cap on my head..."

"Dad!" cried Odette. "You had the bare minimum of clothes on! And then Mom even told me there was a time you did this actually naked!"

"Okay first of all, we were already married and in a remote area where no one could see us," said Mr. Abernathy. His face became serious as he said, "I'd never take my clothes off in front of other people."

"Why'd you even have your clothes off in the first place?!"

"I was sunbathing."

"Oh my gosh!"

"And your mom took a photo of me."

"Okay ew ew ew!" gagged Odette. "I don't want to hear anything else!"

"Then stop asking questions," teased Mr. Abernathy. "Your mother tells me you brought a boyfriend with you."

"Uh... yes...," said Derik, trying not to be starstruck. "That would be me. I'm Derik Harrison."

"Derik Harrison...," said Mr. Abernathy. He grabbed Derik by the shoulders and began looking him over. "Yes... What do you do, Derik Harrison?"

"I'm a writer?" said Derik.

"A writer," said Mr. Abernathy, his eyes lighting up. He made eye contact with Derik and said, "What kind of writer?"

"A journalist."

"A journalist," said Mr. Abernathy, his eyes darkening a bit. "Have you ever written a screenplay before?"

"I did for one of my classes."

"Would you ever consider writing a serious screenplay? Or do you just like being a journalist?"

"I don't know," said Derik. "I've never given it much thought."

Derik could see the wheels turning inside Mr. Abernathy's head. It was like just being a writer had already endeared Derik to him.

"You and I are going to get along just fine," said Mr. Abernathy. "And you have the look of a little prince. I will call you 'my prince'."

Derik decided to grin and bear it. He hated being referred to as a prince because it brought back to mind the image of that dreadful school photo. The one of his old self. But there was no way he was saying no to someone like Morgan Abernathy.

Mr. Abernathy handed Derik his sailor cap. He had Derik and Odette stand together to take a photo.

"Smile!" said Mr. Abernathy. Derik obeyed, pushing the sailor cap back with his thumb.

When he saw the photo, Derik looked at himself. His hair was back to its normal black color. But his eyes were knowledgeable. Any innocence he had left from his teenage years was completely gone.

After the photo was snapped, they spent a few hours on the yacht before returning to the Abernathy house. It was beautiful and Derik could not believe he would spend the next week living in it.

"Make yourself at home, my prince," said Mr. Abernathy. Feel free to look around and get comfortable with the place."

And that's what Derik did. He marveled at everything but what caught his attention the most was all the family photos in the hallway. Each photo was of a celebrity going all the way back to the old days of film.

"This is so cool," said Derik.

"You think so?" asked Siegfried.

"Yeah!" exclaimed Derik. "Look at all these actors!"

"Yeah" said Siegfried. "These are my mom's people. Most of them were bit actors or acted in small, independent productions. My mom is the first one to really hit it big. Anyways here's your bag. I'll take you to your room."

Derik's room was at the back of the house. He noticed a set of back stairs leading to the second floor.

"There's two sets of stairs to the second floor?" asked Derik.

"No," said Siegfried. "The ones in the front go the second floor. These ones lead to Morgan's room."

"What's the deal with Morgan?" asked Derik. "Every time he comes up you guys act all weird about him."

"There's no 'deal' with him," said Siegfried. "He's autistic."

"Oh."

"Yeah," said Siegfried. "We're not trying to be weird about him. But sometimes when people learn about his autism they try to baby him and treat him like he's less than."

"I see," said Derik.

"You two might get along great though," said Siegfried. "He loves writing and will talk about it for hours."

"Cool."

Derik ended up meeting Morgan a lot sooner than he expected. He had just woken up from his nap and was on his way to the kitchen when they literally bumped into each other.

"Oops!" cried Derik. "I'm sorry!"

"That's alright," said Morgan. He looked at Derik and said, "Who are you?"

"I'm Derik," said Derik. "I'm Rose's boyfriend."

"Her boyfriend?" said Morgan. "When did she get a boyfriend?"

"We've only been dating for a few months."

"Oh," said Morgan. "I'm Morgan. I'm her younger brother."

"Nice to meet you."

"Nice to meet you too."

They made their way to the kitchen for dinner. Mrs. Irina had made them a pasta dish. That was the first time Derik noticed the family did not have any maids or house staff. Apparently, he had stated his observation out loud, and Mrs. Irina explained it was because she was used to doing things herself.

The whole dinner was interesting. It surprised Derik how open everyone was with each other. No topic was off-limits. His family definitely left some things unsaid and there were even some conversations that he and his siblings were expected to stay out of completely.

Mr. Abernathy announced that he wanted to throw a welcome party for Derik, and everyone agreed. Morgan at some point started drawing on the table, before completely disappearing for the rest of the evening.

"He's taking time to himself," explained Odette. "He does that when things start to become a little too much for him."

Derik understood. When dinner was over, everyone started getting prepared for bed. There were lots of "I love yous" said, and Mr. Abernathy hugged everyone, including Derik and Siegfried. It was weird to Derik. He was not used to a father hugging his son, let alone telling his son he loved him. Granddad Derrick was not even that affectionate, let alone Mr. Harrison.

That night, Derik lay in bed thinking about his father. Things between them were more or less the same, with Derik still unsure how his father felt about him. But what was new and interesting was how Mr. Harrison acted as a grandfather. Mr. Harrison with all his lack of affection, seemed to have a great understanding of how babies worked. Derik knew he should not have been surprised since his father *was* a father, but he was surprised to see his father actually parent. He was used to his father being standoffish and hands-offish.

The next few days at the Abernathys' was filled with more new and interesting experiences. Odette took him to see the city, which was like a complete culture shock. There were a lot of things he enjoyed, but he absolutely hated the food. However, part of him felt like an intruder in a world he did not belong in. He and Morgan had also started becoming friends like Siegfried said they would. But Derik was still getting used to some of the things Morgan did.

But what was most interesting were Mr. Abernathy and Mrs. Irina. Derik quickly learned that Mr. Abernathy was the unserious parent. Everything to him was an experience and he always wanted to try new things. He did not mind letting things become uncomfortable because he liked exploring what he called "uncharted waters". However, no matter how free he appeared to be, he did have some boundaries in place, no doubt due to his religious upbringing.

But Mrs. Irina was the complete opposite. She was the serious parent, to the point that her children jokingly called her "The Warden". While they were free to do many things with Mr. Abernathy's permission, she was quick to veto what she did not approve of. And she absolutely *hated* alcohol to the point that she would not even allow it to be served at the party.

"Her mom was an alcoholic," explained Odette when they were alone. "She died from cirrhosis of the liver when my mom was eleven."

"Dang," said Derik. "That's sad."

"Yeah," said Odette. "My mom's pretty sure what drove her to it was how her acting career dried up after blaxploitation went out of popularity. After that, it was hard for her to find roles and she didn't know how to handle it."

"I'd probably be the same way about alcohol then if it killed my mother," said Derik.

"What's your mom like? You never talk about your family much."

"You don't either."

"To be fair, my parents are famous. And as you can see the way they act in public is just a slightly toned-down version of how they act normally."

"True," said Derik. "My parents are nothing like yours. My mother is very prim and proper and very ladylike. Her family is also the richest family in our town. My dad is... I don't know how to describe him other than 'closed off'."

"What do they do?" asked Odette.

"They co-own a hair salon and barbershop, but it's really my mother's. My dad owns a gym and also has his own tech repair company."

"Wow," said Odette. "Your parents must make a lot of money."

"Nowhere near as much as your parents make."

"Well yeah," said Odette. "What about your siblings? You've talked about them a little but not that much."

"I have two brothers and a sister," said Derik. "My oldest brother, Matthias, is a mechanic but he's recently started college. My other older brother, Deidrick, is a barber and he's got three kids. And then my sister, Allison, is also in college."

"But what are they like though?"

"I don't know how to describe them. You'd just have to meet them."

Odette had a thoughtful expression after he said that. Derik wondered what she was thinking about, but the conversation kept moving after that, so he let it go.

That Friday was the day of the party. Derik spent the whole day getting pampered, and it was so unusual to him. He was used to just getting a haircut and that was it. But the Abernathys put him through a whole process. When he saw himself all done up in the mirror that evening, he could not believe it was himself.

"That's not me," said Derik.

"That is you, my prince," said Mr. Abernathy.

Derik smiled and turned to Mr. Abernathy.

"Uh sir...," said Derik. "I hope this doesn't come across wrong but can you stop calling me that? It brings up bad memories."

"Oh!" said Mr. Abernathy, growing embarrassed. "Why didn't you say something sooner? If I had known, I would've never done that."

The party was nothing like Derik had ever seen before. Even the winter balls the Perrys threw could not compare to the Abernathys' party. And while Derik felt honored to be the special guest, he could not help but feel out of place. He felt like all eyes were on him, looking him over, judging him. Determining quickly that he was a nobody who had lucked up by getting with a rich girl like Odette.

It left him feeling ready to go back home to Creeke. So, when Saturday came, he was more than ready to get on his flight home. The Abernathys had taken him to the airport to send him off. He thanked them for their hospitality and went inside. Odette went with him, so he figured she wanted to be with him until their last second together. When she got in the security line with him, he became confused.

"What are you doing?" asked Derik.

"I'm going with you," said Odette.

"What do you mean?" cried Derik. "You can't go with me!"

"Why not?"

"You don't have a ticket."

"Yes, I do."

"When did you get a ticket?!"

"You said that I would have to see for myself what your family was like. So, I'm going to see for myself. You got to experience my world. Now, I want to experience yours."

"Rosie, this is very last minute. I can't just pop up with a girlfriend with no warning."

"It may be last minute for you, but it's not for me. I'm staying with my sister."

No protest Derik made after that worked. All he could do was give his family as best of a heads-up he could manage. Odette took her seat in first class while Derik went to his affordable seat in the back. It was funny to Derik that their seats matched how their lives went. He had planned for a long time and bought the cheapest middle-seat ticket. Meanwhile, Odette had booked a seat in the best part of the plane on a whim.

When they landed in the city, Derik was able to get a signal again and found that most of his family was unsurprisingly surprised.

Odette's sister, Camille, picked them up from the airport. Derik was not prepared for how different she appeared to be from the rest of her family. While the Abernathys' mostly were easy-going, and dressed casually, Camille seemed more like a mini-Mrs. Irina. She wore a T-shirt, an ankle-length denim skirt, and brown sandals. Her curly hair was pulled back into a bun.

"Camille!" cried Odette, running to hug her sister.

"Rose!" cried Camille, embracing Odette. "I was so surprised when you said you were coming to visit! I haven't had any time to straighten up."

"It's okay," said Odette. "It was a spur of the moment thing."

"Things usually are with you," laughed Camille. She looked at Derik and asked, "Who is this?"

"My boyfriend."

"Oh," said Camille. "Hi boyfriend, I'm Camille."

"I know who you are," said Derik.

"Oh, she told you about me?"

"Well yeah, but I also see you around here preaching all the time. You're the Wisdom girl, right?"

"I am," said Camille, her interest piqued. "So then, you're from around here?"

"I'm from Creeke."

"Oh," said Camille, looking at Odette knowingly. "I see. Very spur of the moment indeed."

The conversation continued when they were in the car.

"So, how long are you staying, Rose?" asked Camille.

"Only a few days," said Odette. "I wanted to meet his family since he just met ours."

"Okay," said Camille. "You know you're going to church with me tomorrow, right?"

"Why?" whined Odette.

"Where else do you have to be other than the house of The Lord on a Sunday?"

"I was hoping to meet Derik's family tomorrow!"

"Derik?" said Camille. "That's your name, boyfriend?"

"Yes," said Derik.

"Are you related to a Pastor Derrick Harrison? My friends told me he was on of the pastors at the church down there."

"Yes, that's my grandfather."

"Mhmm," said Camille, nodding. "Rose, his family's going to be in church probably longer than we are."

"Aw man!" cried Odette. "I'm only going to be here until Tuesday!"

"We could go meet my family now," suggested Derik. "If Camille doesn't mind driving us to Creeke."

"Of course not," said Camille. "I have some friends down there I can go visit."

Derik's family had instructed him to bring Camille to his grandparents' house. He hoped they would make a good impression on her and not do anything to embarrass him.

"We're in the town," said Derik as they passed the gas station that served as the entrance mark to Creeke. He felt glad to be home.

"There's so much open land out here," said Odette.

"Well, we're still on the edge of the town," said Derik. "As we get farther in, there will be more buildings."

As they drove through the town, Odette marveled at how "quaint" it was. At the stop sign outside the church, she asked about the hole in it.

"It's always been like that ever since the old music minister shot a hole through it," said Derik.

"The old music minister?" questioned Odette. "As in for the church?"

"Yeah."

"What in the world?"

"That was my friend's great-grandfather," said Camille. "Apparently, he could have a bit of a temper sometimes."

"I see that," said Odette."

When they reached his grandparents' house, Odette gasped.

"It's like a farm!" said Odette.

"It is a farm," said Derik. "My great-great grandfather was a farmer. But my grandfather doesn't know much about farming. If you go down the road, you'll come to the creek. That's where everyone hangs out."

"I'd love to see that!" said Odette.

"I'm just going to say hi very quickly before I go visit my friends," said Camille. "I let them know I was coming, so they're expecting me."

"Okay," said Derik.

As they approached the house, Nanna Kiana came out on the porch to meet them.

"I thought that was you!" said Nanna Kiana. "Derik Tremaine Harrison, how you going to come back from school with a girlfriend and not tell anyone she was coming? You gave us no time to prepare!"

"I didn't know she was coming!" whined Derik. "I found out when y'all did!"

"A mess!" said Nanna Kiana. "Get over here and give your Nanna some sugar."

Derik hugged Nanna Kiana. When they let go, she looked at Odette and Camille.

"I thought you said girl*friend*," said Nanna Kiana. "Why I see two girls here?"

"That's my girlfriend," said Derik, pointing to Odette. "That's her sister. She drove us here."

"You made this young lady drive y'all down here?" gasped Nanna Kiana. "Why you didn't ask one of your brothers to come get you?"

"I didn't mind ma'am," said Camille. "I was coming to visit a friend anyways."

"Oh," said Nanna Kiana. She looked at Camille closely and said, "Wait, have we met before?"

"Possibly," said Camille. "You may have seen me witnessing dressed up as Wisdom."

"Oh!" said Nanna Kiana. "You're the girl I gave my coat to!"

"That was you?" cried Camille. She ran to her car, saying "Wait there!"

Camille returned with Nanna Kiana's coat and handed it to her.

"I've been holding on to this, hoping I'd run into you again so I could return it," said Camille. "Ain't God good?"

"All the time," said Nanna Kiana.

"I was so glad when you gave me that coat. I had forgotten mine at home."

"That's alright," said Nanna Kiana. "So, what are your names?"

"I'm Camille Abernathy," said Camille. "This is my sister, Odette."

"I go by Rose though," added Odette.

"Camille and Rose Abernathy," said Nanna Kiana. "I used to go to a church under a Reverend Abernathy in the city."

"That was our grandfather," said Odette.

"It could've also been our great-grandfather," corrected Camille. "They were both reverends."

"It was probably the great-grandfather because I left there once I got married," said Nanna Kiana. "What a small world this is!"

"A small world indeed!" agreed Camille.

"My name is Kiana," said Nanna Kiana. "I don't know if I said that already. Some people call me Kiki, some people call me Danette. I'll answer to any of those three as long as you put a "Mrs." in front of it."

"What does Derik call you?" asked Odette.

"I don't know what he calls me behind my back, but to my face he calls me Nanna," chuckled Nanna Kiana.

"I call you Nanna all the time," said Derik.

"You better," said Nanna Kiana. "Come on inside and meet the rest of the family."

Derik and Odette followed Nanna Kiana inside. Camille came too, and after greeting everyone, left to go meet her friends.

"So, how long have y'all been dating?" asked Granddad Derrick.

"A few months," said Derik.

"A few months," said Granddad Derrick. "And y'all met at school?"

"Yes," said Odette. When the word "sir" did not follow, everyone stared at Odette.

"What are you studying?" asked Granddad Derrick.

"I'm studying theatre," said Odette.

"Theatre?" said Granddad Derrick. "So, you want to be an actress or something?"

"Yes."

"You said the second Reverend Abernathy was your grandfather, right?" recalled Nanna Kiana.

"Yes."

"Isn't his son the director Morgan Abernathy?"

"Yes. That's my father."

"Oh," said Granddad Derrick with surprise. Derik noticed that Deidrick seemed to perk up too. "Well, then you'll have no problem becoming an actress then."

"You don't know my dad," laughed Odette.

As the day went on, it became more obvious that Odette, like Derik when he was with her family, was out of her depth. When she asked a rather personal question and got weird stares from everyone, she learned quickly that his family was not as open. At dinner, she only ate half of her food, saying it was too much, and gave the rest to Derik.

"Am I making a good impression?" questioned Odette as they sat on the porch waiting for Camille.

"Yeah," said Derik.

"Then why does everyone stare at me every time I say something?"

"They're not used to someone like you."

"What's someone like me?"

"Someone who asks the kind of questions you ask. Doesn't say ma'am or sir. Doesn't eat all her food."

"Oh dear," said Odette, beginning to blush. "They must think I've been very rude."

"You're fine," said Derik.

"No, I should go apologize," said Odette.

"Rosie, that's really not necessary."

But Odette was already on her way into the house. He followed her into the kitchen where Nanna Kiana, Mrs. Harrison, and Allison were.

"Excuse me," said Odette. When she had the women's attention, she began her apology. "I just wanted to say I was sorry for how I've been today. I didn't realize how rude I've been."

The women stared at her. Then Allison glared at Derik.

"Did you tell her to come in here and do this?!" snapped Allison.

"No!" cried Derik. "In fact, I told her *not* to do it!"

"I can't believe this!" said Allison. "Got this poor girl apologizing to us and she didn't even do nothing wrong!"

"I didn't tell her to apologize!"

"Well, you didn't try to stop her either!"

"What is all the commotion?" asked Granddad Derrick, coming into the kitchen.

"Dee-Three's girlfriend is in here apologizing to us!" said Allison.

"Apologizing for what?" asked Granddad Derrick. "What'd she do?"

"Nothing!" said Allison. "She said she was being rude but I didn't notice."

"I didn't notice either," said Granddad Derrick. "Do y'all think she was being rude?"

"No," said Nanna Kiana. "I thought she was a nice, young lady. Still do."

"Oh... I...," said Odette. She blushed and ran out of the room.

"I'll go talk to her," said Mrs. Harrison, following Odette.

"Now look at what you did!" accused Allison.

"I didn't do anything!" said Derik.

"You must've said something to make her feel like she was rude to us!"

"I did not! All she did was ask if she made a good impression and I said yeah. I just told her why everyone kept staring at her."

"You big dummy!" cried Allison. "Why would you tell her that?!"

"She asked!"

"Men!" huffed Allison. "None of you ever think about anything!"

Once everything was sorted out, Derik and Odette were once again on the porch waiting for Camille.

"I can't believe I made such a fool of myself!" cried Odette.

"It's alright," said Derik. "It was just a misunderstanding."

"Your mom is very nice though," said Odette. "You weren't kidding when you said she was a prim and proper lady."

"Nope."

"And you said she comes from the richest family here?"

"Yeah."

"But you've never been on a yacht?"

"Do you see any water to go on a yacht around here?"

Odette laughed. It made Derik glad to hear her laugh. He had started to worry that she regretted coming with him and was very uncomfortable.

"Your brothers are also nice," said Odette, when she settled down. "And your sister has already made me her new best friend. Your grandfather, your uncle, and your cousin are also pretty cool. It's scary how much he looks like you though. I can only tell you two apart because he's a lot beefier than you are."

"He spends more time at the gym than I do," said Derik.

"I can see that," said Odette. "Your dad doesn't say very much though."

"Nope."

"He seems kind of nice though."

"I think you're first person to ever describe him as nice off the bat."

"Really?"

"Yeah."

Odette went quiet for a moment. Then she spoke again.

"Do you think we're a good match for each other?" asked Odette.

"What do you mean?"

"We just... we don't seem to fit in each other's worlds."

"Maybe not yet. But if we give it some time, we might."

"Maybe," said Odette.

The rest of the visit was not as dramatic and full of misunderstanding. But on Monday, something happened that changed the trajectory of Derik and Odette's relationship. He took her to see the creek. And Danielle was there.

After their second breakup, Derik had kicked himself for letting her get away from him a second time. He figured a third chance was out of the question after how he acted during the second chance. But once he had gotten with Odette, Danielle had been the furthest thing from his mind. At least she had been until he saw her at the creek.

They did not speak. But after he saw her, she was on his mind. Then, when he looked at Odette, Danielle was no longer a factor. As long as Odette was around, he did not think about Danielle. The minute Odette was out of sight though, Danielle returned to his mind.

And Odette must have noticed. After a while, they sat beside the creek, and she brought Danielle up.

"Who was that girl you saw earlier?" asked Odette.

"What girl?" asked Derik, hoping to avoid the discussion.

"The cute brown-skinned one," said Odette. "With her hair in a braid."

"Oh her?" said Derik with a laugh. "Nobody. Just my ex."

"Just your ex?" asked Odette, raising her eyebrows questioningly.

"Yeah," said Derik. "She's nobody to worry about."

"Uh huh," uttered Odette.

Derik looked at Odette. He took in her dark-brown skin and her beautiful afro. Her lips were plump, and her nose was cute. She was in every way, the girl of his dreams. But he could almost see Danielle sitting beside her, taunting him to pick which one of them was really the one he loved. And that was not good for their relationship.

"When y'all broke up...," said Odette. "Was it sudden?"

"I guess," said Derik.

"Did you take time to process it?"

"What?"

"Did you process the breakup? Or did you just move on?"

"What does that–!"

"Derik," said Odette bluntly. "I like you a lot. But I won't be with you if you're not over your ex."

"I am over her," said Derik.

"Doesn't look that way to me."

"Rosie."

"I'm just saying. I'm going back home tomorrow, and you'll still be here. If you have unresolved feelings for her, I'd rather we not be together so you can figure it out, than for you to end up cheating on me and making everybody mad."

"I don't want to break up though."

"Can you look me in the eye and tell me you have no feelings for her?"

Derik looked her in the eye. He knew Odette was who he wanted to be with. But there was still that question of what could have been with Danielle.

"I don't," said Derik, willing the words out.

"I don't believe you," said Odette. "Not yet anyways."

"Rosie, you're the one I want to be with."

"There's only one way to find out for sure," said Odette. "I'm breaking up with you so you can figure things out. When you can believably tell me after being here this whole time that I'm still who you want, then I'll get back together with you."

Derik could not believe it. His girlfriend had just broken up with him. And he had not even done anything wrong.

Odette at least allowed him to see her off at the airport. As she walked away from him and Camille, it took everything in him not to break out in tears right there.

"Don't worry Derik," encouraged Camille. "Rose can be a bit spontaneous, but she's always been a woman of her word. If she's giving you this chance to figure things out, then it's because she really likes you and really wants to be with you."

It was supposed to make him feel better, but it only made him feel worse. The first few days after the breakup were hard. He started out sad, then he became mad. Derik wanted to blame Danielle for the breakup, but he knew it was not really her fault. It was his because he kept pushing the women he liked away with his antics. As time went on, Derik became numb. One day he found himself standing in the creek, staring at the sky.

He had just finished reading some poetry from the book Matthias had given him for his seventeenth birthday. Having that book inspired him to write his own poetry to express himself. And he was considering writing a new one to express his feelings about the breakup.

"What are you doing?" asked Derek, coming to join him.

"Watching God," said Derik. "Trying to figure out what's He's doing."

"Learn anything?"

"No," sighed Derik, dropping his head. "Why does life have to be so complicated?"

"I'm trying to figure that out myself," said Derek. "Maybe we can figure it out together."

The one thing being around Odette's family had done was expose him to a family unlike his own. While Odette had told him to figure out his feelings with Danielle, all he could really think about was how open and loving her family had been. Especially Mr. Abernathy. He had been a dad that Derik was not used to seeing. Derik could not get the image of Mr. Abernathy and Siegfried hugging and saying they loved each other out of his mind.

"I just don't get my dad," sighed Derik.

"What do you mean?" asked Derek.

"I don't know if he loves me. He probably doesn't even know himself."

"He knows," said Derek assuredly. "What he actually doesn't know is how else to show it to you."

"What do you mean?"

"What I mean is that he loves you."

"Let me guess, he told you that?" scoffed Derik jealously. "What'd you do, force it out of him?"

"He didn't tell me anything."

"Well, I wouldn't be surprised since he seems to prefer you over me."

"Uncle Marlin doesn't have favorites."

"I can't tell."

"You do know I've only really gotten to know him these past few years, right? He was the scary uncle I barely talked to for years."

"Well, you seem to know him better than I do. Because you're convinced he loves me and I'm just plain confused."

"You're not confused," said Derek. "You, like Auntie Leya, just want him to say it out loud."

"Is that too much to ask?" complained Derek.

"For him it is."

"Why?"

"Like I said, he's not used to showing love that way. He's not affectionate like that."

"Then how are you so convinced he loves me?"

"Because of his actions," explained Derek. "He got arrested fighting over you. He put himself into debt to try and rescue you when you got kidnapped. He doesn't lie to you to spare your feelings. And the biggest one was him admitting in a room full of men that he cared about you."

"He didn't say he cared," said Derik. "He said he didn't hate me and that I was part of his life."

"Which is the closest you'll ever get to him saying he loves you."

"Why?"

"Because he's an old-school man raised by an old-school man," said Derek. "Listen to the older men around here and their stories about their fathers. Their fathers weren't hugging and kissing them and telling them they loved them. Their fathers were toughening them up and teaching them their feelings came second to their survival. Uncle Marlin is no different."

"Then why isn't Uncle Falcon like that?"

"Because Dad had a different version of Granddad," emphasized Derek. "One that was older and wiser than the version that raised Uncle Marlin. Granddad will tell you. He treated them differently and that's why they're the way they are."

"Why are you so good at reading people?" sighed Derik. "It's like you can easily connect with others and make friends in no time."

"You can do some things too," said Derek. "I'm not smart like you are. You're doing great in college, while I dropped out after one semester. And I'm not good at hiding my feelings like you are."

"I'm not good at hiding my feelings either," said Derik. "Otherwise, I'd still be in a relationship. In fact, I'm terrible at it just like I'm a terrible person."

"How are you terrible?"

"I...," began Derik. He stopped to contemplate his words. Then, he just started speaking everything he had kept inside for the past few years. "I hate Devon."

"Really?" said Derek sarcastically. "I never would've guessed!"

"It's terrible!" cried Derik. "I shouldn't hate him, but I do! He looks like her and I hate him for it. And I know it's wrong because the baby didn't do anything to me, but I can't help it. Sometimes I dream that what happened to me wasn't real. And I wake up and believe it. I believe what happened was all a bad dream and in reality, I'm fine and everything's okay. But it wasn't a dream. I really was kidnapped, and that baby really exists. And I feel my heart grow cold and I hate that baby being around, reminding me of what happened. I'm a terrible person and that's why I don't blame you if you're mad at me about your leg. Because I'm a terrible person and I deserve it for hating that baby. And then I can't seem to pick a girlfriend and just stick with her. It's like every time I'm in a relationship, here comes a past girlfriend and it's like I can't help but wonder how things would've turned out if we were still together. It's terrible!"

Once he said it all, Derik felt better. But he became worried when Derek did not respond right away.

"I'm angry," said Derek. "Because my cousin was kidnapped and the people who took him tried to kill him. But instead of hitting him with the car, they hit me, and everything I've worked hard for and ever dreamed of has been taken from me. And I know it's not his fault, but I can't help but wonder how different everything would be if he'd never tried to run away in the first place. So, I'm also a terrible person for being angry at my cousin for running away and getting kidnapped, which led to my leg being broken and ruining my dance career."

"I really am you, and you really are me," said Derik. "Even when we're mad, it's similar."

"Because we're connected," said Derek. "What hurts me hurts you and vice versa."

"But what do we do?" asked Derik. "I don't want to be full of hate and anger."

"Me either," agreed Derek. "What do we do?"

"I was hoping you'd tell me," said Derik. "You're the one who's good at fixing stuff."

"If I'm so good at fixing things, then why can't I fix my life?"

"You always know how to fix relationships and make people laugh," said Derik. "I can't do that because I don't care to be liked."

"You ran away at sixteen because you thought your whole family hated you."

"I ran away at sixteen because I felt unwanted. And that's the point I'm trying to make. I don't stay where I'm not wanted."

"Well, maybe you should stop doing that," said Derek. "If you wanted to, you could fix relationships too."

"I don't know," said Derik.

"Just try it," said Derek. "You never know what could happen."

Derik decided to take Derek's advice. The first person he started with was his father. He asked his father to talk with him, and after a few seconds to build himself up, he began.

"I just wanted to tell you that I think I understand how you feel towards me now," said Derik. "I know you think I'm soft. I know I probably can't change your mind about that, but I hope that we can try to have some sort of relationship as father and son."

"Okay," said Mr. Harrison. "I've already told you before that you are part of my life."

"Yes, I know," said Derik. "For the longest time, I've wanted you to tell me that you loved me. But I've come to accept that you probably will."

Mr. Harrison's eyes fell.

"I just want you to know, it doesn't matter anymore if you say it," said Derik. "Like I said, I think I have a better understanding of how things are. But whatever you feel towards me, you'll always be my father. And even though you may not feel comfortable saying you love me, I can at least tell you that I do love you and I do care about you."

Derik felt really good saying that to his father. Putting words to what he felt made them make sense. He had loved his father all along and felt hurt when he did not feel that love reciprocated.

Mr. Harrison did not say anything. He just nodded. But that nod told Derik more than enough. It was hard for a man to say he loved someone when he was not used to saying it. And it was also hard to receive love when he was not used to outright receiving it.

That's why Derik decided he would have to start loving Devon too. Devon was already at a disadvantage because Deidrick was turning out to be as unaffectionate a father as Mr. Harrison. Derik knew what it was like to be on both sides of that kind of relationship and he could not live with himself if he inflicted that on his nephew. Especially when he was not that way toward Bianca and Car'drick.

"Your girlfriend," said Mr. Harrison. Derik had been so caught up in his own thoughts that he was surprised when Mr. Harrison spoke. "She's gone?"

"Yeah," said Derik sadly. "She's gone."

"Do you want her to be gone?"

"I don't know," said Derik. "I'm not sure what I want."

"Hmm," said Mr. Harrison. "Can I give you some advice?"

"Sure..."

"While you're figuring it out, don't look so sad," said Mr. Harrison. "Never let anyone see you sweat. No one respects a man that let's everyone see him sweat. Especially not your woman. If she sees you sweat, she won't trust or respect you. No one will."

Derik thought about that advice long after leaving his father. On the surface, it may have seemed like his father was telling him to hide his emotions. But when Derik considered that the advice came from his highly unemotional father, he figured it made sense. It was his father's way of showing he cared and that comforted Derik.

With that advice, Derik went to fix his relationship with Danielle. He stood on her porch, preparing to once again attempt a relationship with her. Although he was still hurting from his breakup with Odette, he knew he could not sit in it forever. She had given him a chance to figure out what he wanted. And the only way to do that was to find out if he still felt something for Danielle.

So, he took a deep breath and knocked on her door.